# QUEENIE

## LC Van Savage

**BeachHouse Books**

Chesterfield Missouri, USA

# Copyright

Graphics Credits:

Cover by Dr. Bud Banis. based on a drawing by LC Van Savage.

Publication date 2017

Printing 3

ISBN 9781596301078 BeachHouse Books Edition

Library of Congress catalog number 2017952301

BeachHouse Books

www.beachhousebooks.com

an Imprint of

Science & Humanities Press

Saint Charles, MO 63301

# FOR:

Dylan, Zoe, Darby, Jordan, Tommy and Hannah,
the lights in and of our lives.

# CHAPTER 1

The steady, gentle whoosh of the BMW's air conditioner was the only sound as I sat parked on the deserted street outside my old high school. Even in the mechanically cooled air, the leather seat felt hot. My back stuck to it and my dress peeled away like wet cellophane when I leaned forward. I folded my hands in my lap, looked around slowly and blinked hard, remembering how I'd stood rigidly still back then, frightened, desperately wanting to vanish, to be invisible, to be no one.

The street was quiet. It was very hot outside the car. Tall trees now nearly obscured the sand-colored, two-story building with the huge windows, now fitted with neat, white Venetian blinds in place of the huge, crooked and cracked yellow shades I remembered. A white metal sign with a business's name in blue almost covered the letters chiseled into the lintel over the red-painted metal doors, but I could still see the NE to the left and the OL to the right; New Town High School.

It surprised me to see those same old red metal doors, the color darker than I remembered. I'd walked through them alone that day, shaking, my mouth so dry I thought my tongue would split apart and I'd choke on the blood. I recalled looking helplessly back at my beloved Fred, seeing the sweetness in his kind, black face as he'd nodded encouragement. He could not help me this time.

I squinted at the building through my windshield, then gripped the steering wheel hard and lowered my forehead against it. My dark hair now webbed with silver slid across my cheeks and eyes.

"Forty-four years?" I thought. "Forty-*four*?" I looked into the rearview mirror, at the grey in my hair, and there was lots of it. Neck wattles, too. When was I going to get around to having them sliced off by that New York surgeon? And those crow's feet, looking to me more like eagle's talons. I'd have him do them, too. My throat became swollen as memory pressed hard into my heart.

"My God."

I leaned back on my palms and faced the night sky, and my long, dark hair brushed against my bare back, tickling my skin. I sighed deeply, curiously aroused and confused, and yet pleasured by a new sensation sliding through me like soft, melted chocolate. The stars were clear and thickly clustered as if smeared across the night heavens with a cosmic butter knife, there was a nearly full moon laughing down at me, and I stared up without blinking until I lost the focus and the heavens became a blue/black and silver shimmered blur.

Music from the small orchestra playing on the club's patio up the hill looped down through the soft, dark air, around me, into me, and I softly hummed the gentle melodies. *"Or would you like to swing on a star/ Carry moonbeams home in a jar..."* The songs I loved were now more than ten years old, but I knew all the tunes and words. The emancipated, raw rhythms of that new music called Rock and Roll embarrassed me, made me uneasy. I would not listen to it and most certainly would never dance to it.

It was early August, 1955 on Staten Island New York, I was nearly sixteen years old, and my world that night, was perfect.

*Bliss. Yeah, bliss. God, what a nerdy word. No one ever says that.* I swished my feet in the turquoise water. Tiny green bubbles swirled around my calves and popped to the surface. The pool's underwater lights turned my skin to a milky turquoise, my red toenail polish vivid purple. Tilting back on my hands, I stared into the sky and breathed deeply. I looked down at my body and saw myself reflected in shimmered, scrambling shards in the aqua colored water. Dark long hair, dark eyes, I knew I was too plump but my generous curves pleased me anyway. I was very aware of them now, unashamed and even proud.

A doddering old uncle had once said to me, "You know my dear, you possess an engaging winsomeness," and I secretly often practiced what I hoped was an "engaging winsomeness" in front of the mirror in my locked bedroom, and while I was a little unsure just what "winsome" was, I was pretty sure it was a good thing. I'd look it up in my father's eight-inch-thick dictionary someday.

I knew my lips were too-full, my mouth too wide, and my white teeth protruded just slightly. I had also been advised by that same uncle that this tiny imperfection was appealing, gave me "an endearing Huck Finn look, and besides, didn't you know? All magazine models have buck teeth."

2

I'd laughed out loud at that. Model indeed! But from then on, I smiled almost constantly, so others might enjoy this toothy allure I was now so sure I possessed.

"Hey! Court!" A huge bellowing head suddenly burst through the water's surface, propelled upwards by wide, muscular shoulders and a broad chest streaked with curling, water-flattened hair. A big hand grabbed my ankle roughly and began to pull.

Bracing against the pool's edge, I looked down and grinned at the frothing, hormone-engorged behemoth causing all the commotion: Remington Nathaniel Richardson, my first real boyfriend.

My heart pounded and my eyes widened. Remington was tall and brawny. Dark blond hair topped his big square face split by a wide grin. His large, remarkable eyes were swirls of blue and green, like game marbles called "Clearies" I'd seen boys playing with on The Academy's playground when I was very young. I stared into his face, and felt my heart swell and smiled to cover my nervousness. I reached out and touched Remington's massive wet head, aqua moon reflections rippling over his face. He tightened his grip on my ankle, grinned and jerked hard.

"Ouch! Come on, Rem, let me go!" I shrieked down at him. "Please! Let go! I really don't want to swim. Honest I don't!" Laughing, I clung to the pool's edge, my body nearly horizontal as I tried to squirm away, fully aware that my movements were exciting him, and knowing this, pleased and sort of scared me, but mostly pleased me. I laughed and writhed a little harder, then a lot, and suddenly knowing how, not really knowing how I knew, I pushed my arms hard against my sides so my breasts bulged together and bounced, and he looked and I saw that he saw.

Remington Nathaniel Richardson was considered "a very good catch" by my friends' mothers, and by their daughters too. Every female past puberty who walked by Remington in school flashed hopeful, flirtatious glances in his direction and were thrilled if he flashed one back, which he often did, instinctively understanding his grin's effectiveness and using it to get all he wanted in life, whenever he wanted it. Now, water beading on him like diamond chips falling from the moon, he flashed his best look at me – and kept on tugging.

"Remington!" I shouted at him again, laughing. "Wait a sec! I just want to sit here and listen to the music, and watch the kids swimming. Remmy! Come on, Rem! Stop it!" I twisted my body hard and got my bottom on the edge of the pool. He stopped pulling and drew close to me, gripping both my ankles and propping his chin on my knees. Drops of water trembled on his long eyelashes and he gazed with unabashed admiration down the length of my solid, tanned thighs and into the hard V of my bathing suit and I saw him do it and knew I should pull away, and didn't. I reached out and combed my fingers through his wet hair, pulling clumps into points.

"You look like Alfalfa," I said. Then softly, "Come on up here next to me and let's just sit and talk. It's so nice here, really. Come on Remmy, please?" I was flirting hard to convince him to let me sit in peace, knowing he would not, and not really wanting him to anyway.

Remington was nearly seventeen and well-loved by his teachers in the private school we both attended, and especially by the coaches. These men knew "our boy" could always be depended upon for consistently playing a dazzling game of football, heroic and damn-the-torpedoes, and for often being personally responsible for the team's victories. He maintained excellent grades in school, and planned to attend one of the best Ivy League colleges, although he was never quite sure what that phrase meant. Sometimes I knew he wondered if lesser schools also had ivy growing on their buildings, or if he was forbidden to attend a school that was ivy free. But he never dared to ask about all this, because to ask would have shown ignorance, and that lapse, for him, would have been unforgivable.

Remington had a bright and well-planned future which included making a substantial fortune before he was thirty-five with only a smattering of help from his father, although "smattering" had perhaps a different meaning for him than for others outside of his world.

Remington looked up at me from the pool's edge, then suddenly churned backward in an explosion of water, pushing off from the pool's side with both feet, tugging hard on my ankles. With new shrieks of protest, pretty ones I hoped, I finally splashed down next to him, going under, coming up, spluttering, hair flattening over my eyes. Now breathless, we held onto one another, treading water, our hands sliding, lips brushing, young, strong bodies sliding neatly together, legs corkscrewing tightly, briefly, then flailing to keep from sinking. Pretending to grope for the pool's edge, I let my hands slide furtively over Remington's young bulges. Large drops of water bounced between our faces as we bobbed, and I felt his growing hardness against my belly and I knew with absolute certainty that I loved him.

4

Tiring, we finally pulled and pushed each other out of the pool, our skins slippery and cool. We dried off, rubbed each other's backs, snapping the country club's thick monogrammed towels at each other's bottoms. I knew Remington was staring at my rounded, bouncing backside as I dashed from him, and was sure he earnestly wished to cup his hands around it, to kiss, taste, to bite it, and wondered if I'd love to let him, but he didn't do that, couldn't, not there. Not yet. Remington grabbed my wrist and pulled me back.

"Come on Rem," I pouted (again prettily, I hoped.) "I gotta get to the ladies' cabana to get dressed. I want to dance, Remington, and it'll be over if we don't hurry!"

We parted, backing away, stretching our arms toward one another, fingers sliding on fingers, tips touching to the last second, a melodramatic departure copied from the movies. It felt silly, but we did it anyway, and laughed at our drama as we separated.

When I finally emerged from my cabana, shiny-faced, wet hair combed back, I wore a sheer, peach-colored blouse over a lacy camisole. My black taffeta skirt, noisy, was topped by a wide patent leather belt with an enormous rhinestone buckle. Under it was a bouncing, white crinoline woven through with pink ribbon, so stiff it pulled hundreds of tiny pulls in my nylons.

I had gartered my stockings up tightly, and had wiggled and tugged the seams on my still damp legs so they would be straight, knowing that to be seen with crooked seams was perhaps one of the greatest of social gaffes, along with wearing pearls before six, or sporting gold and silver jewelry on my arms and hands at the same time. My shoes were black patent leather pumps, pointed at the toe, with pencil-thin four-inch stiletto heels, and that they caused my feet great pain was of no consequence. My jewelry consisted of a single strand of perfectly matched pearls, (acceptable, because it was now well after six), smooth and luminous around my neck, and two smaller pearls clipped onto each earlobe.

As I moved toward Remington, I wobbled slightly, struggling to walk on the balls of my feet so the spiked heels wouldn't stab themselves into the grass, and this made my calf muscles burn. I ran my hands lightly, quickly, over my body, enjoying the sensual smoothness of my clothing, and the way my skirt whispered silkily as I walked. I felt wonderful, feminine, happy. My heart beat in quick, sugared spurts. I felt a strange yearning. *I feel as if I'm waking up. From something. What?*

Remington swayed slowly toward me, keeping an easy, sensual rhythm with the music from the club's patio, snapping his fingers softly. He wore a seersucker blue-and-white striped summer blazer, charcoal grey pants and scrupulously clean white bucks, topped by navy and red argyles. His tie was red, blue and gold, striped on the slant, and his shirt was white button-down broadcloth, and the shirt and shoes and his beautiful teeth shone purple-white in the moonlight.

We came together, quickly shy.

"Hi," he said, his voice low. He looked deeply into my eyes, the way he'd seen Alan Ladd and Farley Granger do it.

"Hi," I whispered back, my throat catching the small word, the way I'd heard June Allyson or Ava Gardner do it. We smiled. Looking splendid and knowing it, we joined hands and headed up the banked lawn from the pool to the patio, where we danced amongst our friends, and whispered together until the soft music and the gentle night ended. I absolutely knew that sweet night that the world, my world had stopped still and everything from now on to forever would never change and I was content to let it be.

# CHAPTER 2

The country club where Remington and I danced under the summer stars that evening also held many seasonal events, the most important of which were The Holiday Balls, held, of course, on major holidays: Christian observances like Christmas and Easter, and all-purpose holidays like Thanksgiving, Hallowe'en and Valentine's Day, the last two of which were not official holidays but were celebrated nonetheless, because to hold a Ball was an important rite of passage for both chaperones and young people, and all of them knew it. As I swayed slowly in Remington's arms that summer night my mind drifted to the Holiday dances and I smiled, knowing that now I'd be going to them with Remington, proud I had a serious beau and as a happy bonus, I'd maybe make a few of my girlfriends jealous. I knew thinking that way was wrong but I did not care, not then, not that night.

The Ball I knew began in the early evening after a long and impeccably prepared dinner, served by the club's waiters. Begowned and dewy-eyed young damsels were given hand-painted dance cards, later saved for lifetimes in attic-dried scrap books, looked at maybe once and never again. But on this night, they'd hang from slender kid-gloved wrists by a shining silken strand ending in a tiny golden tassel atop a slim lavender pencil. The young ladies always wore beautiful, long, flowing dresses, in delicate, pale colors, although some wore pure white, perhaps secretly rehearsing their wedding days they hoped might not be too far in the future. They all fluttered about the country club like flowers floating on a shimmering lake, hair gleaming and rippling, faces glowing, jewelry sparkling.

In the trembling breasts of these anxious maidens burned but one thought, that their cards would be quickly filled with the names of twelve nervous, perspiring tuxedoed gentleboys, who, after requesting permission for a numbered dance, scribbled their names on the blank lines, sweaty shaking fingers sliding repeatedly to the point of those damnably tiny pencils, until the smudged name was firmly in place. Having accomplished this, these young bucks could safely and with barely constrained macho, swagger about the ballroom knowing they'd done the manly thing by rescuing the ever-so grateful young maidens from the shame of being wallflowers.

Thus, the intensely relieved young ladies, cards filled, could quietly exhale and lean languidly against the backs of chairs or mahogany newel posts, and rightfully resume airs of calm superiority. Their cards were filled, and they cared not a fig for anyone, not even (and especially not) for friends who hadn't been as lucky as they.

For the less than desirable young maidens however, these cards remained painfully empty. These unfortunates stood stiffly about the ballroom like pastel paintings, their hearts burning with shame, chatting with feigned nonchalance with the other wallflowers, pretending not to care, pretending not to notice the other girls, the chosen, pretty ones, floating by, laughing up into their dance partner's grinning faces, the sound like the tinkling glass of old chandeliers.

One fact always remained achingly obvious to these partnerless young ladies; they had not been asked to dance. But they held their chins high with false pride while smiling stiff, bright fake smiles, laughing brittle, high-pitched and panicky laughter, all the while hoping they conveyed that they cared nothing in the least about being so obviously swainless. But care they did, and so wanted to have been asked, to be able to dance with the others, the beautiful ones.

But they were never asked all through their high school years. Never. These tragic girls were the Holiday Ball regulars, who bravely showed up at every dance because mothers forced them.

Ah, but help, embarrassing, awful help was always hovering nearby in the form of the Ball chaperones who considered it their God-given responsibility to make absolutely certain these less-than-perfect young ladies had their cards filled. Any young men unschooled in the techniques of avoiding these formidable Defenders of the Empty Dance Card were straightaway snagged, and pressed, with a sweet, nail-hard smile, into compliance. There was and is no name for male wallflowers, but many of the male attendees at The Holiday Balls were exactly that, and their hearts bled also, although from their facial expressions, no one could possibly know. On average, most of the uncarded young men were not handsome, certainly many were not very bright, and all were not popular.

They were, they knew, assuredly not beggars and, unlike the shunned girls, these equally shunned boys at least had the chance to choose, or so they'd persuaded themselves. They knew a flawed female had far less market value than a flawed male, having had that fact taught them scrupulously from birth by their all-wise fathers. Left to their druthers, however, they would pass over these wallflowers with scant regard for their feelings and happily spend the evening in stag mode punching at each other and laughing raucously.

It would never have occurred to these young bucks that these languishing girls had small desire to spend time with them either, although being empty-carded at a Ball rather predisposed them to other standards, at least for that evening.

Thus, the aching girls no one wanted to dance with were passed over by the aching boys no one wanted to dance with either. It was the boys' job now to pretend to not see Remmie dance smoothly by with a gossamer vision in his arms, and for the standing girls to glance indifferently as their friends floated past them, held tenderly in the arms of an adolescent Adonis.

I squeezed my eyes shut and pressed my face into Remington's shoulder as we danced in the summer night, trying not to think about the Holiday Balls coming up. I knew some of the wallflower girls from The Academy and even though my upbringing told me it was none of my concern, I was concerned in spite of myself and tried to make up for their pain by being excessively sweet to them during the upcoming weeks, but I knew they knew and that made it worse. I pulled my head back and smiled up at my first real boyfriend and soon those sore and guilt-riddled feelings drifted away from me like the music in the night.

As at any Holiday Ball, a reception line was imperative, comprised of fabulously appointed and bejeweled grand dames. These country club doyennes stood rigidly in a row, coifs high, jewels flashing, and judgments more finely honed than a double row of teeth from a mature Great White. At their sides stood bored and sweating husbands, hapless gentlemen squeezed miserably into tuxedos tailored for them several decades before, but which now cut and squashed them mercilessly.

As soon as these grand men and women greeted each other and all the young Ball attendees, and the line, thank God, came to an end, these luckless patricians would bolt en masse across the ballroom and through the enormous dining room to the Men's Grille where women were not allowed, and where there was always a bottomless supply of very hard liquor which satisfactorily helped them through the evening. How these woeful husbands hated those Balls and even secretly thought them unnecessary and not needed under any circumstances, although they knew better than to express these sentiments to their steadfastly resolute wives.

Some long time later, with rosy glows, bleary, guilty smiles, and in considerably improved fettle, these husbands would return to their livid wives who would fix upon them glares capable of melting plate steel. Now able to endure the Ball ordeal to the end, with an occasional quick revisit to the Men's Grille for re-libation, the men stood (or swayed) in obedient, congenial acquiescence, an occasional snort of mirth escaping them.

Dancing couples at these affairs were forbidden to have any body parts below waists brushing even lightly together, and if the orchestra dared to swing into something with an actual beat, it was immediately silenced by the Country Club's Guardian of Purity and Righteousness, an uptight, perpetually frowning, grey old goat named Mr. Caswell who was literally thought to be, at least by all those under the age of 20, to have somehow once had a ramrod implanted in his spine and left there. He was astonishingly rigid.

"It simply isn't done," was the repeated clarion call with relentless regularity throughout the evening whenever a couple tried to convince the orchestra to play something somewhat livelier than a Fox Trot from the early 1900s. It was a phrase the young people had heard from birth, and for them, it had, against their wills, a certain thrust.

The chaperones meanwhile, kept a watchful eye on the dancers. Like every young couple there, Remington and I obeyed these rules, but when we thought the coast was clear and the hawkeyed chaperones were looking elsewhere, we allowed our young bodies to press together, while we chatted and laughed, pretending it wasn't really happening, thrilled that it was.

The etiquette of these Balls did not permit young attendees to come as couples, so we quickly learned to sneak out and join each other behind a tall, dense hedge at the side of the country club's property. Here we would neck wildly as long as we dared, hoping our absence was not noticed, although it always was.

One night when the Ball was nearly over, Remington and I passed a secret signal to each other, and nonchalantly left the dance floor at separate times. We met at the back entrance of the ballroom and ran hand in hand in the darkness, the hem of my gown bunched in my free hand and pulled high over my knees. My high heeled satin dyed-to-match shoes gouged holes in the grass and became dirty, but I didn't care. The peach-colored dress I wore, with its long creamy ribbons tied at the waist streamed behind me, making me think, hope, making me know I looked exactly like Scarlett O'Hara.

Suppressing shrieks of laughter, Remington and I sped over the spacious lawns toward our new secret place in a thick stand of pine trees. Our breath coming in great spurts, we stopped abruptly at our spot, and stared at one another, suddenly shy. Reaching out, our hands bumped awkwardly, and then our fingers wound together as we gazed meaningfully into each other's eyes and laughed and fell into an ardent, bumbling embrace.

Suddenly, headlights sliced through our hideout. "Get down! Follow me!" Remington hissed. He bolted away, but I tripped on the hem of my gown and fell. I crawled clumsily beneath a tall pine tree, tearing my Ball gown's skirt from its bodice. Twigs and stones shredded my hands and knees as I scrambled close to the tree's trunk. I crouched beneath its low-hanging branches and began to pray I was in a safe hiding place, prayed I would be unseen. The car's headlights pinioned me between the low growing branches. *Oh God, oh God!!* I was clearly being seen by that driver! The car hesitated. I froze in mid-crouch, eyes bulged, staring into the headlights, horrified. My heart hammered painfully against my ribs as I envisioned the chaperones' wrath when they discovered my transgression, when they told my parents.

"I'm a dead duck," I breathed aloud.

But then, a miracle in agonizing, slow motion. The car edged away! I watched it slowly pass and saw the tail lights disappear down the long circular driveway. Collapsing to the earth, I exhaled in gratitude and sucked dirt and pine needles into my mouth and nose as I gasped and gulped air. Small sharp twigs wedged into the top of my strapless gown, stabbing me, but I didn't care. I lay on my belly under the big pine for some minutes. I would never know who it was that had decided to keep my secret that night, but I'd never stop being thankful, and I thought about that person, that saviour, all of my life.

Remington drove me home that late summer night after the dance at the Club and kissed me goodnight chastely, awkwardly. I wanted to ask him if he really had his driver's license or had just sneaked off in his parents' car but I did not want to ruin that evening with a silly technicality. I walked up the flagstone path to my front door, turned, waved and blew a kiss hoping I was doing a great imitation of Ingrid Bergman, but Remington had already backed out of the driveway and was moving away, so he never saw my performance. No matter. I was happy, completely convinced I would never be this happy again. Happy in my future? Yes, but this happy? Impossible! Remington was the love of my life forever.

I awakened late as I always did on weekends. Languorously sliding my fingers through my long hair, I let it fall over the canopied bed's side. I was giddily blissful, my thoughts only of the ball and beautiful, dear, wonderful Remmie. My torn and dirty ball gown lay sprawled on top of my chintz covered chair like an exploded, pastel balloon, pine needles sticking from it like quills. I'd make something up if my mother questioned me about the gown, if she actually came into my room and saw it, which wasn't likely. The lie would slide out casually, effortlessly, as my lies always did to my mother. Besides, I would make sure my dear, indifferent mother never saw the gown anyway. *There are advantages to being ignored!* I smiled.

And then sighed. Time for lunch soon. Time to get up and face my boring parents in the dining room. Time, too, to prepare for my tennis date with Sally. We'd play a few sets, and would attend a Tennis Tea afterward. *Gee, I hope Mary cleaned my whites.* I pulled myself slowly from the bed.

Humming as I dressed after my shower, I became slowly aware of my parents talking in the breakfast room below my bedroom. The thick walls of the old English Tudor home muffled their words in winters, but now their voices carried clearly through the opened windows. The faithful Wolcott staff happily cranked open all the casement windows in the big, old home to bring breezes through. It felt good to them after a long sealed-in winter.

The voices from the breakfast room became louder, and were obviously angry. *"Angry? Mumz and Dadz are angry? Nah, that would mean they'd have to be alive!"* I laughed quietly at my own joke and then stopped moving and raised my eyebrows in surprise. My parents very rarely argued. My mother knew her place.

Somewhat older than the parents of my peers, my small, mousy mother and loud buffoonish father generally appeared happily married, always attentive to each other's needs, while often cool and indifferent to mine. They quite nearly always ignored me, treating me as a guest they sometimes enjoyed, but more often wished might soon leave. I was always aware of this fact and had become quite used to it even while wishing way down deep they could be like normal parents, loving and involved. But finally, as I grew older, I quietly accepted these constant parental detachments, indeed was mostly comfortable with them and had long since given up the yearning to be "someone's little girl." Sometimes though, it saddened me when I'd let it, especially when I visited friends' homes and saw the love, laughter and attention their parents gave them.

I had long speculated my birth had been unexpected, and wondered sometimes if I'd been adopted because I simply could never imagine my parents joining together in passion and actually "doing it." My girlfriends and I had often discussed the possibilities of getting pregnant by means other than the norm, although we weren't completely clear about what "the norm" actually was, but were actively pursuing all methods of learning; books, rumors, movies, forbidden magazines, and the ever-revered "gutter." Some of the more advanced of our group actually had gotten the information straight from their parents. Some from teachers. And a few rare ones, from their doctors, and they were very willing to share the titillating information to those of us who asked, and we all asked.

Eventually, I came to the irrevocable conclusion that my existence could only be credited to a shared toilet seat, or perhaps by a renegade sperm that had somehow escaped my father's unimaginable testicles and had resolutely and without notice, chased my mother around our swimming pool, and surreptitiously climbed aboard and within.

As I walked down the stairs and toward the breakfast room, I heard my mother say with an edge of shrill hysteria, "But Walter! You promised me the problem was taken care of, that this would never happen again! You *swore* to me!" *Problem? My father has a problem? Is being a gasbag considered a problem?* When my father answered, his voice was low and thickly sad. I strained to hear.

"Helen, I'm so …. I'm so very, very sorry. I couldn't help it. It just happened. I'll take care of it, dear, just like before. Please. Don't worry about it. Just don't worry."

"Don't *worry* about it Walter?! Don't worry about it? You told me you'd gotten help, shots or something, pills. A psychiatrist. Walter, what if everyone finds out, what if our friends, club members ------Oh! Hello Courtenay darling." My mother turned quickly toward me, her anguished expression changing instantly to an eager, warm smile, but not soon enough. I had seen my mother's white, frightened face.

*Fake. God, I hate that fake cheerful grin of hers. How the hell does she switch so fast?*

"How did you sleep, my dear?" my mother asked sweetly. "Did you have a wonderful evening? Come and sit down and tell us all about it." She patted the chair next to her. I stared at her. *What?? She means me?* I took a few hesitant steps toward her.

"Well Mother, Father," I began, grinning, "it was just a simply fabulous evening." I slowly began to lower myself into the chair next to my mother. "The music was divine, and just everyone was there. And my card was filled almost immediately. And, oh, Mother, the flowers were--" I paused, and then sighed quietly. They had already turned back to each other, this time to discuss some problem they were having with the printed invitations to their upcoming black-tie party. *Invisible again. So what else is new?* I sighed, loudly this time, hoping it would be noticed. It wasn't. I stood and began to walk out of the room.

"Never mind," I said, but they did not react. I said it again, one more time, softly, when I reached the doorway, but again, my parents didn't hear. Couldn't hear. Wouldn't hear. What did it matter, really, my being invisible to my own parents? I often thought I hadn't ever really been born somehow. Was I really here? I'd become used to their doing this, I would tell myself, wishing it were otherwise, but then realizing yet again that if my parents ever actually listened to me for more than four minutes, I'd be rendered speechless from the shock.

My parents, the Wolcotts, I knew and had certainly been reminded of, were in great demand socially, considered one of the "better couples" in their circle. Married a long time, they did the myriad things financially secure people are privileged to do: they took long trips, threw lavish parties, owned expensive cars, jewelry and clothing, and indulged themselves (and occasionally me too) in every new gadget and creature-comfort invention that came on the market. They had several gardeners to attend the lengthy terraced lawns and the profusion of flowers, plants and imported, exotic trees. There seemed to be a staff member to look after every single thing in and around our home.

14

Considered a "handsome couple" by their peers, I had to admit they actually sometimes were. Always impeccably dressed, even putting on a jacket and tie to eat leftovers in his own home, even when the staff was not home, my father Walter Wolcott was tall, grey haired and in certain lights, at certain angles he actually did resemble The King, Clark Gable, or at least thought he did. In fact, was sure he did. Everyone said so, after all. He occasionally tried to do the Gable squint and smirk into his mirror when my mother couldn't see. I caught him at it a couple of times and I laughed and he turned and stared blankly at me. But then he always stared blankly at me, so it didn't much matter.

My father had several close friends and a few of them were teachers at The Academy where I was in the 10<sup>th</sup> grade. They golfed together on Sundays on the Country Club courses, and seemed to belong to a kind of secret man club, sharing secret man things, laughing at secret man jokes, giving each other secret sly man grins, manlike slaps on the back. I was always weirdly uncomfortable at their closeness but decided it's what men did when they were together. Or something. Other men I knew didn't seem to behave so oddly in groups, although lots of them acted kind of stupid together, I thought. And when I was in school all this never happened because my father was never in The Academy, probably because I was there. He almost always seemed to want to be anywhere other than where I was.

My mother, Helen Wolcott was vacuous, at least with me, and her eyes, when she bothered to look at me, were dull and uninterested, grey, and her mouth was always turned down at the corners. She often made me feel as if I'd been an unfortunate accident, and perhaps I had been. My mother was one of those women who never aged; she looked perpetually old. She was short and had beige-grey streaked hair cut with no particular style, sallow skin, a non-smile when she bothered, sort of tight and forced. She was constantly arranging parties and trips but did it all in a kind of Johnny One Note way, only enthused about "doing the right thing" but not even enjoying doing that very much. She ran the house well because she didn't really have any other goals and spent a large part of every day lying on the twin bed in my parents' bedroom talking on the phone. Hour after hour; no one seemed to know or care who was at the other end of the line and I often wondered if there actually was anyone. She did it so often and for so long each day that the side of her bed sagged in the shape of her body and she lay exactly there for

15

each phone call as if it were her own personal cradle, and it was. My mother was colorless within and without. She worked at being stylish but it never took very successfully. She'd layer on lots of make-up, clipped, pinned and hung many jewels onto her body at various locations, and wore highly fashionable outfits when she and my father were entertaining, but it was all strange looking compared to other women. She didn't seem to be able to make it all come together very well. My mother always seemed bored and out of touch and did not appear to have much joy in her life. I often wondered if she had taken on maybe just one of the physical chores in our home if she'd have been happier having at least something to do during her long days, but the extent of her life was planning parties, packing for trips, keeping our home clean and in order, giving meal orders to the black people working for us, and walking to her bedroom to dial the phone. Sometimes, when I guess she thought I wouldn't notice, she'd stare at my father with a vaguely troubled expression of fear, maybe shock, always a sort of strange helplessness. A questioning look. It was hard to define, but she'd slip into that facial thing sometimes and I'd wonder if she thought maybe her handsome husband was having an affair or something, but no, I could not imagine any woman being interested in my father. He indeed was handsome, but he was aloof and boring. Except for his vanity, wealth and playing golf, he seemed to me to be distant, sparkless, of no interest and having none. He was always somehow pre-occupied. I so often compared him to my friends' fathers, and he always came up wanting.

During weak moments, I let myself yearn for a normal father and mother, who would hold, love and cherish me, but I would quickly run mentally from those thoughts knowing it was not to be, not ever, that wishing for those things would not ever make them possible and I'd sigh and look up at the sky. I'd then shake it off. I was pretty sure I had a very good life anyway.

My parents had two maids in their hire, Negroes, Emma and Mary, and one black man, my beloved Fred who handled all the repairs and the outside work, and he drove me anywhere I wanted to go. Emma lived in her own quarters in a small wing of what I knew she thought was our splendid house, so she could more easily attend the mundane and unpleasant housewiferies my mother eschewed. Mary came from her own home every morning, Thursdays off, and took care of laundry and other chores my parents asked of her. And Fred showed up every day because our huge old English Tudor needed perpetual care.

I loved these people even when I caught them all giving each other curiously knowing looks, but I never knew what they thought they knew, or maybe did know. Those exchanged looks always startled me --- they knew something about my parents I did not know, but I knew they'd never tell me. And then they would smile reassuringly at me and touch me lovingly.

My father was, la de da, THE Mr. Walter Hancock Wolcott and his wife, the woman who insisted she was my mother, was la de da THE Helen Avis Wolcott and were typical of their peers in their narrow and velveted world. I happily and warily realized sometimes they were not entirely unhappy about my place in their lives. Sometimes they even liked me---I think. I was tolerated, expected to conform, to absolutely unfailingly do the correct thing in any situation, and to be a never-wavering credit to my parents. In return, I was given a sheltered life with all possible comforts. There was one more important recompense I had known as far back as my memory began; I was expected to marry well, continuing the tradition to which I'd been born.

As I grew, I gradually and then thoroughly understood my place in the universe, especially vis a vis NOOK-D's. I'd always been told by my parents how proud they'd been that one of my first baby words had been "NOOK-D's." This awful word was a wealthy family's code word spoken at family and social gatherings often right in front of the servants and others of their ilk because it was presumed they would not know what it meant. "Not of Our Kind, Dear." But the servants knew. They always had. I knew they knew and hated that they knew. But knew they did.

My la de da parents carefully taught me the basics of The Good Life they expected me to lead: Correct manners at all times; how to unobtrusively remove a bone from one's mouth during a formal dinner without offending the sensibilities of the other guests; to always blow one's nose before one enters a host's gracious home when coming in from the cold, (thus to avoid the indelicacy of the other guests having to see one's nose run); to always send thank-you notes; to never completely finish one's meal at a dinner party implying that one was wealthy enough to waste food; to observe the rules of *Noblesse Oblige* at all times, and that I must never, ever cross over the invisible line separating me from those of lesser station. The list was long but I knew it perfectly and always would.

Proud, I knew my parents felt that I was now able to properly follow in their wake, and could quite soon be safely launched into a socially well-fitting marriage to exactly the correct young man from exactly the correct family with exactly the proper amount of money; lots. I sensed they were not displeased with Remington Nathaniel Richardson.

# CHAPTER 3

In September, I would finally be a junior at The Academy. The private school was small, with classes usually of no more than ten students, most of whom I'd known since kindergarten. We knew our fathers' money would easily take us to college, even if our scholastic accomplishments did not. Life presented few pressures and most of our concentration centered on how, where, how much and how often we could indulge in life's pleasures.

The headmaster of The Academy was Mr. Winston Raleigh, a squat, light-haired hawk-faced gentleman with grey metallic eyes, impeccable dress, correctness and credentials, and a sudden, violent temper that exploded viciously with no predictability. The only certainty was that it would, and with horrifying frequency. The student body learned early on how to avoid the man completely, since the causes of the headmaster's savage outbursts were never consistent or even logical. When walking by him was unavoidable, it was best to keep one's eyes cast down, one's expression obedient, submissive and polite.

The principal's outbursts came frequently and each were much like the last ones; the man's performances could be depended upon, if nothing else. This day would not be much different and yet we could not stop staring. Our principal was like looking at a car wreck; we knew we should not stare but we simply had to.

"Look! Oh my God, there he goes again," I whispered to my friend Sally as we walked down The Academy's long hallway. "His lid is about to blow!" It was Friday. The students were restless. Some, in a lax moment, had let their guard down in front of Mr. Raleigh.

A luckless student passed by, and the seams holding the headmaster's black neon temper began to slowly and unreasonably split. The very air became electrified as students stopped to watch with frightened, unmasked glee, the way gazelles will stand and watch silently as one of their own is being torn to shreds by a lion. Sally and I watched, mesmerized, as the headmaster loomed over the young boy, his face slowly draining of color as if being sucked back through his skin and into his skull. Mr. Raleigh chewed fiercely on his lower lip, and his pale, tin-colored eyes popped as if set on springs.

At some unseen, unheard signal, we students began to slowly make a wide circle around Mr. Raleigh and his victim, walking so slowly it was difficult to tell we were moving at all. We watched the gruesome scene warily, silently exulting that *we* had not been the ones pinioned. Our eyes darted between Mr. Raleigh and the wretched child who stood rigidly, face white, eyes wide, as if he'd been submerged in cold cement.

"Wow Sal, Raleigh looks bad this time. Worse than usual," I said.

Mr. Raleigh never discriminated. Both sexes were equally selected as the objects of his white fury, though they were subjected to slightly different behaviors. Mr. Raleigh forced girls to stand rigidly in front of him to be impaled by his wrath. If the student were a boy, however, Raleigh would sit in his high-backed oak and black leather swivel chair, forcing the young man to sit directly opposite him, their four knees touching. As he screamed, Mr. Raleigh would grasp the boy's thighs in both hands, inflicting excruciating pain. He would then, in a piercingly high pitch, list the child's sins, extracting shrieked, frightened promises from the tortured and thoroughly humiliated lad that they would never occur again, whether or not they'd occurred in the first place. By the end of the tirade, Mr. Raleigh's terrible hands would have slid to the very tops of the boy's thighs.

Sally and I moved on to class, looking back over our shoulders at the headmaster's contortions. I sat at my desk, silent, and thought about Mr. Raleigh's rages. My hands were wet and cold, and I could not quite focus my eyes. *God, I wish he wouldn't do that. It's so terrible. I wish he wouldn't. Why does he keep on doing that?*

The other kids were laughing about the way our headmaster's tongue would slowly begin to protrude when he was about mid-rage, the tip folding back against his lower teeth, at least an inch beyond his whitened lips. Everyone, sometimes even the victim, would stare in fascination as spittle sprayed from each side of the man's tongue, showering the horrified youngster from head to chest. We students chortled gleefully about the pulsing purple veins in Mr. Raleigh's temples, how they contrasted with his beige hair which in turn contrasted with his florid face.

"Like a science fiction monster," we laughed. "Yeah, like that!"

I turned my head away as the kids relived their headmaster's latest and most creative tantrum. I'd been a Raleigh casualty a few times myself, and I remembered, and shuddered.

For as long as I could recall, my father and Mr. Raleigh were in the habit of playing golf every weekend with Mr. Harold Tonaschell, The Academy's Latin instructor, weather permitting. One steamy summer day when I was twelve, my pals and I went on a picnic into some nearby woods, while my father golfed again with his two player pals. As we sat in the soft, dappled shade, my friends while giggling, told me about something they'd overheard their parents whispering at a cocktail party.

Some years before, it seems Mr. Tonaschell had suffered through a difficult time, referred to tactfully by the students' parents as "the incident." It involved the testimony of a young boy, then in the fifth grade.

One late fall afternoon, Mr. Tonaschell had apparently offered the boy a ride home after soccer practice. The boy lived nearby, but it was cold and he was tired and dirty. His parents had not come to see him play, so the child was grateful for the ride and the chance to discuss the game with an adult who had been there. During the course of the short drive, my friends told me, Mr. Tonaschell suddenly turned into a dead-end side road. When he got to the end, he abruptly slammed on his brakes, then reached across the car seat and shoved his hand roughly up the leg of the boy's soccer shorts. Confused, frightened, and suddenly fearful of showing disrespect, the boy apologetically pushed the older man's hand away, imploring Mr. Tonaschell, "please, please sir, I'm sorry, but please, could you---- stop doing that?"

Not knowing what else to do, the boy wrenched the car door open, jumped out and began to run. Tires grinding into the dirt of the road, Mr. Tonaschell roared up behind the boy, slammed to a stop and leapt from the car. He caught the boy, grabbing him violently and spinning him around by the shoulders.

Tears began to streak down the young boy's cheeks leaving white stripes on his dirt-smudged face. He stared in terror at the older man, not knowing what to do, how to scream, where to run. He stood rigid before the man. Then quite suddenly, to the boy's utter horror, Mr. Tonaschell fell clumsily to his knees, wrapped his arms about the child's body, squeezing hard, and began to plead with the child to forget what had just happened, hugging him, pushing him away. Weeping, the teacher offered the boy money, his shaking hands digging into his pockets, bills and change scattering across the ground. Mr. Tonaschell

21

offered the boy everything, anything he wanted, even a new bike, if he would only promise to not tell.

When the child was unable to answer through his frightened sobs, Mr. Tonaschell grabbed the boy's shirt with both of his hands and jerked him off his feet. Shoving his livid face into the boy's, Mr. Tonaschell, his voice now hoarse with rage, then threatened to kill him, his baby sister and his parents too, if he ever dared to tell. He shook the child violently, and demanded to know if he was being understood. The child responded through his terrified sobs that indeed he did. The enraged teacher shook him once more, hard, snapping his head back and forth to make his point absolutely clear. Then he dropped the boy into a heap on the roadway, got into his car and drove off, savagely spraying the child with stones and dirt from his tires on the roadway's surface.

When he was certain Mr. Tonaschell was really gone, the boy scrambled to his feet and ran home. Apparently, he believed the Latin teacher's threats because he didn't tell his parents what he'd been through until finally, weeks later, the nightmares he'd managed to keep unknown to his parents began to result in his shrieking incriminating words into the darkness. His parents convinced him after hours of persuasion that it was OK to tell, that in fact he had to. How could they help him, they begged their son, if he didn't tell them what had happened and why he was so afraid? They loved him so much, they assured him, that he'd be safe if he told. And so, in long shuddering breaths and flowing tears, the boy told his parents.

"Oh, come off it! You think I'm stupid or something? That never happened," I said, looking at my friends, but I could see by their faces they weren't joking. I didn't really understand why Mr. Tonaschell would put his hand into the young soccer player's shorts, why a man would want to touch a boy like that. Worst of all, I could not understand why nothing happened after the parents reported Mr. Tonaschell.

Apparently, Mr. Tonaschell had been glib, calm and amused at the accusations. He convinced everyone who mattered, students and faculty alike, that the boy had made it up to get back at Mr. Tonaschell for reprimanding him in front of his friends after a soccer game. Students and faculty immediately believed the teacher and mocked the child. The matter was dropped. Shortly afterwards, the boy and his family moved away.

I sat with my head bowed as the awful story ended. My chest was constricted with revulsion and fear I hoped my friends wouldn't notice.

"So that's it?" I asked. "It happened exactly like that? You know this? You're sure??" My throat was dry. To hide my disquietude, I bit into a sandwich Mary had made for me that morning. It made me gag.

"You mean after that---that thing ----that happened, everything went back to normal?" I asked, trying to hide the fact that I was choking, not doing it very well. My friends assured me the story was absolutely true and that everything in fact had gone back to normal. The matter was forgotten, they told me, "except at cocktail parties."

Why, I wondered, did this story make me feel so afraid? Why, I wondered, were my eyes spilling tears?

The three men--- Mr. Raleigh, my father, and Mr. Tonaschell – had remained friends after that, and anyone who bothered to think about it would have noticed that all three had similarly explosive tempers. Mr. Raleigh's was by far the worst and most infamous, but I convinced myself that his friendship with my father might protect me from the headmaster's wrath, although there would come a time when I came perilously close to being caught in the net of his wild rage.

It was in 1951, the year of the Korean "Police Action," when President Harry S Truman fired General Douglas MacArthur as Commander of the United Nations forces for publicly advocating the bombing and blockading of Communist China. We'd been told that MacArthur had openly disagreed with the plans President Truman had in place to declare war on Korea. Our teachers said that the President did not want China involved in the war, no matter what. MacArthur disagreed with his boss's plans, wrote and sent many letters to Congress about this and finally sent a strong letter of ultimatum to China without asking permission of the President first. And then, the great and mighty General Douglas MacArthur quickly lost his job.

The entire student body marched on Mr. Raleigh, demanding they be allowed go to the home of a teacher who had one of the new television sets everyone was always talking about, but did not as yet own, their families somehow connecting having "one of those things" in their homes with having a bawdy, common vaudeville show in their great rooms. The students wanted to watch the ticker-tape parade that would commemorate the General's triumphant return to the United States even though the great General was disgraced for disobeying a direct order from his boss, Harry S Truman. The American public was supportive and adoring of the renowned wartime leader and gave him a fabulous welcome home in spite of their President.

I, at eleven years old, and in the 6th grade, was moving rapidly into the confused, smart-ass echelon of adolescence. As the crowd of students mutineered in the hallway outside Mr. Raleigh's office door, demanding the day off from school in order to watch the historic event, I turned to my about-to-explode principal, flashed a sugary smile at him and said in a sing-song voice, "Well, Mr. Raleigh, you can't blame us for wanting to see history in action."

A ghastly silence swelled the hallway. The student body froze to a solid unmoving block and all eyes burned on Mr. Raleigh and me. His secretary's fingers hovered like frozen commas above the typewriter keys. Mr. Raleigh's face turned slowly to chalk and his eyes began to bulge. Saliva collected at the corners of his mouth in wet seed-pearls. The famous tongue slowly emerged and folded itself backward. As his hand moved toward my shoulder, he glared down at me and I stared back with a bravado not in the least matched in my guts.

But then, astonishingly, Mr. Raleigh spoke very quietly and dropped his hand. "Do not be impudent, Courtenay Wolcott," he said. Keen disappointment filled the hearts of the watching students as Mr. Raleigh's face slowly returned to normal. He looked through his pince-nez glasses at the children massed at his office door, and smiled.

"Well, then, children, get on with it," he said hoarsely, "you really must see this bit of American History as Miss Wolcott has suggested, albeit somewhat rudely I may add. I'll notify the school bus drivers to take you. See each of you in the morning. No running. Haste makes waste!"

The stunned kids stared at me, suddenly their hero, and I stared back, my knees buckling, realizing that a sort of history had been made right there in The Academy's hallway, of more import to me than the return of the mighty, and fallen, General Douglas MacArthur.

# CHAPTER 4

The Academy was an enormous old Victorian building that sprawled and towered at once in the center of town like a great brick queen. Originally built as a private residence and converted into a school about 80 years before my enrollment, the building boasted "great character," with pointed, steep slate roofs that mirrored the hills it sat upon, and massive, cathedral doorways surrounded by deep carvings of mighty battle scenes. Inside were wide, graceful marble staircases, gentle depressions worn into their steps, mostly on the right, by the footsteps of generations of Academy students.

On either side of the echoing hallways were high-ceilinged classrooms, all former bed and sitting rooms, boudoirs, whose huge, ornately carved fireplaces had been blocked with fitted squares of heavy, black painted wood. The hallways, wide enough for students to gallop six abreast when the mood hit (and Mr. Raleigh was not about,) had loudly creaking wooden floors, making sneaked trips to anywhere in the building nearly, but not always, impossible. Each hallway ended in huge, floor-to-ceiling mirrors, framed in heavy gold baroque, whose chiselings were chipped and overflowing with decades of black, oily dust.

The bathrooms were the students' favorite rooms. The acoustics were perfect because of the floor-to-ceiling porcelain tiles. There, we students with the anonymous abandon we loved, liked to sing or howl in hopes of aggravating our teachers, and these efforts were generally successful. The toilets had wooden seats and water closets high above, with long brass chains that ended in a wooden tear-drop shaped smoothed-from-wear handles for flushing. These chains were also successfully and frequently used to tie up our fellow students' gym clothes. We were in the eighth grade now, meaning we knew everything, and nothing could hold us back. We were immortal.

The classrooms were warmed in winter by tall, black radiators covered with bas relief scenes of noble stags, pheasants in flight and wild boar hunts, and they hissed and banged loudly all day from October through May, when they worked at all. The heat was overpowering but poorly radiated, causing the luckless students nearest them to drift helplessly into a thick, sleep-tugging torpor, while the students across the room slowly atrophied from the cold. Because we were all seated alphabetically and my name began with a W., I got to sit close to those hissing behemoths and spent a lot of my years in those classes trying to force myself to stay awake and alert. It wasn't easy and I was frequently unsuccessful.

The school's two huge auditoriums, one more a gymnasium than the other, were former ballrooms when the wealthy owners lived there. The lower one was large enough to hold two tennis courts, its walls covered with climbing devices. Hanging from the high beams were the knotted ropes on which boys climbed hand-over-hand to develop upper body strength, and of course for showing off too, with displays of snorting disdain for any of us girls who happened by.

Students ran laps on the balcony that circled the top third of the great wooden gymnasium, and the room smelled of sweat and hemp, old wood and decades of dust. The upper track had a deteriorating metal railing, ostensibly to keep the runners from plummeting to the gym's floor below, and when the young students ran their laps the entire structure shuddered with exhaustion.

Edward Judson, an excruciatingly shy student, was one of my Academy friends. One day after months of sleepless planning, he decided to act on his year's long fantasy of impressing his female classmates, with some daring athleticism. I knew he wanted to impress me in particular because he "liked" me as they said back then. He often tried rather feebly to do this, and never succeeded. But I always made a point of chatting with Edward. I knew he was lonely.

Edward was a slight boy and would be a slight man, but at 15, he was a frail, hopeless snarl of acne, elbows, enormous bony hands and well-spaced hair sprouts. He possessed a voice that continued to crack from high to low for years beyond his adolescence, and on occasion, he honked an uncontrollable, inappropriate maniacal laugh. His hair was thin and colorless. He had huge feet, no height and wore thick black-framed glasses. Edward had an ever-present, sour odor about him, known to everyone who came within 3 feet of him, but clearly unknown to him.

On Edward's chosen day of reckoning, a group of my girlfriends and I were clustered on the gym floor, preparing for a badminton tournament, choosing partners. Edward coughed loudly as he leaned nonchalantly from the balcony's rickety railing above. He looked at the ceiling, coughed again. It was an ugly sound, and wet. Almost a snort.

Sally and I looked up, and then at each other.

"What do you think he's gonna do?" I muttered, with no particular interest. Even from the floor below, I could see Edward's heart thudding in his thin pigeon breast beneath his thin plaid shirt.

Edward glanced down and made a crude, sharp sound in his throat, louder than the cough, worse, awful, determined to get all the girls to look up at him, not just Sally and me. When everyone finally obliged, Edward smiled down at us, took a deep breath, climbed the shaky balcony railing and sat on it, his legs and huge feet dangling above the parquet floor of the gym below. We stopped talking, our faces continuing to turn upward toward the boy sitting on the old railing above us, swinging his skinny legs and big clumsy sneakers back and forth.

"Jeez," I said. "What a jerk! He's trying to look cool, but he's really scared to death. I can tell."

"Yeah," whispered Sally. "He's giving me the creeps! He really ought to come down. Should we call up to him or get a teacher? What? What should we do?"

"I don't know, Sal, I just don't know." My mouth was beginning to get very dry, and my neck hurt from peering up at Edward. I felt dizzy.

Still sitting on the railing, Edward stared for several moments upward toward one of the steel beams that stretched high over the gymnasium, from wall to wall. Some of the girls gasped, a few tittered nervously. I could see that months of planning and mental rehearsing were flashing quickly through Edward's mind. Slowly, wobbling, he managed to stand on the top bar of the ancient black metal railing, tottered and grasped the steel beam above him an instant before he would have tumbled to the floor below.

With a loud grunt he swung his legs up and around it, hung there for a moment like a hairless monkey from a branch, and then, with another loud grunt, hoisted his thin body onto the beam and straddled it. And then, with an awkward, quaking scrambling of his legs and arms, he then stood atop it, arms extended to each side, a novice high-wire performer on his first gig. I could actually see the thrill of joy shoot through him when he heard the gasps and smattering of high shrieks from the girls below. I knew life for Edward at that instant had meaning at last, and I could see by his face he found it breathtakingly delicious.

His sneakered feet firmly on the steel beam, arms extended to each side, stick-like wings, Edward edged out past the safety of the balcony, out over the gym floor and then slowly sank to his hands and knees and began to crawl across. He swayed and glanced down at us girls below him.

I could see Edward was pleased at our expressions of fright and wonder. He was being noticed at last! I knew it was a moment more exquisite than Edward had dared to dream.

It was also the moment, he discovered, that he was a lot higher than he'd thought he'd be when planning his performance from the safety of his bed late at night. The floor below was bigger too, an ocean of wood. It looked really hard.

Eyes widening with horror, I saw Edward suddenly freeze. Fear, like an icy, steel hand, began to squeeze his heart. I could easily see that Edward was unable to move forward or backward, to speak, to cry out. He stayed still, a terrified statue, hands clamped rigidly, skinny knees shaking on the beam.

His face slowly changed to grey-blue and his mouth fell open. He drooled, and the liquid hung down like a long, shiny, transparent worm, stretching past the steel beam, then splattering unevenly on the gym floor. I looked down and stared at the tiny wet spot, and looked back up at Edward. My mouth, like his, also hung open in horror. I could see his eyes popping from his head.

So desperate now, Edward stared down at the gym floor and slowly lost control of his bladder. The hot, yellow liquid ran down to his knees and onto the beam, then dripped to the floor below. When he realized this new mortification, Edward began to weep in dry, heaving sobs, his frail body bucking while he clutched the beam. He appeared to be vomiting, but mercifully, no vomit came out.

Now truly frightened, the other girls and I laughed in nervous, soft hysterics as we saw Edward's urine begin to drip over the side of the beam. We quickly moved away from the unpleasantness of his urine possibly splashing on us. Standing still again, we craned our necks to watch, silent now, unable but wanting to help, not knowing how to anyway.

Like the Cavalry in the movies, Headmaster Raleigh suddenly burst from a doorway at the side of the balcony. He stood still, looking quietly at Edward, his arms folded across his chest, a small frown on his face. He nodded slightly. The gym became quieter than death. Even the temperature seemed to drop in the huge, wooden room. Two more drops of urine fell to the gym's floor and splattered there in tiny wet starbursts.

"Ick" someone said faintly. Mr. Raleigh began to speak softly to Edward--easily, soothingly, the way a person will calm a frightened animal. I stared at him. No one had ever heard this man speaking so kindly, so gently. He told Edward not to be afraid, to remain cool headed, not to look down, whatever he did, not to look down. The students turned to stare at their principal, stunned at the gentleness of his voice. Mr. Raleigh tenderly, softly urged the boy to begin crawling again, slowly, slowly now, toward the other side of the balcony, where he, his loving and concerned headmaster, would meet him and help him down to safety.

Edward did not respond. The minutes dragged, but the boy was too hardened with terror to heed the headmaster's cajoling, soothing words.

No one spoke. Mr. Raleigh waited. "Come on, boy," said the headmaster, "come along now, son. Just don't look down. You'll be fine." And finally, with agonizing slowness, Edward began to crawl. I could hear him breathing, a sucking sound. Out. In. Out. Short, hard rasping gasps pushing from the black hole of Edward's open mouth. Mr. Raleigh was droning softly, encouraging the boy forward in a gentle sing-song of no urgency. Edward wobbled along robotically, tipping from side to side, his audience gasping and shrieking with each quaver.

And gradually, so very gradually, Edward Judson made it safely to the other side where both of his hands weakened, his bowels too, and he fell sideways from the beam to the floor of the balcony, flat onto his back. Mr. Raleigh walked slowly around the bend of the balcony toward Edward, as the boy scrambled to his feet, shaking violently, out of control, ashamed of the stain on his pants, struggling to cover it with his trembling hands. It was awful to see and I could feel my throat constrict in painful sympathy for my poor, dear friend Edward.

Mr. Raleigh stood above Edward and looked down at the humiliated boy. Slowly, very, very slowly, he leaned backward and to one side while bringing his right arm way behind him. Edward looked quizzically at his principal. What was he doing? Why was he leaning back that way? He shook his head, frowned and laughed slightly.

And then, with a speed so sudden no one could see it coming, Mr. Raleigh balled his right fist and swung it hard, smashing it against Edward's puny chest. I felt a scream coming from my own chest but it never came out. The intensity of the blow lifted the boy into the air and shattered him against the back wall. Stunned, silent, his eyes not leaving his principal's face for an instant, Edward slid slowly down the wall, leaving a long, wet, brown streak from his shorts on the varnish behind him. Edward stared up in fear at the Headmaster and struggled to right himself. Mr. Raleigh glared at him for a full minute, turned and walked away.

I tried to laugh but the sound stuck in my dry throat. I was sure my heart had stopped.

"Sally----"I croaked and tried to be cool and to laugh again, but the sound that came out of me was terrible.

The school's other auditorium was used for basketball games, dances and graduations. Bleachers stood high on both sides and at one end was a tall wide stage, where all of the school's dramatic productions were held. The curtain was a ponderous, dusty rag that took at least two students to pull open, and to which Mr. Raleigh would occasionally touch a lit match to be sure the asbestos was still working. There was a panel for the lighting at one side of the stage, and behind all of this was a mole's paradise of unlit, unswept, winding, narrow stair-cases, accessed from the sides of the stage and from the basement. These staircases led to a small, dark, windowless rooms occupied by the coaches, and used for showing hygiene class films on the very serious problem of awakening sexuality and how to squash it before it got too woken up.

Originally designed as servants' quarters, not all of the rooms were occupied by school personnel. Some stood empty and idle, smelling like ageless dust that had finally given up trying to accumulate. They easily afforded countless students who might be so inclined, many hours of undetected hard-breathing, clumsy gropes, and perhaps even more, much more if they were lucky, and they often were.

My friends and I giggled uncontrollably for weeks over the story of a sophomore couple's trysts in one of the third-floor rooms. The besotted lovers came together every afternoon after school for the purpose of some intense physical reconnaissance, their steamy scenes habitually enacted in the ell of a storage closet off the south side of the music room. There they stood amongst the clusters of trombones, drums, violins, flutes and a crate of ukuleles, clutching each other tightly and exchanging wet, loud kisses.

One afternoon to the young lovers' horrified consternation and in the very midst of some intense squirm and gruntage, an unscheduled class thumped into the music room. The couple froze in position, hands stuck to various body parts, not their own. Their eyes popped.

"Oh shit!" they whispered in unison.

The assemblage began a tediously long and ceaselessly off-key musical rehearsal, each instrument playing its own squawking melody which broadly missed nearly all of the notes on the music in front of them, while the teacher insisted the students go over and over their passages so they'd be perfect for an upcoming school recital. The hapless couple waited, and waited in that dark storage closet, their ardor evaporating like steam leaving a cooling kettle.

Finally, late for appointments and with no other choice, they burst from their tiny huggermugger room, causing the rehearsing students to blast off-key bellows from their instruments and the music teacher's baton to point, motionless, at the ceiling. Wild-eyed, the mortified couple raced down the hall and staircases with adrenalin-heightened speed, charged out of the building and continued all the way to their homes without help from the school bus, and without stopping once.

"Can you believe it?" we all screamed at the story. I was so overcome with the thought of those kids roaring out of The Academy that I could not stop laughing for nearly an hour.

"Courtenay!" laughed Sally. "You're losin' it, you nut. It's not that funny, y'know!" But to me it was hysterical---or was I just jealous that it was not I locked in an illicit embrace with a boy? I'll never really know, I guess.

All the school sock hops and other informal dances were held in this upstairs auditorium, and I passed many happy hours there, dancing in kilt skirts and cardigan sweaters worn backwards. For the more formal dances, I wore silky, pastel gowns, corsages pinned to the bones of strapless tops, my what I hoped were elegant young shoulders wrapped in tulle stoles and rabbit fur jackets. My hair would be swept high, caught in jeweled barrettes.

31

Remington had started to ask me more often to attend these dances with him and I was almost certain it would not be too long before he asked me to wear his school ring. I had rehearsed many times in front of my long bedroom mirror how I'd react when and if Remmie offered me this cherished piece of metal and semi-precious glittering gem.

I would be prettily surprised, perhaps I'd gasp enchantingly, and I had absolutely no intention of playing hard to get. Doing this, I'd been told by my trusted friends, invited the dangerous risk of causing the ardent young buck to back off in disgrace and begin pursuing someone a bit more acquiescent.

I was not planning to throw a perfectly good opportunity away. Besides, wearing Remington Nathaniel Richardson's school ring would be the coup of my young life, and I did not dislike the idea of the other girls' guaranteed envy of me.

# CHAPTER 5

Sally and I loved our summers together. We had been best and dearest friends since we were younger than we remembered. This summer in our early teens would be like all the others; full of fun, laziness and ourselves.

That day, we enjoyed what we assured each other was a "great game of tennis," as we did each time we played regardless of what the level of "great" was, and only we knew. The day was clear and shining and hot and the clay courts scalded through the thin rubber soles of our spotless white Keds, and we were anxious to pull them off.

"Nice shot," shouted Sally when I smashed the ball into the far corner of the court, mercifully ending the way-too-hot game. Laughing, we ran toward each other and shook hands over the net. Best friends forever, we retired to the side benches and peeled off our sneakers and white socks.

"God," said Sally. "I'm gonna play on the grass courts from now on. That clay is like running on hot coals."

We stood and slowly walked barefooted through the soft grasses of the landscaped grounds toward the Country Club's entrance, speaking softly, lazily swinging our sneakers in one hand, slapping the ends of our tennis rackets at the tips of the grass with the other. The cool grasses felt glorious on our hot feet.

Huge ancient elms and oaks lined the serpentine driveways designed two hundred years ago for the viewing pleasure of the occupants in elegant horse-drawn carriages. Back then, making a memorable entrance was a seriously important part of our lives. Birds called in the soft, dappled summer air. Beyond the stately white Greek Revival Country Club building, we could see the expansive proper¬ties where fox hunts were once regularly held and occasionally still held when the members could indulge themselves in this cruel and useless extravagance without the local newspapers first finding out.

I remembered once questioning my parents about this "gruesome sport," I'd called it, insisting that local foxes were hardly a threat to anyone's chicken coops or "gentleman's farms," since those in their circle of friends, I reminded them, certainly did not own any chicken coops, or even lived on, owned or ran any farms that I knew about, so why not leave the foxes alone?

My parents responded as they always did when what they regarded as their "annoyingly sentimental daughter" passionately demanded answers to what they perceived as pointless questions; with no comment and tolerant smiles. Those smiles filled me with rage. All I could do was to simply turn and leave.

In the ladies locker room, Sally and I changed for the afternoon Tennis Tea.

"Sal," I said. "Do you hate these tiresome teas as much as I do?"

"Yeah, I do Court," she answered me, "but my folks insist they make ladies out of us or something. Don't yours make you go?" Sally didn't wait for an answer. "Yeah. Ladies. Like we'll be great ladies if we learn how to pour a pot of tea properly without slopping it on people's shoes. But God, Court, don't you hate it when Mrs. Henderson spears a piece of banana bread with those huge, ugly nails of hers? I won't go near those platters after she's been doing that. Looks like she's harpooning live fish. Makes me practically barf!" And we laughed.

We showered, and as we dressed, our conversa-tion turned to the usual: discussions of boys, clothes, current music, school, boys and clothes.

But as we chatted, my mind inexplicably began to drift back to my parents' discussion from that morning. I pretended to listen to Sally, nodding and smiling, making appropriate sounds, but I had remained uneasy about what I'd overheard and was unable to focus completely on my old friend's conversation.

My parents never seemed to disagree about anything more serious than where to plant the newest azalea bushes or what part of Europe they should next visit or when they'd leave for the south of somewhere, and, of course, in which season, so I just could not shake the thought that this argument between them seemed, well, kind of ominous.

"Sal," I said, suddenly interrupting my old friend. I cleared my throat, looked away, looked back. "Do your parents ever fight?" Sally looked at me, her head cocked in surprise, and then she smiled.

"Of course they do, silly. They always tell me that fighting blasts the carbon from their engines so it's a good thing to have a big fight sometimes. Isn't that just too weird sounding? Jeez, parents can be such lamebrains. But yeah, they fight sometimes. I don't think it's ever serious so I don't worry about it much. Umm-- how come you're asking?"

I began to comb my long hair slowly. When I saw in the mirror I was frowning, I stopped and smoothed my fore¬head with my fingertips, remembering my mother's admonition that if females frowned, the wrinkles would stay forever and nothing short of plastic surgery would remove them. Frown marks were forbidden. Wrinkles after all, were for the working class. It was common knowledge that if a person's face was heavily wrinkled it meant of course that they worked with their hands, and often outside. Smooth skin, it followed, meant a person was a business man or a lady-of-the-house and did not do manual labor, or even better, if born well, they did not have to work at all. The rules were quite clear.

"Well," I said, as I rubbed the spot between my eyes to 'start the circulation going and chase away those ugly creases,' "it's probably nothing," I said to Sally, attempting to sound unconcerned, "but when I got up this morning, I could hear my parents in the breakfast room. I couldn't hear their words exactly, but they sounded real mad at each other. I mean really, really pissed! Mother was kind of yelling and so was Father. It was so strange. And then, when I walked into the breakfast room, they stopped, right in the middle of whatever they were talking about, and then Mother asked me something or other about the dance last night, but as usual didn't take the trouble to listen to my answers."

My throat began to contract, but I controlled it. I couldn't let Sally see how much this was actually upsetting me, so I looked down at a bottle of lotion, picked it up, pretended to read the label, and forced a smile.

Sally laughed at me, rubbed her hair with a white towel and then snapped it at me, but I pulled back just in time.

"So what's the big deal, Court?" Sally laughed again. "You call that a fight? That?" she said. "Honey, that was conversation. Your parents? We're talking about Tweedle Dum and Tweedle Dee here. Those two having angry words? Impossible. Come on, Court! Give me a break! It was nothing. Don't look so concerned! Your father's toast was probably cold, or his eggs were runny, he got cranky about it and Emma wasn't available to whup. You know how our fathers are. I'm sure it was no big deal. Just forget it." Sally began to comb her hair also, shook it back and ran her fingers through it.

35

"Yeah," I said absently, not convinced. "Yeah."

We reluctantly attended the Tennis Tea where the redoubtable Mrs. Stanley, whose family name generations ago was the never mentioned "Stanislaus." She was the club's wealthiest woman member, and often "poured" while Sally and I daintily and surrepti¬tiously swiped far too many cookies and petits fours. We would then turn our heads away and cram them into our mouths to the point of choking.

During one Tennis Tea, laughing uncontrollably at our gluttony (which we both knew from its being hammered into us in St. Andrew's Episcopal Sunday School, was #2 on the Deadly Sins list and we didn't much care,) sweet crumbs sprayed from my mouth onto the Country Club's elegant old dark velvet drapes. They stuck there, unnoticed for years, until so old and crumbling the window dressings were finally replaced.

When the tea was at long last over, finally sated, content and smiling, Sally and I ambled home past sprawling family estates, watching our long shadows in the late afternoon setting sun.

Standing at the end of Sally's long driveway, we gossiped and planned our futures, lazily unfocused, lazily satisfied with our lives.

Eventually, with a mutual "See ya," we parted, and humming, then frowning, I walked the rest of the way, cutting through gardens, ducking under fences, running across vast carpets of lawns, until I arrived at the private road leading to my home.

# CHAPTER 6

My parents and I shared our enormous brick and stucco English Tudor home, located atop sprawling lawns and gardens massed with heirloom and wildly colored flowers and overlooking the Country Club's golf course. The gardens were attended by our faithful Fred and others hired to manicure, suggest and plan. There were "picking gardens" to supply blooms in vases throughout our home during the warm months, and spacious gardens heavily manicured and made to look casual. And British.

There was also my mother Helen Wolcott's fabulous garden of prize-winning roses through which she occasionally languidly strolled, outfitted in her large straw hat, flat bloom-carrying basket over one arm, wearing a summery, flowing pale dress, gloves and Wellington boots, the perfect bloom picking ensemble, presentable for all viewers. She would load the basket with cut blooms but rarely went about in that ensemble unless she was certain neighbors would be available to notice.

But dressing for the garden was about the only connection that this Grande Dame actually had with it, as she did not care much for those nasty bugs the roses kept accumulating, or for all that tiresome pruning and weeding. No, it was for her to admire, to be admired in, to take the glory, and I have to admit, she carried it off well. Sometimes my drab little mother could be downright queen like.

It was for Fred to keep the blooms blooming and the blossoms coming into the house daily for Emma to arrange into lovely, beautifully balanced floral gatherings in my mother's graceful, deeply cut Waterford glass bowls and creamy Limoges vases. When company commented on the artfully arranged lavish bouquets in each room of our large home, dear mother thanked them graciously and spoke glowingly of her "jewel of a picking garden," but never once spoke of the jewels she had in Fred and Emma who made the entire garden bloom and glow from early spring until late fall and to remain, of course, altogether bug and weed-free.

My mother also never bothered to mention to her peers that it was Emma's tedious chore to carry all the heavy, flower filled vases into our cool basement each night and then haul them all back up again in the early morning. As "dearest mama" (this was what some of my friends called their mothers, but not I,) explained to the tired black woman as she trudged endlessly up and down the long staircases one evening, "that will keep them blooming longer and they'll remain fresher." Emma had no concerns whatever for the welfare of her employer's efflorescence, but did as she was ordered. She knew better than to protest. Like so many people of color in that part of America, jobs were vital, difficult to keep because getting fired was commonly done for any reason whatsoever, and many were eagerly waiting to replace them. It was prudent to do the work, always smile and look down, and to never complain

Our old home contained 32 rooms, each filled with priceless antiques, and what I always called "Popeye furniture," since it looked to me to be exactly like the overstuffed 1930s furniture depicted in the Popeye cartoons I saw at the local theater with my young friends on Saturday afternoons, days which I know allowed beleaguered governesses and nannies some respite.

None of the rooms in our home went unused by us, even though we were such a small family, and each had its own title: Sun Porch, Breakfast Room, Good Parlour, Master Bedroom, Mother's Bedroom, Everyday Parlour, Library, Maids' Rooms, Father's Study, Milady's Dressing Room, Garden Room, Butler's Pantry, Gun Room, Bar Room, Mud Room, Morning Room, Conservatory, Music Room.

It was the only home I had ever known, and I am not proud to say I was completely unaware of how the rest of the world, including the household staff, lived, and wouldn't have cared much had anyone the temerity to attempt explaining it all to me. No one ever did. And even as I looked at far more modest homes from car windows, I never actually quite saw them. For me, back then, they did not, and really could not, exist.

I walked into my huge home that day, hung my tennis racket on a hook in the vestibule and was surprised to find my parents waiting for me. They called me into the Good Parlor, of all places. I responded that I'd be right in, as soon as I'd gotten a snack and a glass of milk, wondering why I was deliberately stalling. My stomach began to knot.

"No," my parents cried sharply in unison. "We'd prefer it if you'd come in here immediately," said my mother, followed by a softened, "Courtenay dear."

Sighing, I walked through the imposing dining room to where my parents waited in the good parlour, seated together but somehow not really together, in front of the broad fireplace. *How can two people sit together and yet be on different planets??*

Something--what was it? --alarmed me as I moved toward them, and I trailed my fingers nervously across the keys of the grand piano knowing it would annoy my father. I kissed each of my parents drily by way of greeting. It was the sort of physical affection, affectation actually, allowed when it seemed appropriate, and evidently it seemed appropriate now, since it provoked no reaction.

"Sit down, Courtenay," my father said, and I obeyed. "Your mother and I have something to tell you and," he sighed and straightened, "we expect you to be strong and to accept what we have to say, the way any well-bred young lady would." My father looked very grave. I felt my stomach shrink, and I began to be afraid.

"Is one of you sick?" I asked worriedly, standing. "Are you OK? What's going on? Please tell me--you're scaring me!"

"Courtenay dear," her father said, "we are both quite well. Sit down! Sit! It's nothing like that, nothing at all. Don't worry. But I do have some news for you, and I know you won't like it, but you know, sometimes we all have to pull together. If we work hard we can make it. Yes, indeed, we'll pull out of it. We are Wolcotts after all, and we'll weather this thing-----." My father was rambling, not looking at me or his wife. "Oh God NO," I thought. "Please not the stiff upper lip crap, please no. What's happened this time?"

"FATHER!! I shouted again, jumping up. "You know I hate it when you talk in those -- those platitudes, or whatever they are. Don't do the stiff upper lip story until I know what's going on. Please! Tell me! What's happened? *What* will we pull out of? My God! TALK to us! Me. Talk to *me!*"

My mother sat still, staring blankly into the cold fireplace, not reacting, not looking up. It appeared she did not even hear her husband or me. I had never seen my mother's eyes so cold, so blank. She was a beige marble statue, frozen, unmoving, awful.

"Daughter," my father began, exhaling a long sigh. My jaw clenched, just as it always did when he called me a female noun. "Things", he said slowly and rather a bit melodramatically, "have not been going well. As you remember, I sold your grandfather's business to that big firm in New York City, and they allowed me to continue heading the company until I retired. Well, I did retire--remember? A few years ago? --and I took a great deal of our money, actually almost *all* of our money, and invested it in something that unfortunately has gone completely bankrupt. We'd been living on that income rather well, as you know, but now it's gone, it's all gone and I must rebuild that part of my fortune."

I stared at him and frowned. My heart was beginning to beat faster. What was he saying?

"What did you invest in, Father?" I asked.

"Now don't you bother about that, young lady. It's really none of your business and besides, you couldn't possibly understand. Why, I haven't even told your mother. It is simply not proper for ladies to know of such things. It's my affair and I, and only I, will take care of it. Women, ladies, do not get involved in this sort of thing." My father spoke firmly, I suppressed a laugh. He was using his "don't argue with me" tone, and I knew it was futile to press him. I heard a soft sort of snort come from my mother and she turned to look at me, but then turned back to stare at her personal nothingness. She continued to sit, in waxen non-response.

My father continued. "We will be all right, but we have to tighten our belts. Now, I don't mean we'll be eating potatoes and beans, but we'll have to let some help go and do some of the work around here ourselves."

Now a sigh from my mother.

"No trips for a while, and you girls will just have to make do with the clothing you already own. God knows, you've got enough in those upstairs closets to clothe a small country. Absolutely no more charging on credit accounts. Absolutely no parties until further notice. We will be selling at least two of the cars, don't know which ones yet. We are going to budget and conserve our money until this problem passes. It may be that we have to give up our club membership for a while, but I'll first certainly have to give that some serious thought." He'd begun to pace, to cough softly, to run his hands over the top of his head. He surely didn't look much like Clark Gable on this day. More like Bela Lugosi.

I stiffened. Not be members of the club? What would we do? Who would we see? How would I spend the summer? The club was our

40

whole life. Every single occasion in which I'd ever been involved had somehow been connected to the club. I looked at my mother, disbelieving, but she continued to stare into the dark fireplace, her face still and cold as the grey ashes lying behind the tall, brass andirons. My eyes felt dry. My mouth.

"If we want to continue living here, we can," my father went on, "but we've got to cut corners. Now don't look so stricken, Courtenay. We won't have to go begging. I hope in some short period of time, perhaps a couple of years, we'll get back to normal, but for now, we'll all have to dig in, work together. I know you won't understand for a little while, but after all, during the Great Depression---"

"Oh God! Father!" I shouted. "What does all this mean? I don't understand. Please, no Depression stories now. Tell me--I'm old enough. I can understand. Stop treating me like a child--stop treating me like a *stupid* child! I'm not an idiot. I can comprehend things, figure them out. What will we have to do? What's going to happen to *me*?"

I would remember what happened next as if watching a slow-motion movie, the entire scene slowly unraveling, my father's lips moving impossibly slowly as he uttered the words that would forever change my life.

As he had predicted, I could not comprehend those terrible, cold words. I felt my heart stop and my insides thickened like old and cold Pablum.

Had I actually heard my father say I'd have to leave the Academy and finish out my last two high-school years in—in—*public school?* What? No! *NO!!*

My mind refused to acknowledge the terrible words. I stood staring at my father in cold disbelief, then at my mother who still stared blankly into the fireplace.

She never moved her head. She didn't even blink.

"Mother?" I said, questioning. "Mother?? Can't we do something? Do I have to go to--to that horrible place? Please Mother, can't you fix this? Mother—make this go away...." my mother did not stir. I understood by the set look on my father's face that no discussion was possible. The decision had been made, and my life fell at my feet like a pile of cold, wet rags.

Public school: the worst two words I'd ever heard in my staunchly sheltered, almost-sixteen years. I knew nothing about public school, except what my peers and teachers told me and what I saw outside of The Academy windows.

Students of Rogers High School, one of the area's three public schools, passed by The Academy on their way to their own classes every morning. My friends and I would laugh at what we called the "cheap" way they dressed, and mimic their swaggering walks, the way they snapped their chewing gum, their thick New York low-class accents.

We would gather in front of the open windows, stick out our breasts and wiggle our hips, wanting the public-school girls to know we were mocking them. We were successful. It would have been no fun at all, after all, had our efforts not been understood.

Public school girls wore stockings and flat shoes to school. My friends and I wore white wool socks and shined penny loafers or saddle shoes, "brown and whites." Public school girls' outfits were gaudy, revealing, sexy, tight and far too dressy for school. We Academy girls wore plaid or khaki skirts with coordinating blazers, pullover sweaters sometimes called "Sloppy Joes," or loose cardigans, worn backwards, buttoned up the back.

The public-school girls wore rhinestones, plastic beads and big, tawdry earrings dangling from their pierced ears. We Academy girls would never think of piercing our ears. "That," we would say imperiously, "is for Barbarians or public school girls." And then we would laugh.

Public school girls' arms held rows of clanking bracelets, their ankles one gold chain with intertwining hearts to show the world they were spoken for. We Academy girls accented our sweaters and Peter Pan or button-down collared blouses pinned with gold circle pins or small gold initialed discs, perhaps adding a scarab bracelet when feeling a bit quixotic.

Public school girls wore gobs of vivid, thick make-up, their cheeks often so red they looked bruised. We Academy girls never looked made up before six, although a tiny touch of color to the lips was permitted by day. And we absolutely never looked heavily made up "because," we would say in what we hoped were imperious tones, "that's just for whores," and we laughed, but nervously, not being precisely sure what

42

whores were or what they did or why, but quite certain it was not very polite or nice at all and certainly they had no connection with us.

Academy boys wore a uniform of khaki pants, button-down blue or white Oxford cloth shirts, crew-neck sweaters in charcoal grey or chocolate brown, loafers or white bucks and occasionally sneakers if they wished it known they were jocks, although the word "jocks" was never, ever uttered in front of us girls, considering the article of boys' underwear it represented.

Public school boys wore tight jeans, the cuffs rolled up a requisite two times with a comb sticking from a back pocket. Snug white T-shirts had cigarette packs, usually Lucky Strikes, rolled into one sleeve. They wore high-topped flat soled black boots (having a heel on them would have had them labeled "fag" which would never do,) the boots sometimes affixed with brass rings or chains, or heavy, black shoes with square toes and thick soles topped with short white socks.

Academy boys wore jackets and ties to all after-school affairs. Pink shirts were the rage for public school boys, but only if worn with a pencil-thin black necktie, and then only to dances.

Academy boys wore crewcuts or otherwise very short, tightly combed "English cut" hairstyles. Public school boys applied judicious amounts of grease, frequently purloined from the nearest drugstore, to their long hair, carefully combed back from sides to rear into the coveted "duck's ass" or as was said in more genteel settings, for example in front of their mothers, a "D-A." The top layer of hair was then pushed, bent and cajoled forward until it rose in a jumbled, curly pompadour, kept solidly in place by more grease. One long lock was then pulled forward and teased to the exact proper coil and plastered to the center of the forehead, just above the bridge of the nose. Even the black boys went through the agony of straightening their hair and then curling it forward. Blonde boys often dyed their hair shoe-polish black so they'd also belong to the great, happy world of greasers.

The Academy boys' outer jackets were adorned with large, single fabric letters earned in their sport of choice, all in the school colors which were maroon and gold for The Academy. The dedicated jocks who won letters for a variety of sports found themselves to be the most popular with the girls, that letter being their badges of honor, bravery and heroism on the battle field of choice, and the choice was nearly always football. Soccer and tennis were permitted. Golf maybe.

Public school boys wore letter jackets too, but the sleeves were always rolled up and the collars always pushed up high at the back of the neck.

Academy boys wore long, striped scarves, knitted lovingly with a multitude of dropped stitches by girlfriends in the colors of their favorite colleges, as if by the Wearing of the Colors these colleges would then accept them. Public school boys wore dog tags, if a brother or cousin who "had served" would give them up, or much better yet, if they could be stolen.

Private school boys carried pens. Public school boys carried knives.

Public school boys came to school by public bus, school bus or in souped-up, garishly painted cars, a pair of large, swaying dice hanging from the rear-view mirror, and many of these autos could flatulate great spurts of fire from their tail pipes if they had the proper gizmos to make that happen. Private school boys were driven to school, or they arrived in private school buses with gentle mufflers.

Academy boys were success-driven and, being heavily monied, did not worry about after-school jobs, or in fact, any jobs at all. Public school boys' general attitude was a steadily, coolly threatening, "I don't care. I don't have to care. I don't give a damn." Survival was by one's wits, muscles and machismo, never by conventional accomplishment. And the rules of both camps were brilliantly clear and rigid. Any modifications were at one's own peril. They were absolutely not permitted. Ever.

Would I one day finally and clearly understand these crazy rules? Impossible. At this point it all just confused and sometimes even frightened me.

How could I tell my friends what my father had just said? I sat alone on the floor of my room, hiding, rocking, hugging my knees to my chest. The shades were down.

I knew I had never known such utter devastation. I felt completely abandoned, adrift on a frightening, uncharted sea that would take me to horrible, unspeakable places. "This must be like the fear of death," I thought. *Maybe death itself.* What was I to do? Had anyone ever felt so awful? So frightened? I had never even seen the inside of a public school. I'd heard the public school had thousands of students. Thousands! I simply could not envision that many students in one school. My mind could simply not grasp the situation. My father must have been joking. Ah, but then I remembered---he never joked.

"Public school. Public school! I just simply can't, I just cannot go there. I WON'T go there! They can't make me. I'll die first. I'll kill myself!" My shouts roared out into my bedroom, turned and slammed back into my mouth. I thought I'd be sick and began to sob, and I rocked harder, side to side, my breath coming in rasping, short heaves.

*This can't be happening. It has to be a dream. Like in the movies, like a stupid cartoon. Yeah. I'll wake up soon and it'll all be just a sick dream. Sick.*

Finally, I stood unsteadily and grabbed at the bedpost. I rubbed the tears from my face. *What am I to do? Those awful creepy kids there. Those thugs scare me. So dirty…so stupid and poor and I hate them…. I won't know anyone…they'll all be old friends with each other and I'll be the new one---they'll laugh at me---maybe they'll even kill me with their knives---maybe they'll try to put their hands on me---so many in one classroom—I heard they have maybe fifty in one room---and those cars they drive, and the boys fight so much and those girls, those – slut—sluttish--slutty girls---I can't go! Oh God, what will Rem say? How can I tell Sally? My friends won't like me anymore---I can't let this happen---I'll die first, I'll run away, I'll commit suicide. Oh my God, I am so afraid.* And then with nothing left to do, I shouted aloud "Oh God, please, please save me. I am so afraid!" But nobody heard me, and of course, least of all God.

I felt dizzy, my throat so constricted it ached. I raked the fingers of both hands through my hair. My life had suddenly ended and I thought I was probably already dead. I checked my vanity mirror, relieved and angered to see I was still alive. But I knew with utter certainty that since I had not already died, I definitely wanted my life to end. There was no point in living. None at all.

# CHAPTER 7

"Court? What's the matter?" Remington's face was a mask of solemn concern. He'd gotten into his car immediately after I'd telephoned him that evening, bewildered by the edge of hysteria in my voice, worried he may be asked to help, vaguely annoyed he may have to. He drove, frowning. Something was wrong, and he was busy.

I met him on the front porch, before he'd had a chance to ring the front chimes. Huge summer moths banged hopelessly against the windows and porch lamps, leaving dark powdery winged outlines on the glass. I felt exactly like them, battered, hopeless. Dying. I reached for Rem's hands and tried to speak, my voice hoarse and cracking.

"Rem. Remmy. I don't know where to begin. I just can't believe this is happening. It's so awful. My parents, God, they're such jerks!" I began to sob. My nose ran.

Remington, his look of concern turning to confusion, pulled me against his chest. I smelled the clean, solid cloth-scent of his jacket, and then lost whatever composure I had left, weeping so hard my tears soaked his shirt front. He looked up at the porch's ceiling and grimaced.

"Please Court," said Remington. "Will you just try to tell me what the problem is? What do you mean, `jerks?' You never speak of your parents that way. `Jerks??' Not real ladylike, Court." Rem tried to sound stern, to tease me out of my misery.

His attempt failed. I bent my head back and looked up at him sharply. He resisted another grimace at the sight of my swollen, red and dripping face.

"I don't feel especially ladylike, Remington,"

I choked, "and furthermore why do I always have to be such a goddammed lady all the time anyway? How come I just can't be me? Why can't I feel rotten things and do bad things and say whatever I want to? You can! Boys can." I knew I was babbling, that this tirade had nothing to do with my problem and yet, without reason, it spilled angrily from me. And it felt oddly liberating.

"Sorry Rem. I'm really sorry." Was I sorry for the tirade or sorry for my outburst? I didn't exactly know. My nose became hopelessly blocked and it made me feel ashamed. I knew I looked just awful.

"Forgive me, Remmy, please say you'll forgive me--you must think I'm nuts." I backed from him and drew in a shuddering breath. "OK. I'll tell you all about it. Here goes." I tried to be calm, forcing myself to breathe slowly

"Are you ready for this?" I said. "It's my father. He's got some stupid money problem and so we have to `tighten our belts, all pull together,'-- all that cliché crap he loves to spout off. God, you know how he talks. He sounds like such a stupid fool when he talks like that."

"Courtenay!" Rem shouted. "You're as bad as he is. Stop babbling and for God's sake, tell me!" He fumbledin his pockets for a handkerchief, but all he had was a fairly clean napkin from a hamburger joint named "Bacci's." I snatched it, shredding it between my shaking fingers as I gulped for air.

"Remington. You'll just never believe it. It's too awful. I—look at those moths, Rem. I feel like the moths— wait—there's more." I pulled in a breath, the sound an inhaled moan.

"You know, just because my jerk father has this tiny little stupid money problem, he's going to make us stop having big parties, he's going to sell some of the cars and he may even let Emma or Mary go. Maybe Fred, my darling dear Fred. He says we may have to give up our Club membership. What'll we do without the Club? We're even gonna have to do some of the housework ourselves maybe, can you believe this? I mean, what did *we* do? It's not our fault he screwed up his finances. But it gets worse, Remington, it's much, much worse than that."

Remington let go of me and pushed me back so he could look into my face. He shook his head.

"For the love of God, Courtenay, say it, will you?" Remington was beginning to feel slightly bored, a little put-upon. "What's going on? Is your father sending you away? He didn't sell you into white slavery, did he?"

I glared at him through new tears.

"No, Remington Richardson," I said stiffly. "No. It's not white slavery. I wish it were. I wish it were that simple. Here it is: my father--- he's sending me to--he's sending me to—oh God, to *public school!*"

There. It was said. Shrieked. The filthy, horrifying words finally out.

Remington stared down at me, through me it seemed, as though I had somehow disappeared. He backed up. Blinked.

"*Public* school? Which one? The one near The Academy? You mean Rogers High?"

"No," I sobbed. "The other one. Across town. You know."

"You mean New Town?" Remington said, his voice high with disbelief. "You have to go to *New Town High School*?" Remington began to laugh, throwing his head back so far, I could see his fillings.

"Come on Courtenay, this is some kind of a joke, right?" Remington was practically choking with his laughter now. "Court. We don't *go* to public school! We don't even *know* anyone who goes to public school. You're putting me on, right?" He stopped laughing. "Come on, Court--don't kid around. This isn't funny."

I stared up at the boy I adored. He did not believe me. *How can he speak to me like this? He's not an insensitive guy. He's real sensitive. All the girls say so. What's going on?* I gulped.

"It's the *truth*," I said. "I'm telling you the truth! Yes. I *am* going to public school with the hoods, the greasers. Yeah. Little Courtenay Scott Wolcott. I'm off to public school with those creepy people. You know, the NOOK-Ds. A nice little WASP amongst the riff-raff, as my parents call them--good old New Town High, yay team! I can't wait to begin. Next time you're shopping, pick me up a couple of chains and a nice switchblade, OK? Any color will do. I'm not fussy." I turned away from Remington.

He sat down slowly, feeling behind him for a porch chair. I could hear the moths as they kept banging, and the crickets now too were sounding, but otherwise, the air was quiet. I stared out at the night. I *want the black to suck me away. Away. Now.*

"Courtenay. Oh, little Court--you're really *not* kidding, are you? Omigod, I can't believe it." Remington's head went into his hands, his elbows on his knees. He looked up at me.

"Would it help," he began, "if I were to speak with your father? He knows me pretty well, and I know he likes me, maybe I could ask him to---"

"No, no. Thanks a lot, but no. There's no point. I mean it's really not a discussion type of problem and he's never been exactly a 'discussion' kind of guy, if you recall. It's just that he's sort of out of some amount of money right now, so even if you guys talked, you couldn't make the money come back and besides, it would probably embarrass him. He's a proud man and even though everyone'll have to know about this, with my going to --to that place, well, I think it would make him feel awful if someone just sort of asked him about it or tried to talk about it. It's better if everyone just pretends that nothing has happened, just go on with life, you know, the way we always do." I stopped, out of breath, I looked away and then back at Remington again. I tried to grin and knew it was wobbly.

"We are Wolcotts, after all," I said. I stared down at Remington. He nodded. "No," I continued, "but thanks a lot for the offer anyway, Remmie. I've been his daughter long enough to know that when his mind is set, nothing can change it. I'm going to that horrible school, and I'll graduate with those slimy people and that's that. And you know what else? I don't even dare to ask him about college. He'll probably tell me he doesn't have the money. Gee, maybe some nice vocational school will accept me." I laughed. It was more a wet gurgle. "I can learn to repair car engines," I said, "or maybe even learn some nice cooking, like for a restaurant or something. I hear waitresses get pretty good tips these days." My nose was now so blocked, all my N's and M's now B's and D's. I tried to smile at my weak attempt at sarcasm, but that only resulted in renewed tears, a running nose.

Remington stood and took me gently by the hand and led me off the porch and toward his father's big blue Oldsmobile.

"Let's just drive for a while, Court, and talk this over. We can figure something out. Maybe it won't be so bad. Maybe it'll be OK. Don't worry. I'll take care of you. Every day when I don't have practice, I'll find a way to come get you after school's out at New Town. You won't have to ride home on the afternoon bus with those people. Please. Don't be scared. It'll be OK, I promise. I'll be there for you." Remington's voice was deep and concerned, and I began to feel calmed. His palm pressed gently against the small of my back as he helped me into the car. We drove off into the night, holding hands, not speaking much, but when we did, it was softly.

# CHAPTER 8

Dialing the phone later that night was the hardest thing I'd ever done. My fingers shook and I only half wanted Sally to answer, but she did and the sound of her voice set off another flood of my tears.

"Court!" she shouted. "What's going on? Who died? Why are you crying? Did Remington…?"

"No no," I sobbed and then as if a button somewhere had been pushed, all the words flew out of my mouth in choked clouds, the way bats flew out of the Academy's old chimneys every evening at dusk. I could not stop sobbing. Sally tried to speak but I was unable to hold back my weeping as I kept telling her about the terrible public-school news. I did not give her time to talk.

Finally through my hysterical blubberings, I heard her repeat "Oh my God, no!!" often, and "You are kidding, right? Tell me you're kidding me!" and "Come on Court, this is a joke, right?" My oldest friend Sally was finally getting it. One of our clan, me, was leaving the clique of the People on the Hill and was being sent off to get an education with the people who worked for the People on the Hill. She was having a hard time accepting it, but she did. She was incredulous but she struggled to say supportive and comforting words to me and that made my tears flow even more. I don't even know when we finally hung up, but I know my last words to her were "Sal, please, can you tell the other kids for me? I just can't. I can't. I just can't." And she said, her voice wobbling, "yes, of course I will, dear, dear Courtenay," and I finally fell asleep and think she did too.

Staying alone in my room for days after that, barely eating, not answering phone calls, summer, as it always does, was beginning to end and so I knew, was my life.

# CHAPTER 9

The day arrived. Registration at New Town High School. My parents, as I knew they would, turned away when I asked them to take me, to be with me on this very scary day, but no. I was alone when I was born and even when I was with them, I knew I'd always be alone.

I was embarrassed when Fred drove me to the public school in mid-August on Registration Day, was ashamed to feel that way and did not quite understand why I did. After all, Fred had been with my family for as long as my memory had existed. The big kind-faced Negro did the gardening, driving, and any odd jobs my parents asked of him. He had been driving me places all my life, he was my friend, often my comfort, occasionally my confidant, and it usually felt completely natural for me to be with him, at his side, or driven anyplace by him.

Fred let me off at the entrance to the two-story sand-colored building, with huge windows that went all the way up to edge of the roof. The school's name was carved into the lintel over the large, metal front doors that had been painted red and were badly scratched and dented.

A piece of white paper had been taped to one of them, on which someone had penciled the words "Registration--enter, turn left."

"Please Fred," I said, my voice small and wobbly. "Will you come with me?"

The kindly man stood holding his hat and looked down at the sidewalk.

"Miss Courtenay, little missy, I just can't," he said, not meeting my eyes.

"I'm gonna have to respectfully decline, Miss Courtenay. I'm sorry."

I stared at him, surprised. Fred never refused me anything. I thought of maybe making it more like a command, but knew I could not speak like that to my old friend. I felt weak, abandoned. Why, I wondered, at this most important time, why was he refusing me?

*Well, he's not my slave and doesn't have to if he doesn't want to.* But I wished he would. Feeling even more alone, I anxiously began the thousand-mile walk from the car and across the pavement to the front door of the public school, my new school. Looking back over my shoulder to assure myself that Fred would wait for me, I walked, trembling, up the steps.

At the red metal doors, I turned and looked once more back at Fred's sweet black face, but he was still staring at the sidewalk. I hesitated, reached with a cold, shaking hand, pulled the heavy door open, the one on the right, and walked inside.

I stood in the cool dimness of the vestibule. Up a few worn, dirty steps and to my left and right was a long hall with stained marble floors and very high ceilings. The grey plaster walls were interrupted by rows of dark brown wooden door frames and huge bulletin boards. The enormously high glaring windows threw flat white squares of light on the floors, bending them up the opposite wall. The windows had yellow shades on them, half covering the windows, and slivers of light shot from their jagged tears onto the opposite walls. I had never seen window shades of such size. Long, dirty heavy cords hung from their bottom edges, and I had the ludicrous thought that people, like Tarzan, had to hang from those cords, feet off the floor to haul those shades down.

The sun caught swirls of dust slowly whirlpooling down the hallway. I thought those particles had probably been there for centuries, had been waiting to surround and choke me, to bury me alive in this terrifying place. I felt awfully small.

I looked for doorways, classrooms, but down this long, sun stained and splattered hallway, no doorways led to rooms as they did along The Academy hallways. New Town High School, I would learn, was a U-shaped building, and at that moment, I stood at the top of it. Uncertain, I turned left to find the registration room, hoping, dreading it was there, somewhere.

I clutched a sheaf of papers tightly to my side: birth certificate, medical and immunization records, papers from The Academy, everything I'd need to get into New Town High School. *My passports to hell.*

Finally, my footsteps echoing like dulled gunshots, my hands shaking, I found one door at the far end of the long hallway. This, like the red entrance doors also had a piece of white paper taped to it. I read the words "Registration. Enter."

I knocked once, waited for a response, got none, knocked timidly again, then grasped the door handle with a frozen hand, pushed it down and entered.

The large, high ceilinged room was so cluttered it startled me. It made me feel breathless. Bookcases, shelves and desks were everywhere, squeezed into the room at every possible angle. Every single surface, even the top of the water cooler, was piled high with books, notebooks and papers. Posters with cartoon animals in peculiar poses with odd quotations beneath them were affixed to the walls with strips of yellowed, cracked and curled tape.

Light bulbs dangled on grey velvet-dusty chains with black electric cords woven into the links. Unidentifiable articles of clothing hung from hooks on doors. Rays of dusty sunlight slashed down into the mess, highlighting the chaos. I was temporarily repulsed and fascinated as my eyes traveled around the room.

A sharply accented voice cut through my reverie, and I turned abruptly to look in the direction of the sound. Sitting behind a desk and barely visible between the piles of crookedly stacked papers, was a short, stocky woman with orange beige hair. She wore no make-up; her eyebrows were thick and grey and came almost together over the bridge of her pocked, doughy nose. Rimless glasses fronted yellow-grey eyes and reflected squares of window light, and through them the woman glowered at the me and I knew she realized I was frightened. Her face revealed no compassion. The glower deepened. I squinted slightly, sure I could see a mustache on the small woman's upper lip. Then, the grey lips parted, and a mucous-thickened, too-many-cigarettes voice squawked. "I said, you in here for registration? Come in. Come on. Siddown. Gimme yer papers."

I obeyed, and moved toward a tired chair in front of the woman's desk. I sat and handed over my papers, embarrassed that they'd become stuck to my side and also to my hand that had held them so tightly.

The woman asked me some questions, filled out a few forms, and without raising her eyes, shoved everything back at me, and except for the sound of the pen and paper, the room was thickly silent.

I jumped when the woman suddenly said, "So show up the day after Labor Day and you'll get your homeroom assignment."

I did not know what a "homeroom" was, but was afraid to ask, so nodded as if I understood.

"You live in an area that don't have no school buses so you'll have to come here on public transportation." The orange-grey head bent down over the desk. "You'll need a bus pass."

*Bus pass?*

The woman bent her head and began to write again, and I knew I'd been dismissed. *But wait! I've still got some questions!* The woman continued to look down at her work, then handed me the bus pass.

"Please--uh--," I wasn't sure what to call the woman and briefly entertained the thought of calling her "sir," but imagined that might offend.

With some effort, I suppressed a need to laugh, an intense desire to giggle, maybe even scream a little. I put my hand over my mouth, looked down at my knees, and bit the knuckle of my index finger between my front teeth. The urge to laugh became more acute. It made my chest hurt. I bit down harder. *I'll ask Lady Dracula some questions.* The desire to laugh then became mingled with my fear, and fear won.

"Please--Ma'am," I began meekly. "I've never been to public school before. Actually, I know this'll sound silly, but I don't even know what a `homeroom' is, and, and I've never been in this building before and I was wondering if you might show me around a little bit. If it's convenient, that is--I mean, I hate to bother you. That is, if you're not too busy. Oh, it's OK, if you can't. But, uh, well—um--could you?"

The woman behind the desk looked up at me, and she was clearly startled.

"Do what?" she asked, incredulously. "Do *WHAT?*" The woman's yellow-grey eyes widened, and she laughed. *That is not a very nice sound. It is not.*

I flashed to my etiquette rules. I had not asked anything rude nor had I asked it rudely. *Had I?* Used to having others defer to me, I was bewildered by this horrid woman's response. *Low class dreg.* My heart began to race.

"Well, ummm," I continued. "You see, well, obviously, you already know this, but I've been going to school someplace else, and, well, I just don't know anything at all about this school and was wondering, please, if you'd give me sort of a kind of tour. Would that be OK?" I forced a sweet smile in an attempt to extricate myself from this unpleasantness.

The woman laughed again, a distinctly unpleasant mocking snort. I was simply dumbfounded. That well-practiced smile of mine *always* worked. I was not used to being made fun of; I was used to having my polite requests honored. This was a serious predicament, one I'd never faced before. I frowned and looked down.

The woman looked at me hard across the desk. I knew I looked like a prim young lady dressed in "preppy" expensive clothing. I had the fashionable long dark brown page-boy hairdo, brown eyes, and I understood I had a rich-girl look. I became aware I was sweating profusely. *White water. This will begin dripping on the floor if I don't get out of here.*

"You're new around here, aincha?" the odd woman asked, snorting again. Her teeth were pointed, the front ones so crooked and overlapping each other as if they were switching places. "This is a new one on me, for sure. This is like a joke, right? You want me to show you around, like a kinda tour director on a friggin' cruise ship? You know, you only live a short distance from here, so how come you act like you're from Mars?" She pronounced it "Mozz."

I felt a lump growing in my throat. At a total loss, I looked down, not knowing at all how to respond to this behavior. Tears burned behind my eye lids. No one in my entire life had ever dared to speak to me like that.

"I'm so very sorry, ma'am," I stammered, my voice so inaudible even I could barely hear it. "I hope I didn't offend you. It's only that I've always been at The Academy and now I have to come here to school and I just don't know my way around and all the kids in here have been here for two years and they know everything, and they know their way around the building, but I don't, and I guess I'm scared that on the first day of school I'll get lost." My voice got smaller, and I felt myself get smaller as if I were shrinking into the hard chair.

After a long, terrible silence, the woman said "Oh Gawd," and she sighed. "Christ. OK. Awright. Don't worry. Don't get all upset. Jeez, don't cry now, for the luvvagawd. I'll show you a coupla things so you, Gawd f'bid, don't have to 'look like a total jerk.' Even though right now you kinda do, girlie, an' God knows when school starts, you def'nitly will." She laughed.

55

The woman scraped her chair back, removed her glasses and rubbed her eyes. She suddenly looked not nearly so threatening as tired. She stood up, and I was surprised at how short she was. When she came around the side of the desk, I was horrified to see that one leg was much shorter than the other, but my years of training (one never stares at someone with an affliction) kept me from reacting. I looked away immediately.

The shorter leg ended in a tan shoe, with a very thick, badly scuffed sole that made her legs come out even. I was surprised at myself for my feelings about this woman's affliction, and I felt sad for this pitiful woman who'd appeared so frightening when sitting behind her desk. She walked ahead of me with a limping swinging gait, out into the formidable hallway, and she began to point things out.

"Here's the principal's office. Her name is Miss McArdle, and missy, she's a dragon. Stay away from her, and always act like a lady around her." *But I ALWAYS act like a…*

"She won't stand for no funny business and she'll haul your ass into her office if you look at her cross-eyed. Her detentions are tough—if you screw up, you'll clean the school terluts with a toothbrush while the janitor stands and watches.

"By the way, my name is Miss Piacentino and I run the school business office and compared to me, Miss McArdle is a walk in the park. So I'm warnin' ya. Play it cool and play it by the rules. Don't louse up, and keep your nose clean. You got all that?" The little woman limped ahead of me, not waiting for an answer, and then answered her own question.

"OK," Miss Piacentino said. "I'll assume here you're gettin' the message." We walked down a short flight of stairs, turned a corner and entered a cavernous room with many long tables shoved to the walls, balanced on their ends. Chairs were stacked in front of them. They looked like silent soldiers at attention, waiting to be called to duty.

"This here's where you eat," she said. "It's the lunchroom. Some of yer snottier types like to call it yer cafeteria. But it's always been 'the lunchroom' to me. So. You can bring your lunch or you can buy it. You get milk if you wanna. The lunch periods come in shifts because there are just too damned many kids in this school. You mess up in here, you'll wish you were dead. There're at least five teachers in here during the lunch periods and anyone throws food or makes a problem pretty soon wishes he'd never been born."

I listened to Miss Piacentino, my eyes so wide they dried out and scraped when I finally blinked. At The Academy, everyone sat at round oak tables in Windsor chairs, with one teacher at each table to give instruction on manners and dining etiquette. I'd never heard of food fights, though once, when I was in third grade, my chums and I got in trouble for shoving our Brussels sprouts down through the heat register on the floor. As punishment, the children's lunch the next day consisted of five large terrible Brussels sprouts, and nothing else. I never could think of that vegetable from then on without gagging.

Miss Piacentino was droning on with her guided tour. "Here we have an elevator to get to the second floor. Normally this is used for yer cripples, but special dispensation is given to some other special people to use it. But not you. You use the stairs. Most of your classrooms will be upstairs anyway, and all of the rooms begin with the #2 up there, so if someone sends you to get something in 2-0-3, you'll understand that you gotta go up the stairs to the second floor and look for room three. Got it? Ah, you'll catch on. You're not stupid." Miss Piacentino paused, snorted again, stopped and looked up at me. "Are ya??" A tiny smile forced its way to Miss Piacentino's lips, but quickly vanished.

"I don't think so, Miss Peesentno," I answered, puzzled about the far-away little girl sound of my voice. I cleared my throat.

"MISS PEE-ASS-SENT-_TEE_-NO," the woman yelled. "Just like it's spelt. Say it. Repeat it exactly the way I said it. PEE-ASS-SENT-_TEE_-NO."

"Yes ma'am," I gasped, again looking down. "Pee-yas-SENT-no," I dutifully responded. "No, no--I've got it. Pee-ass-sent-_tee_-no. I won't forget. I promise. I'll say it over and over and over and----."

"Just remember it," the woman barked. "Don't 'splain it to me a thousand times. Why do you gotta say everything a bunch of times? God girlie, you're annoying. Sheesh." She limped away from me and toward the gym.

I was surprised that the gymnasium was so similar to the one at The Academy, the only exception being the absence of a stage at one end. Bleachers ran up and down the sides, and long knotted ropes, ladders, exercise horses and climbing bars were pushed against the walls. Metal rings hung from ropes attached to the steel beams in the ceiling, and I briefly thought of Edward.

"Is there an auditorium in this building?" I asked my escort.

"Yeah, we do have one of them here. We also call it the study hall and it's where you go for your free periods, to study. Not to socialize. To *study*, got that? No wandering around the halls or school yards without a pass, young lady.

"There's a big stage in the auditorium where the awards ceremonies are held and the shows and plays are put on. And it's where McArdle makes all of her announcements, and----- "

"-----Pass? What's a pass?" I blurted, surprised at my courage.

Miss Piacentino turned to look at me, sighed again and shook her head. "Aw Christ, what do they do at that la-de-da Academy anyway? J'mean you're allowed to just walk around any time you want? Students are free to go where they want, do what they want? What kind of a joint do they run over there, anyway? Jeez."

"Well," I faltered, "it's just that there aren't too many of us there, and if we have to walk someplace, it's kind of like an honor system where they sort of trust us to be doing something important and not wasting our time and everything." I knew I sounded like an idiot, so I looked at the floor, certain the look on Miss Piacentino's face would confirm it.

The woman suddenly shot out a rough, stubby hand and placed it awkwardly on my arm. I involuntarily jerked backward.

"Listen girlie," Miss Piacentino said, her voice hard. "I ain't got the slightest why you're here. What, you slummin' or something? You doin' some sort of sociological study or what?" Seeing the complete bewilderment on my face, the woman softened and suddenly seemed almost kind, now filling me with a different sort of panic.

"OK. OK," the orange-beige haired lady said. "I don't know what the problem is, I got no idea. An' it's nunna my beeswax anyway. But you're here, you're signed in, you're on board. Listen though, you're kinda different and it's gonna take a little adjustment on your part to fit in here. But try to tough it out, girlie. Whatever you do, keep your nose clean, stay out of trouble. Just do your work and don't make waves and try not to be noticed." She groaned. "Hell, it may take *you* a *century* t'learn the ropes around here. Tell ya da troot, I don't think you'll ever learn how to do it, but you can survive these two years if you don't let anyone scare you. Once you let 'em scare you, you're a dead dog; you belong to them, and you're gonna hide in the shadows forever. They can smell fear, I swearta Jesus. They'll never let loose of you. They will eat you alive. So be yourself and hang tough. Remember---ain't no one can get at your soul unless you let 'em. Ain't no one can hurt your feelin's unless you let 'em. Now remember all I said, girlie, remember it. You capable of remembering stuff? Trust me. Remember. Take care, ---- you take care now."

I listened, my widened eyes glued to the strange woman's face. Scare me? Why would anyone in this school want to hurt me? I would never deserve to be bullied. I'd never bullied a living soul. My breath began to come in short, shallow bursts. My thoughts flashed to my father. How I hated him, despised him! I would never forgive him for sending me to this hell hole. *Why? What was the real reason?*

"OK little lady, I gotta go back to work. That's all I have time to show you now. From here on, honey, you're on your own. Good luck." Miss Piacentino clumped away, walking rather the way Charles Laughton did in "The Hunchback of Notre Dame," and abandoning me in the huge hallway. I felt as if I were standing in the recesses of a cold, old underground cavern, looking out at an alien world.

Disoriented, I looked around desperately, not recalling where I'd come in or how I could get out. I raised my hand, started after Miss Piacentino, then stopped. The manner in which that woman had walked away let me know my audience with her was over, and my lessons had begun.

I walked toward the sounds of the street, hoping they would lead me to the front door, and to my immense relief, they eventually did. I shoved the door open, and the bright sunlight momentarily blinded me. My eyes ached and I put my palms against my lids. When I thought my eyes could readjust, I lowered my hands and saw my beloved Fred, patiently waiting and listening to the car radio. I ran out and didn't wait for him to open the door for me, but ripped it open myself, a sob rising in my throat. I flung myself into the front seat, sliding close to this sweet, warm man I loved, who I knew loved me. I reached for his satiny, black hand.

"Drive me home, Fred, quickly, quickly, please. Please." I stopped. "Please."

When I arrived back at my home with Fred, I wanted to tell my parents about Piacentino and New Town High, but found only my mother at home. As usual, she was lying on her bed, phone in hand.

I waited on the chaise in the opulent bedroom, intently watching my mother as she talked, her voice the droning buzz of a heavy pollen-laden bee on a sultry summer day. Her ankles were crossed, and one arm was stretched out toward the opposite side of the bed as if reaching for something, or someone, but I knew my parents had not shared the same bed for many years. *If ever.* I thought again I would not be surprised to someday learn that no one was actually on the other end of my mother's conversation.

My mother occasionally glanced over the phone receiver and met my eyes, but her expression was dull. Helen made no effort to end the conversation, and clearly felt no discomfort at forcing me to wait so long. After many minutes, I sighed, got up and left the room. I walked down the long hallway to my bedroom, swallowing my painful need to be cuddled, comforted, to be told it would all be all right. I'd long ago given up the hope of having a mother who would protect and love me. And again, I wondered why I was unable to stop wanting it so when I knew absolutely it would never happen.

# CHAPTER 10

"Hi Court." Remington's voice was softly concerned and the sound made me feel better, a little. "How's it goin'?" he asked.

"I'm OK, Rem," I answered, my voice low, wobbly. I moved the phone to my other ear. "I had to go to that school, you know, to register. Natch, my parents refused to take me so Fred did. Dear, darling Fred. No one was there---I mean no other kids." I curled in the big chair, the phone cradled in the crook of my arm. "You know Remmie, it makes me nervous that I may be the only new one going to that school this fall."

"I know, I know," said Remington. "Court—I..."

"Golly," I interrupted. "Nervous isn't the word for it. Petrified is a better word. Well anyway, this woman was there today---she had one leg shorter than the other one---I asked her to show me around so I'd be able to find my way when I have to go there. It only would've been common courtesy, right?"

"Well, yeah, you'd think so," said Remington, and then "Court, I..."

"Yeah, and well," I went on, "she sure didn't want to at first, but finally, she did take me around and wow, she had a dirty mouth Rem, can you believe that? A teacher? Or whatever the heck she is. I mean, she's showing me that awful place, and she says these words.... well, I should be grateful that she condescended to take me around the place so at least I'll know something about where I am when I have to go there, ugh, and so maybe I won't feel so scared on my first day. But that old bat is definitely no lady, Rem." I paused. I knew I was babbling. I babble when I'm anxious. Remington said nothing.

"But," I went on almost immediately, "there's so much more I have to learn, Remmie. I don't even know where to get the bus or where it'll let me off, and that Miss Pee-sent—oh whatever her name is---she keeps talking about a 'homeroom' where everyone has to go at the beginning of every day, and I don't know how I'll find it, oh Remington this is too horrible I think I'll die, I know I will. I want to die before school starts. If my father thinks this is going to build my character, I don't want it built because it's fine just the way it is. Isn't it? I mean, am I such a terrible person?" I grabbed a breath of air. "I'm babbling, but I'm so frightened, Remmy," I said, and tears pushed from the corners of my eyes and rolled into my collar.

"OK, Court, OK," said Remington. "Calm down. I understand. We'll get through this, and hey, I'll wait for you!" I didn't react. "Isn't ----I mean don't they always say that in the jail movies?" he stammered. Another awkward pause. Remington cleared his throat, grinned weakly, and began again.

"Oh come on, Court, you know what I mean---those jail flicks when the woman always says she'll wait for the guy after he's been sent up? Aw gee Court, don't be mad. I'm only trying to make you laugh." Again, no response from me. Small white fingers of rage began to creep upwards in me.

"OK. Hey, listen," said Remington, "how's about if I pick you up and we go for a drive and then maybe to the beach for a while. Charlie Nichols is having a party at his parents' beach house tonight and guess what? His parents are away in Europe someplace, and they gave him the run of the place. You want to go with me? I know it would cheer you up and I know it'd be great fun!" Rem's voice had an odd but cheerful urgency about it, but I was in no mood to try to understand what that was all about, *and besides, I'm just too upset.*

Quickly pleased at the thought of having some fun in my now very dark world, wanting to forget the gnawing in my guts and wanting even more to spend some time with my friends from school, my real school, where I belonged, I said, "that sounds wonderful Remington. I'll just leave my parents a note. They more than likely won't even notice I'm gone. Give me about half an hour. I want to pack a few things – bathing suit and all, you know, my stuff. I probably should wear shorts and bring a party dress, right?" I didn't wait for his answer. "Wow!" I nearly shouted, happiness now racing through me. "This'll be fun. Thanks, Remmie! New Town begins a couple of weeks sooner than The Academy so I intend to get in as much playing as I can, before my jail term begins. See? Ha! I did get your joke!"

"Great, great!" Remington laughed with relief, but when he spoke next his voice again had that strange tone of before. "I'll pick you up in half an hour. Tell your parents you'll be home late. And Court, if it's OK with you, I'll just honk and not come in. I really don't want to deal with your folks. It's---it's just that they're kinda…"

"No Rem, it's OK, I understand. Just honk. I know they can be a little on the overpowering side. So honk and I'll come right out. See ya!"

Spirits revived, I turned and twirled around my room, anticipating the fun I'd have at the party. I smiled as I moved about, gathering up my things. *But--why did he sound so odd?*

I scribbled a fast note to my parents, told them where I'd be, that I'd be home late and to not wait up for me. *They never have, so why should they start now?* I could still hear my mother's voice droning on the upstairs telephone and I knew it would be hopeless to try to interrupt. Half an hour later, to the minute, the horn of Remington's massive blue Oldsmobile honked out in my driveway, I grabbed my bag and ran out the back door, shutting it softly so my mother would not hear. I didn't want to discuss my plans with her. She never listened anyway.

As I ran down the long curving driveway toward Remington's car, he got out and pulled the door open for me. The way he grinned at me, I knew I looked terrific in the late afternoon sunlight, I knew my hair was bouncing on my shoulders, that my legs looked strong and good, now clad in my Madras plaid Bermuda shorts. My penny loafers were shiny, and my blue knee socks were the identical color of my wide hairband. I carried a large canvas and leather slouch bag over one shoulder holding my salmon colored cashmere sweater, my party dress, bathing suit, hosiery, shoes and cosmetics for the evening. Very aware of and pleased with my image, I felt safe, complete, grown up and wildly happy.

"Hiya, Sweets," laughed Remington as I ran toward him.

"Sweets? Where did that come from?" and I laughed up at him. Once in the car, Remington pulled me toward him and kissed me roughly, missing my mouth, his chin banging clumsily off my cheek.

I pushed at him and his chest felt hard against my hand. "Come on, Rem. Let's just get out of here. I want to have some fun. I just want to forget about what's coming. So let's drive all over the place and look at everything. What time are we due at the Nichols'?"

"Well, let's see," said Remington. *Why does he always have to try to sound like a stuffed shirt businessman?* "Charlie's barbecuing about six. His parents left a goodly supply" *Goodly supply??* "of food in the freezer before they left for Europe, and he's got permission to take whatever he wants. He can even have the beer and booze if he wants it, too."

"Yeah? That's great." I bit into a big apple I'd produced from my bag, holding the other side out to Rem as he drove. He moved his head toward the apple, still watching the road, and bit deeply into it, some of the juice squeezing from the corner of his mouth and onto my thumb.

"So, who's chaperoning?"

"What? Chaperoning? What do you mean?" Remington swallowed the bite of apple loudly, and turned his head quickly toward me.

"*You* know---the adults who are gonna ruin our fun tonight?" I took another bite of apple, and lazily watched the scenery moving past the car's window.

"Well now Courtenay dear," *Courtenay dear?* Remington cleared his throat. "Umm—actually there won't be any adults. I mean…I thought you understood that. That's the good part about tonight. It'll be a party, a great party. A real party! Everyone's coming and we'll have the place to ourselves for the whole night. Great deal, huh?"

I listened to Remington quietly, taking in his words, staring at him, the half-eaten apple suspended in my fingers near my mouth. This was something new. Though I'd often longed to, fantasized, I'd never been completely alone in a house, or really anywhere else, with Remington. All the gatherings I'd attended had always had parents or faculty in attendance; no one ever questioned it. It was, after all, the proper way to be, the proper thing to do. But I hesitated. I didn't want to spoil things. Not tonight.

"Oh," I said, and paused awkwardly. "Well…sure Remmie. I guess so. I mean I…"

"Now don't get all tense," said Rem, back into his favorite stern parent role he so loved. "After all, we're not babies anymore. We can have a simple little party with good friends and no chaperones around, and no one has to know and we don't have to feel guilty. Right?"

"Right. Sure. We're grown up now. Yeah. After all, we're practically adults. I mean, it's done all the time in college after all, and we're practically in college, right?"

I took a deep breath and tried to relax, but something odd was happening, and my stomach began to churn slightly. I put my hand on my belly and smiled casually. *What is wrong with me? Why am I being such a drip?*

We could see the big house in the distance, and soon Remington's father's blue Oldsmobile took us up the grassy, dune-lined driveway, toward Charlie's place. We were surprised to see many cars already there, lining the driveway, parked on the lawn and around the house. I clasped Remington's hand excitedly as he drove to find an empty parking spot and, giving up, just driving up onto the lawn beneath a tree.

The salt air-weathered old house was huge, the slate-tiled roofs tall and pointed high, cathedral-like into the blue sky. Odd balconies stuck out at odd corners, and porches, cluttered with white wicker furniture smothered in blue and white flowered pillows surrounded the house, seemingly built on wherever the owners had a whim to take the sun. Large, wooden porch swings and enormous Boston ferns hung from the rafters. The entrance was at the top of a wide staircase across the front of the spacious porch. Imposing mahogany double doors, each containing an oval flower-etched glass window, stood wide open.

Dark cool air slipped over us like a gentle cloak as we stepped onto the thick, richly colored Oriental rug in the front hall. A heavy, round table in its exact center held a huge, tall vase of wildly colored summer flowers. A small, engraved silver tray gleamed on the table at its base, waiting to accept calling cards.

"Hey you guys!" came a shout from a distant room, and out charged our host, Charlie Nichols, a can of beer in his hand. Short and fat, blond, rich and endearing, Charlie was never without a huge grin and an elaborate plan for a creative atrocity.

"Hi Charlie!" we called in unison. The young men slammed open palms loudly on each other's backs. Charlie and I hugged briefly, our bodies not quite touching.

"Where is everyone, anyway? There're a million cars out there, but the joint's empty. What's the deal?" Remington looked around.

"What do you think, fool? They're all down at the beach, swimming. Why don't you go on down? I'm getting the grub ready for the barbecue and I'll come down later on. Go ahead. I'll catch ya later." Charlie took a huge, loud swig of beer and offered the can to Remington, who drank deeply and passed the can to me.

I looked down at it and shook my head. "Uh,-- Naah," I said. "Not right now. I'll have some later on, maybe." I frowned when Charlie and Rem exchanged a rapid, knowing look. "Yeah," said Charlie, "Okay.

Maybe later." Another look passed quickly between Charlie and Remington. I noticed and gave them a quizzical smile. "What? What??"

No explanation. The two young men turned away, suddenly preoccupied with other things. *Oh well.* I shrugged and said, "OK. I'll go upstairs and change to my bathing suit--I'll meet you in about...

"...uh...what bathing suit?" interrupted Charlie. "Courtenay," said Charlie, suddenly assuming an annoyingly patronizing air. *God, that's what Rem does.* "Courtenay--no bathing suits allowed. We're skinny-dipping tonight. Everyone's game for it. It's almost dark anyway, and hell, everyone's doing it. So just go on down there and, you know, get loose. You'll love it. Nothing to worry about. No one will see--we own all the land around here." He grinned lewdly at me, and turned to Rem. "Unless there's some pervert with binoculars out on his boat..."

I felt red heat creeping from my neck into my face. I tucked my chin in, turned away slightly, afraid I'd look stupid, wanting to be cool.

"Skinny dipping?" I croaked. "You mean here? Now? You're joking, right? Come on, you guys..."

"Court," answered Rem impatiently. "Honey, it's done all the time. I mean, everyone does it in college. This is the fifties, after all. Don't be nervous. We'll just jump right in. Come on. I'll go first." He took my hand, and started to lead me out of the house toward the beach, but I pulled back, feeling more heat, more redness creeping up my neck, spreading to my face. "No, Rem, I don't think so. I think I'd rather wear my suit. So please, if you'll excuse me, I'll just go upstairs and..."

"Court," said Rem in the stern father role again. "If you show up in a bathing suit, you'll look weird. And you'll embarrass me. And everyone'll be staring at you because you'll be the only one wearing a suit. Now think about it, Court, honey, is that really what you want? Everyone agreed to this a long time ago, when we were planning this party. No one's even brought any suits. So come on. It's time we all grew up. Once you get used to it, you'll love it." His voice was slightly higher than normal.

I pulled my hand from Remington's. "*Everyone's* agreed to this?" I said. "I didn't. No one ever asked *me.*"

"God, Court, come on! Get with it, will you?" Remington sounded like a cranky, spoiled child. I looked sharply at him. *Jeepers, he's actually whining!*

"How in heck do you know all this, Remington Nathaniel Richardson?" I laughed and disliked the brittle, phony sound of it. "Oh, what a big man!" I said, hoping for cool sarcasm, knowing it wasn't happening. "You do this a lot?? Wow! I'm learning a whole lot about you today! You're a real hotshot! BMOC!" I again laughed stiffly.

"Okay," I said, smiling, "umm--let's talk about this. What do you mean, it was all planned out? If this skinny-dipping stuff was all planned, how come you didn't bother to tell me when you called to ask me to go?" My voice was too shrill, smile too wide.

"Well, I forgot, is all. So kill me." said Remington. "And about my doing this a lot, well, you don't know everything about me, Missy. I mean, after all, I've been around a little and in a few years, I'll be in the army."

It was with some difficulty that I was able to stifle a laugh at this boyish imitation of an experienced man. My mother had lectured me many, many times about the fragility of a man's ego, how it needed constant feeding and stroking. I knew to avoid winning at games or sports if my opponent was male, and I knew all proper young ladies were expected to defer to men at all times, or to at least make them think they were being deferred to. And all along, she'd advised, just go on and do what you wanted in the first place. (Each time I listened to my mother's advice, I could not shake the feeling that *she sounds kooky!* But being a proper young lady, I'd never have voiced that thought.

So now I simply folded my hands in front of me. I looked at the boys and against my better judgment murmured ancient female sounds of acquiescence.

"Yes, Remington, of course. You're right. Sorry." I lowered my eyes demurely. "I understand. But I guess for now I'll just stay up here at the house and wait for the kids. Anything I can do to help you with the dinner, Charlie? How about if I --- ummm, well I could make a salad ---- maybe?"

"But Courtenay," sputtered Remington, "I want us to go swimming. Come on --everyone's down there. Don't be such a pill."

We stood in the front hall and glared at each other. Remington's face grew dark and his jaw stuck out in a rather well-practiced sulk. He looked at Charlie for support. I again suppressed a laugh.

*God, he's actually whimpering!* "Sorry Rem," I said a bit too loudly, "but I *won't* go skinny dipping. At least not now. Maybe later. Look, I just don't feel like it, OK?" I walked away from the two exasperated young men, and into the large, well-equipped kitchen where I expressed my point by loudly searching for salad-making utensils. I could hear Charlie and Remington out in the front hall arguing in loud whispers. I smiled and made happy busy sounds at the kitchen counter.

I prepared the most enormous salad I'd ever seen, and was proud of my accomplishment, considering it was the first time I'd spent this much time in any kitchen anywhere along with being the first time I'd ever prepared anything edible. I put the greens into an antique breadmaking bowl, and chopped the vegetables into pieces, none smaller than an ice cube. But a salad it was, my own creation, and I stood back, proudly surveying the alarming mountain of ragged vegetation. As a finishing touch, I jammed bracelet-sized onion rings and whole canned mushrooms tightly into the overstuffed bowl, cleaned everything up, then took my bag upstairs to change to my dress for dinner.

The staircase was wide, and the steps shallow, built so Victorian women in long, sweeping gowns would seem to be gliding down, like great, silent swans. I found the huge, old-fashioned bathroom, appointed with heavy, ornate, brass fixtures, at the end of the upstairs hallway. I stepped into the handsome clawfoot tub, which had been updated with a spigot and shower curtain, and turned on the water. It felt so good and its warmth helped to wash away the small sense of grit in my stomach. It would be fun tonight.

Shiny, clean and pressed, I arrived downstairs an hour later wearing my evening dress, satisfied I'd make a great impression on everyone, and especially on Remington. I was not disappointed. Remington, arriving in the hallway on cue, looked up in time to see me floating down the staircase, swinging my body gently from side to side in time to the music coming from the front parlor. I'd pulled my hair back and up into a swinging, high pony-tail, and wore pale pink lipstick and light aqua eye shadow with a gentle application of black mascara to enhance my long lashes, of which I was most proud. I felt confident, marvelous. Rem caught me by the waist at the last step, swinging me around twice, gently setting me down.

"Oh, baby, you look simply marvelous," he growled, his face pressed into my hair. "Marvelous." Seeing Charlie walk into the kitchen, I excused myself and followed him, wobbling only slightly on my high heels. I had, cleverly I thought, avoided shedding my clothing and jumping into the ocean by offering to help with the meal, and I had every intention of honoring my commitment to Charlie, and the kitchen and the food. Surely cooking was preferable to skinny dipping. As we began to prepare the evening's enormous feast for the crowd of kids, many of whom were still arriving, Rem wandered about restlessly, looking bored and out of sorts. Our friends began to straggle in from the beach, laughing, sexy and sexually charged, happy. I was relieved that they at least had the decency to not appear for dinner in their "skinny" mode, but were wrapped in towels or clothed in shorts and shirts. They were my truest and oldest friends, and I greeted them all happily: Marjorie and Douglas, Linc, and Jonne, Janet, Hunt, Thurston and Peggy, my best friend Sally, and Buzz, Ned, Hilda, all my old friends. They'd all heard the news about my being sent to public school and their expressions were of great concern.

"How awful for you," said Marjorie. She put her hand on my shoulder. "Do you really have to go there?" And Douglas said, "Oh Court, those awful people. What'll you do?"

"Maybe some New Town weirdo will hang from the girders in the gym there," said Edward bravely, and I smiled at him and touched his arm, happy to hear him finally joke about his embarrassing performance on the ceiling girders of The Academy's gym. My friends offered encouragement, promises we'd remain friends always, never be separated, that my being in public school made no difference to them at all. I basked delightedly in the glow of these friendships, warmly teary. I looked at the floor, then into their eyes, loving the attention, relishing it, reluctant to end the moment.

"Court!" Rem strolled into the kitchen. "Hey Courtenay. Listen. I'm sorry I was being such a dope before about the swimming. I understand and I shouldn't have tried to force the issue. We'll do it some other time, maybe--"---my look made him stop--"or maybe *not*," he stammered. "Anyway, let's just have a blast tonight and forget it. Now, what can I do to help to get this show on the road?"

"Oh Rem," I answered, and touched his cheek. "You're so sweet. I'm sorry I was a dope, too. I behaved like a baby. Honestly, I don't mean to be a prude, but it's just that I've never done anything like that and I was *so* embarrassed. I want to be adult and mature for you and, oh Remmy, when I think about it a little, maybe I'll be able to do it someday, but it just came as such a surprise. I hope I didn't embarrass you in front of Charlie." I put my arms around his neck, and kissed his

69

cheek, and he pulled me close. We began to sway to the music coming from the front parlor, and after some time, Rem began to kiss me, his mouth pushing hard against mine, forcing it open, and his tongue, oh his tongue was sweet and smooth and warm. His arms tightened around me, warm hands sliding up, then down my back. His breathing became more urgent, and I felt a surge down inside me, far down, and I didn't want it to stop, or him, or anything. Oh.

"Ooops. Sorry." Charlie chuckled when he barged into the hallway from the kitchen. He pretended to back out, but then walked toward us standing at the foot of the staircase, a tray in his arms piled high with glasses and dishes. "So, what's new?" he asked.

"Nothing, retardo. Can't you see we're busy?" Remington pulled slightly away from me, but held onto my hand.

"Yeah, busy. I can see that. You don't have to drop a brick shit house on me!" Charlie was red-faced, obviously drunk. He turned and went back into the kitchen, crashing jarringly into the counters as he made his way to the sink in the butler's pantry. He dropped his load loudly into the double porcelain sinks, sending shards of china and glass spinning out onto the floor and counter-tops.

I pulled my hand from Remington's and followed Charlie into the kitchen.

"Gee Charlie, your folks are gonna kill you if you keep smashing up the china that way." I bent and tried to gather up the broken pieces and I knew the young men were staring at my backside.

"Let it sit, Courtenay," said Charlie. "Katie'll be here in a day or so and she'll get the place back into shape. My parents won't even notice the stuff that's broken. God, there's enough of that crap in the basement to serve dinner to a thousand people. Katie'll just find something and replace the broken stuff and no one'll ever know the difference. Who cares anyway?" Charlie was slurring his words, and his sudden raucous laughter was punctuated by thunderous hiccups.

Tilting, weaving, he came up behind the Remington and me, jammed himself between us and hung a heavy arm around each of our necks, suspending himself, his feet swinging off the floor. He placed his hands behind our heads, grasped us by the hair, and forcing us to face him. He giggled, belched and I caught a very strong whiff of alcohol.

"Lissen you guys. Havva little drinkie, OK? Come on Court. Don't act like such a freakin' virgin. Oh, are you one, by the bye? Don't answer that!" and he chortled loudly.

"All the kids are all over the house, helpin' themselves to Dad's booze," he slurred. "Have some! Can't you see 'em?? All over the place. Partake, my friends. Partake. It can't hoit!!! An' who knows, you'll probly like it, yeah, 's good for what ails ya. Puts hair on your chest. Let's see, Courty Baby--you got hair on that pretty little chest?" Charlie groped roughly at the front of my dress, and when I shoved his hand angrily away, he roared with laughter.

"You stink, Charlie, you know that? Will you just get off me? Remington?!" But my dear Remmie just stood there, smiling stupidly. I felt my face grimace angrily as I tried to back away from Charlie, but he suddenly sagged forward, so I just remained where I was, instinctively raised my hands toward him, afraid he'd fall on his face, hoping he would.

"You know I don't drink," I said, "and besides, Rem and I are having a ball just being here, right Remmie? We don't have to drink to have fun, do we Remmie?" Remington nodded weakly, and I hated his flabby smile.

"So." I turned back to Charlie, smiling brightly, "Maybe we'll just dance out in the ballroom or maybe out on the deck, as soon as I finish in here, and the music's great--really, it's really a just terrific party, Charlie. Don't worry about us. Really, we do *not* need a drink." I wished I didn't babble so when I got nervous but had always feared it would be a habit for life. Charlie was disgusting but I kept smiling at him anyway, not wanting him to know how offensive he really was.

"Speak for yourself, Court," Remington cut in. "Maybe I'd like a drink, even if you don't." He pushed gently on his friend's arm. "Let go, Charlie. Take your big hairy arms off us. I'm going to the bar and I'm fixing one for Courtenay and me. We can get some dinner after that." I glared at him. "Now come on Court--don't let's turn this into another skinny-dipping disaster. Don't chicken out on me now, little girl. And stop giving me that disapproving look. Grow up and just have a drink, for God's sake. Who knows, you may even like it!"

Remington pushed his pal away, and as Charlie shifted his entire weight to my smaller shoulders, draping both arms about me and snorting into my face, Rem walked out of the room with a purposeful, grown-up stride, or so he thought.

"Get *off* me, Charlie." I pushed him away, and stamped angrily after Remington.

Threading my way between the swaying, clutching couples, many barely moving, I found him at the massive oak bar. He had one foot on the brass rail, an elbow on the bar and, of all things, a pipe in his hand. *What is going on with that pipe! A pipe!* I looked away and put my hand to my mouth, covering a smile. Remington put the pipe down to pour himself a drink.

"Oh, hi Court," Rem yelled over the music when he saw me coming toward him. An LP was playing a romantic instrumental by Mantovani, but the volume was turned up too high, making the music garbled and normal conversation impossible.

"Rem! So, you've decided to drink anyway? Liquor?" I was not really surprised, even though I'd never seen Remington drink anything more alcoholic than an occasional beer, and that of course, always from a Pilsner glass. Drinking from cans or bottles was simply not done.

"Here. I'll fix you one too. I promise you won't taste the booze. This is called a rye and ginger. I'll pour some of this rye, just a touch now--don't want you getting tipsy-- into this ginger ale and you'll love it. Here. I'll put a lot of ice in it."

I shook my head slightly and stepped back. Remington took silver tongs from the large wooden ice bucket and placed several cubes, one at a time, into my glass. "Tastes just like soda pop, I promise." He chuckled. "Come on. Trust me. You'll like it." I looked at him doubtfully. I frowned, looked away and then back at him.

"OK." I sighed. "OK, Rem." Still feeling the sting of being thought a prude for refusing to skinny-dip, I assumed, I hoped, an air of sophistication, standing tall, eyebrows arched, chin up, a look I'd practiced thousands of times in my dresser mirror. I took the highball glass from Remington, and raised it to my mouth. And lowered it.

"I can't."

"You can."

"I don't think I want to do this, Remington," I said, but then quite suddenly, poured a large swallow down my throat.

I coughed hard, but only once, and it was with the strongest willpower that I didn't succumb to a paroxysm of wrenching gags. The

72

closest I'd ever come to doing this was the time when I finished a glass of wine left on the dining room table after one of my parents' parties, when the guests had left the dining room for the good parlour to enjoy brandy and cigars. I'd been much younger then, and the taste had been shocking, but this rye and ginger was different. Very different! The bubbly sweet liquid slid down my throat and the burn and aroma made me think of a cinnamon-colored mountain stream. I could see it slide and bubble around the inside of my eyeballs, behind the lids. I had to admit that this was far from unpleasant. I took another large swallow. And another. It was just, *wow!*, so very good. As Rem had promised, I did not taste the alcohol. I smiled up at him, but the right corner of my mouth felt as if it was going in the wrong direction. I touched it with my tongue, convinced it was. I concentrated hard on my smile, and then snorted and thought if it remained crooked, who gave a damn?

"There you go, big boy," I said to Remington, amazed at the idiocy of my words, and I slapped him hard on his upper arm. "See? I can drink with the best of 'em. So don't ever tell me again I'm a kid, or a baby or an innocent, umm, an innocent whatever, or a virgin. Well, actually I *am* a virgin, but who wants to know? I'll stop being a virgin when I'm ready to stop. Being one. A virgin." I paused. "Got it? OK? I'm a woman, I'm grown up and I can have a belt with any darn damn one I want to, so there, Rem, stick that in your poke and smipe it." *God, I didn't know this could happen so fast. I'm bombed!!* And I gurgled and hiccupped out a loud laugh.

And then, very quickly, I slammed the nearly empty glass down on the mahogany bar with such force, some of the ice cubes bounced out and onto the floor. I laughed loudly in a shrill burst, then raised the glass and smashed it down again for the same effect, completely emptying it of ice cubes this time. I then laughed uproariously, at the same time aware that my performance wasn't actually too awfully funny. I coughed, covered my mouth, and laughed horribly again. *I can't help it. I can't stop!* I looked around with foggy bravado, while the backs of my thighs whirled like pinwheels and my teeth walked around in my mouth, and oh lord, didn't I just have to urinate fiercely. *Like a race horse. Isn't that what they say? Piss like one.* Remington chuckled quietly and took the glass gently from me.

"How's about another there, pardner bartender," I bellowed into Remington's face.

"Ah. Happy to oblige there, Courtenay, my dear. I feel like Marshall Dillon and Kitty. OK, Kitty. Here's another," he said, this time making the proportion of rye equal to the ginger. The music from the other room changed to some loud rock and without realizing it, I began to move in rhythm to the sound.

"Hey, in there!" Remington bellowed to the dancing couples. "How's about putting on a little Frank or Tony? Courtenay's gonna rock herself crazy pretty soon. Play something slower, OK?"

Someone shouted "up yours," and everyone ignored him.

I grabbed the glass from Remington, and drained it, tipping my head back so far, I nearly fell over. Behind my lids I saw that nice, cinnamonny river rush over the rocks, the high splashes fanning out in golden-orange sprays. Urgent warmth spread from the soles of my feet, into my groin, breasts, my scalp. I stared out at all of my beloved friends and was amazed at the soft glow that covered everything and went straight to the ceiling where it feathered out into rolling pinkness. Euphoric, I laughed and then laughed again, louder, then pressed my hand over my mouth. I saw a few of the dancers slowing and looking at me, then closed their eyes and danced more.

I hiccupped with a high squeak, then sagged against Remington and looked down at my shoes with absorbed fascination. A new impulse to laugh rose in my chest, since I'd never seen anything funnier, and I knew if I gave in to this burning urge to laugh, I'd never ever, ever stop. Horrified, it fuzzily occurred to me that I could possibly, no, I could *definitely* wet my pants because surely my bladder was fuller at this second than it had ever been in my entire life, even that time when I'd had a Coke-drinking contest with Sally at the beach with no handy bathroom. Just the ocean. Laughing actually wasn't too bad an idea, now that I thought about it. I allowed a small giggle to burst from one side of my pursed lips, sucked it back in loudly, and sagged more heavily against Remington.

"Want another Court?" Remington began to pour more rye into my glass, no ginger this time. "You look sorta cute, you know that?" he smiled down at me. "It'll be OK to have another drink. How about it? Maybe just a small one, OK? I'll have one with you."

Suddenly it felt to me as if some force from behind was pushing me rapidly away from Remington, from the entire room, so I clutched the edge of the bar to keep from catapulting across the room through the French windows and out onto the porch.

"It's nothing," I told myself dully, "it's probably just that little bit of rye that's making me feel like a shocket rip." I watched unfocused, as Rem held the rye bottle upside down over the glass, the contents gurgling rapidly downward. Some splashed out onto my aqua dyed shoes.

"Rem!" I blurted, "Be careful, will ya? I just had these shoes dyed to match my dress. Now they're dyed Rye. Rye dyed. Ryed dye. What the hell." I giggled, looked up at him. I could feel my face going darkly serious. "I sound shtoopid. Yes. I do," I said. And suddenly, inexplicably, tears filled my eyes.

I shook my head, and brightening, said, "Wait! Wait a sec, Remmy-Demmy-Do. I gotta go to the little girl's sandbox. What?? I said that? Cats go to the sandbox. Me? I'm a human girl and I gotta go to the john. The crapper. The loo. The head!" And I ran to the bathroom with such haste, I knocked an unamused young lady straight into Mrs. Nichols' great grandmother's credenza. I didn't slow down to see if anything had been broken but I could hear something glassy shattering on the floor.

Once in the bathroom, I struggled to get my skirt and crinolines up, and when I finally sat, my jaws shivered and ached with relief as my bladder emptied with a great gush of force. A young man opened the door and stared, his hand frozen on the door handle, his face slowly reddening. I smiled sweetly up at him, squinted, and said "Hi,--who the hell are you? C'mon in!" The rattled young man gulped, muttered something and finally backed out, slamming the door. I frowned and could not remember ever having seen him before, but in fact, he lived only three estates away.

Finished, I splashed cold water on my face and rejoined Remington, who gallantly bent and pulled away a long strip of toilet paper that had become impaled on my spiked dyed to match aqua heel. He poured me another drink.

We strolled out to the enormous parlour where our friends were dancing or sitting around on the Nichols' pale silk sofa pillows. Rem pushed his body against me, holding his glass high to keep the contents from spilling, and we began to dance. A Jackie Gleason record was playing, the trumpet sounds of Bobby Hackett sliding sweetly through the air. The alcohol and music softened whatever was left of my reserve, and I drifted happily around the room in Remington's arms, floating on cartoon clouds. The glow in the room slowly undulated its pastels, the way the Northern Lights do, and I felt detached and happy in a way I had not known before this Glorious Night of the Rye and Ginger. Nothing could mar the sanguine way I felt at that moment. Nothing. Ever. At all.

And then, we weren't dancing anymore. When had we left the dance floor? When had we walked up the long, graceful staircase and entered a dark room along the hallway? I couldn't remember, but here I was on my back on a bed, the knot of my ponytail digging into my scalp, and Remington on top of me making guttural, ugly sounds, his weight hurting me, squeezing the liquor up into my throat, and I was afraid I'd vomit, afraid I wouldn't.

"Remmie!" I gasped, trying to comprehend what was happening. He didn't answer. I moved my hands onto his back, and jerked them away. *Omigod, ogod, ogod, he's naked!* "Remmie!" I said, louder this time, but still he continued making those awful sounds--animal, grunting, peculiar.

"Remington!" I shouted, desperate. My head began to clear speck by tiny speck, my senses to operate sluggishly. Remington slowed his writhing. I couldn't breathe. "Remington--what's going on, what are you doing?" Only my words sounded more like "wuz gone on, wudderu doin?" *Is that my voice?* "Please Remmy, please--no, I want to get up, no... don't." I heard the crackling of cellophane, or foil, something loud.

"What's that?" I half-shouted, and getting scared, I began to cry. I turned my head to see Remington's hand struggling to unwrap some small --- something. "What is it? What are you doing? Stop---what is that thing?"

"It's a rubber, Courtenay. A rubber, for sweet Christ's sake. Can't have you, (grunt,) getting yourself pregnant, nossireebob."

"A rubber?" Those mortifying black rubber overshoes my mother forced me to wear in the rain? *This isn't making any sense to me. What's---what is he unwrapping? A rubber? Rubbers?* I began to twist around, confused, unable to make my mind work.

"God, Court, don't you know anything?" Rem's voice was sharply scornful. "What the hell planet have you been living on, anyway?" Remington stopped struggling with the small packet and his body relaxed somewhat, but he did not move off of me. His legs were forcing mine apart. He was so heavy on me. Where were my panties? *Oh God, please let me have my panties on. Please!* When his movements

76

stopped, his dead weight squeezed the breath from me and I knew I'd shortly smother.

"I thought you wanted this, Courtenay," he grunted. His breath was coming in short, harsh rasps.

"This? Wanted this?" My mind was racing. My heart was beating so hard I felt it hammering against Remington's naked chest. My eyes were so wide with fear they burned.

"Wanted what?" I squeaked. "I don't even remember coming in here. My God, Remington, you're naked, you're *naked*--what're you doing? Where are your clothes? Get OFF me!" I was pushing, pushing against his shoulders, his arms, with my palms, my elbows digging into the mattress, but he didn't move and my hands slid off him from all his sweat.

Remington ground his face against my neck, and he began to snivel wetly, but even in my drunken state, it sounded fake. The bed began to fly, spinning into the air, the way Auntie Em's house flew in the Oz tornado. I grabbed the twisted sheets and clung to them so hard my fists ached to keep the bed from flying away. When my vertigo eased, I again shoved violently against Remington's naked shoulders, trying to squirm out from under him. His voice against my neck was whining, pleading. Nausea filled my stomach and throat.

"Rem," I said. "Rem. Please. No. I don't want you to do this. Please, please stop. Where's my dress? Did you take off my dress? Where is it? Who took it off?" He began to speak. "I had to," he croaked, because he said, there may be another Korea sometime and he'd have to go to fight, and may never come back so girls should be happy to "give it up" to soldiers who may die. And besides, everyone does it, didn't I know that?, and God knows he'd been patient, we'd been dating for a year or more, and don't forget, men have needs, far more needs than girls. How come I didn't know that? he asked me. Hadn't I gotten any of this information in hygiene class? Didn't they tell us girls that a man's balls ache when he doesn't get it? And oh, how much I'd love doing it if I'd just calm down and let him.

"As they say, Court," Remington droned on, "When rape is inevitable, relax and enjoy it."

I stiffened. Was this rape? I stopped moving and slowly tightened my vaginal muscles. Was he inside of me? Was his thing... It didn't feel as if it were, but then I couldn't really know. Nothing was hurting. In all the books it said it hurt, that there would be blood. I hadn't even started using tampons yet.

Bile began to burn at the back of my throat and I shoved harder against Remington's shoulders and finally was able to squirm one leg out from under him.

"Remington!" I shrieked. "I'm gonna puke. I swear I am. Get OFF!" With tremendous effort, I wriggled from beneath him, shoved him off, then rolled and fell with a loud thud to the floor. I looked frantically around, my bleary eyes trying to make sense of the room. I sat on a large flowered rug. The bed next to me was huge, and looked like a cliff with me at its bottom. Remington's blurry, bloated face hung over the edge, staring down at me, eyes popped, red. He reached out and I recoiled from his hand. He looked like a creature in a horror movie. I scrambled away, crablike, and screamed when I realized that I too, was naked. Pulling, wrenching a sheet from the bed, I wrapped it around my body and tried to locate my underwear, anything to cover myself. I found it, scattered everywhere, my dress, shoes, stockings, and I began to dress clumsily. Hands violently shaking, I draped my stockings about my neck, squeezed my feet into my high heeled shoes, left into right, right into left. I felt for my jewelry and was relieved to discover it was still on me. I looked over at Remington who now lay sprawled on his back on the bed, the sheet and blanket twisted around him like the waves of an angry ocean. He was grinning at me lewdly and fondling his erect penis, one arm behind his head.

"You get me out of here Remington, you filthy --- you --- filthy creep," I screamed at him. "Just get up and get me out of here. No, no--DO NOT get up! Don't. Just wait til I leave the room. I can't stand to see you." My voice cracked. I reeled, reached to steady myself, grasping nothing but air.

"God!" I screamed. "I hate you Remington. I'll never speak to you again."

"Oooo," said Remington. "That makes me feel soooo sad, Courty-Worty. Hahaha!" Remington sat upright, swinging his legs over the edge of the bed, his bare feet thumping to the floor. His face was flushed redder now, his eyes bloodshot, hair standing in spikes. He resembled a cat that had barely survived drowning. He stood and staggered toward me, and I could not avoid seeing his swollen, florid genitals, how his testicles bounced from side to side and how his huge penis swayed like a flagpole caught in a wind. He wrapped his hand around it and began to pump the skin up and down, hard, harder, faster. His face became nearly purple with the effort as he bent toward his furiously working hand, groaning hoarsely, and I could see him beginning to sweat and heard his groaning turn to a loud and louder moaning.

"Get *away* from me, Remington! Just leave me alone." I turned my head away, revolted at the sight of his preposterous, black-red maleness, at his sudden pumping and jerking of it, the veins in his hand standing out like thick, blue wires. I turned back to him, began whimpering now. And then, "Stop doing that!" I cried out. "Stop it. What are you *doing*? Let me get dressed. How did this happen? How could you just assume I'd want this? You got me drunk on purpose, Didn't you? Didn't you??" I sucked in a sob and I choked. "You knew this was going to happen. You and Charlie probably planned it! The way you two were whispering about all night. All those *looks* between you. How could you? I thought you loved me. I trusted you."

I shuddered. I clasped my hand to my eyes.

"You know I'm not ready for this," I sobbed. "My God, I'm not even I6 years old yet. Maybe I wanted to wait until I was married. Did you ever think of that? Maybe I just wanted to wait, PERIOD! Did that ever occur to you?"

Remington stopped walking toward me. To my intense relief, he released the handhold on his member and, before my horrified eyes, it deflated like a pricked balloon.

Remington bent, grabbed a blanket and wrapped it around his waist. "Get dressed," he said. His voice was low, bitter, and he looked away from me. "Don't worry. I'll leave you alone. I thought you wanted this. But you have to know something, Miss Perfect Pure Virgin Courtenay Scott Wolcott. There's a name for girls like you. You wanna know what it is? Well, get your pretty little virginal pink ears ready 'cause you're gonna hate it. The name for girls like you is 'cock tease.' That's what you are, sweet little innocent Courtenay. You're nothing but a little fucking bitch cock tease."

I stared at him, stung, confused. "I am NOT," I shouted back, not entirely sure of what I'd been accused. "I AM NOT that!! Now just get out of here and find me a ride back home. You make me sick."

And then, to prove my point, I lowered my head and vomited into the roses and daisies at the center of the large flowered carpet.

# CHAPTER 11

Labor Day weekend. Summer was over. Remington had not called since the party at Charlie's and I spent so many hours feeling shame I could not go to the Club or call any of my Academy chums. I spent this last part of the summer mostly at home, mostly alone, mostly ashamed, lots enraged.

"What in the world is wrong with you, child?" my absent mother asked a few times, as she passed my room on her way to make some calls.

"Nothing, Mother. I'm just tired. I want to just lie here and read," I'd always answer every time, and she would call back with "well, suit yourself, Courtenay, but really, you should get out into the sun. You're so pale." Then I'd hear the dialing of the phone and knew the conversation with my mother had ended and that she really didn't care about my silence or paleness or anything at all about me. I often toyed with the idea of walking into her bedroom (where the upstairs phone was) with my hair on fire and waiting to see her reaction. I knew there would not be one.

Sally had stopped by a few times, and after not much prodding, had gotten me to tell her what had happened that night at the Nichols' beach house.

"Come on, Court," Sally would say. "Let's go to the beach or to the Club pool or something." But each time, I'd turn away and decline. Sally advised me that no one would think any the less of me if they even knew about what had happened, but I very seriously doubted that. After all, I wasn't proud of the fact that I myself had often "thought less" of people because of a rumor I'd heard. And besides the real problem with all this is that I'd heard that Remington was telling everyone that the "act had been completed," and with vigorous enthusiasm on my part. I was hurt and humiliated, and would not, could not, leave my home. I also knew there was no point in denying it; when guys like the charming Remington Richardson told their tales, everyone was a believer.

In some weeks however, I eventually became less ashamed of "the fiasco at Charlie's house," and began to not much care who believed Remington's story anyway. Soon, I found I could even laugh with Sally and our friends about the incident, and actually found I began to enjoy the retelling of it. My version. The truthful one.

Between gales of loud laughter, I would describe Remington's privates. "What else?" I'd howl with glee. "It looked just like a pair of purple plums stuck to the sides of a gigantic purple sausage lying on top of a rat's nest!! All on top of his belly!" and I loved how we all screamed and laughed. It helped.

"Did he come? Did he Courtenay? Did you see it all shooting out? Was it gross? White? Icky?? Did he scream?" Sally shouted between surges of laughter.

"Come where, Sal? He was already there!" I shouted back, not really understanding what Sally meant, but maybe. And we girls would collapse against each other, and gasp for air. But still, even through the laughter, I felt the sharp pain of being betrayed by Remington, the boy I thought I loved, who I thought loved me. It just kept on hurting.

As I often did when troubled, I wandered through the woods surrounding my home. I knew my way around the streams and hills and recognized many of the ancient, huge trees. They were my friends. I often lay beneath them and talked up into the swaying branches and I knew they listened. The woods were my domain, my private, secret place.

Silently moving over the spongy, rich earth, I could hide in the cool dark. Even when I was called by someone in the house, I knew I didn't have to answer since no one could ever find me in those enveloping thickets, and they never thought to look for me there and probably didn't want to anyway.

When I finally emerged, I made sure no one saw where I'd been, always leaving the woods from another angle so they'd never know. An immensely tall pine tree had my initials I'd carved at the very top, and the year too. CSW--1949, and after I did that, saddened that I'd mutilated my friend, I embraced the trunk and apologized. I so loved the solitude of those wondrous woods, my woods, my secret forest place, my own.

The summer ticked on slowly, inching toward the dreaded First Day. I couldn't understand why life at home was business as usual after my father's terrible predictions of a future of near poverty. None of the help had been let go, we still had the same number of cars, and my parents held as many parties as ever. Once I asked my father if I might be able to stay at The Academy after all, since there didn't seem to be any of the ominous changes in our usual family routine he'd warned me were coming, and his answer was a firm and loud "No!"

"And not only that," he went on to say, "I don't wish to discuss the matter with a mere child." But then characteristically, his actions belied his words.

"If you must know," he said drily, "your mother and I have been able to sell a great deal of family estate jewelry. No sense just having it sit in a black box in the bank. Better to turn that crap into cash, to get us out of this mess. We still have to conserve though; don't you agree Courtenay?" he'd asked, clearly not inviting, or expecting, an answer.

A short time after our discussion, my father, ever a lover of new gadgets, and compelled to be the first to have the newest, came home with a bulky Dumont television set. Even though my parents' revered bible, the New York Times, had announced record growth in the number of American homes that had televisions, most of their friends were loath to own one, reluctant to let go more genteel sources of entertainment like the theater, or occasionally the movies, great books, and radio. They considered television only a garish fad and saw little point in having one of the "damned things" in the house, since it would soon end up on the junk heap.

Not so my father. The machine he brought home looked to me exactly like the cumbersome wooden radios of the '30's and '40's with one major difference; a glass screen lay flat on the top of the box and reflected images into a mirror propped and slanted over it.

My friends and I were fascinated with this new toy, but I sensed my father had purchased it out of some mysterious sense of guilt although I could not articulate that to myself. It just felt that way. At any rate, the contraption was a great success. The household staff were so mesmerized they had to be sternly counseled against watching it at the expense of neglecting their tasks.

But even with the new television to distract me, I was unable to think of anything else but public school. By the time Labor Day arrived, I had become resigned to the fact that I would go to my doom in New Town High School the very next Monday. I was so filled with dread for that day I felt continually sick, but was not unaware that the image of a wounded martyr got me a great deal of sympathy and attention from my Academy friends.

I'd always had a habit of rehearsing things when they concerned or worried me. In front of my mirror, of course, bedroom door locked. I always wanted proper responses to be so well-drilled into my mind that when I had to actually do the thing, whatever it was, I'd handle it smoothly and easily, with as little fluster as possible. Making scenes, after all, simply wasn't done. But not knowing the New Town kids at all I had difficulty rehearsing responses to words I had never heard.

I did however, think it would be important to maintain a cool and nonchalant demeanor at New Town, and to keep my profile low. I had no frame of reference, nothing from which to draw, but still, I went over and over all the possible scenarios I could imagine, but it was not easy. The public-school kids were beneath me and I simply didn't know how to converse with who were people beneath me. I'd never been taught.

I rehearsed how I'd speak to them, and tried to plan my wardrobe and how I'd shrink and hide at the back of the classrooms, making myself so small the teachers would never call on me. I would become invisible, a non-person. I'd graduate and get on with my life, then go back with my friends, my own kind. Why was this happening to me? I just didn't get it. Why? *Why won't my parents tell me? Why are they forcing me to do this? There are just no money problems. What?*

I began to worry about how I'd get to and from that school, how would I do that? And the worry was worse when I thought about how I'd be able to get back home at the end of every school day. It made my stomach hurt. Fred, or a friend's parent, had always driven me to the Academy, or I traveled in the school's private van. Occasionally, I'd ridden the local commuter train with my father who would be on his way to his office in the city. We'd board early on weekday mornings, and I'd get off at the stop before my father's, and walk the short distance to The Academy. I'd sometimes turn and wave as the train rattled past me, but all I'd see is my father's profile in the window, his face bent toward his newspaper, and of course never toward me.

I began to consider taking that same train to New Town. It would allow me to be inconspicuous, and I would not have to suffer the humiliation of having to ask for help. It stung when I eventually realized I could not possibly take the train to New Town because I'd have to stand on the platform opposite where my Academy chums stood. I envisioned myself, frail, waiflike, shivering on the wrong side of the tracks, while my Academy pals stood in the sunshine, happy, rich, and content with life, pointing at me and laughing cruelly. I could hear them in my head and the sound crushed my heart. And then I was embarrassed at my own melodrama.

I so wished time would fly so I could get it all over with. Then I'd pray that time would not move so I would never have to go. Never have to go to public school.

"When will my suffering end?" I'd whisper into the night as I lay sleepless, and into the mirror over my dresser in the morning.

Finally, by summer's end, I had become nearly reclusive. I spent almost all my time in my room, shades drawn, squeezing my bent legs to my chest, my face pushed against my knees. I would think about how salty my knees smelled, about the noises my stomach made. I thought about anything that would keep my mind away from what was coming, feeling as if I were caught in a terrible, sucking current to nowhere.

# CHAPTER 12

Monday. I rose after a night of no sleep, or if I slept, I was plagued by colorful, forgettable dreams. I'd lain in my darkened room and studied the patterns dancing behind my eyelids as public-school demons floated in and out of my daze. A hundred times that night I'd forced my eyes open to look at my clock, so frightened I'd sleep through the alarm bell, more frightened I would not. I felt raw and when dawn finally came, my eyelids scraped over my eyeballs whenever I blinked.

I finally got up and sat on the side of the bed, staring at the floor and then sighing, I walked to the pile of clothes I'd laid out the night before and, as I had for days, fretted that the outfit I'd chosen wasn't right.

*I don't know how the cheap girls dress. I can't do this. I don't have the right clothes those awful girls wear. Oh God, I'll look like a freak. I'll stand out like a sore...a sore....*

I stood under the shower, not knowing if the water was hot or cold, not knowing if I even bothered to wash. My mouth was horribly dry so I opened it wide under the shower water but it ran out of the sides of my mouth and it didn't help and made me cough. Hard. I got dressed, frozen fingers fumbling with the buttons on my blouse. I stumbled down the long flight of stairs into the breakfast room. I'd so hoped that at least on this particular day, my parents would join me for breakfast, to comfort and support me, to encourage me, but they did not. I was not surprised, but still it hurt. I knew my parents were incapable of instinctively understanding when they were needed but still, I'd hoped. I mean all this misery and horror were their faults, after all, so I thought the very least they could do was to stand by me on this terrible morning. But no. I sat and stared silently out the window while Emma brought food to me. My eyes burned and my entire world seemed covered with a thick, white fog. I squinted, rubbed my hands over my eyes, and listlessly picked up a spoon and pushed it into my oatmeal. I sat still looking into the bowl, frowning, finally forcing the spoon up to my mouth, and swallowed. The hot, sweet glop stuck in my constricted throat and again, I coughed. And then gagged.

"Honey... Sweetie." Emma's soft voice made me jump. "Miss Courtenay," she whispered, "you gotta eat something, chile! Drink some juice. You'll pass out in that new school if you don't." Emma ran her hand down my long hair. I turned and saw the deep concern in sweet Emma's eyes and I felt the warmth of unquestioning love pouring over me. *Dear darling Emma. Dear.*

"Please Miss Courtenay, please eat something. Believe me, girl, everyone will stare at you if you faint! Now you don't want that, do you Miss Courtenay? Please. Please eat something, honey."

I looked down and then away, staring blankly at the wall. Finally, I managed to turn stiffly in response to Emma's plea and looked up at her again, my eyes unfocused. I didn't blink. Emma's kind, worried eyes gazed down at me, her broad smile nearly as white as the maid's dress she wore. Her familiar warm and mellow scent, like sun-dried clothes and kitchen things, was comforting. In my exhausted stupor, Emma looked to be a big chocolate lollipop. I was able to smile weakly, grateful for the way old Emma made me feel so safe, knowing she could not make the cause of it all go away.

"Oh, Emma," I cried out, taking hold of the wrinkled, dark hand and holding it against my cheek. It felt so warm and soft, like old, worn leather left in the sun. "I know I'm acting like a baby, Emma, but I'm just so scared."

"I know you are, sweet little girl," said Emma. "I know. I'd've felt the same way if I'd been taken out of my poor ol' black school and been forced to go to your Academy. Yes, baby, fo' sho' I know." Emma pulled my head against her big, soft breasts and held me. Tears filled my eyes and darkened Emma's uniform. I knew Emma was and always had been more mother to me than Helen Wolcott had ever tried or ever wanted to be.

The car horn sounded and I jumped. It was time to go. I picked up a new loose-leaf notebook, pen and pencil, put a dollar in the pocket of my jacket along with the mysterious bus pass, and took a quick glance at my school outfit. Praying my clothing was low-key enough to fit in and not be noticed, I felt Emma push a small brown paper lunch bag into my hand. I gave my dear old friend a grateful look, turned and went out to the waiting car.

"Mawnin', Miz Courtenay." Fred still spoke with the heavy drawl of his native Mississippi.

"Good Morning, Fred." I tried to smile as I got into the front seat. Something. Something else began to bother me. What was it? I frowned, looked at Fred and then I knew.

"Can you take off your hat, Fred, please?"

The aged black servant immediately removed his chauffeur's cap, then his necktie, and opened his shirt collar. He understood and didn't question me.

"Thanks, Fred, thanks," I said. My voice wobbled.

"You know, Miz Courtenay," Fred said haltingly. "I know this is gonna be a tryin' day for you, but I gotta tell you now, I won't be here this afternoon when you come back on the bus. I gotta do an errand for your dad at that time. He's been after me for a long time to do it and I promised last month before I knew you'd be goin' to that new school for the first time today. You reckon you can walk home this once? I'll try to be here other days."

"Yes. Sure Fred," I answered blankly, not really hearing him.

As the car moved forward, I stared at the familiar old estates and the Country Club, memorizing the scenes of my childhood, my life, as if I was seeing them for the last time and so I really did have to memorize them. The trip took fifteen minutes, winding around the well-known roads, ending at the bottom of a steep hill, where the public bus would meet me and take me to public school.

I clamped my jaws tightly together when I saw a crowd of public school kids waiting there, but, I reasoned, at least I'd know when it was time to get off the bus and I could follow them to the school.

"Fred!" I suddenly cried out. "Don't!

"What?!" I saw Fred's hands tightening on the wheel. He turned and stared at me, his eyes wide with fright. "What chile?"

"Don't drop me off in front of those kids," I shrieked at him. I pointed a shaking finger in the opposite direction, up the hill.

"Fred! Please! Go up that small side street and let me off behind those trees. Please Fred, please---do it now!" Understanding immediately what I was fearing, Fred turned the car instantly, pulling in behind the stand of trees as I had directed. But instead of getting out, I sat beside him, trembling. I could not make my hands stop shaking. I wanted to cry, loudly, but knew if I started, I might cry forever and would surely drown. I held on.

In an unthinkable breach of servant etiquette, Fred reached across the seat and grasped my hand. I held on so tightly, I knew his gold, old wedding ring cut deeply into his fingers, but blessed man, he did not flinch. Keeping my eyes wide to stave off the tears, I then held onto Fred with both hands. I heard him sigh and then he opened his arms and pulled me against his chest. Oh, he smelled so good, so safe and strong. He rocked me gently and hummed softly. *I want to stay here in his arms forever. I am safe here. Fred won't let me be hurt or scared anymore. Fred....* But in a short while, too short a while, Fred pushed me gently away from him, smiled and told me it would be OK. His voice was so dear, so caring that I suddenly became dizzy. I leaned forward and pressed my face into his shoulder.

"OK," I said in a whisper. "OK, Fred. I can do this." I exhaled a shuddering breath, slid away from my saviour, and stepped out of the car. While Fred watched protectively from behind the stand of trees, I, Courtenay Scott Wolcott, heart painfully hammering, began my descent down the hill.

# CHAPTER 13

With my head up, and having what I so hoped was a cool but polite expression on my face, I walked to the edge of the group. They took no notice of me. Nothing. They were laughing, casually cursing, chatting. Some smoked; others chewed gum noisily. I felt as if I'd been nailed to the asphalt and I didn't know what to do next. I bent and looked down the roadway, making a pretense of watching for the bus.

As if cued by my awful anxiety, the kids stopped talking and all turned toward me in unison. I felt their stares, oh how I felt them, but I didn't dare look back at those public school kids, so kept scanning the street, pretending not to notice as the group examined me in silence. Then one of the girls snickered. Then another.

"Who in hell's the geek?" someone whispered.

"Got me," came the answer.

"She gonna go to New Town?"

"Got me."

"That gawky broad is gonna go to school wid US?"

"Got me."

"Christ, jackass, can't you ever say nuttin' but `Got me?'"

Pause. "Got me."

The group laughed heartily, and went back to their conversation, ignoring me again. I relaxed a fraction.

The bus finally came, not down but *up* the street, and I realized to my abject horror I'd been staring in the wrong direction. I shrugged encouragingly at one of the young girls in the group, palms out, as if to say, "Oh my! Crazy me!"

The girl stared back at me through rhinestone-rimmed cat's-eye glasses, then looked at her companions and shook her head, then back at me, and back at them and she again shook her head in disbelief. They all laughed. I had never before known the agony laughter could inflict, and my mind flashed to the way my friends and I had laughed at the Rogers High School students from the Academy's windows. *Are you punishing me for that now, God? Do it later, do it later. Oh God, please, could you do it later?*

I looked at my shoes, and then my fingers. I wanted to cry. I wanted to run.

The group jammed together at the bus door, and I came as close as I dared to the strange kids. Straggling behind until the last of them got on the bus, I clumsily climbed the high step. Not sure what to do, I waited at the driver's elbow as he pulled the crank and slammed the door shut.

The bus lurched forward with such force I fell backward onto the lap of an extremely overweight and now very angry black girl. When she jumped up, tipping sideways because of the swaying bus, I saw a furious, threatening face under a huge pile of black, greasy hair, straightened in some places, kinked in others. Even though I'd been around Negroes all my life, this girl didn't much look like Emma and Mary. She looked incredibly angry. I'd never seen rage on Emma or Mary's faces. Puffed lids hooded her small, distrustful eyes. She wore a gaudy printed nylon shirt with fluttery short sleeves over arms ringed with rolls of fat, and tight, white pants at the splitting point, stretched hard over more rolls of fat.

Shouting an obscenity I had never heard, the black girl shoved me to the floor of the bus. Again came the laughter, this time louder, infinitely meaner. It stung. I was ashamed, embarrassed, unable to stand, praying my underpants hadn't shown when I fell.

"I'm so very sorry," I stammered to the livid girl glaring down at me.

"Please uh, Miss, Ma'am, I do hope you'll forgive me. I feel perfectly awful about this." With great difficulty, I scrambled to a standing position, and then heard the driver shouting something.

Oh, God, I thought, I've forgotten to pay him. I wobbled back to the front of the bus, reeling as I clutched straps, handles, anything to keep from falling again. My shaking hands fumbled for the dollar bill in my pocket and I handed it in a ball to the driver. He looked at me, then down at the bill, his face twisting in disgust. Then he pointed vehemently to a sign over the coin collection box.

"Exact Change. Fifteen cents," he shouted. "And anyway, girlie, where's your bus pass? You're supposed to have a bus pass. You got one, you only pay ten cents. Show me it."

In a panic, I'd forgotten I had a bus pass, couldn't remember what it was, or where, and I desperately tried to explain. The angry driver made change so I could drop a dime and nickel into the appropriate holes of the coin collection box. Suddenly remembering, I reached into my pocket and found the pass and with trembling fingers, tried to hand it to the driver, but he waved me roughly away. I turned toward the back of the bus, grasping the straps as the bus careened around corners and sped on its way.

No seats, oh God, no seats I thought. *I'll have to stand up where everyone can stare.* I curled my toes inside my shoes so tightly, my arches cramped. I could hear the kids laughing again and my insides shriveled.

*It's OK. It's OK. I'll stand still here and hang onto this strap. God, do they have a rule about using the strap?*

I tried to look bored and stare out the window, pretending to be interested in the blurred scenery.

After some minutes, I timidly looked around, noticed a row of empty seats at the back of the bus and made my way unsteadily toward them.

*Oh God, Oh God, God please God, let me get this seat. Let me be able to sit down and get invisible.*

As soon as I arrived at the coveted seat, a big rough looking boy pushed past me, slid into it and glared up at me through slitted eyes, smirking. He spread his arms wide over the backs of the seats on each side, one leg covering the remaining part I so dearly wanted.

While the others laughed louder at my predicament, I turned and made my way back to where I'd stood before and swallowed hard to keep from crying. I wanted to cry. I wanted to scream and yet I knew if I did, this group of hostile public school kids would make more of a mockery of me than before.

A sharp stab in my arm made me jump. The black girl was glaring up at me. Was that hate too? Why? What had I done that was so bad? After all, I couldn't help...

"Getcher bus pass in the office before classes start," the girl hissed.

I became weak with gratitude. "I—I think I already have one...but I..." My voice wobbled. My knees wobbled. I smiled weakly at the girl, pathetically eager to make a friend, have an anchor, to be a part of something, to blend in. But the girl turned her head abruptly, and looked out the window, sending me the very clear message that she did not wish to establish any sort of relationship.

About five miles into the ride, most of the kids suddenly, and all together, made some sort of crossing sign over their chests. They never stopped talking or changed position in any way or even looked away from each other. I thought insanely that maybe it was some sort of ritual that I'd better follow, or I feared, I might suffer for it. So I too crossed myself desperately, keeping the movement small, doing it awkwardly, and I was sure, incorrectly. I heard more laughter, and blushed in mortification. I, Courtenay Wolcott was unaccustomed to being mocked and therefore knew no defense against it.

"Them wop kids."

I turned my head. The black girl was hissing up at me again. "They gotta cross themselves when they pass their gawdamighty harp church back down the road there."

Again, I had been rescued, but again, the black girl turned her head away when I tried to silently thank her.

I was the last to emerge from the bus when it finally stopped at the last stop before the school, letting everyone push past me in the aisle, letting everyone push me finally into a now empty seat. I stood and stepped off the bus and everyone turned to watch me. A split second before it happened, I felt the trip coming. I would fall. I could not stop its happening. I stumbled, grabbed for the door handle and swung out over the cement, hanging on desperately. The folding door slammed shut and I hung there for a moment, frantic, my feet suspended in the air between the curb and the street. The laughter this time was terrible and shrill. One of the kids shouted, "Take off, driver!" I twisted my hand from the door handle, pain shooting through the bones in stabs. My feet slammed down onto the sidewalk and stung. Thus, with my head down, hot tears of humiliation burning the backs of my eyelids, I followed the crowd as they walked through the town to New Town High School.

# CHAPTER 14

A sea of teenagers swarmed around New Town High School as I approached, trailing twenty feet behind the bus crowd. I had never in my entire life seen such a mass of young people. Most were smoking, swaggering, posturing. A few were even spitting. Spitting! I pressed my back against the high school building, slouched and tried to look small.

*I'm so, oh God, I'm just so----obvious.* My mouth was dry and sour from fear. *My clothes are all wrong. No, the NOOK-D's clothes are all wrong, not mine. No. I gotta always remember that.* I looked down at my saddle shoes and thick white socks, plaid skirt and dark green cashmere sweater. It was early September and hot, too hot for me to have worn that sweater. *Why did I do that? I looked like an ass. They'll have another reason to laugh at me.* A rivulet of perspiration coursed down my spine, soaking the elastic band of my underpants.

Standing apart, I kept my head down, but occasionally flicked my eyes up furtively to look at the kids milling about.

It soon became apparent to me that there were two kinds of girls at New Town. Some were sort of OK looking. *They look like they're trying to be Academy kids. Maybe I can get them to be my friends.* I clenched my teeth. *No, I can't. They'll never. I'll never.*

They wore outfits vaguely like mine but had added or subtracted things. Earrings. With socks! Socks!! Shocked, I caught my breath.

Their opposites wore tight blouses or sweaters, with far too much inappropriate jewelry and dreadfully thick make-up.

Cheap girls, I thought, looking down at the pavement. Ugh. Just like the ones from Rogers that used to strut around and swing their backsides in front of the Academy. I inadvertently smirked, then squeezed my eyes shut. There was a strange sensation in the pit of my stomach. *Guilt. My God, I feel guilty. Why on earth? What's happening?* I shook my head, opened my eyes and looked up.

The cheap girls had on flat black pointed shoes, stockings and skirts. Their hairdos were extreme, stiff, unnatural. Big. Dirty looking. Some of the girls wore straight and tight skirts, others wore full skirts pushed out in stiff circles by layers of scratchy crinolines which caught on their stockings, making rows of tiny runs coursing down their legs like dozens of medical scratch tests for allergies. *Hey! I get those same kinds of runs in my stockings, too!*

I pressed my back harder against the school building's wall, trying to be invisible. The cement cooled the skin beneath my sweater, and its roughness caught on the wool, pulling at tiny strands of the cashmere. Everyone was milling about on the sidewalks. To my shaking relief, no one paid attention to me. I began to breathe more slowly and unclenched my fists.

A transistor radio suddenly blasted with the raucous shrieks and pounding bellows of Rock and Roll. I jumped and instinctively grabbed the wall behind me for support.

"Awright, Daddy!" a voice shouted. Kids began to dance on the sidewalk. Mouth open, I stared, both horrified and entranced at the spectacle. These kids moved so freely--they were sexy and raw. My foot began to tap in time with the music and, startled, I looked down at it. *What am I doing?* I stopped.

A piercing, mechanical squawk suddenly shattered the air and the dancers stopped in mid-step like a still photo, except for their heads which immediately turned toward the sound. The music continued to blast until a second unintelligible squawk silenced it.

A tall, sharply-boned woman with a severe chin that jutted out beyond her hooked nose appeared in front of the red steel doors. *She's...she's the witch from the Wizard of Oz. That's exactly who she looks like. She is that witch—of the West—I know it.* The woman stared out at the crowd, her swamp-colored hair combed rigidly and perfectly against her scalp, several severe, hard curls plastered flat to her temples. Her sharp blue eyes raked slowly across the faces of the students. She wore no jewelry or makeup. Her plain grey dress made no secret of her noticeable lack of breasts, her flat waistline, and sharply angled hips. Her posture was rigid, straight like a post, her legs long, bony and bowed. She wore scuffed black suede pumps with thick, sensible heels. The only relief from all this harsh severity was a small and delicate silver watch, held on her bony wrist with a tight black band.

She stood like a punctilious dictator surveying her about-to-be-vanquished enemy. In her left hand was a battered portable megaphone which she lifted dramatically to her lips, paused, and in an imperious high trill called, "Attention, students! Attention!!"

94

"That's Miz McArdle, the principal," said a voice close to my ear. "You watch yo' white ass around her, cawz she be a nasty old broad. She'd love to bust yo' ass just like anyone else's. White or black, don't make no matter to her. She be a bitch to anyone. She don't discriminate. Believe it, girl, believe it."

I turned to see the large black girl from the bus walk away from me and disappear into the crowd. I reached out my hand, called out softly, but got no response. I turned back to the principal.

Miss McArdle's voice was brittle, harsh.

"All right, boys and girls. Quiet down. Quiet down. SILENCE please. Dominick Di Russo, lose the gum. We DO NOT CHEW GUM AT NEW TOWN HIGH SCHOOL and you know that. You ALL know that. Is that clear?"

"Yes, *MA'AM*, Miz McArdle sweetcakes," came a rough sarcastic voice from somewhere in the crowd. Everyone laughed. I craned my neck to see the offender, but could not locate him in the sea of greasy black coifs, and anyway, everyone was chewing gum.

Miss McArdle sighed into her megaphone, the sound like a rasp on metal.

"Well, well, Mr. Di Russo," she said. "I see you're beginning this year just as you ended the last." She sighed." You are becoming very, very boring. Just come on in to my office as usual, young sir. Surely you remember where it is."

The group tittered.

"Now then," she went on. "We must all obey the rules, mustn't we? All right, all right. Now." I could see the woman enjoyed her Benevolent Dictator role. I shivered at the thought of having to deal with such a despot and vowed I'd always avoid her, and I well knew how to do that. *I guess I learned something from Mr. Raleigh and his tantrums after all.*

"Now then. Today, as you all know, boys and girls," the megaphoned voice was rising, becoming even more shrill, "this is our first day of school and I know we'll have a glorious and productive year together. Just remember to follow all the rules. NO GUM CHEWING! Did you get that Mr. Di Russo?? No running in the halls. No talking in study hall. No defacing school property. All books must be covered immediately. And finally, no smoking in the lavatories." A murmur rumbled through the crowd.

"The what?" someone shouted.

"No children, I did not say `laboratories,' I said `lavatories.' There is a difference, and I think we all know what that is now, don't we. We've had this discussion before. But for those of you who have obviously forgotten, I mean no smoking in the bathrooms, neither in the boys' nor the girls', and no smoking anywhere on school property. This year, we are considering the removal of the doors to the boys and girls rooms if this smoking rule is violated as it has been in years past. If you are caught smoking it is IMMEDIATE expulsion and those of you who know me, understand that I do mean business on this issue. I expect complete adherence to the rules at all times. I will accept no excuses."

She paused to let the weight of her words sink in, but I knew by the sea of bored faces around her that the principal's words simply had no effect at all.

"Miz McArdle, you closin' the teachers' smokin' room too?" The voice was a girl's this time. I scoured the crowd, but the throng seemed to close in on the ones who were courageous enough to shout out. Miss McArdle ignored the remark.

"Ladies," she continued. "I'm sure you'll remember. Skirt hems will fall below the knees, and if there is the slightest suggestion that the skirts are too short, you shall be asked to kneel. If the hem of the skirt does not touch the floor, then you shall be sent home immediately for a longer one. This infraction shall be allowed once. The second time means IMMEDIATE expulsion. Trousers on the girls are absolutely forbidden. Except of course, for any gym classes held outside when the weather is cold. Otherwise, only the usual gym bloomer suits will be permitted."

*Bloomer suits? Did she say bloomers? What on earth? Oh, no, I must have misunderstood.* I dismissed the idea as just too preposterous. *And besides, I just simply won't wear any...any... bloomers, whatever they are...* And then I remembered the trousers worn by my rescuer on the bus that morning and doubted that even Miss McArdle would dare ask that particular young lady not to wear trousers to school. Miss McArdle was maybe weird, but surely she was not crazy.

Miss McArdle continued. "Patience now, children. I know this is a long speech and you're forced to hear it at the start of every year but it's very important that we make everything completely clear from the start so there will be no excuse for misunderstandings. Now. Make-up must be understated and natural looking, ladies. Tiny amounts are acceptable. Remember, we are proper young women and we will *not* look like painted hussies."

"You'd never look like a hussy, right Miz McArdle?" A high-pitched male voice rang from the crowd. Titters turned to loud guffaws. Miss McArdle ignored them.

"We will not wear any clothing that is too revealing, and I'm quite certain I do not have to explain what I mean. Now, gentlemen. You will keep your hair short and combed. Crew cuts are perfectly acceptable. Absolutely no pompadours. Absolutely no dungarees or T-shirts." I looked around at the crowd of boys wearing pompadours, dungarees and T-shirts.

"As for transportation," said Miss McArdle, "no privately owned cars are allowed within one mile of the school. If there is an emergency and one must drive, loud engines or lack of mufflers is absolutely forbidden." Loud chortles punctuated by whoops.

"I will remind you, boys and girls, that this is only a small preliminary of the school's rules. The entire list is posted on all bulletin boards around the school for your review. I'd suggest that you read them all at least once a week."

Hoots of laughter and much rib jostling actually made me feel embarrassed for the principal. As coarse and abrupt as she seemed, surely she did not deserve to be mocked this way. *One does not mock one's principal. It simply isn't......*

"IT IS ABSOLUTELY POSITIVELY FORBIDDEN TO DO ANY NECKING ON SCHOOL PROPERTY OR ANYWHERE NEAR THE SCHOOL. Proper young boys and girls do not do this sort of thing. It is dangerous and foolish and again, ABSOLUTELY FORBIDDEN. I will expect your deportment, especially in this regard, to be completely circumspect. If this rule is broken, there will be no leniency and the students in question will be expelled IMMEDIATELY." The boys standing near me snorted. I looked down at the sidewalk.

"Dat mean US, Miz McArdle?" one of them called out. "You an' me? Geez, we can't be gettin' it on no more?" Again, the principal chose to ignore the comments. I smiled to myself as I watched a pair of young lovers necking rather vigorously behind a nearby telephone pole no more than 25 feet from the principal. If they heard Miss McArdle's admonishments, they gave no indication, and it was clear they didn't much care anyway.

"You'll be given instruction as to fire and bomb drills, class and lunchroom schedules, etcetera, etcetera. Now line up underneath the signs depicting your class level. Good day, students. Please feel free to call on me in my office if you need anything. I always have time for worthy boys and girls." Miss McArdle pulled herself straight into her Convent School posture and the group around her parted. She wheeled and strode like a great and skinny queen back through the red metal doors and disappeared.

I moved slowly with the crowd to the spot where the juniors were to assemble.

A woman separated herself from a nearby group of teachers, and walked purposefully toward the juniors' line. She was young and not pretty, her hair hanging in long hanks, dark and streaked with premature grey, and her small eyes and large mouth were not well balanced by her oddly shaped pointed nose and chin. Her walk had an athletic swing to it.

"OK, kids," she called out, as she approached the eleventh graders. "For those of you who don't know me, I'm Mrs. Jacoby. I teach girls' basketball, volleyball, soccer and personal hygiene. OK, OK, -- simmer down. A lot of you could use my hygiene class so don't be laughing." She grinned. "And you know who you are."

All the kids laughed when she said that and I saw how they liked Mrs. Jacoby.

She went on. "I'll read out the names of those of you who'll be in my homeroom, so listen up. Those whose names are not read just stand by--your homeroom teachers will be right over. Stand still, and quiet down. QUIET DOWN!!" She began to read the names and I was relieved to hear mine being barked out.

Pushing through the red painted metal doors, everyone trudged along behind the Phys ed teacher, laughing and talking, paying little attention since they all knew the way. They eventually stopped in front of a long row of grey lockers. As Mrs. Jacoby read out locker assignments, she pounded her fist on each door and backed her way down the row. Each fist-pound made me jump. I tried to stop and could not.

I noted that almost all of the kids took a padlock from their pockets and put it on the doors of their lockers, twisting the dials. Some had keys. I wished that Miss Piacentino had told me to bring one. When Mrs. Jacoby called out my name she hit locker number 38 with her fist, and moved on, hitting the other lockers loudly. I put my small brown paper bag full of the lunch Emma had prepared for me inside what was now my locker. The bag was crumpled and wet from my hot hand, and had begun to split. An apple began to squeeze from the bottom.

With a small signal from Mrs. Jacoby's thumb, all the kids trooped into what I guessed was the dreaded "home room" and I followed, head down. I looked around the spacious room, number 111, and repeated the number over and over in my aching head, terrified I'd forget. Forty desks stood in rows, and the tall windows were partly covered with those same cracked, dried-out shades I had stared at on registration day. A blackboard stretched from one wall to the other and up to the ceiling. The other three walls were covered with patriotic speeches and inspirational sayings. A dusty American flag stood in one corner. Numerous low bookcases bulged with magazines, books and papers. In front of the blackboard was an old desk, obviously Mrs. Jacoby's, which had seen far better days. The walls were a pallid green.

I hesitated, confused. What should I do? My temples throbbed. Everyone seemed to know what to do, and I lamely tried to copy them. But they all stood at the front of the homeroom, talking and serenely waiting for something. Finally, Mrs. Jacoby sat down, placed a large pile of papers in front of her, and shouted, "OK, OK. Quiet down. SETTLE DOWN!! All right. I'll read out your names, and when I do, you'll sit in the next available desk. You'll be seated alphabetically. Don't screw it up. When I read the name, take the next desk, and no tricks. OK. Got it? Here goes."

I nearly melted with relief: since my last name began with a W, I'd be at the back of the class. I only half-heard the list of names as I worried frantically about where I'd be placed.

"Kort-enn-ay Wool-cott." Startled, I looked at the teacher, turned and walked to the back of the class.

"Miss Woolcot?" I froze. "Oh," I heard Mrs. Jacoby say. "Sorry. I guess that's Wolcott. Miss Wolcott? Where are you going?" I stopped and turned toward her.

"Yes? Oh, --ummm-- I'm sorry, did you call me?" The class tittered. I looked at the floor, and felt the burning starting in my chest and creeping upwards. I felt suddenly as if I'd start to cry. Again.

"Yes, Kortennay, I did." Mrs. Jacoby looked down at some papers on her desk. "Oh. Yes. I see. Kortennay, you're new with us this year, aren't you, dear?"

"Yes, Mrs. Jacoby." I said, my voice barely audible.

"Well, Kortennay, you will recall that I told all of you to take the next available desk when I read off your names. Didn't you understand that?"

I disliked the woman's patronizing tone. I felt my jaw clench. "Well, yes ma'am, I did, but you see, my last name begins with a W and so I was going to the back of the room to where the W's might sit, and..."

"...I understand, Miss Wolcott, but you see John Walinski has the last seat in that row, and then came James Warren who obviously took the next seat at the front of this row and behind him, you'll see there's DiDi Williams, so that puts you right behind her, sixth row over, third seat down." Mrs. Jacoby stood and pointed to the third seat. I gulped and walked over to it and sat down as silently as she could, hoping even my shoes and clothing would not make a sound. I shrunk down low so no one would be able to see me in the sixth row over, third seat down from the front of the room.

# CHAPTER 15

"And don't you agree, Miss Wolcott?" Mrs. Jacoby's voice cut hard into my thoughts.

"What? Excuse me? I'm sorry. I was--I was looking at my--I mean I didn't hear --, I'm sorry--."

"It's perfectly alright, Kortennay. I know you're new here and this is all very confusing, but it would do you well—I mean it would help you a lot if you'd pay strict attention to the teachers when we speak. Now. As I was saying."

The bell rang, announcing the beginning of the first class. My loose-leaf book crashed to the floor. The rings popped and the papers spilled out in a large fan around my desk. I dropped to my knees and jammed them into the notebook, but not before several of the boys good-naturedly stomped on them on their way to the door, leaving filthy smudges on the white papers. No one offered to help.

I finally got all of the papers picked up, stuffed into the notebook, and followed the remainder of the kids, who chatted, laughed and completely ignored me on their way out the door. *They sure pay attention to me when something bad happens, but now that I'd like someone to walk with, they ignore me.* Holding my schedule and looking frantically up and down the hallway to get my bearings, I tried to figure out where my first classroom was. Biology. That would be a lab. Time was flying, the hallway was emptying, classroom doors were slamming and I was alone in the hall. *Oh God, please, help me out here. Please.*

Desperately I turned back and poked my head into my homeroom doorway.

"Please! Mrs. Jacoby! Could you point me in the direction of the lab? I don't know where it is and class is beginning and if I don't get there in a couple of minutes, I'll be late and... " I was losing my breath, begging, pleading...

Mrs. Jacoby put her papers down and got up from her desk. Hearing the terror in my voice, she smiled and that blessed woman took my arm, and pointed me down the hall. "Just go to the end of the hallway, down there, Miss Wolcott, and go up the stairs. When you get to the last floor, go through the door and you'll see the big laboratory down the hall. Can't miss it. Good luck--better run. No! Don't do that. No running in the halls. Walk fast."

"Thanks a million, Mrs. Jacoby." I barely got the words out, and disregarding Mrs. Jacoby's advice, I ran, tore up the stairs, and burst into the third floor hallway. I raced down the empty hall, skidded to a stop in front of the laboratory door and charged through, gasping for breath.

Too late. Everyone was seated. Thirty-six pairs of eyes burned straight into me. My eyes darted nervously around the room, looking for an empty desk. I began to walk down the side of the room hoping I could slink into one and disappear.

"Good morning, Miss--uh--" The white-haired teacher at the head of the room shuffled some papers. "Oh. Miss Wolcott. Courtenay." I stared at her. *Did she actually say my name right?*

"Yes. Courtenay Wolcott," said the teacher, not unkindly. "Well, I know you're new here, so we'll overlook your tardiness, but next time I'll have to send in a report. Alright, will everyone in, uh, let's see, row number eight, all move down two spaces so that Miss Wolcott can take her proper place alphabetically." Groans. Mumbled curses. Papers rustling. Books falling on the floor. The students, already settled, made quite certain I knew of their displeasure by leveling frowns and threatening glares at me as they moved to their new desks.

The new teacher's name was Mrs. Hortense Haywang. It was printed on the board in front of the class, behind the lab benches. A comical name, it was owned by a beautiful and decidedly uncomical woman. Her hair, swept up into a full Gibson Girl coiffure, was obviously prematurely white since her face was smooth, without a wrinkle, and had a rosy, youthful glow. She had kind, pale blue eyes and she was tall, almost regal.

Even though it was a warm day Miss Haywang was dressed in an expensive but subdued tweed dark blue woolen suit, complimented by a mauve silk turtleneck blouse. When Mrs. Haywang spoke, her very fine education was obvious. Her words were rich, her voice moderate and attractive, her language neatly laced with a varied vocabulary. *It is almost like hearing music. I love to hear her speak. I wonder why she teaches here...at this...this awful place. She belongs at The Academy...*

The biology class dragged. *Who cares about the heartbeat of a rat? Or the workings of the human lung. I'm going to fall asleep.* Finally the bell. I found my next classroom easily. It was French class, and I felt confident because I'd been taking French since the third grade at The Academy. I slipped into my assigned seat without calling much attention to myself, and was able to relax for a few moments before the class began.

Keeping my head low, I sneaked a look around the room and was surprised to see that many of the girls were not the cheap girls. These group looked and dressed rather like I did, with some improper differences. And the boys did not all look like hoods. Many were clean-cut, well dressed young men, who dressed a lot like the boys at The Academy. I could not stop staring at them.

"Ma'amselle Wolcott! Ma'amselle Courtenay Wolcott!" I stiffened to attention and responded as I'd been taught at The Academy. "Oui, Madame?"

Tittering filled the room. *This is becoming annoying.*

A loud whisper behind me: "Hey! We got us here an ass kisser, and it speaks in French yet."

Another. "Hey! Annette! How do you say `ass kisser' in French, anyway?"

From the back of the room. "KEESaire dee lay ass-AY."

I looked down at my desk, staring at the carvings. My teacher, Mrs. Brandcamp, ignored the outburst and continued to speak to me in French, but I did not dare answer either in English *or* French. I did not look up and vowed I'd never let anything I'd ever learned at The Academy to surface in public school again.

"Come, come now, Ma'amselle. Do not be embarrassed that you can understand French. You're new, aren't you? And I guess you learned to speak French in your other school. Is this correct?"

"Yes Ma'amselle,--Madame--" I whispered into my desk top. *When will they ever stop making these big announcements that I'm the new one?*

After Mrs. Brandcamp handed out the textbooks and went through the year's plans, the bell rang again, and I followed the crowd out of the room.

During my next class called "Earth Science," whatever that was, I studied my schedule and saw that I had "first period lunch." *Lunch.* Alone with a sea of strangers. *Oh God, I hadn't remembered about lunch.* I tried to hide my mounting anxiety.

When another teacher suddenly entered the room, I immediately jumped to my feet, and then realizing instantly and too late that I'd done the wrong thing. *Again.* Everyone turned to stare. The two teachers at the front of the classroom looked at me quizzically.

"Yes, Miss, uh, oh yes, you're Courtenay Wolcott--is there something I can do for you? Do you have to, well, do you have to leave the room my dear?" My teacher spoke kindly, but to my burning, embarrassed ears, the words boomed.

Mortified, I sat down slowly without answering. A few snickers rippled at the back of the room. Flushing, knowing my face was florid, I stared down at my books, cursing the ingrained Academy training that directed students to stand respectfully whenever an adult entered a classroom.

As the class droned on, I looked up at the huge clock in the corner of the classroom, willing the hands to stop, freeze in place, so first period lunch would never come. But the bell soon tolled for me, and it was time to face the inevitable; lunch.

*Ah, ah, now I will go to lunch with these people. I have to find my way back to my locker to get my lunch. I am so afraid. Afraidafraidafraid.*

I had 45 minutes to get the bag, find the lunchroom, eat and get to my first afternoon class. I raced through the halls, fighting down panic, trying to ignore the pressure from my overextended bladder.

I found locker # 38, wrenched it open and saw my lunch bag sitting forlornly in the dark opening. I took it out, and the apple fell from the split bag onto the dirty marble floor. I retrieved it and looked at the crescent shaped dent in its skin. Hands shaking, I put it back into the torn bag with the rest of my flattened lunch and followed a group of students down a small flight of stairs and around a corner to the lunchroom.

When I saw the rows of long ominous metal tables, I stopped so abruptly that some of the students behind me crashed into my back, causing my over-loaded bladder to ache inside of me. Kids piled behind me or pushed past, cursing me for blocking their way. I stammered apologies, but no one listened.

The students began to line up at the metal food counters. I looked at the counters and saw square, sunken bins full of hot food, others filled with cartons of milk floating in melting ice. A shelf above held a variety of colorful, sweet desserts, most of them Jello with sagging puffs of whipped cream on their tops.

Some kids were carrying trays of food to the long tables. Some already sat, eating from paper bags of food they'd brought. Heart thudding, I stared into the room, clutching my sodden lunch bag. Where would I sit? Everyone seemed to know someone. What if I sat down and they told me to get out? What if I accidentally sat with someone from a higher class? Kids in higher classes always hated the kids in lower. I was *really* afraid now, my mouth becoming dry and sour. Everyone in there had a friend. I had no one and I had never in all of my life until then felt such loneliness. I turned and ran back up the stairs.

The hall was empty. I stood, my head swinging back and forth while I frantically looked for something. Anything!

GIRLS. *Thank you, God.* I saw the sign, and bolted for it, bursting in to find, to my measureless relief, that the girls' bathroom was empty. I charged across the room into a stall, and locked the door. I tore frantically at my clothing. It was almost too late. When my bottom crashed onto the black plastic toilet seat, I nearly cried out with the pain of sweet relief as my bladder released its horrendous overload.

Remaining seated, I stuffed my smashed lunch into my mouth, where it stuck in my dry throat. I had nothing with which to wash it down. I flushed the toilet. O*h God, I have to have water. Should I reach in there and try to scoop some out? Would someone hear me? Would I die if I did this? Oh, God, please … oh what will I do?* I began to weep, praying no one would notice I was in the stall. Several girls came in, used the bathroom, and left. A few stayed and smoked, so busy gossiping they never noticed my feet on the floor of the stall.

"Please, please let the bell ring," I whispered. I pulled my legs up, and hugged my knees so no one would see my feet. I pressed my knees into my eye sockets. My buttocks became numb. Finally, the blessed sound of the bell. I jumped, got up stiffly, and flushed twice to make certain anyone in there would hear, and exited the stall.

*Water. I have to have water. Where are the sinks? Oh my God, what is that thing?* In front of me was a huge grey cement tub, no higher than my knees. Above it was a metal hoop like thing, a hoop pocked with holes. Beneath the cement tub was a metal rail. I walked toward it. A filthy, gummy bar of soap was lying in the bottom of the tub, surrounded by cigarette butts, bumpy clots of discarded chewed gum, and two cardboard tampon inserters. I looked around. No one was in the Girls Room. The bottom of the tub had water in it. I'd scoop some out. I stepped closer, my foot accidentally pushing on the rail and a shower of water shot from the holes in the hoop above. I shrieked and jumped back. I laughed, a dry, small hysterical sound. I put my foot on the rail again, and the water jetted out in a comb of single, curved strands. I pushed my arms into it, cupped my hands and drank, sucking the water deeply, deeply into my throat. I splashed it over my face and neck, straightened, reached for a cardboardy paper towel and scrubbed the wetness from me. I sighed deeply. Throwing the remains of my partially eaten lunch into the waste bin, I pushed through the door and headed for my next class, thankful no one had come into the girls' room while I was there.

Confident no one had noticed me enter the classroom this time, I allowed myself to look around the classroom. My eyebrows lifted and I put my chin into the air a little. *I know I'm better than these jerks. I know it. I'm better. They're nothing but NOOK-D's, every last one of them. Losers. Riffraff. Common. Definitely not PLO.* I composed my face so that my expression would not show what I was thinking, that I was superior in all possible ways to the kids in this public school. *They'll never find out from me they're such low-lifes. They'll learn. They will someday learn.*

Finally, the bell signaled the start of the last period of the day. Wearily, I put my books into my locker, and clutching my precious, now worn schedule, made my way to the gym. When I got there, a very big, very loud woman instantly greeted the class.

"Hello there!" the teacher boomed happily as she gallumped into the gym, her face, split by a gigantic smile, beaming like a spotlight. Two inches higher than six feet in her gym socks, this hulk had a thatch of thick short blond hair that stood out from her head in a straw pinwheel. Heavy, black-rimmed glasses covered myopic eyes. Her name, which she wore on a big piece of tape plastered to her hard square breast, read "HELLO! MY NAME IS BETTY GINOCCHIO. WHAT'S YOURS??"

It was impossible not to notice the gym teacher's long, thick nose. Nature had dealt Miss Ginocchio a cruel hand, I thought, and I knew she must have been made fun of as a child for both her name, its famous rhyme, and her nose. I laughed to myself at the thought of Betty Ginocchio as a little girl. *This woman could not possibly ever have been little.* At birth, she must have been just a smaller version of what stood before the students that day. What a shock it must have been to Mr. and Mrs. Senior Ginocchio when baby Betty was thrust into their loving arms.

Despite her unfortunate lack of decent looks, Betty Ginocchio was a good woman, slow to anger and tolerant of a great deal from her students, who, for the most part liked her and didn't plan to kill her.

"Well, well, well, ladies," she boomed happily. The New Town girls slouched against the walls, well-practiced sullen expressions pulling at their faces.

"Welcome back. "Those of you who don't know me, well—that's me!" She pointed with her thumb to the tape on her shirt, and again the face split into an enormous, toothy grin. She was wearing khaki shorts and a short-sleeved navy blue knit shirt, and the silver Acme Thunderer whistle hanging round her neck bounced from rock hard breast to rock hard breast whenever she moved. Her arms were sinewy and muscular. Her legs were very long, and bulging with substantially veined muscles, and on her feet she wore thick white socks and dark Navy blue tennis shoes. She took a deep breath, placed her hands on her hips, and began to speak. Shout.

"All right, ladies. Most of you know the drill here. Oh, I see one of you is new. A Miss Wolcott? Courtenay Wolcott? Are you here?" My eyes shifted around the room. *Yes, Miss Wolcott is here, and yes, I am once again the target of the day.* Maybe tomorrow I'd be allowed anonymity. I slowly raised my hand part way up.

"Right. Now listen up. I know you all need your gym outfits, and so if you'll line up at the other end of the gym, Miss Gross will measure you and hand them out. Now remember girls, they are to be kept clean and neat, carefully ironed. No jewelry during gym classes. Your gym outfit is appropriate for soccer, and volleyball. Those of you who wish to try out for the field hockey team will be issued the usual plaid skirts and knee socks, and it will be up to you to supply your hockey shoes, hockey stick, white shirt and black nylon panties, which, as you know, will be worn on top of your regular panties." Laughter.

The girls crowded up to Miss Gross to be measured and handed their gym suits. "Just like being in the army," said the measurer, who repeated the phrase at least eleven times, obviously having decided some centuries before that the remark was hilarious and so must be repeated, year after year, over and over, lest one of the girls miss it.

The gym suits were bright green, one piece, belted in the middle, and they bottomed out in elastic-edged balloons. *So those are the famous bloomers. Ugh.* Holding my gym suit up by the shoulders, I stared at it in disgust. I had never worn bloomers before. I hated them. They embarrassed me just staring at them. *They cannot force me to wear this---this thing.* But I wouldn't dare complain, so gritting my teeth, I decided I had to accept my plight with no comment. I followed the rest of the girls to the locker room where I desperately tried to hide behind a post while I changed into the dreadful garment. When we filed back into the gym, we all looked like walking green laundry bags. I stole looks at the other girls. No one seemed to care that they looked ridiculous. *Am I the only one here to understand that we all look like utter fools?? Don't these idiots have any sense of style at all??*

"OK girls," bellowed the affable Miss Ginocchio, "tomorrow, don't forget to bring your tennis shoes. For today bare feet or socks will be acceptable, but only for today." Miss Ginocchio then bawled "OK, line up!" The girls spread out across the gym floor in ragged lines.

Then, as if someone flipped a switch someplace on her back, Miss Ginocchio suddenly burst into a whirling frenzy of activity. She began leaping up and down in a frenetic, sweat-spraying parody of Jumping Jacks, her hands clapping together over her head, each clap like a rifle shot, her feet separating widely with each mighty jump, slamming together with another, smashing down loudly onto the gym floor, sounding as if bowling balls were dropping from the ceiling. It surely was a sight to behold, and most of the girls stood watching her, either bored or stunned. "Come **ON,** girls," shouted Miss Ginocchio. "Count out loud now. One and Two and Three and Four and One and Two and Three and Four. **DO IT!!**"

With the barest enthusiasm, a few of the girls began to imitate her, most of them flaccidly slapping their hands together one or two inches over their heads, their feet not moving at all. Miss Ginocchio, ever forgiving of her jaded students, ignored this mockery of her athletic prowess, and continued flailing the air, counting the rhythm deafeningly.

After she'd exhausted herself, Miss Ginocchio laughed horribly and fanned herself. "That was GREAT! Now, don't we all feel better? OK Girls, let's do a few laps around the gym and after that, we can all sit down and rap about what we want to do this year in SPORTS. SPORTS, as you know, will make you strong, lithe, and will make your brain sharp as a tack! I mean, if you do SPORTS, why, if a taxi is coming at you on a city street, you'll be able to jump back out of the way like a CAT! Couldn't do that, no sir, if you didn't take SPORTS!"

Miss Ginocchio had a way of shouting certain words for emphasis, and it did not take me long to realize that one of her favorites was "SPORTS!" I also quickly discovered how unwise it was to sit near Miss Ginocchio when she was howling over the joys of SPORTS, since those emphasis-words nearly always were punctuated by a large ball of spit which sailed through the air like a tiny comet and landed on the nearest hapless student.

I joined the girls as they began lethargic laps around the gym. Because of my years of playing tennis, and participating in swimming races at the club, I was able to keep up with them, even outdistancing many.

"Christ! I gotta get offa the weed."

I snapped my head to the right to see who had spoken. A young girl was running alongside me. I looked to my left. No other runner was there. The comment had obviously been directed at me.

"What? Excuse me?" I said, breathless.

"What? Excuse me?" the girl mocked me. "I said, I gotta get offa the weed. This running is killin' my lungs. Jeez, you talk funny, you know that? You got a weird accent or somethin'."

"Oh. Oh. I'm sorry. I just didn't think you were speaking to me," I stammered as we ran.

"Oh. Oh. I'm sorry," the girl mimicked again. "Lissen you, whatever your name is, you're new here, right? You don't have to talk like you're always so shit-scared. If you don't stop talking like such a pussy alla time, everyone'll laugh you right outta the place. Or worse. So, talk like normal, cantcha? Christ, what a spaz." We were both panting.

"Well, I didn't realize I was speaking any differently from anyone else in this school," I lied. "And yes, I'm new here, a fact that seems to be one of this school's biggest concerns."

"Right. Right. Yeah." The girl muttered and ran past me. Miss Ginocchio blasted on her silver Acme Thunderer coach's whistle, and the girls flopped down on the gym floor, some running first to the side for a drink from the water fountain.

"Now ladies," began Miss Ginocchio. "As you know, Mrs. Jacoby and I take care of the girls SPORTS"—spit—"in New Town High and we expect you to sign up for whatever SPORT interests you. No one is exempt unless you have some sort of disability, and I can see from this group today that none of you has to worry about that. You're a fine-looking, strong bunch and I know we'll have a GREAT YEAR in SPORTS! So sign up for something, and remember that every Friday, we'll have dancing in the gym."

*OhGod, dancing, what does she mean, dancing? Do we have to dance alone? Ballet? Square? What? Oh God.* I clenched my fingers so tightly, they ached.

The group of girls obediently signed for their sport of choice and trooped back to the locker room, where showers were optional but heartily recommended by Miss Ginocchio. I was suddenly far too embarrassed to get undressed in front of these strange girls, and besides, I hadn't really worked up a sweat, so getting naked on this rather traumatic day would definitely not do.

A siren blast suddenly nearly knocked me into the wall. It was simply the loudest noise I'd ever heard in my life, like having a screaming fire truck roaring straight at me from nowhere. I looked around frantically. Everyone else seemed to know how to react. The girls dove beneath tables, rolled up against walls, and curled on the floor, their arms bent up and over their heads.

"DUCK AND COVER!!" Miss Ginocchio thundered, as she galloped into the room. She bent her knees and executed a mighty and muscular leap into the air, like a stag leap by male dancers I'd seen in ballets, launching herself into a flat, airborne dive straight across the room like a huge, straw-thatched rocket ship. With precise aim and obviously long experience, Miss Ginocchio landed under an old desk in the corner of the locker room, instantly curled her body, arms crooked over her face, and stayed completely immobile. I gasped in awed amazement. The gym teacher's performance was nothing short of stupendous.

And then I began turning in frantic circles. Finally, with the siren still blasting rhythmically, I got down on all fours, and crawled to a corner, where I curled into a position I hoped would protect my vitals from whatever was coming, and I fought down an urge to scream.

Finally, the mighty siren stilled. "Congrats, girls!" bellowed Miss Ginocchio. "Perfect atomic bomb drill! Proud, proud, *PROUD* of ya!" The girls picked themselves up and dusted off, nonchalantly continuing their conversations from where they'd left off before the rude interruption.

*Would a desk and my arms be able to save me from an atomic bomb? No! Nonono! These people are stupid fools if they think that! What is wrong with them???*

Trembling, I dressed and finally heard the wonderful sound of the bell announcing the end of classes and the return to homerooms. Surprisingly, I, who had been planning to secretly place some discreet, small pencil marks on the walls the next day so I could find my way around, actually found my way around, largely accidentally, back to my home room without help.

When the final bell rang at 3:17, I made my way out of the school and through the red metal doors. Disoriented for a few minutes, I had to remember which direction to walk to get to the public bus or at least to the bottom of the hill where Fred would meet me. When I'd gotten it straight in my head, I walked through the side streets, out onto the main street of the town, across the railroad tracks and up to the bus stop. The same group of kids stood there. Some watched me approach, a few of them sneered, I heard the word "retard" muttered a few times, but shortly, all turned away, back to their conversations and friends.

I took a deep breath and approached the fat black girl I'd toppled on during the morning ride. "Hello," I said, hoping my voice was calm, friendly. "My name's Courtenay."

"So?" responded the girl, turning away from me once again. Hurt, embarrassed, I bit my lips. I focused my attention on the bus ride to come. I would ignore the sign of the religious cross ritual this time and avoid more embarrassment. As I fumbled in my pocket for the fifteen cents I'd need for the long bus ride home, my heart flipped. I'd forgotten my bus pass! *Oh God, Oh God, Oh God, please don't let it be the same driver. Pleasepleaseplease. I'll do anything you want, anything. I promise.* The bus pulled up, exhaled an enormous gasp, and the door slapped open. The students jammed into the doorway.

I waited for my turn to pay, then saw it was the same driver. I sighed deeply. "*Well----well---he can just----well, just screw HIM!*" I glanced around furtively, afraid someone would know what I'd been thinking. I stepped up, glared at the driver and said in what I hoped was my most imperious tones, learned from my dear mother, "I do not have a bus pass today, my dear sir. I will have it tomorrow." I dropped my coins into the slots, marched back to an empty seat, slid in and stared haughtily out the window. The driver shut the doors with a loud bus-gasp, and the bus lumbered away from the curb.

# CHAPTER 16

I watched carefully to be sure I would not miss my stop. When it came, I made a lunge for the bus door but not unexpectedly was rudely banged aside by the other kids. I hung back, and was the last to get down from the bus. Some of the kids turned to watch me, no doubt hoping I'd crash out as I'd done that morning, but to my immense relief I made it smoothly and easily, and looked contemptuously at the disappointed group as I walked past them and toward the base of the hill. The group quickly dispersed and with a sigh, I once again began my long walk up to the estates, alone as usual since all of the other kids on my bus lived in the opposite direction, the route that led away from the hills, from the estates.

"Winona." I heard a voice directly behind me and I quickly turned to see who was speaking.

"What?"

"Winona, fool." The black girl from the bus answered impatiently. She glared at me through slitted eyes, her huge lips pursed, then strode away, down the streets and out of sight leaving me to gawk after her. I stood watching her, then turned away and smiled. "Winona," I said. "Winona." I had made a friend.

I looked around desperately for Fred, and then remembered I'd asked him to hide behind some trees on a side street, around the corner. I ran in that direction, but he was not there. I waited for at least twenty minutes, and then finally remembered him saying he'd be unable to meet me that day. How could I have forgotten? Nerves. It was my nerves. Dejected, I began the long walk up the steep hill to my parent's home. I cut through the large side yards of many of the big estates, knowing the owners would not object since they'd known me all of my life. I'd played there, had imaginary friends in secret, magical places on their estates, and the families often invited me to dinner. I was happy there. I loved being alone in those beautiful, serene and meticulously manicured places.

As I made my way through an opening in a long hedge on the MacLain estate, I looked up the long sweep of lawn, and in the late afternoon sunlight, saw a large flock of bluebirds fly by, the first ones I'd ever seen. The sun hit the brilliant speeding blur of their cerulean backs, dazzling me, making me feel amazingly happy. I smiled joyfully as I watched the birds disappear into a grove of trees. I sighed. I was alone in the soft, dimming late afternoon quiet, and as ever, I loved being there. "Thank you," I whispered, grateful for the instant of resplendent beauty on what had been my short life's darkest day.

The sight of my own house thrilled me, and I felt secure again, and strong. I ran up the driveway and through the back door leading into the vestibule and then into the kitchen.

"I'm home," I called out. "Anybody here?" Emma's voice came from her room at the top of the back stairs.

"Dat you, honey? Well well well, little girl, how'd it go?" Emma clomped her way down the narrow, uncarpeted stairs from the maid's quarters.

"Horrible. It was horrible Emma! You don't know how glad I am to be home!" And then, I couldn't help it--I laughed. I actually laughed, and loudly too.

"Come on, honey, sit yourself down. What you need now, chile, is some of my peanut butter cookies and a big glass of cole' milk. Ain't that what I'm uppode-a say?" Emma always laughed at her own jokes.

"Where's Mom?" I asked her.

"Well now Miss Courtenay, you know how busy she is, what with them committees and everything. She's upstairs on the phone, child, but don't worry. I know she's anxious to hear all about your day. She'll be down soon. Hey little honey chile, let's you and me have a little dinner together, just us two, cawz your folks, well you know, they've got that bunch comin' over from the club to talk about ....you know,...the problem." Emma began to pull cookies out of a large ceramic cookie jar and to spread them on a plate.

"What problem is that, Emma?" I asked, holding down a growing thickness in my throat. *Couldn't Mother have been here waiting for me just this one time?*

"Well, you know, Miss Courtenay--" Emma's voice dropped to a whisper, "that Jewish problem."

"What Jewish problem?"

"You know, them Jews what want to get into the country club and one'll let 'em, cawz they be r'sticted." I looked at Emma. *I think she knows what it's like to be restricted,* and I frowned at this sudden and rather odd feeling.

"Oh, yeah," I answered. "That's right. 'No organization has the right to restrict minorities from their membership.' I remember reading that on Father's desk. "Well, I hope it'll all work out. See you later Emma. Yes, I'll eat with you in the kitchen tonight. I'm going for a long bike ride now, and after dinner, I'll do my homework. I'll tell you all about my new school when we eat. You just won't be able to believe how creepy it was!"

The good Emma had prepared my favorite comfort foods as a reward for living through my first day at public school. I shared the delicious feast with her, and we chatted easily. We could hear some of the conversation between my parents and their guests as they discussed "the problem" in the dining room. I began to listen more intently, oddly uneasy with the words I was hearing. I frowned and looked at Emma and tilted my head toward the swinging door leading into the dining room where my parents sat with their guests.

Finally bored, I turned back to Emma and told her all I could about the school and the terror I'd felt all that day. Emma as always would understand and sympathize. She listened to every word, studying my face intently, and she never interrupted or belittled my feelings. Though she was just "the help", Emma's focused attention and genuine concern always made me feel warm inside. I wished passionately that my parents would take such a strong interest in my life. As I had so often over the years, I wished Emma were my mother but Emma couldn't be that because Emma was a Negro and I most certainly was not. Negroes I knew, could only marry Negroes.

After dinner, I went to my bedroom to complete my next day's assignments. When I heard the guests leave, I walked downstairs to speak with my parents.

They were settled in front of the still new television set, snifters of after-dinner brandy in their hands, smoke curling from their cigarettes.

"Hi, folks," I called out.

"Oh, hi darling. How are you? How was school?" My mother smiled at me and raised her glass in greeting.

A rush of words bubbled up and out as I tried to make them understand about my awful day.

"It was terrible!" I began. "First off, I didn't have a bus pass and--

"--Oh, darling, that sounds really fascinating, and we want to hear all about it, every single bit. But you don't look any the worse for wear! Let's talk about it later, shall we? This is Tuesday night, remember, Sweetie? Dinah Shore and then Uncle Milty? You know we just can't miss Uncle Milty!" My mother turned away and looked at the television. My father neither looked at me, nor spoke at all.

"Damn you, damn you," I swore silently, glaring at the stiff uncaring backs of my parents. I turned and walked slowly upstairs to read and sleep. I knew better than to ever try competing with Milton Berle.

# CHAPTER 17

"That don't look good," remarked Fred. "It sure don't look good a-*tawl*."

It was Thursday. As Fred drove me to the bus stop, I noticed the large black and gold sign marking the front gate of the Country Club had been defaced with a huge misshapen Star of David in bright, sparkly white spray paint. Feeling shame, I looked away, but far more concerned with what was awaiting me at the bus stop.

Although my terrors had been gradually lessening, I was convinced I would never feel safe at New Town High. I knew it. There were simply too many unfamiliar customs, rules, and far, far too many kids. I would never belong, and didn't much want to anyway. I thought I'd always feel like a bird forced from the sky to live on the ground. The week crept on too slowly, each hour a week in itself.

The lunch periods were still a horror but I was surprised to slowly notice I was beginning to feel angry that the cheap girls I hated so were forcing me to sit in that disgusting girls room stall which stunk of urine and cigarette smoke. In there, I would breathe only through my mouth. They had no right. After all I was from The Academy and therefore did not deserve to be treated this way.

"Why do I do this?" I would ask myself, again and again sitting on the filthy toilet, my knees as usual hugged to my chest. "I can't eat lunch here for the rest of the year." And I'd clench my teeth and make a vow to go to the lunch room the next day. But the next day, I wouldn't, couldn't.

I knew it was inevitable that someone would eventually notice how long I stayed in the stall; and one day, someone finally did.

"Who the frig is in that crapper for so long? Same stupid shoes hangin' down ferrin hour."

To my horror, I saw a girl's face peering under the door straight up at me. The jig was up. I gulped the rest of my sandwich, flushed the commode and walked out nonchalantly, my lunch bag and its uneaten scraps of food crushed and hidden in my pocket.

Oddly relieved to be out of the girls' room, I froze when a loud-voiced hall monitor full of arrogant self-importance demanded to see my pass. I did not have one of course, and so the boy, heady with the power of his lofty position, wrote down my name with a flourish of great importance, looking up from his labored writing with a squint he fervently hoped was exactly like John Wayne's in "Red River."

In a voice pitched for everyone to hear, he threatened "to send youse in tuddah princpilz's office if I ever catch yiz out in the hall again widout a pass. Got it girlie?"

I got it. Realizing there was still a half hour left in the lunch period, I had no recourse but to walk to the lunch room, or face the tribunal of Fascists Against Students with No Hall Passes.

Thus, I forced myself to walk down the short flight of stairs, my hand clutching the sticky metal railing. I looked quickly around the room, searching for a table with empty chairs. Standing on the tips of my saddle shoes, I saw one, way at the back of the room. Pretending to be not nervous, I casually moved around seated students, clutching my books, only to find there were no chairs at that coveted table after all. Panic rising, I looked around, then reached over and took an empty chair from a nearby table. It scraped loudly across the floor. No one seemed to notice. I breathed a huge sigh of relief and I sat, opened a book, pulled the crushed, soggy remains of my lunch from my pocket and began to pretend to eat. I never looked up once as I did this. Keeping small, keeping invisible and mostly, keeping quiet, would keep me safe.

"Where the fuck is my goddammed chair?"

My eyes froze to the words in my book. My blood froze too. A minute passed. I slid my eyeballs slowly sideways. *Oh God, oh no God!* A tall, skinny black girl, clearly enraged, stood by the spot where I had found the chair. I bent my head closer to my book.

"I'LL ASK AGAIN. WHERE IN THE SHITTIN' GODDAMM FUCK IS MY CHAIR?" the girl screeched.

"Yeah, some stupid cocksucker took her chair. Where's the bitch what took her chair?" I heard the girl's friends' angry voices, mutterings at first, then clearer and louder.

They were saying that I had taken the coveted chair. They pointed at me and accused me, and their fingers in the air felt like daggers in my heart. I glanced quickly up at the girl and remembered her from homeroom. She was Leena and I thought I had never known such terror.

Leena slammed her metal lunch tray down on the table. The sharp report, like a gunshot, shocked the lunchroom into silence. A glob of Jell-O flew from the tray and splattered onto the table, where it shimmered and quivered before oozing to the floor, splashing stale Redi-whip onto the ankles of a boy nearby.

The room grew even quieter, so quiet a car horn could be heard from the street outside. I glanced quickly around, very frightened. The big room looked like the jailhouse scene in the James Cagney movie *White Heat.* I was unable to move, not a finger, not a muscle.

"Well well well," the black girl said, grinning malevolently. "Looks like there's gonna be a fight in the lunch room." Leena walked over and stood next to me, arms folded, grinning with sweet anticipation.

I felt my limbs turn to mush, but I kept my eyes lowered, pretending to read. Finally, despairing of a miracle, and with more exertion than I thought I was capable, I looked up into the face of the livid, leering girl---and to my astonishment, I smiled!

"Oh!" I said. "This is *your* chair? I'm really so very sorry. I didn't know. Here, please, take it back." I stood, pulled the chair out from under me and carried it to the other table. I made a small bumbling effort at picking up Leena's splattered lunch, and smiled reassuringly at her.

"Really. I'm just so awfully, awfully sorry. I didn't know. Hey! I really know how maddening it can be when someone takes your chair while you're getting your lunch. Really annoying. Yeah. I know how it is."

*I'm babbling. Don't let her notice I'm babbling.*

"When that happens to me, I just hate it. There you go. It's all yours. Please. I'll just go get another one. It's absolutely no problem. Really!" I pushed the chair under the opposite table and calmly smiled again at the furious girl.

Stunned, Leena stood completely still, her grin dissolving, black eyes glaring widely at me. She was obviously confused. It was not supposed to be this way. She looked around, placed her hands on her hips, swaggered a little and smirked at the kids who watched nervously. Leena turned back to me.

"Yeah, well. OK then," she said. "See it don't happen again, bitch, you got that?" She hesitated, looked away and turned back. "Nahh. Never mind. Keep your stupid goddammed chair if that's what makes you happy, you fuckin' white trash."

She shoved it roughly at me. It banged hard against my shins, it hurt and the left one bled a little, but I did not react. "I'll forget about it this time, girl. Next time, though, like just ax, OK? You don't ax, I bust yo' white ass." Leena glared and then, finally walked away.

My life was spared. And Leena's face was saved. It was a tie. I nearly swooned with relief, but I'd stayed strong.

"OK. I sure will remember. Sorry for the trouble," I murmured. I knew I'd conquered something, a hurdle, rounded a corner, something, had maybe even survived a brush with death, perhaps death itself. I knew I'd learned in that small space of time how to dance with my aggressors and that things would surely get better from that point on. Wouldn't they?

When I walked out of the lunch room later, I heard a grunt or two from the students. Sounds of admiration? Greeting? I wasn't sure, but finally, I knew contact had been made.

Years later I saw Leena on a ferry boat going to the city and was stunned at the astonishingly beautiful, tall and stylish woman she had become. We embraced and laughed and mumbled quickly about the good old days at New Town, but in the confusion of the moment, neither of us mentioned the incident we both sharply remembered even though, rattled, we had forgotten each other's names.

Friday came. Friday--loveliest of words. I'd made it through my classes, knowing I was still an outcast, still the subject of stares, but I was getting better at ignoring them.

I avoided talking with anyone because whenever I made the smallest of overtures, I got more stares. More like glares. I sort of agonized over this and even tried imitating the other students' speech and accents by simplifying my vocabulary and sprinkling my sentences with occasional ill-fitting and very awkward obscenities, some of which I couldn't even understand.

120

These strained efforts rarely worked. I just didn't get the correct rhythm, the right semantics, and the more I struggled to sound like everyone else, the more I knew I did not.

I answered all the questions my teachers put to me in class in as quiet a voice as I could while still being heard, so my rich-girl accents and language might not be noticed as much. But I gradually and then staunchly refused to pretend I didn't know the answers when I did, even though I suspected that appearing stupid might get the kids to accept me, even while constantly asking myself why I even wanted that acceptance.

Friday gym meant the last class before I could go home to two days of freedom. I put on the horrid green bloomer outfit in the locker room, and walked out to the gym where unfamiliar music was playing. Oh no. It was Rock music. Bill Haley and his Comets were blaring out the rhythmic *Rock Around the Clock* over the gym's PA. I looked around at the other girls who were moving to the beat and singing all the words.

I had not heard a lot of rock music. I was far more used to the tunes sung by Sinatra, Bennett, Torme and Fitzgerald; Big band music, jazz, sometimes even be-bop. I would listen to my radio for many hours in my room, while I read or daydreamed.

Rock music plainly embarrassed me. It was too free and sensual. It made me squirm, made me want to leave the room and it also filled me with feelings I uncomfortably thought no well-bred young lady should be experiencing.

Only the most mellow rock tunes had been allowed and played at the club or Academy dances and they were always accompanied by the chaperones' warning frowns.

As I stood waiting for gym class to begin, I thought about how Sally and I had once ridden our bikes into town to buy 45 rpm's at a new record store called "The Downbeat." I wanted Eddie Fisher's "Oh Mein Papa," and Sally was looking forward to something by Pat Boone.

While we listened to the sample records in the small glass booths, we questioned the young and astonishingly cute store owner (on whom we each had an aching crush) about the new rock and roll music everyone was talking about.

He sagely advised us to not bother buying any R&R records, because, "I only give the phenomenon six months, and then music will get back to normal, to the good stuff." We stood across the counter from him and smiled up adoringly into his face, believed him and did not buy any.

I waited at the entrance of the gym clenching my fists. My nails dug deeply into my palms. The music was pounding.

*What's next? Oh, I'm gonna hate what's coming next. I just know it.*

Miss Ginocchio emerged from her office, and bounded onto the gym floor. "Hey! Hey! *HEY!!!* she bellowed happily.

The large, ungainly woman snapped her fingers and jigged to the music, stopping every few seconds to perform an absolutely grotesque rendition of her version of Rock dancing.

Most of the girls ignored the display--they'd seen it before--but I was unable to take my eyes off the teacher engaging in this unseemly frolic.

Not in the least embarrassed, the happy woman danced by herself, looking for all the world like a drunken Great Dane.

"OK. You know what day this is. It's FRIDAY! IT'S DANCE DAY!! SO LET'S DANCE! YEAH, I'M JUST SO READY!!" the cavorting coach screeched, and the joy on her face all but lit the room.

My stomach clenched. Dance? By myself? In front of everyone? My questions were soon answered when to my stunned dismay, all the girls paired up and began dancing. Together! Girls dancing with girls! *What is this? Where am I?*

How could I get out of this? Maybe I could faint. Maybe I could say I had my period. Maybe there'd be an earthquake or a solar eclipse like Bing Crosby had in "A Connecticut Yankee in King Arthur's Court"! *Maybe I could die. That's it. That would be perfect! I'll hold my breath until I black out and die, right on the gym floor.*

But no. Like a rat in the talons of a hawk, I was doomed and knew it. There was no choice. It would be better to just do it than to just stand there, alone, looking like a freak.

But with whom would I dance? For the first time in my life I understood the humiliation a wallflower experiences routinely, but I did not at that moment think of it in terms of the Holiday Ball.

122

And then, across the crowded gym, I saw her, the girl I had watched with hidden fascination all week. This girl wore a perpetually nervous grin clearly meant to cover the fact that she, like me, simply did not fit in. She always wore the same outfit; a grey dress with a worn lace collar, a frayed patent leather belt and brown leather oxfords with low white nylon socks.

Her breasts could only be described as mountainous, and always on the left one was pinned a small silver horse with a neck so long it more resembled a giraffe. The eye socket of the horse held a cracked plastic turquoise stone, and the tail was made of a few wisps of silver wire that curled down like small fish hooks, and were always caught in the fabric of the grey frock, leaving a permanently frayed spot.

Her arms were abnormally thick and short, and covered with sandpapery skin. She was very short, and extremely heavy, and the grey dress drooped almost to the tops of her white socks. Her legs were as thick as telephone poles, and were covered with long black hairs that curled over the tops of her socks.

Two chipped brown metal barrettes pulled her long, straight black hair back from her face and the rest hung like a long twisted cluster of unwashed black licorice strings down her back almost to the patent leather belt.

I thought she looked like one gigantic box on the bottom and one slightly smaller box on top. I secretly had named her Box Girl.

As I watched Box Girl, dressed now in her voluminous green gym suit and wearing that creepy, perpetual smile showing tiny yellow teeth, she began approaching me from across the gym floor. *Oh no. God no. NO!* I grimly considered the benefits of jumping out of any nearby window and looked around for the nearest one. They all had bars on them.

Box Girl's now visible mega-legs were hairier than I had thought legs could ever be, save those of the stuffed Silver Backed Gorillas I'd seen at the American Museum of Natural History in the city during a field trip with the Academy science classes.

Box Girl rolled eagerly toward me, if square people can roll at all. I could hear her grunting with each step as she waddled close.

"Hi," she said. "My name is Nettie. Short for Jeannette. Jeannette Capinerri. You wanna dance?"

"Uh--Well, I don't know--I mean, I--" I stammered.

"Yeah, I know," said Nettie. "I hate this too, but every Friday Pinocchio Ginocchio makes us do it. She thinks it'll make us better Americans or something--sez it'll prepare us for life. So. You wanna or what?" The question was answered for her when Miss Ginocchio pranced by, arms waving wildly, shrilling, "Hey you girls! Come on! Let's get with it! It's dance time! American Bandstand! Get it on, get it on! DO IT!!"

Nettie then said, "You wanna lead? Or me? Or what?"

I stared blankly at her, my mouth wide, too stunned to speak until Nettie grabbed my arm.

"Well, I don't know. Oh well then, yes. You can lead," I said so with a huge sigh of misery, and not knowing what else to do I awkwardly raised my arms toward the short chunk of girl, dropped them, raised them.

Nettie, grinning broadly, took my right hand in her left and placed an arm about my waist.

When I felt Nettie's hand in mine, I gasped involuntarily. It felt cold and gelatinous, like a raw oyster. The skin on Nettie's arms was reptilian. I gritted my jaws and shuddered, but with the steely willpower of someone trained all her life to react gracefully in difficult situations, I struggled to control my disgust as I began to dance stiffly, my eyes gazing somewhere over Nettie's beefy shoulder.

I was clearly mortified. I heard the other girls stifling giggles as Nettie and I stomped and scraped awkwardly around the gym floor, not even remotely close to keeping the music's beat.

The record changed to a slow romantic song. Andy Williams crooned about unrequited love, and all the girls in the gym changed positions, wrapped arms about each other and began to sway together, their eyes closed in what they hoped looked like uncontrollable ecstasy as they fantasized dancing like this with a real boy sometime, although actually a few had already and were proud to show their inexperienced sisters how it's done.

Burning with dread and confusion, I looked at Nettie. Her smile widened, she began to laugh and the sound was terrible and too juicy and I found myself staring straight at Nettie's wobbling uvula, curtained on each side with waving strings of saliva.

124

I gagged. Nettie did not notice. *Oh, I can't, I can't,* and I wanted to tear out of the room, out of the gym, the school, the world.

Thus I, Courtenay Wolcott, stood staring at Box Girl, not moving toward or away from her. Mercifully, the slow music eventually ended, a thousand hours too long for me.

But Nettie, I knew, had saved me from the pain of being a wallflower and I was hesitatingly grateful.

"Thanks Nettie, for dancing with me," I said. "I'm sorry I'm so--so sort of awful about doing that, I mean dancing, but you see, the school I came from, no one ever danced. I mean, they danced, certainly, but girls never danced with girls, and it just threw me for a second so I'm sorry if I made you feel uncomfortable. Please, do forgive me if I did that."

"Hey. It's OK. I understand." Nettie grinned up happily at me. "I wish we didn't have to do it either, but they do it in all the public schools, y'know. It's like only girls taking Home Ec. I don't think the boys have to dance together in their gym classes though, so it's weird that we have to, but hey, it's OK. I was gladda help out. See ya next time."

Nettie started to walk away but turned. That endless grin was still plastered across her jowls, but it had faded slightly. She looked across the floor at me, and then around the gym.

When she saw no one was close enough to hear, she said in a small squeaky voice, "Hey. Do you think you could dance with me again next week? I mean, you don't hafta, I know you probly don't wanna, it's OK, but maybe, if you could, I mean, you don't know anyone I guess, and I don't have a regular partner like the other girls...."

I swallowed. "Nettie. I'd love to dance with you next Friday. I mean, well, not love--well, you know what I mean. Sure. You can count on me. I'll do it. I mean, I'd really *like* to do it."

And idiotically, I put my hands behind me and crossed my fingers. Nettie looked at me in astonishment and gratitude for my words of acceptance, her smile widening to its usual width, then disappearing immediately. A coldness then filled her eyes and I felt a peculiar weirdness. As Nettie turned and walked away, I sensed within me a perplexing camaraderie for the ugly Box Girl.

# CHAPTER 18

My first weekend at home was the purest luxury. I slept very late, and willingly allowed myself to be pampered and mothered by Emma and Mary. I felt like a conquering hero, returned home from terrible wars. The only blemish on my joy was the knowledge that in two days, I would have to return to the battle.

Still, there were other things to occupy my mind, like the home football game at The Academy. I would attend. I'd be back in the warmth of familiarity, where the gentle moneyed accents would soothe me, and the surroundings would mollify my sorely-tired eyes.

I dialed Sally's number and when my friend answered, I began to laugh.

"Hey! Sal! It's me. I'm all set to go to the game. What're you wearing?"

"Hey Court!" Sally answered, obviously happy to hear my voice. "I dunno," she answered. "Maybe just my grey skirt and big green sweater. What shoes will you be wearing?"

"Oh, I dunno. Maybe my saddles. Nah. Loafers. I dunno."

We two girls talked excitedly, planning the day and the evening to follow.

Sally's parents picked me up and we four drove to the game. The day was glorious, the air so crisp and bright it nearly hurt to breathe it in but I kept pulling in great draughts of that air, washing memories away, calming my heart. I was at ease again, with my own sort, accepted, not the outsider. I rambled on and on to Sally and her parents, as if I'd just discovered how to talk, not waiting for them to respond to any of my remarks.

"Court," Sally said when I stopped talking to gulp a breath, "tell us all about New Town. I mean, what are the kids like? What do they wear? Do they all have those horrid accents we used to hear through the windows? Remember?"

Sally's father parked the car. We got out and began walking to the bleachers, Sally's parents walking ahead of us.

"Oh Sal, you wouldn't believe them," I said. "Most of the girls are, you know, the cheap kinds, but some have the gall to try to dress like we do at the Academy. Can you believe that?" I paused. "Well, I mean *did* dress at the Academy. Me. The way *I* did I mean. Anyway, you ought to see them. And the other ones, they chew gum and curse and smoke. And they're so stupid! Really! Just utter jerks."

I began to imitate the thick New York accents of the New Town kids, and I stuck my chest out and strutted around, wiggling my bottom, pretending to chew gum.

But something inside of me, somewhere behind my ribs pushed and twisted, an unexplained twinge of — what?, and I disliked the feeling. However, my friend's gleeful reaction to my performance allowed me to ignore it.

"And jewelry! Lord, you should see the jewelry. Not a real stone in the bunch. It's nearly all plastic except the glass junk. They like to wear these things called pop beads where they pop these big plastic beads together into necklaces and they make 'em as long as they want. Their stuff is so gaudy!" And I laughed derisively.

"And guess what?" I went on, delighted I had an audience. "They even wear earrings with socks and they wear them during gym class! And speaking of gym, on Fridays the girls have to dance. I mean dance together! Can you believe it?"

"You're kidding!" cried Sally. " Socks with earrings?? And girls? Dancing together? Do you do it too?"

"Not on your life. No way! They sure couldn't make me do anything like that," I shouted back, whooping with laughter. "Look! There are the kids!" I ran toward them, and to my delight, my old Academy pals crowded around me, and continuing my discourse since I had such a captive audience, I kept them all laughing as I mimicked the New Town students and teachers at my new high school.

Not kind in my story telling, I managed to tell all unfavorable things about my new acquaintances, embellishing where I could, inventing when I had nothing more to relate, surprised and pleased at my newly discovered, till then unknown, raconteur abilities.

Now and again I'd feel that strange tightness in my innards but again, I ignored the feeling, pretended to cough. Sally, her parents, all my old friends and their parents too laughed loudly at my mocking, insulting New Town tales.

Turning my head, I saw the beautiful Margo Whiticomb looking straight at me with a look of shock and disappointment. I looked back at her, then looked away. *Why am I feeling so guilty about this anyway? Those horrid public school people don't care. They don't have any feelings, I mean not like we do. They wouldn't care if they were standing here listening to me. They don't care about anything. Anything!* I knew very well that "people like that" had no feelings and could not possibly be hurt by anything anyone said or did to them. My parents had told me so, after all. Those people were different from us, they'd told me. They were lower. Beneath all of us. They didn't go deep, had no future, they were soul-less and crude and only thought about booze and sex and blue collar jobs. My stories about the New Town kids, especially the lies, were obviously making me even more popular with my old friends, so they were at least good for that. I relished the mirth I'd created, and glowed happily in the warmth of my own kind. So then how come I just could not shake that small, disturbing feeling so far down inside of me?

And then I saw Remington on the edge of the football field sitting on the bench with the other players. For an instant we shared a look, but he showed little expression and turned away. I continued my storytelling about "that place," happy my powers had been restored. I was not the new one there, not the oddball, not alone amongst terrifying foreigners. These were my true friends, my only friends, and Monday morning was a million years away.

128

# CHAPTER 19

Time at New Town High School dragged and scraped by, but my fears were gradually lessening. I was slowly, reluctantly learning how to get along with my new classmates. I still knew I had an unshakable, moral superiority, but had learned to keep it hidden. Letting that be recognized could cause me I knew, great harm. At least I did not have to give up the knowledge that I was superior to my classmates. No. I had to just hide it. I even showed more humor toward the New Town kids than I ever dreamed possible under the circumstances, and gradually made a few uneasy and superficial friendships, ones I knew I didn't need and never would, would get rid of later when I did not have a need for them, but at least for now, wanted.

Thus, in October, I made an important decision. I decided it might be wise to try harder to fit in with the kids, the NOOK-Ds. So one morning, as I sat in homeroom awaiting the arrival of Mrs. Jacoby and the recitation of the Pledge of Allegiance, I began pondering which school club I might care to join, a place where I might be liked perhaps a little, and not judged so harshly. Unlike private schools, New Town did not require that one be invited to join these clubs. Anyone was accepted.

"Hey! You!!" The sharp voice chopped into my thoughts. From across the room, a short and chubby girl was looking at me. "Yeah. You!"

"Me? Yes? What? I mean excuse me? You want me for something?" I sat straight. I had often noticed this girl in Earth Science. She was blond, shorter than most, and shaped rather like a fire plug. She often wore a tight grey skirt, slit up the back to what I thought an indecent height, showing a lot of black lacy slip that had seen better days. Above was a white blouse so tight her bra could be seen between the strained buttons. Around her neck she had a huge, ornate silver crucifix, so heavy, I wondered how the girl could possibly stand upright.

She swaggered when she walked toward me and she was hunched over, smiling a sharply V shaped grin, front teeth overlapping. When she sat, her posture was terrible, her shoulders almost resting on the desk. I looked at her and remembered once while walking behind this girl, hearing someone yell, "Hey Rosie, how's it goin'?"

And Rosie had answered, "Oh yeah, hi there stupeedo! You finished your lunch yet?" "Yeah, Rosie," he answered.

"Well good, so please if yiz don't mind," responded the Lady Rosie, "will ya take yer spoon outta my ass?"

The group around Rosie had let out a huge roar of laughter, while I ducked my head so they wouldn't see my shock, and walked rapidly away from them, appalled at what I'd heard, hoped I'd misunderstood.

I steeled myself. The room quieted, knowing they'd not be disappointed.

"You from around here?" Rosie asked me, cinching her wide black elastic belt tightly, closing it with a large paperclip.

"Well, actually, yes, I am," I answered, and my voice shook a little, apprehensive about what was coming next. *Oh, please don't let her say anything horrible or that will embarrass me.*

"Yeah? Well, we tawked about it and we all know where you come from," said Rosie, her voice getting louder.

*God, what is this idiot girl talking about?* I shifted nervously, looked around, looked back at Rosie.

"Oh? Really?" I said, my voice now definitely wobbling. "Well uh, Rosie, actually, it's no secret. I mean, it's no big deal. I'll tell you where I'm from. I was born right here on Staten Island, and I live up..."

"Yeah, yeah, we already know that and we know where you used to go to school, too. But who cares? I'm askin' you where you *come* from. Get it? Where you come from, dummy. You got this queer accent, y'know? No one around here tawks like you do."

*I've got an accent?? Me? Is she actually able to hear herself talk? Me? An accent?* I was appalled but kept my face still.

Rosie waited, arms folded, tapping her foot, while I, dumbstruck, tried to think of what to say.

"I'll tell you where you come from, Girlie. We all know, anyway. It's all around the school. Everyone knows you're from Texas."

I think I went white. I stared at her. I gulped loudly. "Texas? You think I'm from Texas?" I was so startled I could only continue to stare across at Rosie. Finally, I blinked rapidly and again said, "Texas? Me??"

"Yeah, Texas. Don't try to pretend you ain't," said Rosie. She smirked at me, folded her arms. "If you was from around here, you'd tawk like us. But you got this funny accent, so we all figured it out."

I put my hand to my mouth, pushing hard against my lips to stifle a laugh. I pretended to cough and cleared my throat.

Rosie was not finished. "What's that stupid name you call yourself, anyway? Court something?"

I pulled myself as straight as I could while sitting at my desk. "Well, yes," I said icily, "my name is Courtenay Wolcott."

"What? Wool Coat?" Laughter. I felt myself flush.

"No. Courtenay. Courtenay Wolcott. Not coat. Cott."

"OK, OK girl. Don't get in a sweat. Your first name, you mean it's court? Like where people go when they get nabbed by the cops? District court? Juvvie? Divorce?" (Rosie pronounced it "kawt.")

"Or maybe you mean like the place kings and queens go? You know, they `hold court' like we learnt in English class? Like King Arthur's Court? Your name is that kind of court thing? Yeah? Nahh. Really? Jesus shit, that's queer." More laughter.

I clenched my fists. "Well," I said, my voice thick and weak, "I guess so, I mean I guess it sounds like that kind of court." I ran my hands nervously through my hair, and hated that the room had gotten quiet and hated that all eyes were on me. "I suppose that's how it's sort of pronounced, except you say `nee' at the end of the Court part."

"The `Court part'?" chuckled Rosie. "Well, then, lady, if you're a `court part', well, we oughtta be calling you Queen Wool Coat. Yeah. Screw that queer name, Kawt-Nee. Honey, your folks laid a bad name on you. So let's see--we'll call you Queen, now. Yeah, Queenie. And besides Queenie, you act like a dumb-ass queen around here, know that? Ja ever lissen to y'self? Ever see how you strut around with that attitude an' all? Nose in the air? Lah Dee fucking DAH! I mean, you look and sound like queer, y'know? Queenie!" Rosie turned and faced the rest of the class triumphantly. "How's about it, shitheads, let's call the new one Queenie, OK? Wadda ya say??" XXXXXXXX

The entire class cheered. After all, Rosie had once again saved them from another boring homeroom period. They began to chant while pounding their fists on their desks, "Queen-IE! Queen-IE! Queen-IE!"

I kept my head up by sheer force of will, looking wide-eyed around the room, and I forced a brittle smile, understanding the imprudence of angering the natives. I also knew if I ducked my head as usual, they'd never let up, that my life would be one of unending, daily torture. So I smiled at all of them, and without knowing where I got the courage, I looked around at all of them, and spoke;

"How do you do?" I said coolly. The group stopped in mid-chant, quieted for an instant, and then hooted with laughter, mimicking my "How do you do?" in high-pitched voices. Then as they always did, they quickly turned and ignored me. I looked across the room at Rosie, and to my astonishment, we actually exchanged smiles.

Queenie was born. I was not displeased with the name; at least I finally had a sort of identity. Having a nickname was a kind of belonging, ragged at best, but it gave me an existence and I was no longer the new weird one at New Town. I began to respond to the name when I heard it, and as time passed, was able to answer with a sassiness that was better appreciated than the wimpy, frightened response I'd only been able to offer before. These kids didn't care for losers, they had no time or compassion for weaklings, and the daily terror was beginning to bore me anyway.

# CHAPTER 20

It was becoming routine. I was New Town Girl on weekdays, and then slipped easily into Academy Girl on weekends. But I also found I was slipping rather too easily and routinely into telling The Academy kids stories of my new schoolmates and that I was doing it far too often.

True stories or not, it didn't matter, or at least I convinced myself it didn't. When the too-young actor James Dean died in a terrible car wreck, I regaled The Academy kids with stories of the New Town kids' shock and sadness at his untimely fall, mocking their grief.

However, stammering with embarrassment, I had to quickly revise my performance when I discovered that many of my Academy pals shared the same sorrow at the loss of the young actor. I'd found a new and curious sort of enjoyment in being a raconteur, and told my tales with relish, verve and thick hyperbole.

Another unexpected pleasure came to me, but this at New Town High. It was my new name, "Queenie," created by Rosie and her gang. It began to change things for me, and it was, well --- kind of nice. One of the nice things was that it brought me a tentative relationship with the angry girl named Winona upon whom I'd fallen during the bus ride on that first terrible day of school.

Winona actually but only occasionally spoke with me now, and sometimes even stayed around waiting for an answer, instead of vanishing into a convenient crowd the instant her words ended.

While Winona could not be precisely described as being friendly, she was assuredly making not-negative gestures, and I surprised myself to discover that I occasionally looked forward to meeting with her at the bus stop in the mornings.

I also wondered idly if I really needed Winona any longer, then quickly knew I did and my mouth would twist at my *lese-majeste*.

I soon realized that with the tough black girl as an ally, some of the other students actually made room for me on the bus. Occasionally, someone would speak with me, joke, or exchange an opinion. I had begun to experience a tenuous armistice. I had begun to exhale. A little.

It was December 1955, and time for me to serve my stretch as hall monitor. I didn't look forward to this honor since I was positive I'd never be able to enforce any of the rules but I had to go through with it. Everyone in the higher grades had to do a stint.

As the winter wore on, I knew my days were numbered, and I waited for my notice to come. It did. I would be called upon to serve during the students' study hall periods. I had to make plans.

During the winter, the halls were drafty and very cold. The huge windows leaked cold air in great gusts, making the big yellow shades shimmy and rattle. At different intervals in the hall's length, a chair was provided for the monitors.

I finally began my monitor duty on a Monday, and brought many study projects so I'd be able to keep my eyes down, because I wanted to be unable to see students breaking the rules.

I'd rehearsed and memorized for two weeks how I'd handle a gum chewer, a runner, a shouter, a wall defacer, or group fighting, and came up with very few creative ideas.

In short, all I could do was hope the kids would be models of perfect deportment during my duty, although I was realistic enough to know that since this had never happened before in the history of schooldom, it was not likely to happen now.

The hall chair was hard and uncomfortable, and the hall really was cold. Though I ruffled through pages of a history book, I did not read. Instead, I passed the time praying, with no facial expression, that there wouldn't be any trouble.

My prayers, as usual, were ignored. The dreaded sound came. A sudden commotion at the end of the hall made me look up, but I did not turn my head. I just shifted my eyes so it would not appear I was actually looking. Getting involved was the last thing I wanted. But, what I saw made me bite my lip. Hard.

A crowd of greasers, six in all, swaggered toward me, laughing, punching, and cursing. The most sexual one, the loudest, was the leader, and five obsequious followers sauntered behind their strutting leader in perpetual and adoring imitation.

Their warlord was tall, broad shouldered, with hips tapering to a sharp V at his bulging crotch, all encased in worn jeans that were tight to the splitting point, and rolled twice at the cuff. His heavy black boots had two silver chains hanging from one ankle and around the back of the boot, attaching to the opposite ankle.

When he sauntered around the school's halls, they made an attention-getting jangling noise, precisely what he wished, enticing the girls, infuriating the teachers.

I knew it was important to him that the sound be recognized as his identity, to properly herald his approach and that no other student in the school ought to imitate that or they would be soundly thrashed. By him.

His white T-shirt fit over his muscular torso like the skin of a molting snake, and his Camels were rolled into the right sleeve. He'd slung a studded leather jacket over his shoulder.

His hair was so black it had blue glints, and was styled, greased and combed back in a perfect DA, and a perfect, thick curl cascaded not accidentally over the center of his brow. Lowering my eyes, I felt threatened and terrified of him, or at least thought I should be, but a shiver of pleasure touched the center of my back and I frowned from the unshakable sense that I was being confronted by a god, and even my sphincter muscle had tightened to a knot.

I stiffened before the advancing Cossacks. Not raising my eyes from my book, I prayed the group would only stick to simple misdemeanors, things I might legally overlook, since it was more than obvious that this gang could cause trouble as easily as they could draw breath.

As they sauntered near, they loomed above me like muscular black-topped trees, and I felt myself begin to tremble. I hoped they would not notice.

"Well, well, WELL! What have we got here?" said Adonis, as the group braked before me, crashing clumsily into each other, laughing with exaggerated shrieks.

They looked at me as I cowered, and slowly, began to circle their prey, and with a sinking heart I knew I was the prey. I kept on reading, my knuckles white against the blue of my book's cover, my fingers cramped and aching.

"Hey, Sweetcakes! Let's see that pretty face." The big leader's hand, surprisingly gentle, touched beneath my chin, tenderly raising my head to face his eyes-- the better to see me with! I stared into the brightest, bluest eyes I'd ever seen. I tried to turn away, but his large, strong hand kept me facing him.

"Well! Ain't you the cutey!" said the god. "Hey guys! Looka dis! A real honey, right?" He pointed at my face, grinning widely at his pals.

"Oh, Yeah, yeah, Dom, right." "You got it, man. She's a real honey." "Va-va-va- voom!" "Right on! This chick's got what *you* need, that's for damn sure!" came the answers from his toadies in a babbled chorus.

One of the disciples, the shortest with the most zits and too blonde to actually look as if he belonged, interrupted. "But hey, Dom, buddy--you know who dis is? It's that new one. Yeah," the kid squawked in his nearly man's voice. "New-- from The A-caaaaaad-e-mee." He sang out that word in a warbling, cracking falsetto.

I inadvertently flinched. I had not heard the "new" delineation for months. *NOOK-D assholes. Lord, they never change.*

"Dom," the kid went on, "I seen her in Jacoby's homeroom. Always sits in the lunch room in the back, at the end of the table. Hey! One of the chicks told me she sat on the can the first coupla weeks of school durin' lunch, 'cause she was shit-scared. Get it? Huh? Good one, right? Hahaha!"

Another boy joined him, supplying their leader with more information.

"Yeah-- Rosie. You know Rosie. She named this here little chick `Queenie,' you know, like the Queen of England, 'cause she acts so damn snotty."

"Zat so?" answered Dom, staring hard into my eyes. I felt mesmerized, dizzy.

"Well, howja do!" Dom straightened up, moving his hand from under my chin to my cheek. "Queenie, right? Well Queenie, my name is Dominic Nuncio Di Russo, and I'm pleaseda make yer acquaintance."

He stuck out his right hand, and I reached out and shook it, wondering why on earth I'd done something so stupid, wishing I didn't feel so foolish and liking the hard, rough warmth of his skin. I suddenly remembered his challenging the principal on that awful first day.

"How do you do?" I whispered, giving him a wobbling smile, then dropping my gaze.

"Now, ain't dat nice!" Dom released my hand and turned to his loyal minions. "See, jackasses? Now that's the way to do it. You shake hands, nice like. Like you been brung up good. You assholes could take a lesson." They all responded with eager, appreciative laughter.

"Yeah, Dom. You could go have tea now with the Queen, right?" One of the boys pranced around the hall, his hands holding an invisible teacup and saucer. He took delicate invisible sips, and stuck his pinky out. The mime was remarkably accurate, I thought, considering he'd likely never had an opportunity to take tea with anyone, anyplace, ever, and likely didn't even know what tea was anyway. I was impressed.

Dom looked down at me again. I looked up at him, gathered my courage, and stood, forcing him to back up.

"OK, you guys." My voice was someone else's, high- pitched, and it squeaked.

"Ok, you guys," the group mimicked in unison.

**"OK NOW!"** Maybe loudness would establish authority.

"Oooooooo! We're ascairt!" The boys backed away from me, their hands high, faces contorted in mock terror.

Perhaps reason would work. "OK. Look," I said, wishing my voice sounded more controlled. "You can call me Queenie or whatever you want, but I'm the hall monitor and *because* I'm the hall monitor, I've got to ask you to show me your passes, and if you won't show them to me, I'm gonna have to report you to Miss McArdle, and I'M NOT KIDDING!"

The strident (or so I hoped) sound of the last four words made the boys scream, fall down, hit each other, wipe their eyes, laugh and in general behave like a pack of jackals. I was losing ground, as well as face, and I knew it. I waited, head high, eyebrows arched, hoping my expression relayed steely resolve.

"Awright you rat fink assholes," yelled Dom. "Hang loose. Let's give the little lady a break. She's new here, so we won't give her a hard time. Not today. Now you, little Queen," he turned back to me, "you let us go along now, without any passes, and we'll leave you alone, OK? OK? OK?"

I found to my extreme discomfort that the big, sexy greaser with those surprisingly good hands was making my insides melt like butter in the sun.

"Well," I said (haughtily, I hoped), "maybe this time, but only if you promise me you'll honestly go to your classrooms without making any trouble." This bargaining sounded half-witted even to me, but it was the best I could do under trying circumstances.

"Oh, well now," answered the astonishing Dom. "Well now, Lady Queen, we sure do promise, cross our hearts, and hope to fucking DIE!! We'll honestly and truly go straight to class without making any noise at all. We'll be real good. Boy Scouts, that's what we'll be. Ooo, Ooo!!"

"All right, then, all right. Get on your way then. GO!!" I pointed up the hallway, assuming a stern look (I hoped.)

"OK, don't yell at us, oh, please don't be mad at us. DON'T HIT!! We're goin! Oh, just one more thing." Dom reached around behind my head and lifted my ponytail. "Hey, but before we go, let's get a quick look and see what's under this here ponytail. Hey!! Look you guys! It's a cute little pony ass! And lookie at the little bows tyin' the tail right to the pony butt." Pulling the shank of my hair straight into the air, Dom swiveled my head around, leaned down and with a loud grunt, kissed my head soundly at the base of my ponytail.

"There," he laughed. "There now. I got to kiss that sweet little pony ass." He dropped my hair. He and his group of rollicking minions thumped away, leaving me, crimson- faced, glaring after them, speech-less.

"And lemme tell you one thing more, Queenie," the departing Dominic yelled over his shoulder. "I'm gonna do it again sometime. Only next time, I'll be kissin' the real thing. And y' know, what? You're gonna love it, Queenie Baby! I promise you dat! You're gonna love it an' be axing f' more!"

# CHAPTER 21

"So, you live up the hill?"

We were waiting at the stop for the morning bus. I was so surprised to hear Winona initiating conversation I could do little but gawk at her, unable to answer.

Finally, "Uh--Well, yes, Winona, that's right."

"No one else in the whole school goes up the hill. You got no one to walk home with. You got any friends up there?"

"Well, actually, I have friends I grew up with who live up there."

"Oh yeah?" queried the elusive Winona. "Up there? In one of them mansions? You live in a mansion too?"

"Well, it's not... I mean I wouldn't exactly call it...well, it's just a sort of---" Mercifully, the bus arrived. I was uncomfortable at the thought of telling Winona of my background and wanted to avoid any future conversations on that subject, not only with Winona but with anyone else at New Town. I jumped up the steps into the bus, showed my pass, walked rapidly to the back and sat next to someone so I wouldn't have to sit with the suddenly inquisitive Winona. I gazed out the window and with a small shudder remembered my encounter with the mob in the hall.

I had been running into Dominic Di Russo fairly often after the hall monitor scene, and was always left wondering if these meetings were accidental. I'd round a corner, and he'd be there. I'd hide behind my book at the end of the lunch table, and when I'd look up, he'd be sitting in front of me, grinning, eating his lunch. He'd leer, stick out his sandwich, offer a bite, but I'd never answer, and would always look away. I was glad (I told myself) that I had no classes with him because my loathing was so interwoven with fascination that the two became blurred and I sometimes wasn't sure which was what. When he was near, I always blushed and looked at the floor, or walked faster, and I always heard him laugh.

*What's the matter with me? He's a NOOK-D. If the Academy kids knew I was----oh dear God.*

While I would sit in class and wrestle with my ambivalent feelings about Dominic, I often noticed one particular girl staring at me with a decidedly unfriendly look. It was a cold and angry glare. When I moved into the girl's line of vision, her harsh glare burned into me like a flame and left me feeling baffled. We were in geometry class together. The girl always got there early, positioning herself so she could watch as I walked to my desk. I felt myself shrink when I passed her, feeling as if this strange girl was staring holes into me, and that I was beginning to leak.

Martha Commesso had long and frizzy dyed red hair which she pulled tightly away from one side of her face where it was clamped back with a butterfly-shaped rhinestone clip. The other side was teased high. Her eyes were thickly lined with black mascara, and the lids were coated with an iridescent mixture that looked like cars' oil dripping onto a rain wet street. She made her lips look thick with lots of blood-vermilion lipstick, applied at least every half hour in front of a mirror produced from a tremendous black fake-leather handbag kept slung from her shoulder. She clearly had no intention of obeying Principal McArdle's edicts about the application of too much make-up.

Martha wore a tight black leather jacket, sleeves pushed up, and beneath it a frilly nylon blouse unbuttoned halfway down revealed great chunks of breasts so squeezed together they looked more like buttocks. Her skirt was also black leather, and short enough to show a V of pink nylon panties when she sat down and the leather slid up. Pointed, high stiletto-heeled pumps completed the ensemble, the ends of the heels splintered and frayed to shreds. Her nails were long, lethal and very red. She only answered to "Marty," and everyone who knew her knew they'd better abide by her wishes or they might possibly die. I quickly learned to respect and fear this terrifying classmate, to look away when Marty Commesso looked at me, to give her a wide berth when she approached, and to consistently avoid her with earnest and thoughtful intent.

I had made a few friends in geometry, and one of them was with a blonde boy named Teddy Muller, who was also in my homeroom. He was a plain boy, not tall, thin and pale-eyed, and as vain as this may seem, I knew he had become so obviously smitten with me that he often fumbled for excuses to ask me geometry questions. Me! I knew he must be desperate since Geometry and I had never been in the slightest way connected! But I was kind, smiling when I saw him, sitting at lunch with him, occasionally touching his hand across the table. I grinned widely when Teddy wasn't looking, knowing I was his passion and beloved, and it was breaking his adolescent heart that I treated him as if he were a brother.

Teddy had a crew cut and wore glasses and I was both amused and touched to see that he tried for a while to dress like the tough hoods. It never quite came together, sartorially or attitudinally and only ended up with his looking weird. As the school year progressed and poor dear Teddy tried ever harder to please me, I was relieved to see him finally dress more normally, in a blend-in uniform of crew-neck sweaters, button-down shirts and khaki pants.

I remember once telling Teddy that he ought to consider trading in his thick black shoes and short white socks for loafers and argyles, and the very next day, I was so pleased when he appeared in what I'd recommended. When he proudly pulled up his pants leg to show me how he'd complied and proved that my every wish was his command, I just looked down, nodded slightly, smiled and spoke of other things. I wish I'd known that I'd shattered him with my stupid indifference, that he'd shopped until the stores closed for exactly what he thought would make me, his precious beloved, happy, but he smiled bravely at me pretended not to care, loath to allow me to see the pain I'd caused.

I quite often smugly told myself that the New Town kids just never could get it right, but at least Teddy was trying and that's what was important. Maybe there was some hope for him at least. He was still pretty much a NOOK-D, and would probably never escape that, since being that way seemed to me to be genetic, but at least he was a lesser NOOK-D than were the other kids. I hadn't an inkling that my opinions reeked of vicious arrogance. I simply understood that I'd come from far better breeding than the New Town kids. It wasn't their fault, I'd tell myself, but it was a fact, and that irrevocably, was that.

When I entered geometry class one day, Marty was there, as expected. Through slitted eyes she watched me like a lazy snake planning an easy strike. Uneasy and thinking it was the best thing for me to do, I averted my eyes, walked to my desk, and sat down. Teddy entered the room and I beckoned him over. His face split into a huge grin and he trotted toward my desk, not even noticing when he tripped over a boy's book on the floor in front of him.

"Hi Teddy! C'mere," I called out. "Come on closer. Something I've got to ask you about."

I knew Teddy's heart flopped in his chest and that I was causing this to happen and it felt powerful and good. I made my voice liquid satin and let it pour sweetly into his ears, and he was quickly next to me, his own Dulcinea, in an instant, thrilled to do anything—slay dragons, swallow arsenic, chew on hemlock —all for me. I moved over on the bench seat, motioning him to slide in next to me. I could actually see that his heart was beating hard, and he looked at his hands, probably afraid the sweat from his palms would pour to the floor. He appeared as if he were about to have a heart attack. He bent and squeezed in beside me, his hallowed one. Our clothing touched and for the besotted Teddy, I knew it was an inarguably erotic signal.

"Teddy." I leaned close to his head and his face looked as if his in-testines would burst through his ears. "Teddy, look, there's that girl I told you about, what's her name, in the back of the class. She keeps on staring at me all the time, out on the athletic field, in the lunchroom, here in geometry class--just everywhere! What's her name? Why does she do that? To tell you the truth, I'm scared of her. She looks like she wants to *kill* me! "

I could see sweet Teddy Muller's gut settling to its normal state, his heart slowing, and disappointment flowing keenly through his virginal body. All I was asking for was information, not his undying love. However, not one to ignore a thrown bone, I knew he would take what he could get. I was not, we both knew, going to confess everlasting passion for him, of this he was now sure, another of his personal balloons in tatters at his feet. He had assumed that this was why I'd called him over. But no. Disappointed beyond belief, he, in response to my inquiry, turned and looked to where I had directed him. Finding the girl who was so troubling to me, his beloved, was simple. She was still sitting there, still with lids in low slits, still staring hard at me. There was no question as to which girl I referred.

"Oh. Her." said Teddy. "Well, her name's Marty Commesso. Some of the guys call her 'Nails,' 'cause she looks like you could hammer nails with her face." Teddy banged his forehead a few times on the desk to show what he meant and was thrilled when I giggled at the gesture, so happy he'd pleased me.

"She's tough as hell, " he went on, his voice cracking. "Oh, 'scuse my French. But Queenie, please, please keep away from her. And yeah, she is looking at you, and she looks like she doesn't like you much."

"But why, Teddy? What did I do to her?"

"Well, nuttin' much, Queenie..." he hesitated. "Well, you know Dom Di Russo's payin' a lotta 'ttention to you lately, and Marty used to go with him. They broke up last year, but she still thinks he belongs to her. So he pays attention to you, and she don't like it and she's givin' you the evil eye."

"But Teddy! She really doesn't understand. I CAN'T STAND Dom what's his name. Really. She can have him. I don't want anything to do with him. He keeps harassing me all the time. You know, when I first met him, when I had monitor duty, he took my pony tail, and he--oh, never mind." I began to stand. "I have to tell that Marty what's-her-name girl that she can have him! And with my blessings!"

"No. No!" Teddy grabbed my arm and pulled back quickly, astonished at his own boldness. "I wouldn't mess with her, Queenie," Teddy whispered harshly. "She's bad news. She's even been in jail! Yeah, really! I'm not kiddin'. Commesso and some of her friends broke into this store one night, for fun, and the alarm went off, and they got caught and she had a bunch of jewelry in her pocket. She tried to throw it away, but the cops saw it and arrested her. And guess what she did then Queenie? She bit a couple of them. Right down to the bone on their hands. So, because of the jewelry she stole and then making it worse by biting the cops, she spent a few weeks in the slammer. It was really hairy. She's not nice, Queenie. You gotta keep far away from that chick. Trust me. I've heard things. There's more. Lots. I'll tell you sometime."

"No way, Teddy. I don't care what she's done. I'm going to speak to her. Right now!"

I pushed Teddy out of the seat, slid over, and walked down the aisle toward Marty. Teddy made a fast grab at my hand, trying to stop me on my death mission, but he missed, and just stood there, watching helplessly.

"Excuse me," I said, standing over the girl.

"Yeah?" answered Marty, absolutely motionless, keeping her glittering eyes riveted on my face.

"Uh, well," I struggled, suddenly not feeling quite so brave. "Umm, I just heard you're upset with me because of Dom Di Russo, and all I want to tell you is that he means nothing to me, and actually, I wish he'd leave me alone, and if you'd like me to put in a good word for you, I'd be--"

"Fuckin' bitch!" Across the room, Teddy jumped at the words spitting from Marty. His mouth went dry. His Juliette was in danger!

"You get outta my zone, hear me?" hissed Marty at me. "I don't need nobody to `put in a good word' for me, ever, ya got that? Now get lost. Split, or I'll stick you. Got that, Miss Queen Bitch? Stick. Like with this knife I got in my bag." At that, Marty rose to her feet so fast, I stumbled backward. My hands went behind me as I tried to grasp a desk to keep from falling. Marty reached into her bag, and the room became deathly still.

"But really, Marty," I said, straightening myself in time. Hands shaking, I smoothed my skirt and looked at the enraged girl. "I only want you to know that Dom just hangs around me to annoy me," I said and tried to grin reassuringly. My lips cracked. "I really don't even like him. I mean, he's obviously not my type!" I laughed conspiratorially. Marty didn't get it. She put her nose almost on mine, lowered her voice to a hissing whisper, and said, "Lissen. I seen you with him, puttin' on that pussy shy little girl act. He belongs to me, unnistan'? He may not know it, but he's all mine, ALL MINE, and I'm gonna get him back and I'm gonna hurt you if you don't back off, bitch. You got it? Hurt!"

I stared at Marty, my intestines twisting in an oozed knot of fear and anger. *How DARE she? How dare she speak like that to me?? Me! She is a* **cheap** *girl. How DARE.....*

I backed up a few steps, trying to look calm while summoning the courage to defend myself if I had to, and I knew I had to. Footsteps behind me. *Please, let it be Teddy.* I turned my head slightly to make sure. It was. Relief. My friend was near. *Now maybe I can be brave enough to show this—this—thing-- some anger. Teddy will take care of me. Teddy will never let Marty hurt me.* But Teddy took my hand, and pulled me back to my seat.

"Forget it, Queenie," he growled. I looked at him, shocked at his lack of valor. He had not come to back me up after all, only to lead me away.

144

He whispered now, his head close to mine; "She's just no good. She's poison. Dangerous. Leave her alone, Queenie. I swear, it's better you just leave her alone. Don't try to be nice to her. No one can be. I swear, she hates everyone."

The class turned back to their talking, unperturbed by the scene. While Marty continued to slice at my back with her eyes, the teacher arrived to begin that day's consideration of the ancient study of Geometry.

It was Friday again. I endured the final gym class where I suffered one dance with Nettie, and then wiggled away, mumbling an unintelligible excuse. Nettie had looked at me that day with a sad understanding and I felt guilty pain in my heart but turned away from her anyway. I then danced the rest of the numbers with a new friend named Gladys, a beautiful and bright Italian girl who sat next to me in Biology. We'd become friends when Mrs. Haywang had partnered us for frog dissection.

Even though my heart told me what I was doing was wrong, even cruel, I was desperately planning ways to keep away from Nettie on future gym Fridays. We had to work together in Year Book and French Club, and I had developed an uneasy feeling that Nettie was trailing me, stalking, desiring more friendship than I was prepared or even able to give. Or wanted to. It seemed that nearly every day, I'd turn and Box Girl would be standing behind me, wearing the same grey dress with the same ugly horse pin pulling holes into the fabric, grinning the same eager, gummy smile. She looked so hopeful that I sometimes felt compelled to make some effort at kindness, but I was finding Nettie's presence an increasingly disgusting annoyance. I was not proud of feeling like that. After all, I reasoned, Nettie was harmless and I knew she was awfully lonely, but…but…

This day, there across the gym floor was Nettie, standing alone, smiling at the wall, tapping to the music, her foot out of sync to the rhythm. As usual, she was the alone one again. I felt inexplicably unhappy about that, annoyed and confused by the thickening in my throat. I danced past Nettie with Gladys and looked away, promising myself I'd be sure to dance again with Nettie, at least once, maybe next Friday but the thought of doing that gave me a sensation of dread and guilt and even nausea. But oddly, along with the daily revulsion, I had actually come to feel a kind of affection for Nettie. It was all just a tiresome puzzlement.

Final bell. Another precious weekend back up on the hill with my own sort. I could not wait to get there. I smiled as I pushed through the red-painted metal doors, and out onto the snowy sidewalk. I was looking forward to the days off and the basketball game I'd go to with my Academy friends. I'd memorized another batch of New Town stories for my eager listeners and knew I had become quite skilled at this tale-telling. I realized with a weird sort of sour pride that I'd honed my words to razors.

The blast of a car horn broke my reverie, and I turned my head to see Dom Di Russo coasting alongside me in his big turquoise and white Chevrolet. A pair of dice, a baby shoe, and a blue wedding garter hung in a twisted clump from his rear-view mirror. Though the weather was raw and cold, Dom hung out of his window clad only in his unzipped, beloved leather jacket. No uncool cap covered his glorious, shining black hair and the cold wind did not move one hair out of place.

"Hey! Queenie! You wanna ride home?" Cloud vapors emerged from his mouth.

"You've GOT to be kidding!" I strode faster, but the car sped up a little, too.

"No. Really! Hey! You wanna ride home, or what? I could save you the bus fare, and I ain't got nuttin' to do. Come on, Queenie baby. Don't be such a drag! I don't bite. Honest!"

I stopped walking, and turned toward him. "Listen you, Don or Dom or whoever you are. Will you just leave me alone? I don't like you. As a matter of fact, I think you're a creep. A jerk. Go find someone who wants to ride with you. If you can find someone around here who can stand you, that is."

"Ooooh, oooooh, Queenie, baby!! That hoits! You shunta talked to me like that. Hey, don't be a pill. All's I want is to be friends, and give you a little ride home. Come on, you can sit all alone on the other side of the seat. I won't touch you. Come ooonn, Queenie," he let his voice drop to a low whine. "You'll really like it!"

The cold cut fiercely through my camel's hair coat. If he didn't leave me alone, I'd miss my bus and if Fred didn't see me there, he'd go on home, and I'd have to walk up that long hill by myself in the cold, and the wind, and the dimming light.

And then, across the street I saw Marty Commesso standing alone, watching us. We exchanged a long look. I looked at Dom,

146

hanging out of his car window, one hand on the steering wheel, his left arm stretched out, reaching through the cold air for me. I looked up once again at Marty, smiled down at Dom, and said, "OK, Dom, yes, sure, why not? I'd like a ride. I'm cold." I walked around the other side of the car. Dom reached over and opened the door for me, pushed it wide and I got in, slid across the chilly white and turquoise plastic seats. I glanced over at Marty and smiling widely at her, slammed the door. Dom closed his window and turned up the heat and the radio. He then rammed his foot hard onto the accelerator, the car shot forward and we were off. I knew he'd done something to make blasting flames come from two tailpipes at the rear of the car because I'd seen it happen often before, even though the venerable Miss McArdle had forbidden such a display. Dom had not seen Marty, and I had no intention of asking him anything about her.

"So. This is great." Dom hunched over the steering wheel, then ran his hands through his hair and glanced at himself in the extra-large rear view mirror. "So Queenie, where do you live?"

"I live up on the hill. You know where it is? Just go on down here, and I'll tell you when to turn." I shifted uncomfortably in my seat, uneasy about Dom's discovering I was wealthy.

"The hill? You mean THE HILL? Oh, holy shit. So dat's why you talk so weird." He pronounced it "wee-yid." I flinched.

Dom suddenly seemed uncharacteristically shy, and I could think of nothing to say. I looked out the window, motioning a couple of times for him to make turns, and kept completely silent. I felt very uneasy. He was, after all, driving me home, and I felt I should be at least civil to him for that reason if no other. I struggled, trying to think of something interesting to talk about and wondered what Dom was thinking.

"So. Dom. You going to college?" *Oh shit, why did I ask him that? People like Dom don't go to college.* I cleared my throat, spoke again, made an effort to make my voice sound interested and calm. "Um, well, are you?"

"Huh? Me? I doubt it Queenie. People like me don't go to college much. I'll probly just go into my father's car repair business when I graduate. He needs the help."

"But Dom, that's silly. You don't have to be any kind of special person to go to college, and I'm sure if you ask your guidance counselor about it, he'd tell you how you could go. I mean, if you can't afford to go to one of the really big schools, there are the state schools. I mean, you don't have to waste your life fixing cars. You could do so much better."

Dom glanced over at me, frowning. "So, what's the `waste' in fixin' cars? Jeez Queenie, someone's gotta do it. Hell, you gonna tell me your father knows how to fix his cars? He don't, I can tell you dat right now, drivin' around in this here neighborhood."

"Oh. Well, look, Dom, I'm sorry. Naturally, there's no shame in fixing cars. I just thought you might want to think about college. I mean, *everybody* goes to college these days."

"Not everybody, Queenie. You don't get out much, do ya? You ever gone into anyone's home who goes to New Town? Not a lot of 'em look like these joints, lady."

Dom looked out the window as we passed the huge estates, now blanketed with snow, progressing toward my neighborhood. How different he is, I thought, when he's alone and not hanging around with his bunch of fools.

"Well, no," I answered, "I've never been to any New Town kids' homes. Frankly, no one's ever asked me, so how could I know anything about them?"

"You ever asked anyone to your place?"

"Well-- no, --- not exactly," I said, surprised at how defensive I sounded.

"Not exactly? What `not exactly'? You mean you kinda did? A little bit? What does `not exactly' mean?"

"Just like I say--not exactly. Turn down here." The implied accusation infuriated me, and I kept my head turned from him.

Dom drove into my driveway, stopped, and stared wide-eyed at the enormous home before him, my home. "Jesus, Queenie--what is this, you live in some kinda hotel?"

"No. It's where I live, with just my parents-- and a couple of—um -- others too."

"Oh" said Dom. "You got sisters and brothers? So how come they don't go to New Town?"

"No" I said. "I didn't mean sisters and brothers and I haven't got any, anyway. No, just other people who live there with us. They—they kind of help us... well," I said quickly, clearing my throat, "thank you very much. I certainly do appreciate the kind offer of the ride, Don. It was very decent of you."

"Dat's 'Dom,'"

"Oh, yes indeed it is. I do beg your pardon."

Dom listened to my stilted speech, watching me, loving my embarrassment, smiling mildly, his fingers drumming the steering wheel. I jumped from the car and ran up the flagstone path to my door. I let myself in without looking back, and was relieved to hear Dom's car backing out of the driveway. I shook my head as I heard him burn his tires and roar his engine down the private roadway. *Oh, how I hope the neighbors didn't hear that. I hope he didn't do his stupid flaming tailpipe thing.* But I knew he would never have been able to resist the temptation to do something that gauche in my neighborhood.

"Hi Darling! I'm on the phone," my mother's voice trilled from upstairs.

*Yeah, yeah, yeah. So what's new?* I began to make myself a snack.

"Oh Courtenay dear, is Fred with you?"

"No, mother, he's not," I called back. "I got a ride home with someone from school." I slammed the refrigerator door in exasperation.

"Oh, that's nice dear. But you know, Fred was waiting for you at the bus stop."

"Oh really? Oh well, I guess he figured out I wasn't there and he'll just come on home." I went on with my snack making, filling a plate with peanut butter covered Ritz crackers, pouring a glass of milk, slicing an apple.

# CHAPTER 22

I lay in my bed that night while sustaining a marathon conversation with Sally on my private phone. I was most careful not to give Sally all the "good" stories about the New Town students and faculty, saving the best for when I could entertain all my Academy friends at once.

I had to admit to myself that I was very interested, however, in hearing about Remington, who, Sally told me, had been asking about me recently.

"Come on, Court, don't be such a spaz. Give him a break. I mean, what's the big deal? You know where babies come from, and you know perfectly well how they're made, and you know enough about boys to know that they're hornier than girls are and will always try to get into our pants, under any circumstances, any time, any place for any reason whatever! I mean, did you have to break up with him just because he wanted to get some tender lovin'?"

"Sally, listen. Of course I know all that," I said to her. "And we never officially `broke up' because we were never officially going steady. I just never heard from him after that…I mean…the incident. And don't forget, I was really angry at him. After all, he and his big buddy Charlie had this all planned out. I felt like I was something in a store that Remington could just buy and use." I curled under my covers, cradling the phone next to my ear, twisting the wire in my fingers.

"I sometimes wonder if some other girl had been there if they'd have chosen her for this great honor. And all that `boys will be boys' stuff, getting what they want? Just because someone invented that stupid saying, and it was probably a guy anyway, doesn't give them any special rights, you know. I mean, isn't that just like rape? God, he was so drunk. I got sick. Did I tell you I barfed all over Charlie's parents' oriental rug? Into the --- it was woven flowers I think ---who cares? I never cleaned it up or anything, and I'll bet Rem didn't either. I hate to think what the Nichols thought when they saw that disgusting mess." We two girls laughed. Stopped, paused, and then laughed harder.

"But anyway, Sally, really and truly," I continued, "I believed Remington thought more of me than to do that." And then I suddenly began to cry, turning my head away from the phone and into the pillow so Sally wouldn't hear. But Sally did hear.

150

"Oh Court. It was awful, I know. I understand and I'm sorry. I didn't mean to treat it so lightly. But rape? Isn't that sort of strong? I mean, he never put his…his thing…into you, after all. My God, rape is such a horrible word. When you actually know the person trying to do it to you, it isn't rape, after all. I mean isn't that right?"

*It isn't?* "But you know what, Sal?" I said, my voice choking through my tears. "The funny thing is, maybe I would have done it, if he'd just talked about it or something, or asked me--- or something. Or told me he loved me. I don't know. I just don't know."

"Well anyway," Sally said softly, "let's not talk about that any more. What's done is done. So, I take it then that you don't want to go out with him again, right?" Startled, I frowned at my friend's casual reaction. I sighed, wishing I had more experience with such things. Maybe a mother with whom I could discuss this. A mother…

I grimaced. "I didn't say that, Sal. I have no idea how I feel about not going out with Rem anymore. After all, he's the one who acted like a stupid baboon, and then, Sally, *and then* he tells everyone that he actually *did it* with me, and that I *liked* it and *wanted* it! He even told some of the kids that *I asked him to do it!* I'm supposed to be happy about that? And he's acting mad at *me?* How come I'm the bad guy in all of this?"

"I don't know, Courtenay. I know you feel bad. You're right, Rem was an ummmm---ok, an ass. Sorry. He shouldn't have treated you that way. But maybe you could just talk to him, if he asks you to. Let him apologize. Listen to his point of view."

"WHAT point of view? He has a point of view? You're kidding, right? The only point of view Remington Nathaniel Richardson has is between his legs. And I saw it, too! 'Member I told you? And it was slimy and gross!! Purple!!"

This last set off screeching gales of laughter and how good it felt to do that with my oldest chum. Then, calming, we made plans to talk in the morning, and I fell asleep, the phone still in my hand, the wire still twisted in my fingers.

Lately, I'd been dreaming. The same dream, every night, ever since I'd started school at New Town High. Even when I told myself in my sleep it was only a dream, that I was in control of it and could stop it any time I chose, I never did. And if I did wake up, the dream came back easily when I drifted off again, beginning at the exact point of interruption.

In my dream, I saw myself walking down a wide sidewalk, twice as wide as the pure white road running alongside. The road ahead had long, sweeping curves as it pushed into the scenery. Along each side of the road were two parallel and endless rows of trees that went from one horizon to the other. The trees were all the same height, extremely tall, and all had straight umber brown trunks, and on top of each sat a perfect ball of brilliant glistening green. In that dream, I walked along this sidewalk, sometimes winding in and out of the straight, rigid brown trunks of the trees. Suddenly, in my dream, I looked behind me. Something terrified me. Something. And I tried to run away, fast. I could not. I looked down at the sidewalk as I struggled to run, but the scored lines never moved. I was staying on the same spot! I ran and ran and ran until my breath came in stabbing, aching gasps, but I remained in the exact same place, and the terrifying thing behind me was gaining on me. My head whipped around, eyes bulged trying to see what it was, but I could not. It was not there, but still, it was getting closer, gaining, coming so, so near. Fight? Flight? Frantic, I discovered the only way I could move was to get on all fours. Not on knees and hands, but on feet and hands, my butt straight in the air. Embarrassed and ashamed, I would gallop along like a reversed hyena. Ahead of me I'd eventually see Remington, and I would straighten up and run to him. He'd abruptly change into Dominic, but I'd still run toward him. Then, turning, I'd look back and see Remington again. Mr. Tonnaschell would be standing far away, observing this. I'd run back and forth, and each time Remington and Dominic would change from one to the other. I just could never get anywhere, and the space between all of them would lessen, then widen, and I could never get close and did not even really know if I wanted to be or how to do that anyway.

In my dream, I suddenly reversed direction and began to run toward the tall to-the-sky red painted metal doors. They were wide, wide open and I'd tear toward the light shining from them, but the two doors would slam down with a shattering crash in front of me just as I got to them. But they didn't open the way they were supposed to. They smashed down like red metal window shades. This wasn't right. They're supposed to open, left to right, not slam down from the ceiling to the floor. I dropped to my hands and feet again, and from this all-fours position, my head bent up and back as far as possible to see, my neck aching, I reached up and groped for the brass door handles to force the doors up. This time they opened normally, left to right. I tumbled through, but instead of seeing the hallways of New Town High, I saw an endless vastness, all sky. Terribly far below spread a gigantic, gleaming lake stretching into forever, the still surface reflecting huge, flat faces of people I knew, like giant white lily pads. They surfaced higher and looked now like bloated corpses, and then, one at a time, they settled below the surface, sinking in rocking, sliding crescents, the way plates will when thrown into water. They went all the way to the bottom of the lake, and soon resurfaced elsewhere. The faces were so enormous and clear, I could see the pores in their skins. I saw Nettie, and Dom, Rosie, Rem, and Sally. Dark skinned Fred, Mary and Emma floated up at me, Teddy too, and Miss Haywang. Not Mr. Tonaschell because he was behind those doors, on that cement. Miss Piacentino and Miss McArdle slid to the surface, both glowering furiously. I did not see my parents' faces.

Teetering at this terrible height on the inside threshold of the red painted metal doors, I clung to the brass door handle, tipping over, knowing I would soon fall just as I had on the bus that first morning. I turned and looked behind me, but there was emptiness there, complete nothingness, not even a color. But ahead, attached ahead to the threshold, just at the tips of my feet, were thin, transparent ropes, which supported a long, impossibly slender bridge. The bridge's railing was a single rope so flimsy it was more like a string running from the handles of the red-painted doors and attached to the horizon. Some people far ahead of me, some people garbed in 1880's clothing, walked along on this precarious, swaying nightmare bridge. I was compelled to follow and grasped the rope railing with both hands, edging out on the small boards on the floor of the bridge, moving sideways over the abyss, clutching, clutching that string railing. Afraid to pick up my feet, I shuffled like an invalid, frightened to lose the touch of those lurching boards under my feet.

Midway on the bridge, I suddenly changed my mind. Maybe standing on the threshold peering out into the neverland was safer than trying to cross. Suddenly, a man in a derby hat way ahead of me on the bridge slipped and fell, and the flat square wooden floorboards dominoed upwards into a standing position, forcing the people ahead of me to walk atop the ends of the boards while clinging to the thin rope railing that was now near their knees. The bridge began to sway and buckle, as if an invisible devil's hand snapped it like a gigantic whip. As the dream slowly ended, an impossibly huge and brilliantly golden Star of David rose in the west, so bright it blinded me, and I squeezed my eyes shut.

When I awoke, I was not afraid; the dream was exactly the same each time, and I'd accepted it for whatever it was and no longer awoke from it, chattering, wet and terrified. But still I constantly wondered about it, and sat in my bed staring at my windows. Why did it keep coming? What did it mean? Why did it not make me afraid anymore? It was after all, a grotesque, senseless dream. I sighed, swung my legs over the bed's edge, stood and stretched. I had a lovely weekend to look forward to, and was not about to let a stupid dream ruin that.

My plan was to go to a movie with Sally and some other Academy girls, first stopping at The Down Beat to look over some new records. After the movie, we'd get some hamburgers and go to the basketball game, and then on to a no-date dance held in the gym for both teams and their guests. My heart clung tightly to these times with my old friends. They were, I thought, my whole life, and I'd never give them up.

Sally had recently gotten her driver's license since she was older than I, so we two girls roared off in Sally's family car feeling unfettered and terribly grown up. We'd discovered that having wheels and charge accounts was the closest thing to finding one's self in the Garden of Eden with no serpent to louse things up. If we had any cares, they were left behind as we sped off to pick up the other girls, buy some records and weep in the darkness of the theater as we watched our fallen idol James Dean grimace and posture through "Rebel Without a Cause." Life for me was delicious.

"Y'know," said Marjorie from the back seat, "when I get out of school, I may work at this joint next summer." Having finally mopped our tear-stained faces after the movie, we were in a drive-in burger joint, where we sat in our parked car gorging on fries and hamburgers, washed down with chocolate malts, extra thick. We were on our way to the basketball game and dance, and our spirits were giddy and high.

"Yeah, right, Marj," said Sally. "You'd do a great job on those roller-skates with your lardass butt."

"Well now, that's really nice talk, gutter gums. Ever since you got your license, you've developed a dirty mouth, and furthermore, I could too learn to roller-skate and I could skate around in those little skirts and look great. It would be good for me. I could learn how the other half lives. And furthermore, I do not have a large behind, but you do have buck teeth."

I looked at my two friends, tried to appear disapproving, but threw back my head and howled with laughter. The two girls glared at me.

154

"Right. Yeah," said Sally, turning back to the pouting Marjorie. "Sorry, Marj," she said. "I take it all back. Why not fill out an application now for next summer? You should get your bid in early before that `other half' screws you out of the job. Please forgive me, old friend. Here, have a fry. On me. Nah, on you!" And Sally turned and blasted her friend Marjorie between the eyes with a ketchup-laden French fry. Marjorie retaliated in kind, and soon the inside of the car was a blizzard of French fry shrapnel. We all squealed and yelped as we hurled food at each other. Sally was finally forced to call an end to this delight since she did have to return the car to her parents and they would not appreciate finding it festooned with atrophied potato strips covered in dried out ketchup stuck everywhere in the car's interior.

"Party pooper," we shouted at her. Choking with giggles and food, I tried to wipe up the mess with paper napkins, but only smeared it more, and the napkins shredded and stayed on the goo like soft white splinters. Sally honked the horn, paid the roller-skating waitress and zoomed off, still laughing, to the basketball game.

I touched my hand lightly to my chest. I thought my heart would fly from me with joy as I entered my old gym at The Academy. Kids climbed up the bleachers, vying for the best seats and the rumbles and scrapings and thuddings coming from them warmed my soul. I thought I would weep with happiness. I loved the loud rubber-on-wood shrieks of the players' sneakers as they charged up and down the court, the smell of sweat, the screams and cheering. I was back where I belonged. Home. Friends. I almost could not breathe from the joy I felt.

I settled onto a long bleacher bench, loving the hardness beneath me. And suddenly, Remington Nathaniel Richardson was standing over me and the expression on his face ---- could he actually be looking ashamed?

"Can I sit here Court?" he asked. His voice sounded queer.

"This is still America, Remington." I turned back toward the gym floor hoping it looked as if I was ignoring him.

"Thanks." He sat. I did not turn my head but felt the bench dip as he settled next to me. Remington was silent for a while. And then, "Please Court. Don't clutch. I've been wanting to call you, you know, but I didn't think you'd talk to me."

"Ah! Well then, you'd have been correct, Remington," I said coldly, trying to concentrate on the game's beginning, not looking at him.

"Look -- Courtenay." Remington placed his hand gently on my knee. Repulsed, I most un-gently knocked it off.

"OK. I'm sorry. I know I should have said it sooner, but I didn't. I was truly an ass at Charlie's beach house. I shouldn't have done that. It was wrong. It was worse than wrong. I'll never do it again. I promise I'll talk to you about everything if only you'll let me see you again. You have to forgive me, Courtenay. I've been miserable!" *Was that a small sob coming from him? Lord, I'm getting Jerry Vale here. What a dumbbell.*

I turned to look at him. *Do I want to go out with him again? Should I forgive him??* As I stared at him, I felt something hard inside of me begin to soften and it made me think about sand balls I'd made at a beach once, and how the warm ocean waves would soften them and finally make them disappear entirely. I bit down on my lip, pulled in a breath and was about to say "well, --- maybe," when he spoke again.

"After all, Courtenay," he said, "I'm a guy, and well, you know, guys have needs, stronger ones than girls have. But still, I'm sorry. I guess my needs got in the way of clear thinking."

And then I suddenly felt my shoulders stiffen so tightly they ached. *So much for sand balls.* I glared at Remington, remembering his disgusting "needs" at the beach house that awful day. Taking a deep breath, I formed my words carefully.

"Well, Remington, you're right. Your needs did get in the way of something—your tiny brain. I'll just say this one more time. You wanted to score with me. Maybe I'd have liked to do some scoring of my own. Oh yeah, Remmie! Well, dig this. Girls like to score too. Whoop-dee-do, a news flash! But you took my choice away from me. And worst of all, after I denied you your precious needs, you told everyone that I had slept with you anyway! That I'd *liked* it for God's sake, and you even told everyone I *begged* you for it, and that you were MAR-velously good! Well, maybe I could forgive your uncontrollable needs, but lying about me was unforgivable. Know something? You give me the heebie-jeebies. Get away from me!"

Remington's face slowly flushed from his Adam's apple to his hairline. I wondered if that was shame or anger, but didn't much care. He looked down, twisted the edge of his shirt with his hand, the very picture of dejection and shame. *What a hambone. What an ass.*

156

I turned back to the game, and we did not speak again. Eventually, I felt the bleacher bench move again as he stood and walked away. From the corner of my eye, I watched him sit next to another girl.

"Hey Rem!" I shouted after him.

He turned and looked up at me. "Yeah?"

"You wanna lose a quick forty pounds? Yeah? You do? Well, here's an idea. Cut your head off!!" Clapping my hand to my mouth, I snorted with laughter and turned back to the game. I waited to feel jealous because Remington sat down next to the girl. I didn't.

# CHAPTER 23

It was January 30th, my 16th birthday. I found a large pile of professionally wrapped gifts piled at my place at the breakfast table, and I opened them slowly in the presence of Emma, Fred and Mary, as I'd done every January 30th for as far back as I could remember. Those three loving Negros were my family and were more important to me than my own and I knew they knew that.

Three familiar turquoise-colored boxes contained beautiful pieces of jewelry from Tiffany's. One was a pin, shaped to the number 16 and studded with diamonds. I pinned it to my sweater, pictured my classmate's reactions, thought better of it and returned it to its box knowing it would be something they'd mock. I also knew they would probably never receive a gift like that and I did not wish to make myself appear wealthy. There were cashmere sweaters, a mink jacket, and a dressy watch, so tiny the dial was unreadable. In one envelope I found a $200 gift certificate for The Down Beat, enough to keep me in new 45 RPM records for years. I wanted to thank my parents, but would miss my bus if I waited for them to come down, so I wrote them a fast note, propped it on the sugar bowl, and ran to get into the car with Fred.

When I arrived in homeroom that morning, I noticed a jumble of something on my desk but couldn't see what it was from across the room. As I got closer, I saw that it was an immense corsage made up of yellow rose buds, lacy ferns, baby's breath and 16 long, curling yellow ribbons. Sugar cubes were tied to the ends of those ribbons, hung at varying lengths, held on with tiny bows. Stunned, I went completely blank and stood staring down at the jumble, and I knew my mouth was hanging open. I'd seen these things on other girls in my few months at New Town, but had no idea what they were for.

I reached out timidly and touched the odd corsage, then picked it up and held it in my hand. I turned and looked around the room questioningly. Several of the students grinned at me, but most paid no attention. I quite simply did not know what to do.

"Hey, Queenie!" It was Bobby Sotirakis, who'd recently been transferred to my homeroom. "Doncha know what that thing is?"

"I don't think-- I mean it's really pretty, ... what is...I mean.... but where did it come from?"

"Jeez Queenie," answered Bobby. His voice dropped to an even quieter whisper. "It's a Sweet Sixteen corsage, ya stoopit dumbbell, for today, your sixteenth birthday. You forget t' look at the calendar or what? It's January 30th, dopey! Put the stoopit thing on. Summa the girls chipped in and got it for you."

"They DID??" My mouth went dry. I was flabbergasted. My eyes popped. The fact that my classmates were not very well off financially had become something I'd been thinking about more often as my days passed at New Town, so with that in mind I was numbed at their generosity. It was perplexing too, since I'd not thought of myself as being particularly well-liked by the girls at New Town.

"Yeah, they did. So put it on, Weiner Girl," Bobby said, grinning. Awkwardly, I pinned the garish cauliflower-sized corsage to my sweater with its two spear-like pearl-topped pins. It was so heavy the material of my sweater sagged, and the corsage flopped forward, the sugar-cubes swinging back and forth in front of my belly and banging against it. Looking over toward the smiling girls, I croaked, "Thank you so very much," and sudden tears stung my eyes. The girls grinned back and some of them clapped. "Yer welcome, Queen!" shouted Rosie. It was the first time I had felt truly accepted at New Town High School, and it was nice. No, it was sweet and overwhelming. I had never been given a more wonderful gift in all of my life and I knew it.

Bobby Sotirakis was a huge boy of Lithuanian descent, with an abundance of black hair proudly styled like Mo of Three Stooges fame. And he had the biggest, kindest, dark brown, long lashed eyes that always made me think of Jersey cows. Because of his size, Bobby was constantly being wooed by the basketball and football coaches, but he never got any pleasure out of sweating and he genuinely hated pain and considered good sportsmanship extremely boring. Because of his reluctance to pursue his God-given manly obligations, he set himself up for ridiculing hoots and catcalls from his male classmates. But Bobby was possessed of a unique gift; he just simply didn't give a damn. He was amicably immune to the derision of the raging and bellowing jocks who surrounded him daily, not to mention that of the greasers, hoods, or anyone else for that matter. Because of his hugeness and perpetually easy-going disposition, remarks, however negative or scornful, simply rolled off. No one could touch him unless he gave permission, and like the gigantic and harmless whale shark, he was avoided and never attacked. Bobby Sotirakis had a great and most enviable sense of self.

Bobby and I were counter mates in biology, and it was a good thing taxpayers never knew how many Petrie dishes or test tubes he routinely smashed while reaching for something. When Bobby Sotirakis reached, people winced. Jaw muscles contracted and heads flew up. Teachers made every effort to keep him near only unsmashable objects: radiators, refrigerators, cars, lockers, and some of the sturdier walls. Once he'd obliterated most of the breakable things within reach, the All Clear could be safely sounded and people could relax. Everyone knew Bobby had a generous, sweet heart, and a big, passionate crush on me. Everyone also knew he was very, very dull, and that his passionately ardent (and only) goal in his life was to be a mortician.

"Bobby," I asked, as he accompanied me through the side streets of New Town toward the bus stop. "What's the skinny with you anyway? Do you *really* want to be an undertaker? It's so--gee, it's so gross and disgusting."

"Jeez, I don't think so, Queenie," he said, unknowingly crushing an edge of sidewalk beneath his foot as he stomped along beside me. I looked down and then away. There wasn't much point in mentioning it. He often reminded me of L'il Abner in the famous Al Capp comic strip.

"I don't think it's gross at all" Bobby laughed. "I look at it as an art! After all, somebody has to take care of people after they die. I used to even pretend to be an undertaker when I was little. While the other boys played with trucks in the sand pile, I'd bury 'em."

I laughed. I really did like the big galoot, even though I'm ashamed to say I often had to stifle yawns. Bobby was not on the cutting edge of teen-age society, but he was safe and kind, and he obviously adored me and that made me feel good although I could not find it in my heart to return the favor. I wanted to---sometimes---but then I really didn't.

"Sure, Bobby," I said. "I know that someone's got to do it, but ye gods and little fishes, who wants to be around dead people all the time?"

"Well cryminees, I do, Queenie," he answered. "I wasn't kidding when I said it's really an art. Y'know, to make someone who mighta got smashed up in an accident or all sucked dry because of some disease look gorgeous in death ain't all that easy. It's really like maybe making a sculpture, or maybe even painting in a lot of ways. Well anyway, that's how I look at it."

"Jeez, you're so queer, Bobby. Well, OK, if you say so, but keep your tape measure away from me. I'm not ready for that yet. I hope!"

He laughed down at me. "And you know something else?" he continued. "My aunt, well, I've told you that my uncle's in the business too, didn't I? Anyway, his wife, my aunt, loves to use the embalming fluid for her hands. Tells me it makes the best lotion she's ever used. I'll bring you some Courtenay, if you'd like, OK? I could bring it to school in a pill bottle."

"Oh well, gee, Bobby," I stammered. "I don't know, I mean that's *awfully* nice of you, really, but umm--no thanks. I--uh, just stocked up on some Jergens, and that should hold me for a while." Bobby shrugged his massive shoulders and grinned at me, compelling me to think for just a second of a huge adoring, and probably slobbering dog.

# CHAPTER 24

When I saw Teddy Muller walking toward me in study hall, I knew immediately something was on his mind by his expression and the way he was walking. Uh oh. I braced myself.

"Hi there, Queen," said Teddy cheerfully, "how's it goin'?"

"Great, Teddy, but you'd better sit down. McArdle is about to make her presentations---you know, all the kids who won awards--and if she sees you walking around, you'll get creamed."

"Yeah, right," said Teddy, as he found a seat behind me. He leaned forward and whispered in my ear, "Hey, Queenie, if you're not doin' nothin' next Spring, would you wanna go with me to the Sock Hop? Wanna? I know it's kinda far away but ...."

I turned my head around so fast, Teddy jerked backward in his seat, a look of fright on his face. I looked at him in astonishment. "*You* are asking *me* to the spring Sock Hop?"

Teddy backed even farther away nervously.

"Well, yeah, but hey, I can see you don't wanna, it's OK. I just thought I'd ask. You don't hafta, I understand. Anyway, I was just kiddin'."

"No! Teddy! No! Don't be silly. I'd LOVE to go with you!" My enthusiastic response surprised even me, and in my enthusiasm, I knocked some of my books on the floor. I'd seen the posters about the dance, but hadn't given it much thought, or at least I pretended I wasn't giving it much thought. I really wanted to go but knew no one would ask me. I was genuinely very pleased at being asked. I actually wanted to run home to tell my mother. Maybe my father. No. Dumb idea. I knew very well my parents had plans for my future and none of them included the likes of a Teddy Muller. I bent and picked up my books, turned and grinned at the stunned boy.

Teddy looked dully at me, his mouth slightly open. "You will?" he said, his voice gruff. "Honest? You'll go with me?" and I could not help but laugh.

"Of course I will, Teddy!" I beamed at the confused boy. Teddy stood and walked away, turning once to look back at me, his face questioning. I smiled and nodded. Teddy wobbled out of study hall, but soon walked back through the door into the study hall and sat down. He did not have a pass.

*No, Father darling would not be pleased about someone like Teddy Muller in my life.* My father, with typical paternal wisdom, had always advised me that few options were open to me after graduation from college. I could select from five, he said: Wife, Mother, Secretary, Teacher, and Nurse. Ever the obedient daughter, I often asked myself how my father could possibly be wrong about this issue, being my father as he was, and yet it always did not seem right to me. Furthermore, I wasn't especially keen on any of the Big Five. Something always nagged at me about his list, somewhere way back in my mind. It seemed unjust and somehow unfair. There just had to be more to life for me than the Big Five choices. But then, he was after all, my old all-knowing, all wise Father, so of course he had to be right. But …was he?

Anyway, I had a fantasy, a tiny treasured dream tucked behind my heart. I kept it hidden from my father, and from almost everyone else. I had all my life wanted one day in the future to work for a major newspaper, but I never told anyone because being a journalist wasn't anywhere on The List, so obviously, it had to be a bad idea.

I knew better than to mention this to my parents. They had a rather unpleasant way of laughing at me when I tried to explain my dreams, treating them as though they were unimportant, even comical. In fact, they always laughed at me when I tried to say what was in my heart, and deep in my soul too so I learned at a very young age to never share any of my feelings with them. I could tell my dreams to Emma and Fred and Mary and they would listen, and hear me, and they never, ever laughed and even asked questions and gave opinions. But my dreams were serious to me as dreams are to all people who own them, and extremely important too. I tried so hard to not care that my parents did not wish to understand or even accept me, but I did care.

To keep them happy, I obediently enrolled in typing and stenography courses, thinking I could at least keep myself alive with a secretarial job while I pursued my real vision, and furthermore, typing and steno were actually compatible with my secret dream. With that in mind, and without bothering to speak with my parents about doing that, I joined the Journalism Club, one of only five brave girls, hoping it would give me ideas on how to pursue it as a career. The club was headed by the man who was also my guidance counselor, Mr. Clarence Cornish.

Mr. Cornish was tall, pale, and constantly drenched in perspiration no matter what the season or temperature. It was a curse. Forced to be near drinking water at all times, he kept a tall jug of it on his desk. His hands shook. "It's my nerves, my awful nerves," he always said, and he avoided handshakes because his hands were so wet and slippery and felt even to him like cold dead sunfish. When he was anxious—and this poor moist man was always anxious--the sweat from his hands dripped onto the floor into tiny dark puddles next to his shoes.

Mr. Cornish read constantly. He was always reading at his desk during free hours, and he even read as he walked around the school grounds, during athletic events, and even while waiting for public transportation. He wore the same suit every day, only varying his facade with an occasional change of tie. On St. Patrick's Day, he'd defy his rigid reputation for wearing dull, boring clothing by sporting a pale green tie covered with dark green shamrocks. For Christmas, he'd don a tie with small Santas. For Easter, he treated his acquaintances with a pale blue tie covered in tiny faded rabbits, for Thanksgiving the same tie only this time it was covered with tiny faded turkeys. For July 4th, he sported the same tie but this time it had faded American flags all over it. This was the extent of Mr. Cornish's sartorial jocularity. He eschewed St. Valentine's Day.

I had heard that Clarence Cornish had been an unwilling and terrified participant of the Normandy Invasion in June of 1944. That, and being forced to kill people who looked just like he did, caused him to be possessed of his noticeably jumpy nature and nervous sweating problem. These conditions had not existed until after he'd been home from the war for some time, and he eventually understood that they were the result of the horrors he'd seen and in which he'd been forced to participate. Indescribable nightmares, loud, horrifying and even smelly ones came nearly every night, even if he drugged himself with a wide variety of pills, which he nearly always did, trying so desperately to avoid the torturous memories.

Mr. Cornish had gotten his teaching degree on the GI Bill, and would eventually and successfully work his way up the scholastic and education ladder. I could not possibly have known that one dawn in 1962, after one of his war nightmares of a particularly excessive and wrenching nature, he would place the barrel of his father's World War I pistol into his mouth and blow the back of his head onto the flowered wallpaper behind him. There it would stick like a piece of bloody moss until it would be chipped off by his landlady three months later in order that she be able to re-rent the room. Had I known he wanted to do this to himself I like to think I'd have been able to help him. But I was so young. I likely could not.

Nettie was one of the other four girls in Journalism Club, which did not surprise me because Nettie always seemed to be wherever I was, but I'd gotten used to it. She was like a shadow of which I could not be rid, so I chose to ignore her. Occasionally I'd speak with the unpopular girl, expressing interest in some project with which Nettie was involved, commenting admiringly on her ever-present silver horse pin or some other possession when I'd run out of things to say. I well knew if I let her, Nettie would stick to me like tree fungi, and so I sometimes cut our conversations too short, leaving the hungering Nettie standing, bewildered, hurting and alone, and I knew I did that and I did it anyway.

The Journalism Club did eventually bring me a few new girlfriends, as was my plan and hope. I had been making a conscious effort at being warm and friendly but knew I'd never be able to achieve the close feeling with public school girls I'd had with The Academy girls. After all, I'd grown up with The Academy kids. I was ashamed when I told myself that the public-school girls had not measured up, but they simply had not and that was that. I could and would not deny my feelings. Their accents were crude and incorrect. I thought, no, I knew their clothing was invariably improper, and their backgrounds left much to be desired. They remained irrevocably NOOK-D's to me and I could not see that ever changing. I was unsure where they'd come from, where they were going, or what was in their heads. I told myself I really didn't care much, since it was not my intent to make lasting friendships of them. One day I'd graduate and would blast off, back to my old world. But I was finding to my nagging dismay that I sometimes actually did care, and really wanted to be accepted by the New Town kids, even to be a part of their lives. I felt lonely amongst them, and was slowly beginning to understand that I was maybe imposing impossibly difficult standards on them which I gradually realized I had little right to do, and which, I realized, they had absolutely no intention of adopting. And why should they? Would I turn my life upside down for them? I knew the answer.

Sighing, I turned away from the adoring Nettie and went to watch Mr. Cornish operate the mimeograph machine in another room. While waiting for our papers, a few of my sort-of friends sat on some desk tops discussing what young girls have always discussed since males and females came into being: Boys, dates, boys, future husbands, clothes and boys. We huddled together with intense concentration and I was happy to be accepted, our bodies in a circle, faces reflecting the seriousness and importance of our conversation. I was painfully aware of Nettie sitting alone at the back of the room, watching us, not wanted, and smiling, smiling. I cleared my throat, pushing down the guilt that had begun to spread painfully there and told the girls that Teddy Muller had asked me to the spring Sock Hop.

"Do you think he'll ask you to the junior prom, too, Queenie?" asked Theresa Bongiorno.

"The junior prom? Gee, I don't know," I said. "I hadn't even thought about that." Elbows on knees, I propped my chin onto my hands.

"Well," answered Angie, "I'm going with Arty Noa."

"And I'm going with Sal Curatolo!" shouted Dee.

"And guess who asked me?" piped in Antoinette. "Little Freddie Traut!"

"Oohh noooo," they all groaned in chorus. "You're going with Fishy Traut?" And "Him? He's such a yo-yo," and, "Don't make me barf!!"

And so, the chatter continued, happy, pointless and social, while Nettie listened silently, watching us, watching the wall, smiling perpetually, and was as always, the alone one. Years later a hauntingly sad song named "How Insensitve" became popular and I could not listen to it without thinking of my cold and awful treatment of that poor, lonely girl.

It was late when I left the school that afternoon. I shivered as I looked outside and saw the grey cold and windblown snow. I'd have to make the walk alone in that grey-black dusk, through the side streets on to the main street and up to my bus stop, but since there were many houses along the way, I wasn't concerned even though things were in unclear focus, silhouetted. I got into my coat and boots, wrapped my scarf securely around my neck, and gathered my books together. I stepped through the red-painted metal doors.

A movement caught my eye. I squinted into the dimness and could just make out a group of kids at the opposite corner of the property. Next to them was a large pile of snow, darkly outlined in the dimness.

166

The kids were bending over, picking things up from the ground and I thought they might be making a snow sculpture. I walked on up the street, reflecting on the fun of the conversation I'd had with the girls in the Journalism Club. I sighed contentedly. I had friends now and I liked that.

"Hey, Queenie! Hi there!" The greeting was friendly, warm. I peered in the direction of the female voice. It had come from the group I'd just passed a block or so away.

"Hi! Who is it? I can't see you!" I called out, smiling, and I walked toward them.

"It's me, Queenie baby." A pause. "Queenie baby bitch!" The warmth in the voice was gone now as if sucked away by the freezing wind. It was coldly threatening, the consonants like iced shards. A figure came toward me through the dusk. I could see the girl clearly now, and the girl I saw was Marty Commesso.

Marty stopped walking, leaned forward and stared hard at me, inches from my face. I could smell her hair spray, her cheap drugstore perfume. I could feel the sparks from the hatred burning from her dark, glittering eyes and melting into my skin. A bunch of girls, obviously Marty's personal entourage, clustered behind her next to the pile of snow, which I now saw wasn't a snow sculpture at all. It was a large lopsided pyramid of snowballs. Suddenly a laugh erupted from Marty, deep, terrible. She turned and walked back to the group.

"Ladies?" said Marty, waving her hand imperiously, "you may commence firin'."

A wall of snowballs seemed to come at me in slow motion, so many of them I could not see spaces between them. They smashed into me as if blasted from a murderous machine, and they knocked me backwards. They hurt, but then I understood that was their intention. With slow and confused interest, I watched some smash against my coat and saw the rocks inside of them roll down onto my boots. Some of the snowballs were solid pieces of ice. They bounced off my head and one caught me on the cheek, slicing it open neatly with no pain, and blood gushed profusely down my chin and into my scarf where it froze to gelatin. Another spun toward me and this one sliced open my eyebrow. Hot blood slid slowly down into my eye. I stood quietly, fright growing slowly, unable to move or run. Wiping the blood away with my gloved hand, I looked down at it, and in the gathering darkness it looked black. I felt my senses begin to speed up and looked frantically around for help, but my adversaries and I were alone in the dusk. The lethal snowballs kept coming, how *many did they make? Thousands??* pounding and pounding me. The snow at my feet was sprinkled with drops of my blood.

Finally, I got the courage to run, was able to get my feet moving. I tried running to the school, but a split second from possible salvation behind the red-painted doors, Marty burst from the group and charged after me, screaming like an enraged animal. She caught me by the shoulder, spun me around, and smashed me up against the building's wall.

I groped clumsily behind me. My frozen, blood-soaked gloves froze to the bricks, pinioning me there. Struggling to free my hands from the bricks, I flattened my back against the wall, staring at Marty, my eyes burning wide, feeling as if they'd pop from my head. My heart was pounding violently in my ears, my mouth was frozen dry. And yet I could taste blood in my mouth and was surprised at how warm and salty it was, how actually pleasant-tasting.

"Marty," I said softly, my voice a gurgle. The fresh cuts on my skin felt hot against the frozen air. Gradually the blood coming from my skin became stiff. "What is it? What do you want? Why are you doing this to me?" As I spoke, the blood that had run into my mouth splattered onto Marty's livid face.

"Oh! What is it?" Marty mimicked. "What do you want? Why are you dooooooing this to me?" The blood on my face began to thicken into an icy sludge, gluing my mouth, clogging my nose.

Marty shoved her face so close to mine our noses touched.

"Well, let me tell you, Queenie fuck-bitch," she hissed.

I smelled garlic on Marty's breath.

"Me an' my friends are gonna kill you because you can't keep your fuckin' hands offa my boyfriend, Dom. You remember him, doncha? Dominic Di Russo? Ah, come on, Queenie bitch-girl, you know you've been shovin' your cunt at him since you first laid eyes on him." And Marty quickly, with deadly accuracy, punched my breasts hard. I bent forward, clutching my arms across my chest and finally I screamed in pain and fear.

"Marty!" my voice choking. "You've got to be kidding." My voice was thick, now shrieking. "I don't even LIKE Dom. I don't even *know* him. You can *have* him; I don't want him. He's the one who's been after ME! Honest!"

"Oooo, honest, honest. Yeah, right, motherfucker. Well I seen you comin' onto him, and I warned you! So now I'm gonna kill you! You wanna call your nigger driver to come save you? Drive you up to your precious mansion? Well cunt-face, you'll get to ride away from here. Sure you will. But when you leave here, girlie, it'll be the last ride of your life 'cause I'll make fuckin' sure you'll be leavin' here in a fuckin' HEARSE. A meat wagon. You unnerstand? You got that?"

Marty grabbed my now blood-soaked scarf in both hands and pulled the ends in opposite directions. As I moved to protect my throat, I pulled free from the gloves behind me and they stuck, now empty, to the frozen bricks, reaching for me, unable to help. My hands were now bare and I clawed hard at the scarf as Marty pulled it tighter and then tighter around my throat. And then I began to feel everything slow down, and then felt my throat do something peculiar; it sort of clicked softly, wiggled almost imperceptibly, and then it closed shut with the noise a Tupperware lid makes when it is "burped," and I could actually hear it. Feeling my eyes bulging from their sockets, knowing the top of my head was about to burst and shoot my brains into the black air, I tried to signal to Marty that the scarf was choking me, but I knew Marty would not much care. I tugged weakly at its tightening ends, clawed impotently at Marty's rigid hands. I could not speak or scream. Marty's eyes glittered, and she laughed shrilly as she pulled harder, jerking the scarf viciously and bracing herself against my now sagging body.

Eyes now rolling back, I could see a few snowballs arcing slowly over our heads, striking the wall behind us. My knees buckled and became soft as summer worms. The dusk got dimmer, blacker. I fell against Marty, hugging my murderer. But Marty shrugged me off and I felt the cold snow on my knees as I collapsed even more. And then I could fall no farther because Marty held me upright by the scarf, and I dangled from it like an old rag doll. My arms now hung limply at my sides, head flopped backward, my tongue protruding stiffly. I shut my eyes as blackness pushed into me and my nostrils and my soul, and as I began to fall into forever, I was rushing through darkness toward a light, and I absolutely knew nothing could save me. I opened my eyes to look at my executioner one final time.

Something huge loomed behind Marty. Like a military tank, it began to move toward us, and it then shoved hard against Marty, crushing her against me.

The scarf suddenly loosened and fell across my shoulders like a shroud. My windpipe made another strange click as it popped open, and I fell hard onto the snow-covered cement. Coughing, gagging, I sucked in air that wouldn't come and I could hear my chest and throat making horrible screeching sounds as I struggled to pull and pull at the black air. And then the air did come in short, jagged bursts and I began to think I'd live. I retched violently, vomiting blood and half-digested food onto the snow. Recoiling from the mess, my nose now gushing blood, I shook my head, still sucking air. The world rocked and I fell face forward into my own blood and vomit. I rolled to my side and clutched at the frozen stone wall, and struggled to my feet, shaking so violently I thought my arms and legs would collapse. I reached and tugged at my gloves still stuck to the bricks and they peeled away like tape from skin. A sound I could not recognize, a dull violent sort of thud made me look up. There, shoving hard against Marty, smashing on the gang leader's face violently with the palm of her beefy hand, again, and then again, was the big black Winona.

"Yo, bitch Commesso. You got a bone to pick with Queenie here? Well, you can pick it with me, cunt." Winona's voice was growling deep, menacing. I so wanted to get back down on my hands and knees and crawl over to grab my avenging angel by the legs, to kiss her feet, to worship her.

Marty, recoiling from the unexpected ambush, held a hand to her reddened cheek. "Yeah, I got a fuckin' bone to pick. She's tryin'a hump my guy. I WARNED her. She knew I was gonna get her for takin' Dom away from me."

Winona grinned evilly. "I'm gonna clue you in a little, Commesso cunto, and then give you some advice," she hissed. The group behind her edged away. "You and Di Russo broke up a long time ago, an' you fuckin' know it. You're a sore loser, Commesso. You just can't take it that Di Russo hates your little wop ass. This little white tomato here don't want your stinkin' guinea boyfriend. She can't help it if he comes on to her. Christ, Commesso, he comes on to EVERYBODY. Don't you get it by now? You thick or somethin'? Jesus, he'd fuck a donkey if he could. And here's the advice--take your warnings to Queenie here and stick 'em up your ass."

Winona shook Marty so violently, the girl looked like the rag doll I had just resembled. She shoved her hard against the wall of the building and pushed her face up against Marty's, then backed off, holding Marty's clothing tightly in a fist near her neck.

"Ugh," she said. "Holy shit girl, you stink! You eat garlic fried rats for dinner or what?" Winona threw her head back and guffawed loudly, then leaned near Marty again, not loosening her grip.

"Now listen carefully, wop-guinea-ginzo," she said, "Di Russo's always got his dick in his hand. Christ, that asshole thinks with his dick. So, here it is and girl, you pay close attention to me, hear? You touch Queenie again, you even breathe in her direction, in school, in town, *anyplace*, you or any of your other pack of rotten ginzo wop monkey fuckers over there, and I'll come after you. You got that? Not just me. Me and my pals. You know, them big black broads you ain't got no love for? You bother Queenie ever again, I'll grind you up and feed you to my dog, got it? I'll stuff your face into your own shit and make you eat it. Got that too? Good girl. Smart girl." She slapped Marty hard, playfully on the cheek. "OK," she said. "Get lost." And she blasted Marty flat into the snow.

This was the longest speech I had ever heard from Winona, and I listened in stunned admiration, my blood-caked mouth hanging open. Marty now silent and very sullen, struggled to her feet, backed up, then turned and slunk toward her gang, motioning them to follow. As they disappeared into the darkness, they shouted a few lukewarm threats, to which Winona answered in a mocking sing-song, "Nighty-nighty, ladies. Now you remember little darlin's, keep your white asses away from Queenie here!"

"Oh, Winona," I cried. "How can I ever, ever thank you? You literally saved my life. I was…dying…I was….Oh my God, Winona, I----" I reached out, but with an embarrassed shrug, Winona pushed me gently away.

"Yeah, yeah, yeah," she said. "Well, it's good I was here. Don't worry. They won't hurt you again, honey. I've had problems with Commesso before and she always backs off. She wunta kiltcha. She woulda just let you pass out and left you there to freeze yo' ass to death. Then, sheeda blaimt it on the weather." Winona laughed loudly at her joke.

"Very comforting, Winona," I said, my voice hoarse now and weak. I took a few wobbling steps, and had to reach out to Winona to keep from falling. This time my friend didn't push me away. She put a heavy arm around me to steady me, and we started walking. With one hand, I tried to clean myself, discovering rips in my coat from the rocks and ice, and two more holes in my face from the barrage of--what? Fists? Rock-filled snowballs? I couldn't tell. I didn't care.

I let go of Winona, turned and walked back toward the school, hoping to get into the girls' room so I could wash. But at that late hour, the doors were locked. It was minor, this frustration, but as the fable went, it was only one tiny extra straw which caused a camel once to buckle at the knees and the locked door had the same effect on me. It was just too much, more than I could take. I slid slowly to my knees, and put my face into my dirty, blood-stiffened gloves and wept great gobbing, wrenching sobs.

Winona stood awkwardly next to me, trying to soothe me by patting my back and then my head with crushing, clumsy thuds.

"Oh God, Winona," I hiccupped between sobs, "Fred has probably gone up the hill already and the school's locked, and all the public phones around here have been wrecked by the kids. And I don't think I can make it up that hill. It's so dark and I'm so cold. What am I gonna do?" I was wailing.

Winona put an arm around me again and said in a soft voice, "Queenie, come on now, get aholt of yoursef. It's gonna be OK. Tell ya what, we'll get on the bus and we'll get off at our stop and go on down to my place. We got a public phone downstairs there, and we'll call your folks and they can come gitcha."

Flooded with warm relief, I did not think for an instant what that offer might entail. This girl just seemed to keep on rescuing me, over and over again, right from the start of my going to New Town High School.

"OK Winona, I croaked. "That sounds so—just so good. Thank you. Thanks." My voice sounded so strangled but at least I had a voice. If Marty had not come along---I did not wish to think about that just then. "Thanks so much Marty," I said. "I can never ever, ever thank you enough."

Arms around each other, we crunched off on the snow to the bus stop, happily arriving just as the bus did. I was touched to the point of tears when Winona paid my fare. It was warm in that bus, the lights were warm, the atmosphere was warm and we sat close together, Winona's big, comforting arms around me, and I know we must have looked like lovers and that was fine too.

172

When we finally arrived at the usual bus stop and got off, I walked with Winona, away from the hill, the first time I'd ever gone in that direction, and it felt strange to me the way two magnets feel when pushed toward one another in the wrong direction. I turned occasionally to look up the hill, but it looked like a thin and weak grey ribbon off in the distance. *That road back there is what takes me home every day??*

We walked down a long, dark street. Cold and exhausted, we eventually arrived at a dilapidated old store. The place was dimly lit from inside, with a few tired, dusty cans of dog food in the window and a tipped sign stating that Coca Cola was on sale that day for 25 cents off the regular price.

"Well, here we be," announced Winona, fumbling in her purse.

"Here?" I asked, and was apologetic and embarrassed at the tone of my voice. I looked up and down the street and saw no homes, only storefronts. My shivering increased with the uneasy sense of being someplace very foreign.

"At my HOUSE, dummy," said Winona, finding her key, and inserting it into a beaten-up door at the side of the storefront. It swung open with a shrill creak and banged on the wall behind it. I looked up a long staircase made dimly visible when Winona switched on a bare lightbulb hanging from a frayed black electric cord. We stepped into the hallway, the air there only slightly warmer than the outside air, and onto a chipped and filthy once-white tiled floor, and I painfully followed Winona's ample rump up the stairs, and then into her apartment.

I, Courtenay Scott Wolcott, suddenly found myself in another world I had never dreamed existed. It was impossible. I'd read about poor people, seen newspaper pictures, but the scenes never touched my senses. Nothing went into my mind about how other people had to live. Until now.

It smelled different, this place, a smell of oldness and hopelessness, a smell of people, of dirt and grease collected for so long it had finally stopped collecting. The apartment was mostly one small room. Off to the sides, I could see three other tiny spaces, not much larger than the closets I had in my house up the hill. From where I stood, I could see that two of these rooms were apparently bedrooms and one a bathroom. The room I stood in obviously served as a living room and dining area. I saw no kitchen. At one end was a tall wooden bar with two waiting bar stools, yellowed stuffing bursting out of their black plastic tops like puffed cancers. Behind the bar on a protruding shelf was a small rusted gas stove with two jets, and a hot plate plugged in next to it. To the right of that stood a large, chipped enamel sink, precariously attached to the stained wall. It was shaped like a horse's watering trough, and seemed too low for any normal adult to comfortably use. Long rust stains streaked into it, and greasy dishes covered its bottom. A waist-high, brown refrigerator also stood behind the bar, and boxes and cans of food were scattered everywhere. On top of the bar was a cardboard box which contained the family's eating utensils, both for cooking and eating. I realized to my utter dismay that this is where Winona's family took their meals.

"Well now, Winona, this is really--this is--"

"Probly not somethin' you're used t'seein' Queenie, right? I been up the hill to them mansions. I know what they're like inside. And they ain't like this, nossir." And Winona laughed gently.

"Oh, no, I didn't mean, -- well--." I could not continue, and looked away from Winona. I moved my eyes to the ceiling. There were huge, jagged holes in it, exposing old dried out wooden beams. Great strips of wallpaper were hanging down like tired, torn flags. The two overstuffed chairs in the living room were dirty and broken. Magazines and newspapers were scattered about, and a pair of tattered lace curtains hung limply on each side of the only window. A few crooked shelves nailed around the room held several old splayed toothbrushes held together with a rubber band, a jar partly filled with hardened varnish, an empty cigarette package, and a small rolled American flag.

"Go on into the john and wash that blood off, Queenie," suggested Winona, pulling the curtains across the window.

"Where--where's your mother--your family, Winona?"

"Oh, I dunno. Sometimes they be here, sometimes they ain't. My mother works nights and the rest of 'em just show when they need money. I'm the only one who's stayed in school as long as I have. All the rest got out around seventh grade. Couldn't cut it. Wanted ta make money. Me, I want a edjakayshun." Winona moved about as she talked, futilely pushing some of the room's mess into different piles. The gesture touched me and I wanted to tell Winona that it was all right, to leave everything as it was, but I did not speak.

"Now you, go get that blood washed off," Winona said with mock severity. Then she smiled. "We'll go downstairs and wake up the store keeper. He's got a pay phone in there and we can use it to call your family. We can grab something to eat first if you wanna."

As hungry as I suddenly was, I definitely did not wanna. I wasn't at all sure it would be safe to eat anything that had been in Winona's apartment for any period of time.

I gulped and walked into the bathroom to stall for time, but after looking inside, I remained standing in the doorway. The toilet had no seat, its interior was stained brown, and was filled with brackish water. The flush handle hung down from a wire. Tight against this was a claw foot bathtub, its glaze completely gone. The spigot dripped steadily onto a brown patch by the drain, the ring around its inside permanently ground in. Overhead dripped a rusted chrome showerhead. A colorless plastic shower curtain drooped from three open hooks, and there were long crooked fingers of velvet mold growing everywhere on it. Soiled towels lay scattered. A hamper's lid was flattened against the wall behind it, unable to close because of the mountain of dirty clothes stuffed inside and above it. I didn't know what to use on my dried blood. I tried some toilet paper, but it was so flimsy, it clumped and rolled into shreds on my skin. I finally picked out the least foul of the towels, and located a scrap of grey, sticky soap. Under cold water (the hot water faucet blatted out a ball of wet rust) I scrubbed off one corner and used this to wipe off the blood. In the broken mirror hanging from one hinge over a medicine cabinet, I glimpsed my swollen and battered face. Tears filled my eyes and I pushed my face into the grimy towel, now not caring about its filth. It was suddenly all too much, these last hours, and as I wept I thought of how desperately I hated my father for causing me to be where I was at that moment.

Winona heard my soft sobs and came into the bathroom. "Come on, Queenie girl," she said, and her voice was sweet and soft. "It'll be alright. I tol' you, there ain't no need to be ascairt. Them girls won't hurt you no more. Honest! I've had dealin's widim before, and believe me, they never mess with me and they won't mess with you. It'll be awright." Winona stood in the doorway of the dreadful bathroom, her face crinkled with concern and I suddenly thought of all the people I'd known in my life, it was a certainty I'd never known anyone apart from Emma, Mary and Fred, to be so kind. I dried my eyes, smiled weakly, and walked out into the living room.

"Winona," I said, my voice cracking. "You've been so good to me. I can't ever thank you enough for saving my life. You know" --I hesitated ---"I've had a really hard time adjusting to the school and the kids and everything. But for some reason, even though you've always sort of ignored me, I kind of thought you, well, that maybe you understood all that... because of my first day on the bus, and all." I pulled in a shuddered breath.

"Yeah, well, maybe I did, and maybe I dint." Winona shuffled uncomfortably. "Look. I knew you was outta place, comin' from up the hill like you do. You're different, that's for sure. But no matter. I'm different too. Everyone is in a lotta ways I guess, so you ain't so special, Queenie. I once't read somethin' that said we're all alone here, or sumpin'. I guess we are." Winona smiled at me. "And look, don't worry about them girls. They're just dirty sluts, just a bunch of trampy whores. Hang loose, honey, hang loose. Screw 'em. Come on. Let's go call your fambly so they won't worry."

"Oh Winona," I said with a sigh. "They won't worry. But maybe Fred and Emma will, so I guess I'd better call."

"Who be Fred and Emma, your sister and brother?" asked Winona.

"Oh, no!" I started to laugh at the thought, but looked at Winona and changed my mind. "Uh, no, no, they're not. Actually, they sort of---well, they're like my family in a way, but they aren't. They're---"

Winona laughed loudly, her head thrown back. She slapped me heavily on my back, causing me to stagger slightly. "Queenie," she yelled, "say it! They *work* for you. They're your paid slaves, right? They're nigras, am I right again? Look, dopey, you can't help bein' born rich the same's I can't help bein' born po'. It's the luck o' the draw. So don't be 'shamed of it--just BE it. Fred and Emma are prolly nicer to you than your own kin. Am I right?"

I opened my mouth, closed it. Opened it. Where were the words?

Winona laughed again, and led me down the stairs and out onto the sidewalk where she knocked on the store's front door.

"The old geezer closes up at 5, and falls asleep in the back next to his radio an' his bottle o' Ripple," said Winona.

Shortly, the cranky old geezer himself staggered to the door, a bent and wizened man with a food, cigarette and booze stained beard. He grunted something unintelligible as he let us in. Winona understood, obviously having heard it before, since she touched him, smiled lovingly, and walked to the rear of the store, pulling me behind her. The old elf grunted something again. Winona smiled in acknowledgment, looked at me and pointed toward the phone.

I went into the booth, and actually found a coin in my pocket. *Winona. Oh, dear dear Winona.* The phone was one of the very old style with a trumpet-shaped earpiece and a mini-megaphone attached to the center of the wooden wall phone box. I giggled softly seeing this antique and enjoyed saying my phone number to an operator who asked, "Number please?" I heard the strident burr of the ringing phone and pulled the receiver from my ear. "Ouch," I whispered.

Emma answered, so I explained that I'd decided to visit a friend's home, and could Fred please come to get me? Emma said she'd give him the address, and Winona and I went back upstairs.

"You sure you don't wanta have some supper or somethin'?" asked Winona. I looked quickly around and back at my friend.

"No, no I'm not hungry at all," I lied as I felt my stomach pressing on my backbone from lack of food. "Honest. And besides, Fred will be here in a few minutes and then I'll be able to grab something at home."

"Suits me, Queenie. If you don't mind, though, I'm sorta hungry, so I'll fix me something, OK?"

"Oh. Sure. Please, go right ahead. Don't do anything differently because I'm here. Go ahead and eat. I'll just keep an eye out of the window here to see when Fred arrives. Will that be all right with you?"

"Yeah, Queenie, 'course it will, girl. God, you don't gotta ax permission to look outta de window! It's OK. Jesus, you're a oddball." Winona shoved a pile of boxes aside, and located a can of spaghetti. After some minutes of very noisy preparation, she emptied it into a pot, placed it on the hotplate and turned on the heat. She got a bottle of Coke from the small refrigerator, and part of a loaf of white bread. She stirred the spaghetti, poured it out onto a cracked plate she'd pulled from the sink and wiped with a grey dishtowel. She took a fork from the box, sat down on one of the barstools and began to eat noisily. I looked away, embarrassed, unused to seeing people dine this way, and in spite of that wished I could share that meal with dear Winona.

The sound of a horn startled me and through the torn curtains, I saw Fred's car. He blinked the headlights. I grabbed my books and outer clothing, anxious to leave and I stopped and looked at my rescuer.

"Winona," I stammered. "I--I um, I just don't know what to say. I know you said Marty wouldn't have killed me, but I think she *would* have, if you hadn't arrived in time and saved me." I cleared my throat. I felt my eyes begin to sting."So...thank you, Winona, thank you so much. I know I'm not saying this so well, but I want you to know that I consider myself so lucky to have a friend like you." Then I surprised us both by kissing the startled girl. Some of the canned spaghetti sprayed from Winona's mouth onto my cheek. Stepping back, I smiled awkwardly, wiped it off with my hand, waved and ran down the stairs.

Fred's eyes widened with horror as he took in my bruises and torn coat.

"Omigod Miss Courtenay. What *happened* to you? Who *did* this? Chile, you don't belong *here*. What-cho folks gonna say when they sees this?" He slammed the car door and ran to the other side, sliding quickly in and locking the car. He turned the key and drove away so furiously he left a strip of rubber on the icy asphalt. I thought of Dom, smiled and turned my head.

"This neighborhood, chile, lawd-a-mighty, this neighborhood ain't good, Miz Courtenay, ain't good a-*tawl*! Howju get down here anyway, chile?"

"I know I'm a mess Fred. But don't be scared. It's OK. I'm OK. You don't even have to tell my parents. It's a long story, Fred, a long story. I'll tell you all about it maybe later."

It was only a short drive home, but I fell asleep on the way, and when I got home, my parents never noticed how I looked. They waved to me and I smiled at the backs of their heads. They were watching TV. I went to bed that night, bathed and fed and beginning to heal, and I did not dream The Dream.

178

# CHAPTER 25

Finally, after the long winter at New Town High, spring came and was welcomed and celebrated. If I hadn't thought it was just too immature, I would have skipped on my way to school. The long year was finally ending and things were green and soft, I saw the world through a yellow haze, and it seemed that even my blood sang. I was alive, my grades were good, and I felt as though I'd lived through and survived one of the world's most difficult of tests. I also pleasantly discovered I was actually looking forward to going to spring Sock Hop with Teddy Muller, having not been asked to the fall Sock Hop. It would be, after all, the first date I'd had all year. I still kept in touch with my Academy friends, but kept the two schools in separate categories in my mind. When I was in one, I would deliberately forget the existence of the other.

I joined the Year Book Club (so had my shadow Nettie, of course,) and we were finishing up the work on the 1956 book while planning the one I'd be in as a graduate of 1957. The yearbook was called "The Argo," after the ship that took men on a search for the Golden Fleece. I thought it a rather majestic name for the yearbook of such a simple, and after all, public, school. I felt the name would have better suited The Academy's yearbook.

Nonetheless, I worked happily on it, making plans for the Class of '57. I ordered my class ring, and was surprised at how excited I was when it arrived. It was typical for public school-- wide gold band, deeply etched with the school's name and year on one side, a generic embossed high school on the other, and a huge faceted green stone on top. (New Town's school colors were green and gold.) I knew The Academy's senior rings were elegant and understated with a simple gold band topped by a black onyx stone. Delicately etched into the onyx was The Academy's name, and on the inside of the band, the student's initials and year of graduation. These Academy rings were cherished and worn for years, but New Town kids wore their rings for a short while at best, and either sold them for quick cash, gave them to their current objects of affection, or lost them at the beach.

I didn't know then but I would give my gaudy New Town ring to my middle son years hence, and he wore it to the local beach and yes, lost it there. I would be saddened about that, but only for a while.

I stood in the New Town school's doorway on that spring day looking out at the school grounds, running my fingers through my long dark hair and I thought of many things, many memories. I thought about how I'd made friends with people I'd scorned so vehemently in all of my younger years. Yes, had hated. I thought about the boys who liked me, even dated me. I wondered why Dom still pursued me. I'd accepted several rides home with him knowing perfectly well I should not have, but had coolly turned down a number of requests for dates wit him. As strongly as I hinted, Dom Di Russo never seemed to be able to comprehend that he was simply not worthy of my affections, or even attentions. He was harmless I now knew, but his relentless, tormenting teasing was becoming very annoying, and I knew Dom knew that.

Marty and her gang apparently had believed Winona's threat, because Marty now seemed content to simply glare at me whenever the opportunity presented itself, and I courageously made certain it presented itself frequently because I was protected and no longer afraid of her. Maybe a little. Yes. A little. And yet while it never went beyond that, the glares were still slightly unnerving to me and I felt my breath quicken when they were delivered. And Marty knew that, too.

Walking to class one afternoon, I knew without turning around that Dom and his gang were behind me. I walked faster, but it was hopeless so I turned to face my problem squarely.

"Hey there, Queenie, baby," Dom sang out. "How's it goin'?"

"It's going just fine, Dominic, thanks very much for asking. How thoughtful. Now how about getting lost?"

"Oh, Queenie, please, don't make me sad. Why do you always give me such a hard time? I just wanna be friends." Dom began to circle me, running his hands through his curly hair, shrugging, pulling his collar high on his neck. He grinned widely at me.

"Dom." I stood still, trying to look very serious. "Listen carefully to me. I do not, repeat, I do not date guys like you. Do you understand me? I keep telling you. How many ways do I have to say it? I mean, what part of all of this don't you get?"

Dom stopped preening and threw his hands up in mock horror. "You don't? You don't go out wit' `guys like me?' Aw, Queenie! I'm crushed." Dom dropped to his knees, pulled the corners of his mouth down.

180

"Well then, Queenie," he said, his voice filled with sobs, a look of exaggerated sadness on his face. He wiped away an invisible tear, and held his hands beseechingly toward her. "Well, then, Madam Queen, if you won't go *out* with me, will you at least *marry* me? Huh? Will ya? Huh? Huh?"

I rolled my eyes and sighed, mildly irritated at, and more than mildly interested in, Dom. And yes, I was amused.

"Oh Dom, you're as funny as a rubber crutch. What a card. You're so funny I forgot to laugh. Will you please give me a break? What did I ever do to deserve this? For God's sake, GET UP OFF THE FLOOR! And besides, why do you keep after *me* when Marty is so crazy about you? You two belong together. Holy Toledo, Dom, did you know she nearly killed me over you? Why not stick with her? You two are exactly alike. Don't ask me why, but she thinks you're just plain great!"

Dom got to his feet and stood, leaning toward me, quite suddenly listening intently.

"Yeah, Queenie, I knew about dat time. I never tol' you I knew, but when I heard, I went to her house and beat her up."

My books began to slide from my grasp. One hit the ground. I was stunned and my knees began to feel unsteady.

"You did WHAT? My God, you *hit* her?? You crazy jackass! You should never have done that! Can't you people understand how wrong that is? Why do you have to settle everything with violence? And furthermore, don't you know the danger you've put me in by doing that? My God, Dominic! Do you ever THINK? I mean, *EVER??*"

I trembled with rage. Dom moved closer, but I stood my ground. He gently put his arm around me, and put his face close to my ear.

"Aw Queenie. Lissen," he whispered. "I didn't really do that. I wunta hit Marty. I did go to her house and told her that I would do that if she ever bothered you again, but I dint hit her. I swear. The guys were nearby, Queenie. I wanted them ta think I roughed her up a little. I gotta IMAGE, y' know."

"Oh, my GOD!" I glared at Dom, shoved him away and stamped off. "You and your bloody, fucking IMAGE!!" I shouted.

I heard a noise behind me and turned to see Mr. Wright, the janitor, who always came into the school after 3:17 PM, the official closing time. He could never startle anyone since he constantly sang as he worked and walked, the same tuneless song all the time.

Mr. Wright was a small man, whose age floated someplace between fifty and forever, and he always wore a spotted, greasy maybe-green coverall over his spotted, greasy clothing. During the winter months, he wore a deeply soiled red woolen cap, pulled so low on his head his ears stuck out at right angles. Mr. Wright always pushed a big rusted bucket in front of him on small squealing wheels, filled with brackish water of uncertain vintage. The faculty laid bets every year that he never changed the water from week to week, and there were some who believed it stayed unchanged from year to year. A large filthy string mop was shoved into the pail, and Mr. Wright often pushed the whole thing along by the mop's handle, looking for all the world as if he was steering a small, curious ship.

A patient man, he'd write semi-literate notes and tack them up into the bathrooms, begging the girls to put their used sanitary napkins in the metal containers provided, but they rarely would, finding it far more convenient and fun to flush them down the old toilets. Mr. Wright never questioned it when sanitary napkins were also stuffed into the boys' toilets, neither knowing nor caring how they got there. He would never be riled either, when the usual cherry bombs were lit and dropped into the toilets, where they exploded into a huge watery mess, cracking both the toilet seats and porcelain bowls and shattering the pipes.

Plastic wrap, stretched tightly across toilet seats obliging an unwitting girl to sit in her own urine, wouldn't cause the good Mr. Wright to flinch, even when he had to fish the dripping glob of balled plastic from the choking toilet. His work was his life, and this kind, simple man cheerfully accepted every chore and tragedy visited upon him as his due. He had come from a desperately poor background and any paid work, he knew, was an honor.

No one ever called him "Mr. Wright," and not too many even knew his real name. He was "Mr. Wrong" both behind his back and to his face, and he'd had the Wrong name so long, he often could not remember the Wright name. He accepted the nickname blithely, chomping endlessly on an extraordinarily long and thick unlit cigar stuck into the right corner of his mouth.

"Hi, there, Mr. Wrong. How's it going?" I called out to the little man, as I prepared to leave the building.

"Well, fine, now, young lady, an' howzit goin' wit' youse?" he answered. He'd met so many students in the years he'd done maintenance in the school, that he called them all "young lady," and "young man." He often responded without looking up, not seeing which gender was, in fact, addressing him. Woe to the boy with a high voice, for Mr. Wright invariably called him "young lady."

"Well, things're just going great for me too, Mr. Wrong, and thanks for asking." I beamed at him. I loved Mr. Wright. He was so kind and gentle.

"Now, ain't that nice," the man responded warmly. "Say," Mr. Wright continued, "ainchu that new one?"

"Yes," I said, smiling, no longer caring about the year-old label. "That's me. I. But you know, Mr. Wrong, that's sort of old news by now. I've been here for almost the whole year now, so I'm really not `the new one' any longer. I'm just plain old Queenie. Uh--Courtenay. Well, Queenie."

"Queenie? Now that's a moniker for ya. How come your folks named you that?"

"Well, actually, they didn't, Mr. Wrong, but it's a long story and I've got to run. I'll tell you all about it sometime, OK? Gotta go. So --see ya!"

I walked out of the building and my heart sank. There was Nettie, pretending that she had important business out on the sidewalk, but not carrying off the charade too well.

"Oh! Hi Nettie!" I forced cheerfulness, but dreaded having to walk with Box Girl.

"Oh! Hi there, Queenie. I dint know you was in there. I was just--I was just--" Nettie apparently couldn't think of what she was just, and so she stood there, her face twisting in embarrassment. I felt her discomfort.

"Well Nets, I'm glad you're here. There's something I need to ask you," I said.

Nettie, enormously relieved and grateful, said "Yeah? What is it, Queen? Anything!"

"Umm…oh..ah yes! Do you know when the Journalism Club is going on the field trip to visit that newspaper? I don't think I was paying attention when it was announced, and I don't want to ask Mr. Cornish again. You know how he is. He gets so cranky if you don't pay attention to his announcements." I smiled, impressed with my brilliant ad lib.

Nettie, ecstatically happy to be able to help me, her idol, recited the date and time of the excursion, and we two walked off together toward the bus stop, but Nettie stopped at the train tracks since that was her transportation home. Her constant smile was broader than ever as she called out, "See you later, alligator!" and waved goodbye to me.

"Our Lady of the Perpetual Grin," I thought as I walked away and hating myself for doing it, I turned and waved. "After a while, crocodile!" Ugh! I could see Nettie's grin widen even from that distance.

I had to walk home, since I'd missed Fred, but I didn't mind. There was a warm breeze, soft like old, worn flannel against my skin. The ground and trees were turning a pale, tender green, and the gardeners were planting the spring flowers throughout the estates. The air was sweet, and I was happy.

The night before, my parents had called me into the living room, sounding slightly odd, but then didn't they always? I shuffled in, hands in my pockets, trying to show them that no matter why they called me into the room it would have no effect on me whatsoever. I had become quite adept at looking bored and uninterested. I stood in front of them and said "OK, what?"

To my huge surprise and embarrassment, they offered me a long summer vacation sailing with other kids "of my sort" off the New England coastline. All passengers would stay aboard the yacht, but every few days we'd get off at a specific port and go to hotels to clean up, dress up, and go dancing.

Quickly losing my cool bored attitude I was thrilled and from then on, could think of little else. My mother had given me some department store charge cards so I could buy some sailing outfits and bathing suits, shoes and other important things. I wouldn't know any of the other kids on the cruise, but at least this time, I'd have things in common with them. They would be of my sort. My kind. I went to bed that night, my mind spinning with the possibilities, hearing the music, experiencing the fun. I would be with my own kind of people. They'd be like me, I'd be like them. I'd belong! No one would stare at me. People would make room for me at the dining tables. I would not feel alone or frightened! I was anxious to speak with my parents about the cruise at dinner the next night.

"So darling, are you excited about the cruise this summer?" My mother was chirpier than usual this night. She actually sat at the table with me while Emma served us from silver platters.

"Oh, yes, mother," I answered, smiling. "It sounds really great. Who'll be on board with me?" I reached for the water pitcher.

My father looked up from his plate, a piece of chicken cordon bleu speared on the end of his silver, engraved fork.

"Well, my dear Courtenay," he said, doing his Clark Gable squint and pushing the delicacy into his mouth, chewing thoughtfully. "The cruise will put you with children of only the finest families--good connections for you. You have to start thinking about your future, you know. Since you've refused your coming-out party, you'll have to find yourself a suitable husband on your own. This could be a very good start." My father reached for the intricately cut crystal wine goblet and drank deeply, the pale wine vanishing from the glass into his mouth. I watched him, as fascinated as when I was a child. Through the bottom of the glass, I could see my father's rounded lips times ten in the prisms of the goblet.

"Obviously," he continued, wiping his mouth with the large, snowy linen napkin, "I don't have to tell you what this cruise *won't* have on board: No wops. No spicks. Absolutely no kikes on this cruise, and the only niggers (this whispered out of deference to Emma and Mary in the kitchen) you'll see will be the crew."

I stared silently at my father, who didn't notice. He went back to eating with gusto, his head bent over the plate.

"Father?" He looked up. "Why do you have to use those names?"

"What names?" He frowned, not comprehending.

"You know, Father, the names you just called Jewish people and colored people." I was not sure why a lump had formed in my throat, or why I felt defensive and angry. After all, I'd heard him use those awful words my entire life.

"What on earth are you talking about, my dear? Those people don't mind. *Everyone* calls them that. They are amused by it!"

"Amused by it, Father? Are you kidding? Well then, I think everyone is wrong. It's wrong to use names like that on people just because of their skin color or their religion." I forced my eyes wide so tears would not spill.

My father put his fork down and looked at me, surprised.

"Oh *come* now, dearie," he said, his voice slightly scornful. "It's just the way it *is*. Those people don't have any *feelings,* my dear Courtenay. They're not like us. You ought to know that by now, my dear child. We've certainly told you often enough."

I shook my head, and then suddenly decided I might be able to change his mind. I grinned at my father.

"Father, you are SO wrong. Will you let me tell you about something that happened to me a couple of weeks ago in the lunchroom at school? Will you really listen to me? Please, don't shut me out. And you too mother," I turned and faced my mother, "so don't you DARE go talk on the phone."

I stopped and took a long, shaking breath. I was surprised to see my parents sit up straighter, look at each other with amazement, and then astonishingly, wait quietly for me to speak.

"OK. Thanks. Here goes. I was, umm, sitting at the lunch table, you know, eating with a bunch of kids from my classes. There was this newspaper opened on the table, and there was a picture of a girl in a bathing suit, and diagonally across her chest was one of those big wide ribbons, you know, like Miss America, and on this sash in big letters was 'Miss Jewish American.'"

My father, right on cue, snorted. I glared at him and he lowered his head and obediently became silent. I was shocked to see him do that, but didn't let on, and continued.

"Well, anyway," I said, refusing to be rattled by my parents' disapproval, "I pointed at that picture, and I laughed and poked Sue Lewis who sat next to me, and I said, 'Hey, look at that!' And Sue-- she's my friend, she was table captain that week---well, she looked at me, and she said, 'Yeah? So what?' So I said, 'Well, come on, I mean, Miss *JEWISH* America? I mean really!' Sue just kept looking at me and said, 'Well, what's so funny about that?' And you know what? I didn't know what to say. I mean, why *should* that be funny? I guess I just thought I was *supposed* to laugh--that it was *expected*. If the woman had Miss Nebraska on her sash, would I have thought that was funny? Would I have even said anything about it at all? No, I wouldn't have. I just thought people should make fun of people if they're Jewish and because that girl was in some kind of Jewish beauty contest. I thought I was *supposed* to make fun of her.

"And then, Sue Lewis said `Well, Queenie," (I saw my parents exchange a look) "I see you're a bigot. I never knew that about you. So, I guess you don't think a Jewish girl can be beautiful and be in a beauty contest, right?' Well, I started to laugh and--I can't believe I said this--- I said, `Well, yeah, I guess that's right, Sue. Everyone knows Jewish women just *aren't* beautiful and *I've* certainly never heard about a Jewish beauty contest, of all things!'

"And then I laughed and looked around, but no one was laughing with me. Oh God, I just can't believe I said that to her. Everyone at the table got real quiet. I felt like crawling into a hole or something. And then Sue said to me, `Queenie, I happen to be Jewish myself, and I take offense at what you just said, and I will never speak to you again.'

"The whole table stayed quiet and I wanted do die. Sue got up and walked off, and everyone glared at me and turned away. And now Sue Lewis completely ignores me, she won't even talk to me, even though I've tried and tried to apologize. I've left notes on her desk and she just throws them away. And she looks the other way whenever I come near her in school. It's terrible, awful. I've hurt her and I can't make her let me apologize."

My voice had been cracking through the whole story and now was low and uneven. My parents sat looking at me, making no sound. Finally, my father spoke.

"So?" he said. "I don't get it. What's the problem, Courtenay? You don't want to be friends with a Jewish girl anyway. I just don't see that there's a problem here."

"Oh my God, Father." I did not want to believe what I'd just heard, but I did believe it.

"Courtenay!" my father said, now in his stern mode. "Courtenay. Please! Do NOT take the Lord's name in vain. You do that entirely too much these days, young lady."

"What? What did you say?" I looked at my father in disbelief. "I can't say God's name? But both of you can say words like 'nigger?" My parents gesticulated frantically at the swinging door separating the dining room from the kitchen where Emma and Mary were, probably listening with delight. "And," I went on ignoring them, "you forbid me to say God but you can say kike, and spick, and mick, and mackerel

187

snapper, sheeny, and chink, and all of those terrible words you use to... define... people from other countries, or other churches, or colored people, and you're telling me not to say *GOD?!* Daddy, I've heard you use these words while you're standing on the steps of St. Mary's after you've taken Holy Communion, for heaven's sake. NO! I mean for *God's* sake!" I slammed my hand onto the table, and a spoon flipped into the air and hit a water goblet. The musical *ping!* hung in the air.

"And --- wait a sec," I said, reaching for the spoon and pushing it away. "I'm not done. I have to tell you that what you just said about not wanting certain people as my friends, well, you're wrong, Dad, you're wrong. How come you're always telling me what I want and don't want? You don't know what's inside me. And, I DO want Jewish girls for my friends. And Italian, and Negro, and anyone else who'll have me for a friend, but probably no one ever will, now that this has happened. You know, you sent me to that place, even though I still don't know why because you refuse to tell me, and I've gotten to know all those kids, and believe me, they come in all sorts of colors and go to all sorts of churches. Guess what? There are even black kids there—you know, like from Africa. Slaves? Lynchings? Remember? The good old days?? The kids aren't just rich, white Episcopalians at New Town, you know. As a matter of fact, there aren't any as far as I can tell. But the New Town kids, the ones you keep telling me aren't 'our sort,' well, they're just fine." I grabbed some air and my breath was scraping my lungs. "And you should never have taught me to think I'm better than they are, because you're just wrong. You're WRONG father! I am NOT better than they are, and guess what? Neither are you two!"

"Now, now, Courtenay dear, calm down. We're sorry, darling," said my mother, ever the mediator. "Nothing to get all upset about. Let's just talk about your summer plans and forget this little unpleasantness, shall we?"

I stood. The interior of Winona's home flashed through my mind. *Why? Why am I seeing that?* "No thanks, Mother. I don't want to forget 'this little unpleasantness.' And now that I think about it, no thanks to that cruise offer, too. I saw a notice on the bulletin board at school the other day. The YMCA is looking for summer workers to be counselors for underprivileged children. I'm going to sign up for that."

My mother became pale and her eyes widened as she stared at me. And then, my father's hand began to shake, spilling water from his goblet onto the tablecloth. He looked at me vacantly, water dripping from his knuckles. "Now look what you've done, Walter," my mother blurted.

I stared at him. He looked suddenly sick, weird. Not angry. My mother looked like that too--like they'd both been hit from behind by something large and unexpected. They looked jerkily at each other, my mother's eyes wide and white. *What the hell's the matter with them? Are they that hysterical about the YMCA?*

"What's wrong, Father? Are you OK?" I asked him.

He hesitated, stared at me and then shook his head. "Nothing, Courtenay, just spilled a little water. Emma will mop it up. Nothing to worry about. Now, what in hell is all this YMCA crap?"

My mother met my father's gaze for a long second.

"Walter?" she said, and the word was chill and hushed, the way a frightened child sounds an instant before something terrible will happen. Her husband turned and looked back at her. The silence between them lasted too long.

Helen Wolcott turned back to me, her voice louder now, strained. "Your father probably thinks it's unseemly for a young lady of your station to be working at a -- a YMCA, Courtenay. I suppose he feels a little shocked about this sudden announcement of yours. And frankly, so do I. Where, may I ask, did this come from?"

"Well," I said, and my mouth dried. My resolve began to crumble and I feared my parents would forbid this new plan. "It's my own idea. I'm applying tomorrow, and from what I hear, there's a big need, so I'm quite certain I'll be accepted."

If all this had come as a surprise to my parents, it was even more of a surprise to me, but I felt elated and freed as I walked upstairs. I'd stood my ground. My parents had not said yes, but they did not refuse me. I felt five years older. Taller too.

# CHAPTER 26

Finally, it was here; the Spring Sock Hop. Teddy's father drove him to our home to pick me up, horrifying my parents by honking out in the driveway and not coming in. I wore a brand new Poodle Skirt, pale grey with the black Poodle prancing proudly on the side. I wore it with crinolines and my wide black stretch belt, and wore my black and white saddle shoes with pink socks, and a fluffy-collared white blouse. I pulled my long hair back in a ponytail and tied it with a pink ribbon.

Teddy arrived in a pale blue suit and a dark blue shirt with no tie and I thought he looked adorable. He was nervous and so was I. His father dropped us off at the school and when I heard the music while I was walking in with Teddy, I felt enormous excitement and happiness. Holding hands, Teddy and I ran through the red painted metal doors and down the hall to the auditorium.

The band at the Spring Sock Hop wasn't too bad. It was made up of classmates who harbored dreams--didn't everyone?--of being the next world-famous rock stars. They sang, and screamed, swiveled and gyrated in a desperate imitation of Little Anthony, and The Four Aces, with just a touch of Elvis and a soupçon of Bill Haley and Harry Belafonte. The result was a deafening musical mess, and I was thrilled by it and could not wait to begin dancing.

I was having a wonderful time I kept telling myself, and I knew I really meant it. I'll admit I disliked the feeling of dirt collecting in my new socks and grinding into the soles of my feet. Some of the girls also wore the new Poodle Skirts, which were full and swingy atop their crinolines, and some even wore their hair in the new "poodle cut." But the guys remained uniformed, as usual, in their standard jeans, boots, white T-shirts and leather jackets, except for the jocks who wore crew neck sweaters and khaki pants. Some, like Teddy wore suits but none wore shirts and ties.

Teddy opted for the suit out of deference to me, I knew, and we danced to everything, fast, slow, and in between. (I gave grudging mental thanks to Miss Ginocchio for those horrible Friday afternoon dancing classes.) The dancing I'd learned at The Academy wasn't quite appropriate for New Town.

The school crawled with chaperons, but still one of the kids was able to follow the time-honored tradition of spiking the punch bowl. The transgression was soon discovered, the large bowl emptied and refilled, and three acutely scowling parents stationed themselves at parade rest at the bowl's sides, prepared to annihilate anyone who looked even mildly predisposed to adding hootch or a touch of Sneaky Pete to the sweet liquid.

When the kids decided to do "The Stroll" I demurely declined, hating the thought of having to dance that gauntlet with Teddy and being stared at. But Teddy finally convinced me, and down we danced between the two lines of swaying, finger-snapping kids, a step forward, a step back, turning from each other, our backs touching, arms slightly intertwining, then turning again, our fronts touching, hands joining, everything sliding softly together, all the time smiling and smiling. I instantly began to love the dance, did not want to give the moment away to the next couple, but I did, and Teddy and I stood at the end of the line and watched as the next couple came floating, snapping by.

I loved being at that Sock Hop. The music was sweet that night, soothing and kind to my ears. I was happy in New Town, but I couldn't-- wouldn't give in completely to liking it, hated that I couldn't, but oh, so wanted to.

My feelings about my two schools had become jumbled. I could really see good in both, importance in both, and that made me feel disloyal to The Academy and my old friends there. I thought I was supposed to be 100% loyal to just one, and I could not.

Dominic Di Russo came stag to the Sock Hop and he and his proselytes hung on the sidelines to mock and sneer at the dancers. As I danced past him with Teddy, I cast my eyes down when I saw Dom watching me. After a while, Dom pulled himself tall, tucked his shirt into his pants, combed his hair, and gave the thumbs up signal to his gang. They all laughed knowingly, thumbing-up and elbowing each other, and I heard them loudly assure each other that they didn't need to go dancing around with those geeks, but I knew they wished they'd been asked.

I looked over Teddy's shoulder, and saw Dom making his way toward us. *Oh no! Oh no no no!* I stiffened.

"Teddy!" I whispered. "Just keep on dancing. Di Russo's coming over. I know he wants to cut in, but I just don't want to dance with him. So ignore him, OK? Please? Please Teddy??"

But Teddy was no fool, and made a snap decision that living was more important to him than honoring my pleas. Therefore, when Dom reached forward to tap his shoulder, he whispered rapidly into my ear, "Oh, come on Queenie, now don't clutch. He's not such a bad dude. Give him one little dance. I'll be right over there watching you. What could it hurt?" Giving me no time to respond, Teddy turned and showed all of his teeth to Dom, saying merrily, "Hey man! How's it goin'? You wanna dance with Queenie? Hey, buddy, be my guest. I'll just go get me some punch."

"I shall kill you, Theodore, you worm, you traitor. Remember it," I hissed just before whirling away in the unyielding arms of the grinning Dom Di Russo.

And then, to my annoyance, the music slowed. The Five Zits on stage moved into a lame rendition of The Tennessee Waltz, and I felt Dom's arms encircle my waist. Not wanting to look foolish by letting my arms flop limply at my sides, I stiffly placed them above his shoulders, locking my hands together behind his head holding my arms several inches out in a yoke, while maintaining an expression of disdainful boredom. And so we danced, moving slowly and awkwardly to the butchered rendition of Patti Page's newest hit song, "The Tennessee Waltz." I knew how to waltz, had been taught years before in Miss Tate's Dancing Class at The Academy on Sunday evenings. Dom did not. It was an awkward, clumping pairing at best, with my following the rules of the waltz and Dom following his own.

"Queenie," Dom whispered, "You just gotta relax your arms. Don't be such a yo-yo. Christ with your arms out like that you look like you're dryin' your pits. And, you gotta put your head on my chest, near my shoulder there. You got it bent back so far, you'll getta nose bleed. Come on. Stop being so square. I ain't gonna rape ya, y'know. At least not here in front of everyone." He laughed.

"Oh, yuck, yuck, yuck, Dom. Dream on, fella. You wish." I had enough friends around that I did not have to let this great greasy posturing hairball one-up me.

"You want I should give you a ride home tonight, Queenie?" Dom asked.

How I hated his arrogance. "Are you kidding? No! Teddy is driving me home, of course."

"Hoo Boy, Little Teddy-Weddy. Say now, I'm impressed, Queens! Better carry a club or sumpin'. I hear he's a passionate dude, can't keep it in his pants, has AWLL the girls beggin'! "

"Look, Dom. Lay off, will you? Just because someone's different from you, knows how to read without using his finger, and has plans to do something with his life, that is no reason for you to make fun of him. How come you *always* do that, anyway? How come you and that gang of stupid, wimpy thugs holding up the wall over there always *do* that? Are you afraid of the jocks? I think you are." I pulled away from him, folded my arms, leaned against a wall and smiled sarcastically at him.

"So what's the deal, Dom? If you're so cool, how come you can't live and let live? How come you can't stand on your own, Dom?"

Dom put his hand under my chin, squeezed my jaw, leaned forward and looked closely into my eyes. But he did not speak. I could smell his skin, his maleness, and my heart flipped. For once he seemed wanting for words.

Finally: "Who, me??" he asked, eyebrows up. He put his hand behind my neck and pulled me close and then closer to his face. The music mercifully ended, and I knew I'd touched a nerve in this self-made god. *Maybe he's human after all.* And then, *nahh.* I reached up, wrapped my arms tightly around Dom's neck, and hid my smile against his shoulder.

When the Sock Hop was over, Teddy drove me home. At my back door with the light from the vestibule glowing down at us, he kissed me once, sweetly and softly. His hands on my shoulders, he looked up at the huge house and said, "Jeez Queenie, you live in this place? It's a hotel, right?" Then he told me he'd had a nifty time, touched my cheek and walked away. It was nice. Very, very nice.

Early the next week, we girls circled again in the Journalism Club, and did a thorough post-mortem on the dance: who kissed whom, who groped whom, who begged for what. Giggling, then laughing raucously, we all re-enacted the sweaty gropings and pitiful pawings of our lusting dates, imitated their love-sick promises in falsetto, whining voices. Mr. Cornish tried to break up this bonding rite between all of us, but as soon as he'd leave the room, we'd clump again, filling in the details, laughing, confessing all. At the back of the room Nettie sat alone, smiling, holding a pile of papers, wearing a strangely new string of pink pop-it beads hanging against her familiar old dress. Under the desk, she twisted the material of the grey dress with her fat, rough fingers. I looked over, saw Nettie, and went to the back of the room to speak with her.

"Oh, hi, Nets. Didn't see you there. Say, um, you got those clippings Cornish was talking about? Let's have a look at them. We should really go over them together, OK?"

For the first time, I saw the girl's perpetual smile fade. And to my dismay, her chin began to tremble.

"Nobody will ever ask me to a dance," Nettie said softly and huge tears trembled on her lashes.

"Aw, Nettie," I answered as tenderly as I could, and it was painfully easy for me to do that. "Oh gee, Nets."

# CHAPTER 27

School would end in a few more weeks. Almost everyone, or at least all the popular kids had been invited to the junior prom, and so had I. I was happy, although my date was not Teddy, but was someone I'd never expected.

He was Al Scaramoozo, a young man easily able to breach the gap between the greasers and the jocks and who also had enough sense of self to allow himself to be seen at a junior prom even though he was a senior. Neither tall nor short, with pale eyes and hair, Al had an everyman's face that was mostly kind and often happily blank. Al Scaramoozo was non-threatening and well-liked by mostly everyone in the school, and I was one of them! He heartily enjoyed selecting a different girl every day with whom to walk around school, his arm casually about her waist. No one took him very seriously, and he was forgiven an odd and messy handicap: Al Scaramoozo had malfunctioning tear ducts. They just could not shut down. A constant stream of salty tears ran perpetually down his cheeks and into his endlessly soggy and wilted collar. During all of his waking hours there appeared a crystal teardrop hanging from the tip of his nose and chin, and he was keenly aware that his school pals laid bets as to when one would fall to make room for the next. All his school papers had ink smudges. Al had long since given up trying to control this problem, and had the tenacity to expect his peers to accept him as he was, tears and all. They did. Al was very popular in spite of his malady, and was smart enough to make light of his affliction, occasionally talking vaguely about "an operation after graduation." Over the years, I would wonder about Al and whether he ever got the operation to dry his eyes. I wondered what would happen if he ever cried after that surgery--would there be any tears left?

And one day, it was my turn to be escorted around the school. I felt Al's arm go around my waist as I walked to my homeroom, and I looked into his smiling, wet face.

"Hi Al! So, I'm the Chosen One today?"

"Sure are, honey, you lucky duck. And since we're being so lovey-dovey, Queenie, there's something I've been wanting to ask you all year." He cleared his throat.

"No thanks, Al, I don't want to marry you," I smiled at him. "I want a career in journalism first. But once I'm famous, call me and we'll talk, OK?"

Al laughed down at me. "Oh, you dreamer! You should be so lucky, Queen! No, no--actually, I wanted to ask you to be my date for the junior prom, if you'd like."

I stopped and disentangled myself from his clutching arm. "You want to what? Hey Al! I didn't know you cared!"

"Well, Queenie, really I don't. To tell you the truth, I'm a homo and wanted to ask Ralphie, but I didn't think they'd let me in to the dance with him, and even if McArdle had let me, I just knew he'd never tell me what flowers he wanted. Pink-- or pink." And then, eyes spurting as if from minuscule water pistols, Al threw back his head and laughed at himself.

"No, Queenie, really, I'm just kiddin'. I'd really like it if you'd let me take you. Woodja?"

"Well, Al-- I hardly know what to say! Uh, sure, I'll go with you. It'd be fun. Really! Thanks!" I smiled at Al's drenched, shining face.

And so I joined the select girls in the school who'd been asked to a prom. My dear mother, who told me with her face turned away, that it was less stressful to forgive me "for that unfortunate outburst about the silly awful YMCA business" than to force me to go on the cruise, reluctantly gave the charge cards back to me. Thus armed, I selected a strapless aqua gown with a tulle stole, and a hoop slip to hold the ankle-length taffeta skirt out in a wide circle. The most peculiar thing about strapless gowns, I sometimes thought, was that they moved to the left when the wearer turned to the right. And they hurt too, sometimes leaving scars, but the style was "in" and so I would wear it with resolve and pride.

It was a week before the prom and school was nearly finished for the year. I had made the honor role three out of four times, and had begun to send out college applications.

The mood at New Town was light and happy, the halls filled with giggling young girls, heads together as they walked. The boys walked in groups too, earnestly discussing their chances of getting laid before school was out, or better yet, after the prom, or even better than that, during.

It was Friday. No one was concentrating on school work. Most were staring out of the windows, or doodling lazily on their book covers. My homeroom class jumped at the sound of an early bell. Miss McArdle's voice scraped over the PA system.

"All boys and girls will meet immediately in the auditorium. Please leave everything on your desks, and file out quietly. No talking. No running. No gum chewing. I shall meet with all of you there in twenty minutes."

"Must be another atomic bomb drill or somethin,'" someone offered, as we trooped out. Even the teachers seemed perplexed as they struggled to keep law and order amongst the large group of kids.

"Jeez. You t'ink there's a war on?"

"Nahh. Maybe Miss McArdle is gonna announce her engagement."

"Yeah. To Piacentino."

Blasts of laughter erupted down the line.

I was surprised, as we all were, to see Miss McArdle and Miss Piacentino up on the stage, waiting for the arrival of the student body. A local priest was there too, along with a rabbi and a minister, all looking extremely solemn, their eyes casting long looks at the kids, then looking down quickly. The hooting and yelling stopped abruptly as the kids arrived in the big room and saw who was on the stage.

Miss McArdle walked to the microphone, and tapped its metal front. A high-pitched screech blasted from it. She stepped back, glared at someone offstage and began to speak.

"Boys and girls," she said. "I'm afraid I have some very sad news. The clergymen behind me are here to help you through this tragedy, so please feel free to come up and speak with them after I've made my announcement." She took a deep breath.

"Your beloved classmate Jeannette Capinerri," she spoke slowly, paused dramatically, "died over the weekend."

"Who in hell is Jeannette Capinerri?" I wondered. Then my heart stilled and electrified ice froze my guts. I grabbed at my chest. Something sucked the moisture from my mouth, the breath from my body. My eyes froze in my head. The room was quiet, like in a tomb. I knew.

Miss McArdle, obviously shaken, looked expectantly out over the silent crowd. No one moved. No one spoke.

"Jeannette." She paused. "*Nettie*," she prodded.

The crowd moved. Faces turned toward each other. A few students laughed nervously. I heard some sobs, and one muffled scream. There were gasps like air escaping from tires. A few curses.

"Our poor, dear Jeannette just could not handle some personal problems. Brace yourselves, children. It seems she took her own life."

The room again became silent. I gripped the arms of my seat. A scream began at the back of my throat, but it didn't come forward. I sucked in air. *Nettie! Nettie!*

"I'm gonna pass out" I murmured, my tongue like wood. Through a fog that seemed to have quickly filled the room, I heard Miss McArdle speak again.

"There does not seem to be much point in hiding it. You'll read it in the newspaper anyway. Jeannette swallowed two large bottles of aspirin, Bayer, I think. She did leave a note. We haven't been privileged to read it, but the police reported to me this morning that she'd said something about no one liking her, or wanting her, that she felt as if she just didn't belong. And that ultimately, she knew she wasn't important, that she didn't matter. Apparently she'd been feeling quite badly hurt. This is something all of us must think about carefully over the next few weeks."

Some of the girls began to sob. I was shattered, and then enraged to hear some of the boys laugh and whisper about how repulsive Nettie must look dead. I heard one boy say "But hey! As a stiff she might be an improvement!" and they all laughed again, but it wasn't real laughter, it was forced and weak, and I understood.

Miss McArdle announced that we were dismissed and must return to our homerooms. Morning classes were to be canceled she said, so that "students wishing the assistance of a clergyman might avail themselves."

Soft rubber replacing the bones in my legs, I got up and stumbled out. Silently, the students returned to their homerooms, some to brood about the fragility of life and to wonder if they'd in some way been party to this strange, fat, boxy girl's terrible decision, others to happily plan how they'd spend their time off from classes while Nettie, whom they'd completely ignored and disliked anyway, was starting to be mourned by at least a few. I sat at my desk and stared at the words carved into the top. Obscenities, messages, initials. Years, opinions. I read them all. They made fascinating nonsense. I knew if I concentrated on the graffiti my mind might stay balanced and clear. That way, perhaps, I would not feel the terrible pain I knew for a certainty would devour me.

It hurt so, so much. I had not known anything could burn into my soul the way this did. I traced the words on my desk top with a shaking finger and then let my head sink down, and I folded my arms over the carvings. Silent tears spilled out of my eyes and my heart. They mixed with the ink in the deep grooves of the carved words, collected in slender puddles, and slid like tiny crystal threads where the letters curved.

I groped for a tissue inside my desk but my fingers touched a small, paper bundle. I pulled it out sluggishly, not really caring, I unrolled it. Something hard was inside of it. My eyes stared at it but didn't see it and did see it. Hidden inside the tissue was a silver horse brooch, its neck so long it looked like a giraffe, its eye a cracked turquoise, its tail a few long wires of silver that once had hooked into a worn spot on an old, shabby and shapeless grey dress. A small piece of soiled paper lay beneath the sad, tiny piece of jewelry, words written on it in smudged penciled letters: "This is for you. You were the only one who was ever nice to me. N."

# CHAPTER 28

It seemed after all, that the entire school attended the services for Nettie, which included a wake. I was so anxious-- I had never been to a wake, let alone an Italian one.

I went with some of the other girls from school and was afraid, because I had never seen a dead person before. All of my grandparents had had the good grace to insist on closed coffins when their time came; and anyway, they'd died when I was much younger, so I had not been expected to attend. But this was Nettie, someone I'd touched and talked with, someone my age. Someone. A human being my age. I was coldly trembling and everyone could see.

My friends genuinely tried to comfort me, told me going to a wake was nothing, they'd done it plenty of times. A dead person, they told me, just looked asleep, and usually looked a whole lot better than they'd ever looked alive.

My knees were actually knocking, just as I'd read about people's knees knocking when they were frightened. I was and they were. I can't even remember how I got to the Funeral Home, but I did and entered it and stood next to my now good friend Rosie, the one who'd baptized me "Queenie."

The funeral director directed us into a long, dark cold room, filled with Victorian furnishings and packed with people, friends of the family, relatives, New Town students. A line extended outside the door onto the sidewalk. Even through my fright, I thought this was odd. Most of the high school kids in attendance hadn't given much time to Nettie, except to shout terrible things at her, or make her fall down, or steal her books and lunches. But now, the whole school was paying attention to her. Finally. I knew I was there for the same reason they were; guilt. That, or just the chance to skip school.

I recalled with a stab of pain what a chore it had been for me to try being nice to Nettie and that Nettie had probably known that. I cringed again when I remembered the last Valentine's Day when Nettie had left a tiny box of red candies and a sweet card in my desk. I had been embarrassed, had not known how to react, and of course, had been unprepared to give Nettie anything, and wouldn't have anyway. So I thanked Nettie quickly in an offhanded, brusque way, not addressing the kindness of the gesture, not really looking at her, knowing if I did see her sad disappointment to my reaction it would have been too much for me. Me. It was all about *me* in that moment. I recalled Nettie's joyful eagerness as she'd watched me discover that gift in my desk, and how the homely girl's face had crumpled like a flower in a flame at my brief, harsh thanks. I stood there in that funeral home overwhelmed with grief and self-hatred.

How I wished with my very soul I'd told Nettie I'd liked and appreciated her, even if it had been just a small white lie. Silently, I swore repeatedly to myself that from that day on I'd tell everyone I cared about how much I loved them, even if it was an overstatement, just in case they died too soon. *Thank you for teaching me that, Nettie.*

I glanced around the room. Nettie's relatives looked just the way she had; short, squarely built, and wearing outfits so drab, Nettie's daily grey dress was a veritable rainbow by comparison. Many of them stood, crying quietly, not understanding. Nettie, I discovered from overhearing bits and pieces of hushed conversations, had been one of nine children, all much older than she. *Had she also been a mistake in her own family?*

My friends and I shook hands with Nettie's relatives and whispered stammered condolences. Their hands were cold and gelatinous, just like Nettie's had been on that day in Miss Ginocchio's Friday gym dance class. After the first few handshakes, I hardened to it and was able to go through with it without flinching. Much.

Rosie leaned close to me. "It's time now, honey. Let's go."

"Time? Time for what?" But I knew. "Oh, no, Rosie, I can't. Please, I can't. I want to remember Nettie as she was, not like--not like--"

Tugging at my gloved hand Rosie pulled me to the front of the huge, hushed room where the flower covered coffin rested I had so far avoided looking at.

"Oh, Rosie," I whispered to my friend. "Rosie. We don't have to, do we? I mean, there are so many people here, no one will know if we don't go up there. Please. Don't make me do it. I can't. I just can't." Something bitter was rising into my throat.

"Yes, Queenie, you can. Grow up! Don't be such a wimpass. You'll have to do it sometime, so you might as well do it now. I'll stay with you. Just do everything I do. I'll get you through it." Rosie grasped my elbow and when I tried to pull away, Rosie's grip became a steel band.

I sighed and because I had little choice, I obeyed my friend as we joined the long line waiting to approach the coffin. It crept along with agonizing slowness. I so wanted this torture to be over with. I desperately wanted to run. I kept my head bowed, following the shoes of the person ahead of me, and then my shins banged against a low kneeling stool. Suddenly, horribly, there in front of me was Nettie. I heard a blast of loud, terrible waterfall music in my ears that came and as quickly disappeared and then a crashing calm from nowhere washed over me. When my eyes rested on my dead friend, fear floated from me like smoke in a breeze.

With the soft lights beaming down on her, Nettie lay on tufted pink silk, a pillow beneath her head. The coffin was as big as a piano box, and Nettie, for the first time, looked tiny. She wore a lavender lace dress, with a neckline that reminded me of Kate Smith. A lavender bow pinned back her hair, and entwined in her waxen fingers was a white Rosary. A small white Bible had also been balanced in her hands although I could see that her fat fingers did not actually touch it. I wondered, crazily, if it were propped somewhere under there with toothpicks. Someone had made up the square face in a clumsy attempt to make Nettie beautiful. It did not. Never beautiful in life, expending this tremendous effort at making Nettie beautiful in death was, I thought, just simply insulting. And creepy. The funeral people had used thick make-up on her arms and all other exposed areas, apparently to hide the alligator skin. They'd curled her hair around her face, and it had been cut and styled.

I stared into the coffin and began to feel sick. I could not take my eyes away, could not blink. I felt a tug on my sleeve, and Rosie pulled me down to a kneeling position on the low, padded stool. Again I obeyed, folded my hands demurely and continued to stare in disbelief at Nettie's piteous remains, now so frighteningly close to me, bitter nausea rising higher in my throat. I was too close. I could see the large pores in Nettie's nose skin. I half expected Nettie to yawn, stretch and sit up because even with all the phony stuff piled on and around her, she did still look enough like Nettie, and she looked only asleep. I stared at the huge breasts, willing them to move up and down with breath. Certain they were moving, I turned excitedly to Rosie, who was rising now, pulling me up with her. Rosie, to my hanging icicle horror, suddenly leaned down and kissed Nettie on the forehead. I gasped. Straightening, Rosie gestured with her head and eyes that I was to do the same.

202

"No way, Rosie. There's no way in hell I'm gonna do that!" The whisper was hoarse and shrill, some of the words cracking. I looked around, my head jerking nervously, but no one was looking at me, or listening, except for a few impatient people in the line behind us.

And then, Rosie did the unforgivable; smiling sweetly, she pretended to place a comforting hand on the back of my neck. Not too gently, she shoved my head toward the corpse. *Oh, I can't. I can't. No.*

"Rosie!" I hissed at her. Rosie pushed me farther, closer to Nettie's head. I could see the layers of make-up clearly. It was thick, and made me flash to Silly Putty. I could smell the sweet, thick deadness of Nettie. Rosie's hand did not leave the back of my neck. I knew that if I didn't kiss Nettie, Rosie would shove me head-first into the coffin and I'd be stuck there, butt in the air, legs flailing.

With a strangled "Rosie, I'll kill you," I kissed Nettie's icy, dead forehead. Horribly, my lips slid on the thick makeup, now melting from the lights over the coffin, and the cold cement of the dead girl's skin made a new wave of nausea rise in my throat. I gagged. I was so terrified I'd vomit into the coffin, ruining even this moment for Nettie.

Finally allowed to stand, I wiped my mouth hard with the back of my hand and glared at Rosie. "I will hate you forever" I hissed. Then we gazed down at Nettie for a minute more. Feeling the bile rising in my throat, I concentrated on what Nettie might be wearing on her feet, hidden under the lower half of the closed coffin lid. Could it be that below this elegant dress (that Nettie would never have worn or even been seen wearing in her lifetime,) she was wearing her sensible brown Oxfords and short white socks? Or worse, was she barefoot? And were her feet big and sausagey, wet and cold and scaly the way her hands always were? I pushed my palm against my mouth to suppress the nervous thunder roaring from my guts to my throat where I knew just then that it would erupt not in vomit but into clamorous laughter. *What is wrong with me? This is my dead friend Nettie in front of me. Nettie—why do I want to laugh?? Why can't I swallow this down?* As I looked again at that terrible dress, the idiotic hairdo, the Kate Smith neckline and the gobs and gobs of make-up, I struggled to choke back weakly stifled laughter. But then it was Niagara, terrible, the force was terrible, and I then knew I would not be able to hold it in once the laughter blasted out of me. It would be only seconds until my body would split like a watermelon dropped from many stories up onto a cement street. I clamped both hands over my mouth. Rosie looked at me and thought I was trying to not regurgitate. She grabbed my arm and steered me rapidly outside.

"Queenie, Queenie," she pleaded, "For God's sake—don't puke, breathe, breathe---please--Jesus you'll make a mess…"

When we got out into the air, I unapologetically collapsed against Rosie, the laughter finally whooping out of me in huge blasts. I could not stop; it was utterly unstoppable and obscenely loud. I could feel my face becoming distorted. Rosie held onto me, concerned, laughing too. My eyes poured water and I thought of Al, which set me off into another paroxysm of screaming, shrieking laughter, and I was drooling, my screeches getting higher and higher. I wet my pants, and that caused more laughter. And then I began to collapse to the ground, dragging Rosie with me. In terrible pain, my abdomen and ribs ached brutally. Rosie began to laugh again and finally we were both on the ground, rolling, pounding, screaming, bellowing and hollering with uncontrollable, unstoppable mirth. Some of the guests came to the door, looked out at us, shrugged, and went back inside.

We began to lose our breath and laughter stopped abruptly. From flat on my stomach, I looked over at Rosie.

"Why are we laughing, Queenie?" asked Rosie, her voice soft and very somber. "Is this sick or what? What is wrong with us?" Both of us now had deadly serious expressions. At the exact same split second, we both erupted again, and it ripped out of us, exploding, raucous. We staggered to our feet, clutching each other. "Kee-Riste, Queenie, what was that all about? I thought I'd crap my drawers." Rosie tried to scold me, but could not, and we began to laugh again, but the energy was leaving us. We gasped for breath, brushed ourselves off, looked at each other and laughed. But only a little now, and softly.

"Honestly Rosie," I said, wiping my eyes with the heels of my hands, "I just don't know what happened. I began to think about Nettie, and her shoes and socks, and then that *awful* dress, and her hair, and I just lost it. I'm so sorry. Really, I'm sorry, but it got started and I couldn't stop it, and the harder I tried, the worse it got. Really, I won't do it again. Do you think this happens to other people? Maybe we should go back inside or something."

"Not on a bet, Queenie, not after the scene *you* just made. No, don't worry--I think we've done everything that's expected of us and

204

anyway, I got us a coupla mass cards. We can send 'em to the family. And know what? I think I read somewhere that when ya laugh like that at a sad time it's---well kinda good or something. Gets all the bad stuff out. Or something. I dunno. But it sure felt good, right?"

"Well Doctor Frood, thank you very much for that brilliant diagnosis," I said haughtily, and my friend Rosie and I came close to losing control again, but held tightly to each other and got the laughter to stop.

I was not sure what a mass card was, but decided to let it go, and to do what Rosie said. We joined a large crowd of New Town kids and went home. School would begin again. Time would wash away the guilt we all carried in varying degrees. Shortly, the hole Jeannette Capinerri had left in the student body would close. Jokes, creative, funny, crude, would begin about her and the way she'd left us. The desperate humor would maybe obliterate the guilt and justify the roles we students suspected we might have played in causing her death. And the jokes would, of course, let us hide.

I went to bed exhausted that night, after telling my parents about the funeral service. (They were distractedly concerned: The television was on.) As I lay in the dark, Nettie's small, forlorn horse pin lying next to me on the night table, I remembered that strange girl, and began to weep. "Aw Nettie," I sobbed. "Oh, Nets."

# CHAPTER 29

One night Thurston, a nice boy from The Academy called and invited me to his senior prom. I was just so excited and accepted immediately, but then realized that The Academy prom was the same night as New Town's junior prom. I was so sad that I had to decline.

"You can't go with me? How come?" Thurston asked, disappointed and clearly miffed. I could hear it plainly in his voice.

I thought for a minute about making something up, but then opted for honesty.

"Well, to tell you the truth, Thursty, I've been invited to the New Town junior prom and it's the same night. I was asked a couple of weeks ago. Sorry, Thurst, really. It would have been such fun to go with you. I hope we can go out together sometime. Can we? I mean would you want to?"

There was silence at the other end of the phone wire, and then he spoke again, a new tone in his voice. This time it was incredulity.

"You're going to a dance with a guy from *New Town??* Courtenay, are you kidding me?"

"Well, no, Thurston, I wouldn't kid about a serious thing like this. No way. I've got to go to the New Town prom because I promised."

"So, who's your date, Court? Some creep out on bail?"

Anger quickly bubbled from me.

"No, Thurston." My voice was a knife. "He's not out on bail because the cops never caught him after he stabbed his grandmother in the eye. Maybe next time he won't be so lucky. So for now, I'll go to the prom with him. Lucky for me I get a chance to date him before he gets life!"

There was no response on the other end.

"By the way, Thurston, the date of the Academy prom isn't very far away. What's the matter, couldn't get a date? So what did you do? Settle on me, the poor slob from New Town? Well, don't do me any favors, you simple tool. I've got better things to do than go to a dance with you." I hung up hard.

The big night arrived and the New Town gym had been transformed from a hard, wooden smelly room into a magic place. It was the only time of year the coaches and Mr. Wright would allow shoes to be worn in there. The huge ceiling lights were dimmed and tiny lights, like stars, twinkled from the overhead beams. The prom's theme was Springtime in Paris, and over in one corner stood an uncertain Eiffel Tower, constructed of Papier Mache and dozens of bent coat hangers. It listed precariously to the right, slowly bending and cracking under its own unwieldy weight. It would quite dramatically crash to the floor precisely as the last strains of "Good Night Sweetheart" played. No one was hurt except the feelings of the students who'd slaved over it for months.

In the center of the room stood a tall Arc De Triomphe, made of cartons from the supermarket. The dancers could dance under and around it, as occupying armies had marched under and around the real thing not so many years before. But who was thinking about that now?

The walls were decorated with enormous Henri de Toulouse-Lautrec can-can Moulin Rouge posters and up on the stage stood a long, flat boat, also made of boxes, earnestly attempting the look of the barges on the Seine. Everywhere were renderings of the City of Love. Huge life-sized drawings of artists at work painting Paris scenes hung on the walls.

The Prom Squad had gone into the woods in the dead of winter to pilfer young saplings which they'd stuck into big buckets of earth. These had been placed all around the gym floor. They had decorated each branch with paper leaves and paper pink blossoms, and had hung even more tiny lights amongst them. Long swaths of soft peach-colored netting swagged along the walls from all four corners of the big gym and were also hooked into the basketball hoops. It was lovely, a dazzling sight and it all even melted the hearts of the toughest greaser although they went to great lengths to not let that show.

The band members were all dressed like French Apache dancers in striped boat-necked collarless shirts with long sleeves and tight bell-bottom pants. Thin, curled painted mustaches decorated their hairless faces, berets perched on their DA's, and cigarette stubs stuck from the corners of their mouths. The girl singers wore tight red satin blouses, cut low, tight black skirts, belted and slit to one hip. They wore fish-net stockings and spike heels, and their hair was pulled back with wide, sharp curls glued to their cheeks. The fake moles fell off their faces constantly, and the dancers spent time vainly searching the floor for them when all the while the black dots were stuck to the bottoms of their shoes. As they undulated provocatively to the music, these young damsels gave the audience sweeping up and down looks with their long false eyelashes, the way they'd seen French dancers do in the movies.

I stood transfixed, looking and looking at the scene. I felt all soft inside and the scene made me so happy. I grinned and felt an odd kind of love down on the inside of my heart, a soft thrill. I'd never felt that before.I quietly watched the couples in tuxedos and floating, diaphanous dresses. *How beautiful—it's like--- like visions.* I did not think even once about the Holiday Balls.

The full dresses were a boon to those ardent young bucks desirous of copping the occasional "accidental" feel. Their thoughts were riveted on some post-prom action, and thus, the unfortunate young studs were given to premature, brassbound erections. To cover them, the afflicted boys desperately held tightly to their partners--during the dances, in between dances, during the breaks, and on into the night, burying their persistent shame in the folds of the girls' skirts. Some girls knew, some liked it, some were merciful and let it continue. The young bucks remained in that condition until the bewildered and finally cranky young ladies broke roughly away and ran into the girls' room, leaving the mortified, tumescent young men frantically searching for cover, cursing the fates that caused this problem and would do nothing to make it go away.

Al Scaramoozo had gone all out for me that night. He'd even consulted an optometrist to see if there was something he could take to dry up his eyes for just that one night. The doctor gave him a prescription for some pills, which Al dutifully took before the dance, resulting in his spending the entire night fighting an overpowering desire to sleep and to swallow huge amounts of fluid, any kind at all. But he was the perfect gentleman nonetheless and laughed casually when I mentioned that he seemed to have "lost his edge." And through it all, his eyes poured more than they'd ever done before.

I didn't mind, as long as he didn't try to dance cheek-to-cheek. That could get messy. I was having a great time. Al had brought me the perfect corsage which didn't stick out too far in front of me. I'd had my hair curled at a beauty parlor for the first time and was quite pleased with the way I looked. As I danced with Al, my head pressed into his shoulder, I truly didn't mind at all that my new hairdo was being flattened on one side by the prodigious and involuntary weepings that constantly dampened Al's collars and occasional shirt fronts. I grinned. For a year that had begun in abject terror for me, Courtenay Wolcott Scott, it wasn't ending badly at all.

# CHAPTER 30

It was the first Saturday in June. I'd driven myself to the Y two days before, so I could apply for the job for the upcoming summer and felt no nervousness at all as I walked into the small, cluttered office at the YMCA. The interview had gone well and easily and the young interviewer named Amy didn't seem to care that I'd attended two local high schools in 4 years. Nice relief, that. For once it didn't matter.

She asked a lot of questions like how had I heard about the job (newspaper) and how did I know I'd do well at the job. I told her I had no idea how to answer that, but that I'd lately had an overwhelming need to do something for other people instead of myself and for even more reasons I didn't understand, I wanted to work with kids, "normal or poor or handicapped." Even I cringed when those words came out, but Amy reacted as if she were impressed, and after what seemed to be a few hundred more questions that I suppose I'd answered well, she stood up, I stood up, we shook hands and she said "Courtenay, we would love to have you work for us at the Y. Welcome aboard." I grinned and squeezed her hand perhaps a bit too tightly. Amy handed me a pile of papers and said "Take this pen and fill all these out. You'll be paid every other Friday and we never let any of our employees down on that issue. You can count on us!" She smiled widely and left the room. I sat and began to fill out all the papers. I had gotten a job. By myself. I felt grown up and Amy, my new boss, liked me. And so, surprisingly, did I.

Days later on that first Saturday in June, Sally and I sat on the edge of the club's pool, trying for the first tan of the year. Soft, warm water bubbled against our legs.

"But Court!" Sally was wide-eyed. "I can't believe this. You turned down a tropical cruise with other kids and NO PARENTS for a job at the YMCA? That awful shabby place? What?? You're putting me on, right?"

I couldn't adequately answer that, because I didn't fully understand it myself. I did understand that of late I was experiencing an uncomfortable sense of trying to balance, to make everything come out even, and to have everyone like me, everyone in both schools. I was beginning to realize it wasn't working out so well.

"Yeah, well Sal, what the heck. Those cruises can get pretty boring. I don't know." I sighed and looked away. Sally liked tropical cruises with rich people. So did I. I mean, what's not to like? But things were different now, and I sensed they'd never be the same as they were a year ago. I was confused, and I was beginning to notice lately that I didn't feel as if I belonged anywhere. And too, there was no one to whom I could explain this. No one who would understand, anyway. And I often feared I'd have this in-between, not fully belonging anywhere feeling for the rest of my life.

"Well," Sally said, swinging her legs through the turquoise water, "OK, I suppose cruises *can* get boring. But Court, I mean, how boring can it *get* with great guys, terrific food, parties day and night and gorgeous scenery?"

"I don't know how to answer that, Sal." I looked at my friend and knew that Sally thought I might be crazy. "I guess working at the Y is just something I've got to do. And no matter what reason I give for doing it, it comes out sounding like I'm Florence Nightingale or Joan of Arc or somebody. But hey! Maybe it'll be one of those 'Great Life Experiences' kids are always supposed to be searching for! I mean, my parents tell me I'm supposed to be looking for those. Don't yours?"

"Yeah, sure," murmured Sally. "All the time." She shook her hair and sighed. "I sure hope my folks don't make me get a job."

"Oh Sal, my parents didn't make me. I came to this conclusion kinda on my own."

"You did? What on earth made you decide to do that?"

"Honestly I dunno. Anything I say about this sounds so lame, but it's kinda ---- well---- OK don't laugh--- I have so awfully much in my life and I never did a thing to earn it—I just got it---born into it---so I've been thinking lately that I oughtta maybe do some kind of---well, payback or something. So the Y was a good chance to maybe do that."

"Oh Courtenay, for heaven's sake. You don't have to pay anyone back. You and I were just born lucky, right? Who says we have to pay people back?"

"Well, no one Sal, not anyone really. It's just this queer feeling I can't seem to shake."

"That stupid public school has screwed up your thinking, Courtenay. Your parents should never have sent you to that public school. You're not thinking straight. Why did they do that anyway?"

"I still don't know Sally. Every time I bring it up they change the subject or begin to look like scared rabbits. I don't think I'll ever really know why I had to go there."

"All the kids at The Academy keep talking about it, wondering what happened. Why it happened."

"Me too, all the time. Every single day. But one thing I have to make kinda clear Sally--- I really want to work at the Y this summer and I really do want to do some good in my life, something good for other people, or something. Know what I mean? I know this all sounds icky."
"Actually Courtenay, I do not have a clue what you mean. That awful place. That New Town High School and those disgusting, dirty hoods have messed with your head and I'm beginning to think you'll never be the old Courtenay again."

We two old friends sat and stared at each other, not comprehending, a huge band of thick, hard air had formed between us and I began to realize it would likely never vanish.

Sally straightened up and cleared her throat. "Hey, Court," she said, obviously wanting to change the subject, "all the kids wonder how come you never tell us any more stories about those New Town pigs anymore. Don't tell me they've all gotten smart or something. Come on, Courtenay, you're not starting to *like* those creeps, are you?"

I stiffened at the sting of anger I felt toward my oldest and best friend. Taking a deep breath, I suppressed the feeling. "Ah, I don't know, Sal, I guess they're all about the same. Nothing much new going on down there. I'll fill you in next fall."

"What do you mean, `next fall'?! You mean you're going back there in September? No! I thought your parents were OK about sending you back to The Academy, and had finally made their point, whatever that was. We've all been expecting you to come back to The Academy for your senior year!" Sally leaned forward, gaping at me.

"Well, Sally, I --" I stalled, running my fingers nervously through my long hair. Again, I just didn't have a reasonable answer. "Well, Sal, when they told me I had to go there they said it was for a full two years, that I'd graduate from there, so I've never really thought it would be any different."

"Oh but Courtenay, you've *done* it. I mean, you've had the `public school experience.' Won't they let you come back where you belong now?" asked Sally.

I looked at my old friend, uneasy with the intensity of her questions. *Where do I belong? Where?* To ease the situation, I stretched and yawned. The warm sun was making me sleepy anyway.

"Well, you remember Sal, a couple of years ago, my parents asked me if I wanted to plan a coming-out party, and well, I know it's the thing to do, but I sort of just don't like them. I sort of think they're kind of old fashioned, don't you? Girls don't `come out' anymore, do they? Well OK, yeah, I guess some do. But I thought that stuff went on back in the old days when girls had to 'come out' to find a husband. Well, that's just not for me. It embarrasses me kinda, you know? And besides, I don't want to get married. I really and truly want to pursue a career in journalism."

"Journalism? Really, Court? That sounds wonderful!" But Sally's face did not match her words. I looked sharply at her, confused, feeling patronized. "Whatever that means." Sally laughed. "But as for me," she went on, gazing dreamily at the clouds, "I intend to marry a filthy rich man who loves horses, so I can own a whole herd of Arabians or Thoroughbreds and spend my days riding, going to shows and traveling around the world. You know, stuff like that."

"Gee. I'm impressed, Sally. Sounds as if you're planning on contributing to mankind in a really big way."

"Yeah, well, ya do whatcha gotta do, doncha know." We both laughed. "And you know, Courtenay, you and all this new `save the world' stuff you're doing; first public school, then the YMCA summer program, and now this journalism junk... you sound like you're turning into one of those beatniks or something."

I turned my head away, unwilling to have Sally see my unexpected smile. Why did this accusation flatter me? I cleared my throat and turned back. "Yeah, right, Sal. That'd be the day. Beatnik! Ha! Wouldn't old Walter and Helen love that!" I held my nose delicately and giggled.

"And you know what's really queer Sal? The whole reason for going to public school just hasn't happened! You remember they gave me all that `we'll have to tighten our belts' bull last year? Well, I've been waiting for something to happen, but we've still got Emma and Mary and Fred and all the other ones who come to work around the place.

We never got rid of any cars either, and my God, the parties are coming more often than they ever did! I just don't know what gives. You got a clue?"

"Me?" answered Sally, eyebrows raised. "How would I know? You don't think your father thought it would be `good for you' to hang around those awful people, do you?"

Again, I bristled at Sally's description of the kids I'd come to know. "No, no," I said quickly. "It *can't* be that. I mean, my father still can't get through five seconds without saying something nasty about my friends----umm--I mean the kids at New Town." *Why did I change that?*

"So, I still can't figure out why he sent me there," I went on. "I mean, it really puzzles me, but if I ask him, he has a cow and gets really mad and won't talk to me. But then he never talks to me anyway, so what's new? Oh well, I guess that's the way the cookie crumbles."

We left the pool to lie down on a couple of nearby chaise lounges, to cover ourselves with suntan lotion, and to begin the very serious business of boy-watching. And as I lay there, the sun baking through to my bones, turning the lotion to molten ooze, I looked around at the familiar families reclining and playing around the pool, and I felt separate from them all and experienced a yearning loneliness, as if I were on the outside looking in.

The next day when I walked through the door at the YMCA, I thought about that sunny afternoon with Sally at poolside and smiled. I walked up to the desk and announced my arrival to a smiling Amy, eager to begin my work with underprivileged and perhaps handicapped children.

# CHAPTER 31

Had I been suddenly thrust through the door of the YMCA without the calluses I'd acquired in a public school, I would have found myself far out of my element, and afraid to be there, too. But I went through those Y doors at the end of June 1956, with a bold and eager smile. I felt strong and courageous. I was aware I was beginning to learn to function smoothly in different worlds although never quite in balance with either.

"Dammit all, Joanne, get the hell up. Stop faking. I know you're faking." But I could not stop the grin spreading across my face. This kid was good at what she did!

I stood over the limp body of the small ten-year-old blonde girl lying at the YMCA's pool's edge. She was as still as the tiles beneath her tiny, wet body.

"Get UP, Joanne," I shouted, prodding her leg with my foot.

"OK, OK, lemme alone, OK?" the child whined, and then, "Bitch."

Joanne Walniski finally stood up, glaring at me, whom she'd decided to hate. Despite the fact that she was an orphan being raised by an indifferent aunt, no one took pity on her. Perhaps in retaliation Joanne had developed a remarkable act; she would go about her business, then suddenly her head would fly back, her eyes would roll up into her head and she'd go completely limp, collapsing to the floor in a dead faint and not responding when people screamed and rushed to her side. She could lie still like that for an hour or more if she chose. No slaps, stabs, or shakings ever got a response until Joanne felt she'd gotten the attention she desired. Her performances were the stuff of Oscars. It took me two faints to catch on.

"Watch your language, Joanne. Show some respect, or I'll throw you out of here."

"What language? Wuh? Wuh? Me?" Joanne suddenly became a bewildered little girl, wrongly accused, stabbed to her tender heart.

"But you swore at me just a minute ago," she said in a tiny voice, her lower lip stuck out so far it looked like a tiny red shelf. A fat tear coursed down her cheek. *How in hell does she do that, anyway?*

I sighed. "Look. Joanne. I know I swore. I'm sorry. But I'm an adult and I'm allowed to. You're a kid and you aren't. So drop it. I'm unimpressed by your dramatics. Now look. We've got a lot of kids to deal with in here. I can't pay constant attention to you, you know. I mean you're a cute kid and all, but it's my responsibility to teach swimming to *all* those kids out there. So, if you want to faint, could you please do it outside, or after class or something? You're really becoming a big pain in the ass, you know?"

"Ah, OK, Miss Wolcott," said Joanne, taking my hand. "I wuz on'y kiddin'." She let my hand go and leapt into the pool. I went on with my swimming class, keeping a special eye on Joanne. I understood the child was hungry for attention because I myself dearly understood that craving, but there were too many kids and not enough counselors. But still, I loved the little expert swooner.

I had never felt better. At the Y, I was finally doing something that mattered. The feeling was new to me and I reveled in it like an athlete with a trophy. Each day flew past and I grabbed at the hours as if they were bubbles in the sky, hating to see them disappear. I couldn't wait to get up and get back to work every morning and even chafed at accepting my paltry salary, thinking it was somehow wrong to be paid for doing what I loved.

Amy finally introduced me one day to Mr. Clare Savage, the Y's director. He was a kind man, balding, with nice eyes and he seemed to like me right away. He had a habit of staring hard into the eyes of the person with whom he was chatting and I kind of liked that. He had the gift of making people feel important and I was glad he was Amy's boss and therefore mine too.

The YMCA offered an excellent program for kids that included a variety of athletic classes. I was so delighted to see that Mr. Savage made certain that each child, regardless of how badly he or she performed in a sporting event, would go home with some sort of award. He understood the importance of that and the kids at the Y responded happily to this knowing they'd never be mocked or made to feel like lesser people for being prize-less.

Clare Savage also instituted a somewhat controversial new policy: he insisted that "mentally retarded and Down syndrome children" be allowed to enjoy certain hours at the Y, time reserved just for them when they need not feel the discomfort of being compared to the "normal" kids. The board of directors had held many meetings on this delicate issue and Mr. Savage had fought hard to win. Some of his esteemed and learned colleagues had insisted that "those" kids best be kept in their own environment, that normal people had no need to be subjected to those troubling sights and sounds. Angrily, Clare Savage prevailed, writing long impassioned letters and filibustering the board members. Finally, one evening, exhausted and wanting to get some sleep before they had to get up for work in the morning, the board reluctantly agreed, and the local YMCA opened its doors to "retarded, physically handicapped and Down syndrome kids." The irritable men gave the handicapped kids all the Y had to offer, with special instructors to assist them. But there was a stipulation: the "normal" kids were at all times to be segregated from the "not normal" attendees and to have their own special hours. And that seemed fine with Clare Savage who knew it was prudent to move slowly in this matter.

Clare Savage seemed in every way a good man, loved and admired by everyone. In spite of his being so pushy, the board of directors was pleased that he was in charge of the YMCA and spoke often about how well he was doing and what a splendid addition he was to their fair city. They congratulated themselves on their excellent choice. They relented even more by letting the Y stay open during evening hours just for these "special" kids. Parents felt comfortable with leaving them there for two hours and coming back for them later giving them some free time from the intense care required for these challenged and loving kids.

And there were so many kids at the Y! Like Scotty, the little boy who stole everything. Scotty liked to boldly insist that any item that went unclaimed during the Friday Lost and Found announcements was his. His timing was superb for one so young. He'd "steal the pennies off a dead man's eyes," Mr. Savage would often say. Years later when Scotty was killed while flying a rescue mission helicopter during the Viet Nam war, his wife found many of these small treasures from her husband's besmudged past in a tightly taped and tied box on a shelf under his basement workbench.

And there was Dana, a kid too small for his age. Dana fought with everyone and anyone, for any reason or none. I sometimes wondered if maybe he'd developed a need to prove himself because of his lack of size. He was desperately poor, never knowing from one week to the next where his home would be, where he'd sleep or eat, and I surmised it must have made him restive and defensive. His parents, who lived on welfare, had decided years before they'd had children that it might be nice to travel around the country and see it all, especially if they could somehow manage to make "the Gummint" pay for it, and they did. And so as their family grew, they'd work at menial jobs, get some money together, pack the kids into their rusted, broken trailer, and take off "to see something new." They'd stay in each new place for a while, just long enough to get their children into a new school, see them make friends and establish roots and identity, then off they'd go again on their endless quest. Dana had to fight at each new school since he was new and small, both conditions perfect excuses for the established kids to beat the crap out of him. Dana discovered years later that his parents were not exactly the roving free spirits they professed being; they were really constantly running from the law, just one or two days ahead of the sheriff. It seems Dana's distant cousin's daughter had been raped and the cousin and a friend went after the man who'd done it. They found him asleep in his car. They shot him. But eventually, they got caught. The jury was unsympathetic; they'd shot the wrong man.

I used to try to get through to Dana, to talk with him, show him I could be a friend to be trusted, but my overtures were met with derisive, childish put-downs. I understood. I knew how it felt to be alone. He was too young to have established a vocabulary big or clever enough to destroy another human being, so he used his small fists and smaller lexicon of mostly curses as courageously as he could, especially when I tried to show that crazy boy affection or interest. He trusted no one. But not completely understanding my motives, I persisted, even though I was never sure I got through. Occasionally, I'd actually see a tiny glimmer of acceptance in his eyes, and I had the satisfaction of knowing that for a couple of short, hot summer months, I had been able to convince young Master Dana that with me, he need not prove anything, and that he was safe, respected and even loved.

I never told anyone at New Town or The Academy about my fragile connection with little Dana, but I loved him. I did. Did he know? Yes. Did he care? Yes. Was he able to acknowledge it? No.

Many years later, twelve people sitting on three long rows of benches told Dana he would be spending the remaining two thirds of his life in Alcatraz off the coast of San Francisco for stabbing his employer to a nearly instant death at a barbeque celebrating Dana' five exemplary and successful years with the man's trucking company. Dana it seems, had flown into a rage when his mildly inebriated employer who'd been hoisting a few and who was cooking Dana's steak to medium rare, just the way he liked it, began to poke good natured fun at Dana's small size. Dana, never terribly good natured about this issue, wrenched the barbeque fork from the man's hand and made it quickly and abundantly clear that he was not amused, by shoving it straight into the man's heart. Mercifully his boss died almost instantly there on the grass, the long tines of the fork and the wooden handle sticking from his heart and staining the grass around him while the steaks cooked to a more well-done degree than Dana would have preferred.

I recall reading about this and not being too awfully surprised but definitely feeling sad that during my time at New Town, I had not been able to penetrate that small boy's dark and angry heart. Shortly after Dana's sentencing, "The Rock" was closed down by Attorney General Robert F. Kennedy because the men in the suits decided it was too costly to keep it going. Dana was therefore sent to Leavenworth Prison in Kansas, where he stayed until he was too old to be set free, after serving a sixty-seven-year sentence.

There were only a couple of weeks of YMCA camp remaining, so I took the $200 gift certificate I'd gotten for my last birthday to the Down Beat and invited all the Y kids in my charge to come into the store to pick out a couple of records to keep. I'd had the foresight to warn the store's owner about the arrival of this fractious group, and he was able to evacuate the store minutes before the onslaught. The boisterous charges spent a wonderful two hours listening to (and ruining) many of the sample listening records, and walked out with the tunes of their dreams clutched tightly in their arms. That many of them had no record players was a minor consideration.

# CHAPTER 32

"All work and no play, y'know, Court," said Sally on the phone one evening in August. "Come on, I've got tickets to see My *Fair Lady*. It's got Rex Harrison in it, and they say he's fabulous even though he can't sing or anything. I heard all he really does is talk all the songs. Anyway, there's this new girl, what's her name, Julie something, who's in it too, and everyone says she sings like an angel! I don't like that opera kind of singing, but oh well. It must be good though--it's always sold out. Everyone's seen it except us, even my old fogey parents. Oh yeah, Andrews, that's it. So let's do it. Be there, or be square. My treat, Court. Let's go."

"Well sure Sal," I began, and stopped. I knew when my old friend was on a roll, little could stop her.

"There are only a couple of weeks left 'til school begins," Sally went on, oblivious to my trying to speak, "so let's live it up! The old man got me six tickets, can you believe it? We're in like Flynn. Probably wants me out of the house so he and Mom can make whoopee all afternoon. Ok, I know, that's totally disgusting. So! Let's get the rest of the gals and make a day of it, OK? Come on! Say yes. You know you want to and I am not taking no for an answer!"

"Oh, Sally, you won't have to! I'm ready!!" I was thrilled at the idea. It had been a long time since I'd had a chance to get dressed up and go into the city with my oldest friends. We sat, heads together, laughing, touching, happy to be making plans to meet our dearest friends under the clock at the Biltmore Hotel in New York City. We'd have tea by the potted palms at small tables with gleaming silver and glassware on thick, pure white linen tablecloths. Dinner would be at The Tavern on the Green. We'd then charge outside to flag down a taxi, and get to the theater in time to see this glorious new musical we'd read so much about. I just could not wait for the day to arrive.

And when it finally did, we girls all met under the famous old hotel's clock, squealing and greeting one another as though they hadn't seen each other for years. We sat down to tea, full of gossip and laughter and requisite boy-talk. But I felt weirdly out of rhythm with my old friends. I would not, however, let this annoying feeling ruin my day.

*I just haven't been in a lot of these things they're laughing about. I feel like I'm a step behind everyone. What is wrong with me?* None of them seemed to notice my discomfort, however. Brushing away these thoughts, I grinned, listened happily, and made all the appropriate noises at the all the proper times.

*How pretty we all are!* I gazed with love at my chattering, glowing group of friends. How really, really pretty. Excited! Happy! *I'm going to memorize this.* But my New Town friends' faces inexplicably flashed into my mind. Again, I brushed those thoughts away.

My friends and I all wore small, expensive hats, that day, some with veils, and our dresses were understated and pretty. Each of us had on real jewelry: a small pin, a string of pearls, small gold earrings. Spotless short white gloves and purses that matched our shoes completed our ensembles. I felt so secure to be back in this genteel circle. Off in a corner musicians in white tie and tails played chamber music just loudly enough to be enjoyed.

"Hey! Ladies! We gotta go!" Sally rose so abruptly she knocked her teaspoon onto the marble floor. She never glanced at it.

"We'll miss dinner if we don't get going. And I don't want to miss the beginning of the show. Curtain goes up at 8:40 sharp, y'know, so we've got a couple of hours to go stuff ourselves up at the Tavern. Come on. Let's run to the Ladies Room, and then go grab a cab."

Our group rose obediently, and trooped through the venerable hotel to the elegant Ladies Room. Made up, coifed, shined, brushed off and brushed up by the starched black woman attendant, we, behatted and begloved young lovelies deposited a noisy handful of change into the porcelain bowl left for that purpose on the dressing table. We then swished through the hotel, knowing absolutely we were making a glorious impression.

When we reached the sidewalk, one of the girls asked the doorman to fetch us a cab, and handed him a dollar. We stood in a row and leaned forward slightly, waiting for his piercing whistle. I glanced over at the doorman. He was standing quietly, grinning at the line of pretty girls, so taken with us that he obviously had temporarily forgotten his assignment. I knew we looked so fresh, young, and very innocent, and of course, perfect. Not a single item of our clothing was even wrinkled as we stood with our gloved hands folded, tiny purses tucked properly under our arms. The late afternoon sun shown on our small, perfect hats and our hair and on our eager glowing faces, and a soft summer breeze blew our skirts into gently billowing ripples. The doorman breathed more quickly and the noises and smells of the big city were not there for the moments he stood and watched us all in a row of glowing, shining young girls. I could see he was mesmerized.

I looked down at my hands. My short kid gloves needed buttoning, so I turned my left palm up, tugged the glove into place with my right hand, and began to button the cuff.

It was so soft and swift, silently speeding past my face so fast that I could not believe it at first. I hardly felt it and then did, felt the breeze of it as it sailed past my face, and then I definitely saw it. A gentle, warm splat on my upturned palm. I looked up at the sky, frowning, and then back to my palm. I looked at my friends, but they were watching the street for the cab. I looked back at my hand with a blank, non-registering expression.

"Hey girls," I said quizzically. "Will you look at this? I can't believe what just happened here." I was completely calm.

The girls peered over at me with interest, and there, lying squarely in the palm of my left hand was a large, multicolored pigeon deposit. A healthy young pigeon, lusty bombardier with perfect and feckless aim, had let one go, and it had sailed down neatly into my upturned and pristinely gloved hand. *What are the odds??*

Suddenly, the girls in line next to me screamed so loudly the doorman jerked from his reverie to eye-popping alarm. They laughed, they screamed, and howled. "Eeeeeoooo, my God, it's a turd, pigeon shit, a bird took a shit into Courtenay's hand!" "Yuck, I'm gonna barf!" "Don't tell my parents I said shit!" "Oh, will you look at that, look, a bird laid one on old Courtenay." "Hey Court! It couldn't have happened to a nicer girl." "Save it Courtenay! Put it in your scrapbook. You know how you love to memorize and save everything. This'll be perfect!" "Hey! I got it! Let it dry out and make a pendant of it! You can wear it to the Holiday Ball! Keep your hand out—maybe you can get some matching earrings!" "I think I'm gonna be sick!" They would not stop. Their shrieking ad-libs came so thick and fast that passers-by stopped to listen and laugh along with them, some applauding. My friends laughed and choked, and laughed more, not stopping, while I stood silently, a quizzical look on my face, looking blankly at my upturned palm, not at all amused.

Gingerly, I pulled the glove from my hand by the tip of one finger. And then dropped it, like a queen, into the gutter. I peeled off the other one, and dropped it next to its mate.

I said, "Those gloves are kid leather, they are expensive. And, they are gone!" I turned, gave the group a murderous look, and swept back into the hotel to scrub the offending hand in the Ladies Room. My oldest friends stood in a staggering group, laughing, coughing, gasping for air, falling all over themselves. Their hair was askew, hats hanging over one ear, a couple of high- heeled shoes had fallen off, and their purses lay on the sidewalk. They had not seen anything ever as funny, and their hysterical laughter during the acclaimed Broadway musical comedy that night was much louder and longer than it really had to be.

# CHAPTER 33

I charged around the corner of a hallway in the YMCA building. I was late, running quickly to an evening meeting. I'd always hated being late and was really late that night. I skidded to a stop, my shoes squealing on the linoleum flooring. I saw a man---I squinted. It was--- no—was it? I began to walk fast toward him.

"Father!!" I shrieked. He suddenly turned and I nearly collided with him. *Why is he here? He has never been in this building before. And--- why does he look so different?* He was wearing casual and rather colorful clothing, startlingly unusual for my parent. I stared up at him, my mouth hanging wide. My father stopped and looked down at me with a very surprised scowl.

"I…. I… Oh my God, I thought you were here only during the day," he said, more like blurted. He looked confused, sort of even frightened. His voice was forced, choky. *What??* I wasn't sure if he was scared or confused. He leaned to the side and looked around me and up and down the hallway, behind me, over my head. *What in the world is going on here?? And why is he carrying a camera? When did he ever get interested in photography?*

"Well, I usually am, Dad," I stammered. "Here. During the day. Yeah, you're right ---- but umm-- they have meetings here at night once in a while to talk about the kids and future programs. You know-- ideas and everything. You remember, I told you about it at dinner tonight. Dinner? Tonight? At home? Remember?"

"Oh, yes," my father stammered. "Of course. Well there Courtenay, I guess I forgot. Well, no, I remembered. As a matter of fact, I—I---- dropped in to see--- to see how you're getting along!" He coughed and again looked rather wildly up and down the hallway. Then behind him. Then behind me. *What on earth is going on??*

"Are you enjoying your summer job?" he asked me with a forced smile. *What?? He doesn't give a damn about my summer job.* My father looked so helplessly flabbergasted, I felt an oddly strange pity for him. He never asked me *anything* about my job, not ever, so what was this all about?

"W---well Father," I stammered uncertainly as I glanced up at him. "Thanks ummm—thanks for asking, I do enjoy this job a lot. It's been just great." *Why am I embarrassed? Why is he embarrassed? I'm hating this.*

I looked up at him quickly and grinned. "Hey!" I said, "since you're here anyway Daddy, would you like to come to the meeting with me? There's coffee, ---I'd avoid the brownies—always stale---and you could meet the other counselors and the director and everyone. Come on! This'll be great! Maybe you know the director, Mr. Savage. Do you know him? *Why is he blinking so hard? Why are his eyes so wide?* "It would be fun," I stammered on, "and I'd be so proud to have you there." I smiled encouragingly and tugged him toward the meeting room.

My father stiffened. "NO!" he said sharply. Then more softly: "No, thanks, Courtenay," he said more softly. "As I say, I just stopped in to see how you're getting along." *What??*

I absolutely knew he was lying, but *why* was he? I could see he was agitated, very upset so I knew not to press him to come with me, to let him get on his way, but I was awfully puzzled.

When I turned to wave on my way to my meeting, my father was nearly running in the other direction toward the exit. *What on earth was that?? He's never----I've never seen him like this. I'll ask him tomorrow.*

But I knew I'd never know why my father was at The Y that night and why he was acting so strangely, and I knew I'd never ask him either.

The final night of YMCA day camp at the end of August was a poignant one for me. The kids were subdued and downcast, some even cried. Many of them had either bought, borrowed or perhaps stolen small gifts for me and some of the other counselors. A tiny plastic change purse. A vibrantly colored Pop-It necklace of plastic beads. An ashtray made from a seashell. A broken Zippo cigarette lighter. A snapshot of one of the campers. Several sweet poems. The pile was pathetic and small, so different from the glittering, opulent piles of gifts I'd become used to at home. But I kept every single gift from those Y kids for the rest of my life, hidden like a priceless treasure in a box at the back of all the closets in all of the homes I'd ever own. I hugged them all good-bye and told them how much they'd meant to me, how they'd made my life happy and better, how I expected them to stay strong and focused. Many of them clung hard to me before they got into their parents' cars. It was the hardest and saddest and happiest evening of my life. Those kids had loved me unconditionally and did not care if I was wealthy or poor. I knew I'd never forget them and I never did.

The ending of the YMCA day camp marked a new beginning for me. It was now time to prepare for my Senior year at New Town High School.

# CHAPTER 34

I hadn't had "the dream" for the entire summer, and its sense of horrifying helplessness had finally begun to disappear from my memory. But the night before I was to begin my second and last year at New Town High School, it returned. In this version, when I was running to and from Remington, I turned to him, dreamwise, and asked him why he was still in the dream, since I'd only seen him a very few times during the summer. Remington didn't answer, and his expression did not change as he came close to me and drifted away again in slow motion as if attached to a flaccid elastic band. I turned and asked the same of Dom, having not seen him at all during the summer, and his response was the same as Remington's.

So I made a decision, dreamwise, to go through the dream to its end--lake, bridge and all--then to wake up and get on with the first day of my last year at public school. A clean sweep.

On that first morning of my last year at New Town High School, I recalled my feelings on that September day in 1955 when Fred had first driven me down the hill. *How childish I was. What a baby.* I had grown and the kinds of things that had upset me a year ago could not possibly faze me now. I was certain I would never be afraid of anything again, because I was certain I'd never face anything as bad as those experiences. I'd made it through, and because of the things that had happened to me, I was positive I had at last become a woman. A real grown-up.

Fred and I drove past the estates and the Country Club, with its big black sign at the entrance. The Star of David had been removed, but its outline could still be seen on top of the gold lettering. Jews had at last been accepted into the elite Country Club. But I knew "accepted" was not the correct word to be used here. They had simply gotten into the Club because even rich people had to eventually stop taking stands on old worn out prejudices.

When I saw the sign with its rubbed-out Star of David, I remembered something troubling I'd overheard in my family's living room one summer's evening several years ago. Just as all children always have, I had found the perfect spot at the top of the stairs on the second floor, where I could hear and see everything that went on in the living room, without anyone knowing I was there.

Mr. Meyerson, a good friend of my father's, had stopped by with the express purpose of insisting he be allowed to join the Country Club. He had young children and lived near the club grounds, and he wanted his kids to have access to the Club's pool, tennis courts and other summer activities. "To be with their friends," he'd said. "Our kids are so left out of everything, Walter."

I physically cringed when I heard his lamentable request in a soft, imploring voice, remembering one night when my Academy friends and I, including the Meyerson kids had arrived at the Club's gate. I remembered how we'd stood there, uncertain, embarrassed, then all the other kids and I entered the Golden Gates, leaving the Meyersons behind.

"Come on, Sam," my father had said that night as I hid at the top of the stairs. "You know I'd love nothing better than to get you in. But my hands are tied. You know that, Sam."

"But Walter, come on, you can put me up for membership. You've got influence at the Club. God, you've been a member there forever. No one would dare to blackball me if you gave the nomination." Meyerson's continued pleading made me acutely uncomfortable. The two men talked for a long time, sometimes with raised voices, sometimes with sadness. Eventually Mr. Meyerson left, his request not honored.

"Mother?" I'd said the next morning.

"Yes dear, what is it?" my mother answered, studying her newly polished nails.

"Why wouldn't Father allow Mr. Meyerson to join the Club? I sort of heard them talking last night."

Helen Wolcott sighed and shook her hands in the air to speed the drying time.

"It's a shame you had to hear that Courtenay, but Mr. Meyerson really had no business speaking about this to your father. No business at all. He knows better and has for a long time." Her voice was cold.

"But why, Mother? He's a perfectly nice man and I really like his kids. We hang around together and we..."

228

"Courtenay dear, you're old enough to understand, and so I'll tell you. Mr. Meyerson cannot be put up for Club membership because his grandfather was a Jew, and no one having even a trace of Jewish blood can be allowed to join the Club."

"Oh Mother, for heaven's sake!" I began.

My mother looked at me sharply. I nearly laughed. She hardly ever looked at me, but now it was sharply!

"Now don't get all huffy with me, my dear," she said, her cultured, soft voice tinged with uncharacteristic anger. My mother rarely displayed emotion, so this was a surprise.

"Your father and I have nothing to do with this. We don't make the rules at the Club and we cannot change them. Nor do we want to. Furthermore, Sam Meyerson had no business putting your father into that awkward position. It was extremely embarrassing. Club membership indeed. What gall! And imagine, his grandfather being a Jew and all. Really, he should have known better. I can assure you, Courtenay my dear, we shall be having precious little to do with the Meyersons in the future." With that, she stood, patted her short beige hair, swept grandly from the room, and I never hated her more.

As Fred drove me to the bus stop, I remembered with shame that I had not reacted at all to what my mother had said that morning. I knew I would always have strong feelings on the subject, were the scene to be replayed. I wished it could be. I fantasized that if it all could happen again, I'd rush dramatically down the stairs and defend poor Mr. Meyerson and his deprived children, and insist that my father make certain that club membership be offered them. I'd take a stand. I would not hide or delay my reactions. I'd be Mr. Myerson's hero. *Why didn't I do it anyway? How come I even care?* I frowned and looked at my hands and I felt a searing shame.

Finally, I leapt from the car after Fred had hidden it behind the same stand of trees, and ran down the rest of the hill to join the New Town kids waiting at the bus stop. I never turned once to wave goodbye, but I know Fred grinned anyway at my running figure and got back into the car to drive home. "That chile is gonna make it. Yes, she is," he said aloud.

Everyone at the bus stop greeted me happily and asked about my summer at the Y. They all laughed and shouted, filling each other in on all the happenings of their summer.

"Hey Queenie, you get any this summer?"

"He means did you get laid, Queenie, in case you didn't understand him."

"Naah, rich bitches from The Hill don't get laid. They do INTRACAWSS. It's fancier for rich people! For us scum 'o the earth types, it's called plain ol' fuckin'!"

"Yeah! I hear rich people's shit comes out in little pink silk bags. Wid a string! An' a tassel!" While I laughed, my mind inexplicably flashed to the cards hanging from the wrists of the girls at the Holiday Ball.

"Yeah. I know what dat intracawss is. We loint it in Hygiene. I'd'a never known if they dint tell me in hygiene. Hey, you seen them films of the diseases you could get?"

"Hey Queenie, you adopt any of them retardos you took care 'o from the Y?"

"Hi Queenie, I gotta idear. Why don't you marry one of the colored kids from New Town? Don't tell your parents, just bring him home an' see what happens. Hahaha!"

I looked around at the grinning faces of my New Town friends in the early morning sunlight, the ones I'd been so frightened of before. Grinning back, I slowly raised my middle finger high into the air. They all laughed, and so did I, and it was very good. I was joyful to be back with this earthy, rough and endlessly interesting crowd of young people, and loved being the object of their jocularity. I reached out to touch some of them. They touched back. It felt good.

I hadn't gotten my bus pass again, but this time I'd get one immediately from Miss Piacentino and would not allow that ugly bus driver to give me a hard time about it. I saw Winona at the edge of the crowd and stood on my tiptoes to wave at and greet my old friend, but Winona turned her head away as she aways had, despite last winter's experience. I dropped my hand and turned away, wondering if she still lived in the same place, wishing she'd talk to me.

When I got my class schedule in homeroom, I was nonchalant and barely looked at it. I already knew about my classes and all I had to do was show up. I didn't have to be afraid that I wouldn't find my way around. My mind flashed to Nettie, saw the grin and hopeful eyes, but after an instant of ripping sadness, I felt OK again. I was gratified to see a section of the school's library had been dedicated to my friend, and I ran my hands through my hair and grinned broadly so no one would know I was still hurting and raw and feeling so guilty about Nettie.

Without warning, a strong pair of arms came around me. I turned and looked up into the broad milk-white face of Bobby, the future undertaker. My heart wobbled as I saw the yearning love in his eyes.

"Oh, Bobby. How wonderful to see you again. Did you have a glorious summer?" I reached up and touched his face and nearly giggled out loud when I saw that the gesture made him nearly crumple.

"Yeah, Queen," he said hoarsely. "I sure did. I see you're still saying fag words like `glorious.'"

"Oh well, Bobby, it's hard to let all that go, y'know? Anyway, did you have fun? What did you do all summer?" I knew the second I asked the question I shouldn't have.

"No! No Bobby, I don't want to know. Oh, please don't tell me!!" Too late.

"Well," he began, ignoring my pleas. "I apprenticed over at Shipley's Funeral Home, you know, down in Tompkinsville. Jeez Queenie, it was great. I got to do some of the drainin', the embalming y'know, and I--"

"All RIGHT," I shouted. "Please, Bobby, dear friend Bobby, spare me the gross details. God, I'll barf, I swear I'll puke right on your shoes! Just tell me you had a nice summer, you know, like a normal person. I mean I know you're in orbit because of your summer---activities,--- but I'd rather not hear. Tell me you found a girl to worship. That'll be enough. Honest, it will. My God, you could gag a maggot!"

My big friend roared with laughter. He looked at me so lovingly, I nearly caved in. A look like that, his kind face flushed with hilarity and adoration, threatened to melt my heart, and I had to be very careful to not let this happen. Getting involved with Bobby Sotarikis would be a mistake, and I knew it. I also disliked the idea of necking with a guy who'd been handling dead people. We walked down the hallway toward our homerooms. I really enjoyed being with this behemoth for short periods, but I would never love him, although I knew he'd love me forever.

I walked into homeroom, and there, in all his glory, sat the object of my disaffection, Dominic Nuncio Di Russo. *Oh shit, the fungus among us.* In fact, the room held several of my most unfavorite people. Marty Commesso was there, glaring at me as usual, her eyes hate-filled glittering slits. *Jeez Louise, has she been sitting here all summer waiting for me? Doesn't she have to go to the bathroom sometimes?'* The ostentatious girl wore approximately the same outfit as always with perhaps a small variation here and there. Across the room sat Sue Lewis, who glanced briefly at me, then looked away. My ethnic gaffe had gone unforgiven, and I had to resist the impulse to go across the room and apologize yet again. I knew it was hopeless and that I did not much deserve Sue's forgiveness. The great snob Courtenay Scott Wolcott was learning that I, and the people who had brought me up, could never apologize enough, that nothing could be done to atone for all that had gone on before. Nothing.

I sat down, gave Dom a warning look, thought about poor, dead Nettie, and settled in for the start of my senior year.

"Helllllllooooooo, Queenie Baby." (Oh God, how I'd been dreading this.) Dom was still wearing his trademark jeans and white T-shirt, still combing his hair constantly, still carrying cigarettes rolled up in his sleeve. And, still able to swagger while he was sitting. *How does he do that, anyway??* I feigned distaste, but my heart quickened, making me look away, making me annoyed, making me glad. *What is it about this big greaser that makes me feel this way? Ugh.* The bell rang, and we all walked down the hall to the first class of 1956. Dominic Di Russo stood and followed me so closely I could feel the movement of his hard legs against the backs of mine.

"Now Dominic, first, get away from me. Second, before you start, let's get things all straightened out between us right from the first," I began.

"Oh Queenie Baby, I'd LOVE to get something straight between us!" Laughing at the keenness of his own wit, he sounded to me like a braying donkey. I held my hands over my ears.

"God, you never change, Dom. Could you possibly *be* any more boring? Why don't you grow up a little? Look! Look at you! You're still dressing like a low-class hood. You know? That just frosts me. Come on, Dom, get with the real world. Why not indulge yourself and get a shirt with buttons? Oh, never mind." I took a deep breath and looked up at the grinning boy. "Look. It's nice that we're friends, I mean I wouldn't have it any other way. Honest Injun. But do you think you might not

232

hassle me this year? I want to work hard, and here's a flash, Dom--I want to graduate! Go to college. Make something important of myself!!"

Dom looked at the ceiling and sneered.

"Yes, Dom! Graduate!! You remember that word. It's that ceremony they hold at the end of each year. You know—finals, diplomas and everything? Those funny flat black hats? I'm sure they explained it to you when you came here as a Freshman ... what, was that seven? Eight years ago? Anyway, I want to make plans for college. I really have a lot on my mind, so please, leave me be, OK? There are plenty of great girls out there. Why pick on me? I'm nothing special."

I reached up and pinched him playfully on the cheek. He grabbed my wrist and held it but I quickly pulled my hand away, feeling the blood burn in my face.

"Oh, Queenie, you're wrong there," said Dom, his voice filled with surprising tenderness. "You *are* special, you really are." He smiled and tried to put his arm around me. "Queenie, you ain't gonna believe this, but you're about the best thing I ever seen. You turn me *on*, Sweetcakes, you really do. So gimme a break, will ya? Go out with me? Just once? How do you know you won't love it?"

I pushed his arm away. "Not on a bet, Dom, not for a zillion bucks. And I turn you on? Sure, Dom. Any woman with a pulse turns you on. Get serious! And, get away!" I walked rapidly down the hall. I could hear him laughing. At least this time he didn't have his little gang of apostles hovering around him. I put my hand against my cheek and clenched my jaws to feel the red heat that was there. I could still feel his fingers on my wrist.

# CHAPTER 35

The college acceptances had started to come in. My parents were pleased to learn I'd been accepted at several of the better schools but I was confused as to which to choose. My father wasn't much help because he kept insisting I only consider the one that had the strongest secretarial programs, or at least a school that would adequately prepare me for one of the Big Five; "Wife, Mother, Secretary, Nurse, or Teacher," he'd drone. I am not proud that I believed him and did for many years.

I had taken shorthand and typing the previous year, and felt I had mastered those skills well enough to get a job after graduation. I could get nowhere with my father on the subject wanting a career in journalism since he doggedly persisted it was an unsuitable job for a "nice" young lady, and that people of "our kind" do not just go off and do "that sort of thing." The phrases were so predictable, and so very boring.

I decided to discuss the matter with my guidance counselor, Mr. Clarence Cornish, hoping he'd be able to advise me. I'd always liked him, mostly, I knew, because he bore a striking resemblance to the movie star Jeff Chandler. Tall, muscular, he had a cleft chin, tight, curly grey hair and dark blue brooding eyes. Most of us girls in New Town adjusted our hair, smoothed our sweaters, walked a little provocatively, giggled or even stuck out our breasts when we were near him, desperately trying to send him "the signal." He never reacted.

I arrived for my appointment at Mr. Cornish's office at 9:30 a.m. It was a tiny office, cluttered and filled to the ceiling with his beloved books. There were so many volumes in so many stacks they all but obscured the only window in his office, since he'd piled them on each side, and from the floor up, leaving only one small opening for the dirty glass panes.

"Good morning, Courtenay," Mr. Cornish said, looking over his half-eye glasses at me. He smiled, and I had a sudden feeling he'd rehearsed how to do that many times in his mirror at home. *The way I do.* But although it was still a stiff, dry effort, I really appreciated the awkward attempt.

"I've got a small problem, Mr. Cornish," I said with a bright smile, "and I was hoping you could help me with it. I've been accepted at some good schools, but I've decided that I'd really kinda like to be a journalist, working for maybe a magazine or a newspaper or something like that, and maybe eventually write some books. I thought you could help me select the proper school for that."

Mr. Cornish smiled back at me, and there was almost some warmth in it this time. "So, you want to be a newspaperman, do you?"

"Well, sir, maybe a newspaper*woman!*" I answered, proud of myself.

"Hmmm?" he responded, looking confused. "Oh. Well, yes, certainly, a newspaper--um---woman. Of course. So, let's see the list of schools you're considering."

I handed him the list and was flattered to hear him remark that it was an acceptable collection, very impressive indeed.

"Frankly, Courtenay, I'm a little surprised at this list. Not many of the children from this school ever go to places like this. They really are very expensive places to attend, and I'm rather surprised that you were accepted, even though your grades here at New Town are exceptional." Mr. Cornish frowned down at the list and looked up at me.

I felt immediately embarrassed. Squirming slightly, I said, "Well, Mr. Cornish, actually my father, well, he knows some people at these schools, and he once gave one of the colleges some money for something or other, oh, I don't think it was much, but you know, well, umm—oh dear."

Mr. Cornish's face softened, and his eyes became kind. "Oh yes, Courtenay, now I remember. You were new to us last year-- you came from The Academy, didn't you? Now my dear, you have nothing to be embarrassed about. You don't have to be defensive about being born-- well, being born with perhaps more than your classmates here have. After all, it is no sin to have money. Never mind. I understand. So—" he turned his eyes to the list of colleges "—let us consider these schools."

I felt relieved that this man understood and that he did not insist I fully explain my background. Of late, I had been having some difficulty with the facts of my "past" which I'd always taken for granted. I was experiencing feelings of guilt and could not neatly put them away someplace in my mind as I always had before. These feelings were becoming rawer by the day. I took a deep breath and pulled my thoughts back to the matter at hand.

Mr. Cornish and I talked for a long time. With his help, I decided to give serious thought to attending a small girl's college in New Jersey because it offered the strongest curriculum for journalism hopefuls, including help with job placement after graduation. Eventually, our conversation drifted to books. Mr. Cornish gave me a good reading list of classics, which, he promised, were fun to read. I smiled and looked out of the window and my mind began to wander. I was getting bored.

"And so," Mr. Cornish droned, "in the *Red Badge of Courage*, we see the hero wrestling with the problem of—"

Mr. Cornish suddenly stopped speaking, and looked away from me. He began to sweat, and his skin was releasing floods of it. It ran down his face, dripping from his hands onto his desk blotter leaving dark blotches. He drew in a quavering breath, began again, glancing at me and rubbing his hands on his pants legs.

"He—the hero, *The Red Badge of Courage* hero, that is—put this bandage around his head with a red blood stain on it because he'd, you see, he'd run away, he'd been so--so afraid, he'd seen such horror and just couldn't-- and so he pretended---"

It was becoming clear to me the man could not continue. I stared at him, unable to help. Mr. Cornish looked out his book-framed window, struggled again to speak, but his words were garbled, disjointed. I felt scared, but I had to rescue him. I looked at my watch, got quickly to my feet, and announced I was very late to my English class and that I'd get detention if I didn't leave immediately.

"So! Thanks a lot, Mr. Cornish," I said. "You've been so awfully helpful. I know I'll be able to make up my mind about college really easily now." I quickly gathered my books and the list, thanked Mr. Cornish again very much for his help, and bolted from the room, pulling the door shut behind me. I stood out in the hallway and leaned against the wall, breathing fast with relief, while on the other side of the door, Mr. Cornish drifted dangerously into the memories of the horrors he'd experienced during World War II and how his story so stirringly resembled that of the young soldier in The Red Badge of Courage, who had run away from the war.

# CHAPTER 36

The clatter of the rows of old black Singer sewing machines in my Home Economics class was deafening. Snippets of clipped thread surrounded all the chairs like thin, colorful collars even though it was forbidden to "clip and drop." The rules were "clip and drop into the trash," but no one bothered. Each female student was expected to make one article of clothing by the end of her fourth year, or she would not graduate. In this case, it was "she or he would not graduate," since the sewing and cooking classes had one courageous male student, the young and very brave Ralphie Volonnino.

Ralphie sat alone at a sewing machine in the back, completely absorbed in the Western- style shirt he'd chosen to make. It was to be made of different shades of denim, and the chest pockets would have mother of pearl buttons at the points of the flaps, he told me. There would be a row of these same style buttons along each of his cuffs, and he'd have leather fringes hanging from each arm from the elbow to the wrist. Ralphie swore he'd wear this garment for years until it fell into threadbare rags which he did, such was his love of this shirt he made in his New Town High School Home Economics class in 1956.

Ralphie was a secure guy, and knew himself well. He cheerfully endured the giggles he knew would come during his first week in the class and they did. However, the girls soon accepted, and then completely forgot he was a boy. He became one of us, welcomed to participate in all bull sessions (at which he could "dish the dirt" better than most of the girls,) and his opinions were valued during discussions of everyone's future plans. He became a remarkably skilled sewer, and in the cooking classes, he always finished making his meals first and his preparations always tasted better than anyone else's. His meals even looked beautiful, too.

"Ralphie," I'd laugh. "You're a boy. You're not supposed to be better at this stuff than the girls are. You even make everything on your plates look good, too."

"Appearance is everything," he'd say. "Appearances do matter."

Ralphie was enjoyed by the girls and teachers alike, and this was almost enough to take him past the worrisome knowledge that his male peers regarded him in most unsavory ways. Ralphie, after some considered discussion on the subject by the strong and very macho New Town males, was labeled a "fag," and because of that, his life was in constant jeopardy. Ralphie was forced to constantly prove he was heterosexual, but he failed these tests since it was surmised that his association with girls was just a cover. My pal Ralphie Volonnino had to spend his entire four years of high school in perpetual, exhausting terror, his back to all walls. But to his credit, Ralphie persevered with his love of the "feminine arts."

"Now, if you'll just ease that seam a bit, it'll all come together nicely." Miss O'Sullivan was the pretty, young Home Ec. teacher, and everyone liked her. She was slim and had short strawberry blonde hair, white marble skin, and very large feet. She was engaged to Mr. Schattsneider, who taught Algebra, and the New Town kids watched them like vultures to see if they'd ever pass a look or a touch during school hours or school dances, which would indicate that they might actually be "doing it." The couple was circumspect, however, and nary a glance nor touch were exchanged between them while in the presence of the student body, although they did arrive at school together each morning. Miss O'Sullivan always wore a small blue hat that looked like a bread and butter plate with one quivering daisy sticking about six inches out of the top center of it. They were a perfect couple, clean cut and pure, and Miss O'Sullivan wore a simple diamond solitaire from Mr. Schattsneider on her ring finger. They finally married in late June of 1956, and their first child was born on Christmas day, proving once and for all that they in fact had been doing it with regularity in the way-back of Mr. Schattsneider's station wagon after school on one of the wooded side streets surrounding New Town High School. When the new Mrs. Schattsneider began to show a considerable belly in early October, and it was clear that she was not newly pregnant, the outraged principal Miss McArdle demanded the couple's instant resignation, which they submitted without protest. They went on to run a very successful dog breeding and boarding kennel in a city far away, where no one knew or even especially cared about their unfortunately soiled pasts.

I was very proud of my homemade Home Ec. dress. I'd selected black corduroy, and had designed and made a jumper dress in an eased no-belt style that skimmed but did not hug the waistline. This "princess style," with its full skirt, flattered me well, and I knew it and loved the dress. I bought a pink-checked long-sleeved shirt to go with it, since it was all the rage that year to wear pink and black together, for both males and females. I wore stockings and flat black patent leather pointed shoes. A pink headband held my long brown hair back, and I'd found some tiny pink plastic button earrings. I wore this outfit to one of the New Town dances and received many compliments, which I shrugged *off*, but wallowed *in*. (My dear insensitive mother referred to it as that "nice little frock," but her tone told me she'd prefer to see it in the rag bag.)

Weeks later, I wore the same outfit to an affair at The Academy. I saw my old friends glance at it quickly and then look away. Not one person commented on it. *They could at least pretend to like it. That's what I'd do.* Embarrassed, I realized my mistake too late. My wonderful outfit did not fit in with the Academy girls' ensembles and apparently screamed PUBLIC SCHOOL!! I could hear their muffled snickers as I walked past them and I never wore it again. Seventeen years later, when I gave the entire outfit—jumper, shirt, shoes, stockings and earrings—to the Salvation Army, I remembered the sharp pain of that night when I began to finally accept the fact that I could never completely belong in either group.

All the girls in Home Ec cooking classes were issued white cotton aprons, on which they were asked to embroider their names on the left-hand pocket. I had never embroidered anything before, but knew what it was from the damask linens my mother used at dinner. I laboriously sewed on my name and was rewarded by Miss O'Sullivan's saying that it looked as though I'd been doing embroidery for years. I beamed at the unexpected praise; I'd never done anything creative or with my hands before.

In cooking class, each girl, and Ralphie too, wore a white cloth hat, resembling a shower cap. Ralphie hated it as much as I did but Miss O'Sullivan became murderously punishing if she discovered a hair in the prepared class meals, so it was much safer and far more prudent to just suffer the embarrassment of wearing the ugly thing. One afternoon after class when we'd finally been able to strip off those horrid caps, some of the girls expressed concern about one student who had open and encrusted sores on her hands, arms and legs. The students asked that this afflicted girl be removed from cooking classes, since they were fearful some of what they perceived to be a truly horrendous disease might somehow seep and drip into the prepared foods. Not really wanting to do it, Miss O'Sullivan finally and reluctantly confronted the hapless girl. So humiliated by the experience, the girl left New Town that day and was never seen again, even around town. After that, rumors were rampant that the wretched, spotted girl had actually been a Leper so all students who'd known her tugged nervously and surreptitiously at their fingers and toes, convinced they had caught the germ, convinced their appendages would one day separate and fall off. I am aware that we all have regrets in life but mine seem to be too centered on my participation in hurting people back then, and I regrettably have no way of fixing that. I have always wondered about that poor wounded nameless classmate and still today wish I could speak with her.

Ralphie received an A+ in both courses, while I received only B's.

"Hey Ralphie," I said in Home Ec one day, grabbing his arm and laughing loudly, "I'm the girl here. I'm the one who's supposed to get good grades in this cooking and sewing stuff. Not you!"

"Yeah, yeah, yeah," he said. "Well, surprise there, Queenie! Maybe I *am* a girl!" I laughed but had no idea why. Ralphie sauntered away and looked back at me and winked.

One week later, I was two halls away and could neither see nor hear as Ralphie came flying—he was literally horizontal and face up in the air—out of the boys' room. He crashed head first into the wall opposite, and fell to the floor with a dull thud. A pack of snarling greasers followed him out, and continued a beating that had begun while Ralphie had stood deep in thought at the urinal. His fly was still open, and he desperately tried to zip it while his attackers kicked and beat him. A crowd of bloodthirsty kids stood shouting "Fight! Fight," as a gang of seven screamed rejoinders between blows and kicks. "Hey Fag!" one shouted. "We don't let fags live around here." "Don't try to zip your pecker in, faggot. Keep it out so you can find a pussy boyfriend to suck it." "Yeah, but ya won't find no one in this here school, so why doncha go to one o' them faggot bars in Greenwich Village?" "Hey, Homo, you found any nice little boys around here so you can pull his pants down?" "Get outta this school, queer-bait. We got no room in here for dick suckers."

Ralphie told me much later that visions of his parents came to him then, even through his indescribable pain. He told me how his father had told him how ashamed he was that his son was taking "girlie" courses in high school, while his mother, proud of her boy for bravely doing what he loved without regard for his reputation, encouraged him.

The blows continued, but now Ralphie only heard them. He was beyond pain. He heard his father's voice, accusing him of being "a fag, a queerbait, and a homo." He thought of his mother, and how he loved her. The blows to his body became distant, unconnected. Blood clouded his eyes and ears, and he could do no more than curl into a ball, hold his arms over his head and pull his knees up. He thought he would die there on the floor, surrounded by the jackals he'd thought were his friends. His biggest worry at that instant was that this torture would never end, and he began to pray through bubbled blood for a teacher to come around the corner and rescue him. He could feel some bones break and was vaguely surprised at the sound. He heard, he was sure, his spleen split. He chewed on some loosened teeth and they were hard and salty from his blood, and he later said, "I should have tucked them into my cheek and saved them. Maybe a dentist could have put them back in place." He smiled and then felt the toe of a greaser's thick soled shoe crush his cheek like an egg.

I rounded the bend, curious about the noise and I saw the crowd of kids cheering the brutal beating of my sweet, gentle Ralphie. Incredulous, I could do nothing at first but to stop and stare. And then, with a surprising sudden shot of numbing rage and unknown strength, like a furious engine being started up, I shoved my way through the mob in time to see Dominic Di Russo raise the semi-conscious Ralphie from the floor by the front of his shirt, and punch him viciously in the face. Ralphie's head flopped loosely off to one side like a dead bird's would and the horrible but oddly delicate sound of Dom's fist connecting with Ralphie's nose was a memory I knew I'd never lose. It was terrible: soft, crushing, mushy, the sound a wooden mallet makes smashing into a rotted, wet log.

And then as if standing outside of myself, I heard my own voice scream Dom's name and saw my body charge toward him in slow motion, enraged and out of control. Dom straightened when he heard me, blood on his face and hands, some smeared on his white T-shirt. He dropped the limp Ralphie to the floor like a sodden, broken cloth doll, and turned to see me roaring toward him, and I knew my face was contorted in rage. I raised my loose-leaf binder with both hands high over my head, and with a crushing force seconds before I would never have believed I had, I smashed it violently down on Dom's head. Its metal edge ripped through his flesh, from his temple to his lower jaw. The wound spurted blood. I did it again. I screamed out his name, over and over until my voice broke into a rasping shriek. The notebook's rings sprung open with the force of my blows, and my entire year's papers flew out everywhere across the floor, some landing against Ralphie, becoming stained with his blood. Dom stood frozen, his eyes wide and white with shock. He put his hand up to touch his wound, looked at the blood in amazement, and then looked at me in total confusion. "Jesus Queen," he said. "Jesus God." He held his sticky hand out for me to see, but unmoved by what I'd done, I smashed him again with the notebook, and this time the sprung-open rings ripped into his shoulder like circled claws and drew immediate blood. I could hear myself screaming more, and my throat burned from the intensity of it. The kids in the crowd moved back, looking at each other, some laughing nervously, not knowing whether to run or cheer.

Finally, a teacher, the football coach, rounded the corner, and the situation instantly lost its fervor, a pricked balloon. I felt myself recede back into my body, and the crowd dispersed silently as only uneasy teenagers can do.

"You help Ralphie, Queenie, and then come to Miss McArdle's office right away," the coach shouted over his shoulder as he punched, kicked and shoved Dom and his gang down the hall.

I sped off for the nurse. When I found her on the phone talking to a friend, and my mind flashed to my mother, I quite nearly tore the instrument out of her hand, refusing to wait respectfully for the conversation to end. Dragging the protesting and flabbergasted nurse to the shattered and nearly unconscious Ralphie, I then charged off full speed to the principal's office, furiously determined to testify against Dom and the bunch of bloodthirsty greasers for so cruelly beating my dear little friend Ralphie.

Miss McArdle paced in front of the cowering gang, glaring at them, her eyes nearly white with rage. Their heads were down, all except Dom's; he chose to smile sarcastically up at her.

"Ah. Miss Wolcott. I'm glad you're here," Miss McArdle said as I skidded to a stop at the door. "Please come in and tell me exactly what happened out there. Sit."

I sat. I glared at the boys and with no fear I willingly related all I'd seen of the fracas.

"I didn't see it all, Miss McArdle," I said, my voice hoarse but strong. "Obviously I couldn't have been in the boys' room where it all began." I related that I'd seen Ralphie being beaten horribly and that I'd lost control and had bashed Dominic over the head a couple of times. The football coach stood in a corner of the room, listening quietly, his muscular arms folded across his chest. When Miss McArdle looked at him, he nodded affirmatively.

"And what pray, Mr. Di Russo, had Mr. Volonnino done to deserve this treatment? What made you decide to gang up on him and hurt him this way?" Miss McArdle leaned over Dom, who, I was satisfied to see, crumpled ever so slightly under her searing gaze.

He shrugged, sliding down in his chair. "I dunno, Miz McArdle," and he looked away from her. "I swear. I dunno. He was, well, he's a—jeez---a---."

The venerable principal bent close to Dom, and shrilled in his ear, "What? What was that Mr. Di Russo? AND STAND UP WHEN I ADDRESS YOU, YOUNG MAN, YOU UGLY LITTLE SNOT, THIS VERY INSTANT."

Like a shot, Dom was on his feet, towering over this skinny woman, obviously afraid of her.

"I sez `I dunno, Miz McArdle.'" His voice was barely audible, his eyes shifting nervously from her to the ceiling.

"Oh? You don't *know*, Di Russo? You beat a boy nearly to death and you don't know why? Well then! I have always known you were a stupid lout who only stayed in school to kill time until you got into jail, but even *I* thought you'd be smart enough to know why you'd beat someone up! Ah, Mr. Di Russo, you really are a fool with no brain, a jackass, probably retarded. I've always suspected that. Mother of God, I so long for those sweet days of yesteryear when caning was the thing." She sighed, smiled sadly and sat in her desk chair.

"You know, Mr. Di Russo," she continued, shaking her head slowly, "in my beloved motherland, caning is still an accepted practice. There are no problems with the children in Ireland like the one you've given me today." She sighed again. "Ah but then you have no idea what 'caning' means and for certain you have never heard of Ireland.

"Well then, Mr. Di Russo," she went on icily, "perhaps after I call the police and your parents, you'll remember why you did this, and why you let this pack of jackals help you in your brave cause."

A whisper from the others. "Wuzza jakilz?"

Since "parents" and "police" were two nouns that could loosen the foggiest of high school students' memories, Dom immediately said, "Yeah, yeah, yeah, OK, OK, I *hadda* hit him," still refusing to look her in the eye.

"What? What was that, Mr. Di Russo? You 'hadda' hit him? Reeeallly? My, my, my. How come you 'hadda' hit him, Mr. Di Russo? You hadda send him to the hospital? Maybe for weeks? You hadda??? I shall be very anxious to hear all about it. Please! Commence! We're all fascinated to hear." Miss McArdle sat back at her desk, folded her hands and smiled broadly at Dominic Di Russo.

"It's because he's a fag. OK? He's a fag. Now you know." Dom sighed and looked away impatiently.

"Pardon me?"

"I said, he's a fag! A homo. You know!" Dom stood hangdog before his tormentor.

Miss McArdle's eyes narrowed. "So. You and your gangsters took it upon yourselves to beat up Mr. Volonnino because in your astute perception, he is a *homosexual*?" Dom nodded once.

And then, "a homosectional?" Dom sneered, pretending to be perplexed. "Zat the same thing as faggot?"

"Don't mess with me, Di Russo" she hissed. "You know perfectly well the word is 'homosexual.' Now, we all obviously know this is abnormal and a sin against God. If we had any *proof* that Mr. Volonnino had this problem, you can be certain he would be a candidate for expulsion; but he's never given us any indication...even though he does take classes which customarily are attended by female students. But that of course is not proof. Tell me, Mr. Di Russo, how do you know that Ralph is a homosexual?"

"Well," began Dom, "everyone knows it. It's like common knowledge, or wudever." Dominic's face reddened. His sneer weakened.

"Really! Well now, that's very interesting. The boy is homosexual because everyone knows it. Well, Mr. Di Russo, since homosexuals prefer the company of the same sex, I can therefore only surmise that *you* are one *also*."

Dom's head shot up. He stared at the principal in utter shock and furious denial.

"Who, me? Waddaya, crazy or sumpin'? I ain't no queer."

"Oh? Really, Dominic? Is that so? Well then, how can I think otherwise? After all, you're rarely seen without your gang of snotty little worshippers over there. And since you're always together, I can only assume that you and your boyfriends over there are all homosexuals and doing whatever it is that homosexuals do with one another. There can be no other conclusion for me to draw. None at all." Miss McArdle ran her fingers through her hair, patted it down and smiled at Dom. My hand flew to my mouth to cover a smile.

The room became as still as a tomb. Miss McArdle walked back to her desk and sat down. Her chair creaked as she rocked back and forth, grinning cruelly at the group. The boys looked suspiciously from one to the other, shook their heads and tried hard to sneer, to look tough. A couple of them laughed, but it was strained and false. Their expressions clearly showed they all wanted to kill their principal. They were also filled with fear that perhaps the witch of a woman knew something about them that they did not. After all, they did all hang out together all the time. They turned and searched Dom's face for guidance. But Dom looked plainly thunderstruck, unable this time to guide or counsel his loyal minions. The coach turned and gazed out the window.

Suddenly as if someone had signaled them, the nervous boys burst into loud protestations, gesturing angrily, shooting threatening looks at Miss McArdle and the coach, and especially at me, the stoolpigeon. After a sharp warning look from Miss McArdle, they quieted and then began to mumble protests. An old hand at this, Miss McArdle ignored their threats and grumblings.

"We shall discuss this at a later date, gentlemen." The principal's voice was low, ominous. "As for now, you will return to your classes. You will all report to my office every day after school for three months' detention, where you will assist Mr. Wright in his janitorial pursuits. You will take orders directly from him, and do everything he assigns you. Mr. Wright will report to me each day regarding your progress. If you do not follow through on this assignment, the consequences will be very grievous indeed." Her face lit with the pleasure her words gave her.

"Now, as for you, Mr. Di Russo. As ringleader, you shall have some extra chores. I'll arrange a special assembly this week. Thursday, I think. Yes, Thursday will be perfect. That is, if Mr. Volonnino's wounds have healed sufficiently for him to walk. You will publicly apologize to Mr. Ralph Volonnino in front of the entire student body and you will make no reference as to his sexual preferences. I shall be quite close to you on the stage as a gentle reminder that your apology will be heartfelt and will hint at nothing other than complete shame for your actions. If you make even the smallest of lewd suggestions, you shall find yourself in very, very serious straits."

He had no idea what "straits" were, but Dom paled anyway as he listened to his sentence. He knew they couldn't be good. His gang waited, expecting him to make some show of bravado, but he did not. They were deeply disappointed in their god, disbelieving. Their glorious hero quite suddenly had developed feet of mud.

"I've just thought of one tiny addendum," Miss McArdle chortled, and she was delighted to see that Dom was embarrassed that he flinched when he heard her sinister snicker.

"And," she continued happily, "during the assembly this Thursday, *all* of you gentlemen will file onto the stage to stand next to your hero. You and Mr. Di Russo shall each read twenty-five lines from your own composition on the following subject: you will tell the students why it is wrong to hurt anyone because he or she is different from you. Different in any way, gentlemen. Color, religion, looks, preferences, size, etc. You will explain to everyone that this is a free country, and that we are all God's children. And, when you are all finished," she threw back her head and laughed sharply as a new and sudden thought came to her, "you shall all kiss each other soundly on the mouth. This act will show all of us that you are contrite and sincere. After that, your punishment will be over, except of course, for your term with Mr. Wright. If you choose not to accept this invitation from me in the study hall, I shall be forced to call the police to have you arrested for assault and battery. And that, gentlemen, is that." She glared.

The room was silent for several minutes. The coach continued to stare out the window, and I saw that he was swallowing hard to keep from bursting into uncontrolled laughter. I stared at Miss McArdle and was suddenly filled with an unexpected admiration. *I think I may have misjudged that woman. What a classy old broad she is!* The boys, stunned by their sentences, looked at each other and back at their despised principal in uncomprehending disbelief. Their mouths, to a boy, hung open. I began to laugh and again stifled the sound with my hand. I looked hard at the ceiling to calm myself and then back at the principal. And then, like the queen she always prayed she would one day be, Miss McArdle, with an imperious wave of her hand, said, "You are dismissed." Her voice was pure frost.

246

The vanquished warriors shuffled through the door, heads down, Ralphie's blood drying on their hands. Miss McArdle had the coach escort them to their respective classes, then directed him to check on Ralphie's condition. I left the room. My head was beginning to ache.

# CHAPTER 37

Two days were left until Dom's stage debut. The school was abuzz with rumors, since almost everyone knew, or thought they knew, what was afoot. Since I had not been sworn to secrecy, I told anyone who would listen all the juicy details; my popularity soared. There was of course, a small constituency who sided with Dom and his gang of thieves, but it was a tiny and non-threatening faction that most of the kids ignored. I had some concern about having to confront Dominic, knowing he was volatile and unpredictable, but I'd never thought him dangerous until I witnessed the horrible scene with Ralphie. Then I knew his true depths.

The time for reckoning would be Wednesday. New Town High was holding its collective breath. Dominic was waiting outside when I left school the Tuesday before The Big Day with Bobby Sotirakis.

"Hey! Queenie. See you a minute?" Dom was standing near the outdoor basketball court. He'd obviously been waiting for me. I looked around but he was surprisingly without his buddies.

"OK, Queenie," said Bobby anxiously. "Just stay here. Don't move. You don't have to talk to him. You want I should go over and tell him to back off?"

"No, Bobby, thanks." I waited, looking at Dom, then back at Bobby. I was not afraid.

"I know he seems scary Bobby, but Dom is really nothing but a big bully, and I read in a psychology book that bullies always back down when you push them back. I'm not afraid of him. Really, I'm not. He won't hurt me." I casually pushed the hair back from my forehead and smiled at Bobby.

"Let me go hear what he has to say," I said. "But keep on looking back at me, OK? I mean, as you're walking along, OK? Thanks Bobby. You really are always so sweet to me. Don't think I don't always notice that, honey."

Startled at "honey," he looked at me, a lovesick moose, and I knew he desperately wished Dom would make a move so he could kill him and be my everlasting hero.

I walked over to where Dom waited.

"Hello Dom," I said in what I hoped was a confident, superior tone. "Now don't start. Just don't you dare start with me. I know you're really pissed off, but it couldn't be helped. What you did was terrible, and damn it, you *know* it. You had *no right* to hurt Ralphie that way just because you think something about him which may not even be true! You acted like an *animal*. No, I take that back. No animal I ever heard of would *ever* do the cowardly, vicious thing you did."

Dom listened quietly to me, staring hard into my eyes as I spoke. He straightened and looked away.

"Yeah, yeah, I know," he said, his voice rough. "I expected you to say that shit, Queenie. You can tell your boyfriend over there to go on home and play with his stiffs. I ain't gonna hurtcha. I just wanna talk." He looked back at me, and his face softened.

Dom seemed docile, maybe even remorseful, and I felt completely safe with him. I glanced over at Bobby, smiled and waved to indicate my safety, and turned back to Dom.

"Come on. Let's go sit down on the bleachers. I really want to talk too," I said, and I touched his arm. "Don't get nervous. I won't preach at you. Well, maybe a little. But I do think we should talk about this thing."

Unused to being steered anywhere by a female, Dom hesitated, his body stiffening a little.

"What about your bus, Queenie?" His attempt at sarcasm was not a good one. "You have to get up to your precious mansion, doncha? Won't the maids and butlers be lookin' for ya?"

"Yeah, right, Dom." I sighed. "Look. Could you please drop the asshole stuff? I know it's the only thing in life you're really good at, but it won't work today. But nice try. Now Dom," I said trying to sound at least a little bit kind. "Come and sit with me, and let's talk. Besides, you can drive me home, right?" I looked up and shot him a lopsided grin.

He grinned back, gave in, and we walked to the bleachers and sat in the cold sunlight. To my delight, we actually began to communicate. Bobby lurked protectively in the background.

"Look Dominic," I said, shifting, smoothing my coat beneath me. "I'm sorry about what happened-- well, not exactly *sorry*. You *deserved* it. And probably a lot more, too. I know it's gonna be awful for you to have to go up on stage and apologize to Ralphie--and then to have to----" I knew I'd never be able to say "kiss your friends" without laughing, and I was sensitive enough to recognize that Dom was newly vulnerable. I would not cause him more distress, although I knew it was richly deserved.

Dom looked at me, squinting his eyes.

"But Dom," I said, "what you did was just--it was just terrible! How could you do such a thing? I mean, your whole gang picked on that poor kid. Jesus, how *brave*, Dom. I wonder if you'd have had the guts to fight him one on one. I doubt it. You always have to have your stupid-ass gang of morons with you to make you feel brave and manly. Why do you hang with them anyway? They're so stupid. Dumbbells. None of them can walk and chew gum at the same time, you know."

My throat was beginning to thicken. I felt my face growing hot.

"Please," I said, my voice trembling with anger. "Tell me. Make me understand what makes you this way! I'll listen to you, really. I'll try to understand, but you know, it'll be hard for me to comprehend why you'd hurt someone so helpless, so badly. I'm listening."

"You say you're listening Queenie? Cripes, you *never* stop talkin', do you know that? Jesus H. Christ, you babble like a magpie." I could see Dom struggling to regain his usual cockiness.

"Who the fuck died and made you the Holy Mary, Mother of God?" he said.

I sighed. "All right, Dom, I can see there's no point in talking to you. All you do is try to make someone else take the rap for the rotten things you do. Or you change the subject. Like now. When're you gonna grow up, anyway?" I started to get up but Dom put his hand on my arm. I glanced at Bobby in the distance and saw him tense in hopeful readiness.

Dom gazed into the distance, a rare, thoughtful look on his usually sneering face. He took a deep breath, and, not looking at me, began to talk.

"Y'know, Queenie, just because you live in a big house up on the hill don't give you no special permission to be a bigshot, y'know. You ain't nobody special. Hell, you ain't nobody at all!"

"See, Dom? There you go again, twisting it all around. I'm not talking about me here, or where I come from or how much money I have or anything like that, and you know it, so drop it. We'll talk about that some other time if it's all that important to you, OK? What we *are* talking about here is you and what you did to Ralphie, and you really can't talk about that, can you?"

Dom's face paled as he shifted on the cold bench. He squinted sideways at me, and sighed.

"OK. I shunta hit the little fag. I shunta. But you gotta know something, rich girl. Down here in my neighborhood, we don't like faggots. We got a big problem with them. Some of 'em have hurt little boys."

I started to speak, but Dom held up his hand.

"Now don't start on me again! Shut up for once. Shit, you know everything, don't you? I awreddy know what you're gonna say. You're gonna say that just because one guy done something bad to a little boy don't mean all fags are the same. I know, I know. Christ Jesus, I know. But maybe all fags do dat, maybe they don't. I dunno, but believe me, when they go after a little kid, they treat him bad, real bad. You don't wanna know."

"But Dom--you don't know that *Ralphie* is that way. Just because he likes to cook and sew doesn't automatically make him someone who hurts kids. And what about *your* male friends?"

Dom bristled. "Hey, now Queenie, don't get started on *that* again. My friends--hey, they're my pals. That's man stuff. We just do man stuff together, and everybody knows it."

I sensed I'd said enough. I leveled my eyes at him. Dom squirmed.

"Yeah, sure, awright." he sighed. "You're right. You're always right. Anything you say, Queenie. But Jeeziss, them fruitcakes do disgusting things---"

"Look Dom, I'm sure those people do terrible things and maybe I don't know much about that. The way I was raised, no one ever talked about it. I mean sometimes my father said such awful---well, never mind." I turned my head away and then looked back at Dom.

"But" I said, "if a person is a faggot as you call them, and they hang around together and don't bother other people, can't they just be left alone? Why do they always get beaten up? How come they get sent to jail? Whose business is it anyway what they do if they do it by themselves? Why do they always have to get the crap beat out of them?" I drew in some air, and it surprised me as it came as a sharp sob. I knew I was way out of my depth but still I felt these things keenly.

"OK. Don't say it. I'm talking too much, I know." I looked into Dom's now-solemn eyes. "I really worry about you, Dom, honest! Don't ask me why, but I do!" Dom looked down briefly, then at me, his face suddenly flushed at the tenderness of my words.

He said, "Christ, can you just stop talkin' for a second, Queenie? Can you try?" He put his arm gently around my neck and pulled my face to his. I tried to pull away weakly, but he looked into my eyes for a second, then kissed me softly on the mouth, pulled back and looked again into my eyes and kissed me a second time. His mouth against mine was soft, and I thought it felt like the rabbit fur mittens I'd loved as a child and I liked it, liked it a *lot*, and I kissed him back.

Off in the distance, Bobby's eyes widened, his nostrils flared and his jaw clamped. He definitely did not like what he was seeing.

Dom stood but I remained seated, staring up at him. He smiled down at me for a minute, and walked down the bleachers before he turned.

"Awright, Queenie, I'll think about what you said. Don't ax me to do nuttin' except think about it, OK? An' that's all I'll do. For now. See ya." He waved and sauntered off toward the sidewalk.

"Dom!" I called after him.

He turned. "Yeah?"

"Dom? Those little boys who got hurt by those...was that little boy, I mean, did that happen to you?"

Dom opened his mouth to speak and then stopped, his face tightening. "Wadda *you* think?" he said, and he disappeared around the corner of the school and my mind flashed to my dear friend Ralphie lying broken and smashed on the floor of New Town High School.

# CHAPTER 38

That Wednesday was maybe the only day in the history of New Town High School when there were no absences, no one had to see the school nurse, and no one played hooky. Everyone was seated in the auditorium and the room was unusually quiet. Eager anticipation thickened the air. Up on stage sat a row of eight downcast and humiliated young men, their heads bent low, looking with great interest at their folded hands. Dom occasionally looked up and sneered weakly, shook his head, and looked down again. I thought the shock of seeing them in shirts and ties was almost worth the wait. (One rebellious young man wore the requisite tie, but with a T-shirt. Seeing it tied around his bare neck caused a roar of laughter from the delighted student body.)

Miss McArdle stood and walked to the front of the stage. Like vampires hungry for blood, everyone sat at the edges of their seats, straining to see and hear every utterance of the anticipated humiliation. Finally, after an excruciatingly long pause which she clearly enjoyed, Miss McArdle spoke into the microphone.

"Boys and girls, as you doubtless know, we had a very unpleasant incident recently. Today we have the perpetrators on this stage and of their own will--- make note of that, please---- of their own will, they have agreed to speak to all of you about what happened, and to assure all of us that they have mended their ways. First, Mr. Dominic Di Russo would like to say a few words." Miss McArdle gestured toward the mike, and primly took her seat next to Miss Piacentino, her knees clamped tightly together. A few people started to clap when Dom was introduced, but were immediately silenced by a withering icicle glare from Miss McArdle.

Dom did not move, but sat with his head down, his face and ears crimson. The room became quieter. Miss McArdle cleared her throat. I couldn't help feeling pain for Dom as I silently willed him to co-operate. His head shook a little, and he looked up at the principal and then out at the student body. His eyes finally rested on little Ralphie Volonnino, who sat in the front row. Dom could see the black bruises. A crutch lay next to Ralphie, and a thick white cast covered one arm. One hugely puffed eye was black and completely shut and his nose was swollen and purple. There were stitches in his scalp and neck. Ralphie's internal injuries could not show, but they existed and would heal in time, although the memory of that beating would haunt and influence him the rest of his life, and he'd never be able to be brave.

Dom swallowed hard. I could see his Adam's apple move in his throat. Slowly, he got up and walked to the front of the stage where he looked down at Ralphie, and turned his head toward Miss McArdle. He opened his mouth and began to speak, but no sound came out. He coughed, croaked, and tried again.

"Awright. So I'm up here. I cudda not come, but I did." His broad shoulders squared back, and he tugged at the unfamiliar tie.

"Somebody tol' me I gotta own up to my--whadayacallit, my mistakes. So I'm doin' dat. Ralphie Volonnino, I'm very, very sorry I beat you up and I know it's wrong to hit people just because they're a--" Miss McArdle cleared her throat loudly. Dom shot her a black look.

"Yeah. OK. So, Ralphie, I'm sorry I did that to you. I shunta and I know that now. It won't never happen no more." He bowed his head and walked back to his seat.

"Thank you, Dominic," Miss McArdle said, her voice sharply edged. "That was very nice. I'm sure everyone appreciates your sincerity. And now, the remaining young men wish to convey their apologies to the victim, and they will express here in their own words why it is unacceptable for them to continue this bestial behavior."

In halting, ungrammatical phrases, the six boys struggled through, looking up occasionally at the snickering crowd and then over at Miss McArdle who would clear her throat in warning and force each back to his prepared text. One of them even announced his intention to become a priest because of what happened. (The audience roared with mocking laughter at this, some throwing balled up paper at him, most of them content to hoot and catcall. But in fact, that is exactly what he became, years later.) One said that even though he was unsure of what "'beestchill' means, I won't beat up people no more." I cringed to see them so humiliated, but I knew if it would possibly change their behaviors, it was worth every painful minute.

Finally! The moment all had been waiting for. The room became still once again. Savoring the moment, Miss McArdle waited for just a little longer than necessary, then got up and strolled slowly to the mike. Her job definitely had its moments.

"And now, ladies and gentlemen, these young men have a desire to show you how sincere they are about this issue. As proof of their deep earnestness and their wish to take full responsibility for their appalling misdeeds, they will now give each other a loving kiss. No tongues, please."

I thought the ceiling would crack from the huge roar of approval and laughter that erupted from the student body. "Yeah!" they shouted. "All right! Go for it! Do it! Do it! Do it!"

The taunts fell like hundreds of sharp arrows on the bowed heads of the group on stage. The entire crowd stood and gave Dom and his gang a standing ovation, shouting and screaming. It was a mob scene no one tried to quell, since the teachers were cheering along with them.

The Misses Piacentino and McArdle sat rigidly still and upright, and smiled indulgently at the crowd, then at the greasers, who had become pale and then began to perspire heavily. Miss McArdle got up and beckoned them to the front of the stage. Like chunks of granite, they remained frozen to their seats, their eyes pleading. Miss McArdle gestured a little more strenuously, a lot more meaningfully. Still they sat. Her eyes widened into a searing glare. Her shoulders hunched forward. (Miss McArdle was gifted when it came to the art of body language.) The crowd got louder, clapping in unison, chanting "Kissy time, kissy time, kissy time."

Finally, Dom miserably, slowly rose to his feet. I felt a tremor of compassion for him. He was brave to go first. *He's finally taking some responsibility.* It was too painful to watch I thought, too mesmerizing not to.

He shuffled to center stage. Turning to his gang, he raised an eyebrow. They understood the command, but no one moved. Dom then beckoned with an old Italian gesture implying the laying on of a hideous and disfiguring curse, and this did get his cohorts' immediate attention.

Reluctantly, the first of the group walked toward the dethroned leader, and his doom. Dom bent, and with a furiously reddened face loudly kissed the lips of the revolted boy. Backing away, wiping his mouth and looking as if he'd just chewed dung, he shuddered and slunk back to his seat. The next victim approached Dom, and the next and the next, until the entire group had completed the repellent deed. The crowd cheered and screamed, stomped and clapped, the din building with each buss. In the front row Ralphie laughed and cheered to such a degree I feared his facial stitches would pop open. But I could see by his expression it was worth the pain. I saw him wince when his eyes teared because they ran into his facial cuts but it must have smarted sweetly because he grinned so hard his face looked nearly rent in two. The kids around him clapped him on the back and gave him the thumbs-up signal and he grinned widely through his pain.

# CHAPTER 39

The year moved on with no outstanding incidents, or at least none with the impact of the stage kissing event. I was content to study hard and keep myself on the honor roll. Bobby still hung around, and so did Teddy Muller, and even teary-faced Al surfaced now and again. Dom drifted in and out of my life more often than I would have liked (or not as often as I'd have liked, depending on what I was thinking at any given moment.) New friends were added to my list at New Town. One was Pansy Junko.

Indeed, this was the name she'd been given by her parents who had lived in Greenwich Village when their daughter was born and who supported themselves by trying to peddle radical and not very good poetry, handmade sandals and clay beads from within a beatnik cooperative. Among Pansy's many idiosyncrasies was the small female white mouse stolen (she preferred to say "saved") from imminent dissection in New Town's biology lab right square in front of the nice, balding and absent-minded biology teacher. She carried that little rodent around in her bra, oblivious to the accumulating deposits of mouse droppings and urine.

I often but quickly wondered what the inside of Pansy's bra looked like when she took it off at night, and gagged softly at the thought. Pansy told me that at night she always kept the mouse in a desk drawer where she'd place a mayonnaise jar top full of water and another full of peanut butter, bacon and dried pieces of cheese for her beloved pet's cuisine. Consequently, the animal had become hugely fat, a baseball sized lump of white hair. Its pink eyes, nose, and tail poked from the appropriate places, nearly obliterated by the rolls of fat. This happy, lazy animal more often than not found it easier to roll from spot to spot than to bother with the more recognizable rodent scamperings. It had also become completely nocturnal from spending long daytime hours asleep in its mistress's pink brassiere. While snoozing between Pansy's breasts, it would release from its tiny intestines the digested goodies from the mayonnaise lid offerings of the night before, shooting infinitesimal spurts of mouse urine and loosing minuscule blasts of effluvia. She rarely woke up even when Pansy was in the midst of a rigorous basketball game. She simply snuggled down deeper while her athletic mistress made swish baskets from two thirds out on the court. The mouse had been christened Elizabeth.

On Wednesday and Friday nights, Pansy was routinely taken to the local cemetery by a group of love-hungry young chaps from New Town and surrounding schools. There, in the back of a pick-up parked next to a wealthy family's huge Grecian marble mausoleum, Pansy would contentedly avail herself of the lined up male students, one at a time, for five dollars per.

However, before her evening's labors began, Pansy was always careful to first place Elizabeth safely in a glass jar with a perforated cover where she would reside, clearly bored, until the evening's revelry was finally over. Pansy Junko always had wads of money, and her girlfriends considered her a competent consultant on the great variety of sexual joys, condoms, birth control, abortion and the odd social disease. Pansy Junko sneered at abstinence and why she never got impregnated by the willing and eager High School males to this day remains a clouded mystery although she managed to give birth easily and often once she married the man of her dreams, the biology teacher from Rogers High School across town.

Sylvia Frothingham, another new friend, was perhaps the most beautiful girl I had ever seen. She was tiny, with a delicately curved figure and hair the color of canned mushrooms. Her eyes were huge with sparkling light blue centers outlined in dark greenish blue, all sur-rounded by naturally curling, thick lashes. Sylvia had a sprinkling of pale freckles across the bridge of her upturned, perfect nose. She utterly dazzled everyone when she grinned and everything she touched seemed to be better because of her attention. I thought she really belonged in The Academy with that British-sounding name but of course never spoke that thought aloud.

Sylvia and I worked together on The Argo, creating appropriate poems to go beneath the graduate's pictures. Sylvia begged Mr. Cornish to allow us to use quotes from famous poems, speeches or plays but he'd have none of it, insisting it would be better for all of our minds were we to create the poetry ourselves. So Sylvia and I worked together many afternoons after school, laughing at our at-first inept efforts and sometimes inventing what we were certain were cleverly disguised obscene limericks. We also thought many of our efforts were deathless prose destined to end up in great, heavy leather poetry volumes on the shelves of wealthy families and great, ivy covered institutions.

258

I'd always thought I was a fair poet, but compared to Sylvia's efforts, mine seemed turgid and ponderous. Sitting at a desk, always perfectly dressed in softly colored cashmere sweaters and plaid woolen kilts, Sylvia would gaze at the ceiling or out of the window. Slowly, she'd begin a poem, swinging her dainty foot. She'd make a few halting, false starts but would soon finish with a perfect jewel of a poem, four lines that exactly captured the personality of the graduate and what his or her future would hold.

I was impressed, and jealous, too. Sylvia's language was so educated, grammatical and pure that I often wanted to ask her if she'd also come from wealth, but I never did. I did think it odd however, that Sylvia never volunteered any personal information either. She vanished off the bus in the afternoons, she did not climb the hill with me, and she reappeared the following mornings looking beautiful and perfect. The New Town kids liked Sylvia but I did notice that they never seemed to give her the hard time they gave to me because I was different, but because Sylvia was who she was and because she had a sort of untouchable aura about her I decided I did not mind. I was grateful she let me be her friend.

Years after graduation, my precious, delicate friend Sylvia would be killed in a bizarre accident while demonstrating against the Viet Nam war at her alma mater, the University of California at Berkeley. When the demonstration had become unruly, firehoses were turned on the crowd to quell their violence. Standing too close to one of the hoses, tiny Sylvia was knocked backward by the tremendous force of the water, her head smashing against the corner of a cement memorial bench and shattering her temple. She died instantly, and her lifeless body was borne to the ambulance on the upstretched arms of her compatriots, as in the primitive funeral of a great queen from antiquity. While being held high in the air, Sylvia's long mushroom-colored hair cascaded and rippled down one side, swinging silkily against the arm of one of the pallbearers, the other side hanging in long hanks of dripping blood. Her face was peaceful, her square mouth open, showing perfect rows of snowy teeth. Sylvia had been and still is the most impeccable female I'd ever known and I tried to be like her and knew I never could be.

Sometimes in the idle trance of walking up the hill on my way home from school on familiar roads, I'd think about the female friends I'd made at New Town, remembering how I'd never have dreamed such a thing to be possible on my first day. For example, I found the Le

Mieux cousins to be completely irresistible. Everything about those two New Town seniors was always hilariously funny. They realized that people regarded them this way, but they took it in good stride, laughing along with the joke. No one ever asked these good-natured oddities for a date, but they were not in the least embarrassed to would go to dances together. They would dance all night with each other and some of the more secure boys, and they'd have a wonderful time, accepting their respective lots with good grace.

The taller cousin was Myrtle. She stood a hair or two (or maybe even three) above six feet in her socks, if they were thin socks, but had adjusted to this handicap with cheerful resignation. She was "painfully thin," as all parents labeled this condition, but she regarded her frame as that of a magazine model's, and that's precisely what she saw when she looked into her mirror. She wore her thick, curly hair high on the back of her head, accentuating her tallness, of which she was genuinely proud, having decided early in life that she'd been given something unusual while other girls had been dealt merely average stuff. Because of her hairstyle, curled tightly and swept high, held by velvet ribbons, Myrtle had the regal appearance of a nineteenth century woman. She never shunned high heels when she dressed up, and when she saw men staring at her, she told everyone cheerfully and without the slightest embarrassment that it was because she was awesome, like a goddess, and often she was correct.

Myrtle accepted all life handed her, even enduring the same old height jokes, year after year, throughout her long and productive life. They came from everyone and were predictable and boring. But Myrtle Le Mieux was always kind, and allowed those voicing the old tall clichés to think they were the first to have ever said such things to her. She would laugh and laugh at this "brand new" tall joke, because Myrtle Le Mieux was always good to everyone.

She was also an extremely intelligent young lady, so bright she sometimes answered questions incorrectly in class so her brilliance wouldn't be quite so noticeable. She would go on to get her medical degree and work in the shadow of some of the country's great scientific men and women. Many years later, Myrtle contributed greatly to research needed in the struggle to find a cure for the new and frightening disease killing so many of her friends, Acquired Immune Deficiency Syndrome; AIDS.

Myrtle's best friend was her cousin Heather. Their mothers were sisters, who were ecstatic when their baby girls were born on the same day and almost at exactly the same minute. The births made news in the local paper, and copies of the article hung in both mothers' homes, framed and faded. Myrtle had been born long and skinny, while her cousin Heather was round and fat and dimpled, shapes both girls maintained for their lifetimes.

Heather Le Mieux looked as though she'd grown up to a normal size and shape and then had been squashed in some terrible accident. Heather's eyes were almost invisible between fat puffs of eyelids, and her eyebrows were way too low. Her nose was flat, her perpetually grinning mouth was wide and flattened, and even her teeth were wide and short. She had dimples all over her cheeks as if she'd been scarred by buckshot, and her head sat directly on her shoulders, with very little neck between. Heather's wide and fat shoulders hunched down too close to her waistline which was wider than her hips, and all of this rested on great, fat legs. But in spite of this peculiar build, Heather got around the school with amazing rapidity and grace, and when she danced, there were few who could match her easy, floating rhythm and suppleness. She was living proof that the cliché "fat people are light on their feet" was quite true.

Occasionally, when she looked up at something, it was actually possible to see into Heather's eyes beneath the sausaged lids. They were snapping brown. She had a mass of thick curly dark blonde hair which she kept bundled around her face with wide, brilliant ribbons, and she always wore her nails long and painted, and there was never a chip in the polish. She possessed a sunny disposition and was very nearly as bright as her best friend, Cousin Myrtle, but she never would do as much with her mind. Instead, Heather would marry a staunch Irish Roman Catholic who refused to practice any kind of birth control, not even the rhythm method, causing Heather to give birth to seven sons in nine years. She was, however, eventually brave enough to have her tubes tied while her husband was on business in the orient, a deed for which he never forgave her, after he'd nearly beaten and kicked the guts out of her.

Years after graduation, Heather cheerfully ran the New Town High School Alumni Association, sending out thousands of letters at her own expense, begging graduates to send in information about themselves. She ran all the fund-raising drives too, always pleading for money from graduates, business people and anyone she could cajole or corral. She rarely got much, but on some levels, she felt her life to be satisfying and productive. (Maybe as much as her cousin's, although Heather never saw the inside of a lab in her life and was confused by "all that research stuff Myrtle insists on doing.")

It was only natural that the two cousins were always called Mutt and Jeff but in their case, the names were drolly switched, making Myrtle Mutt, and Heather Jeff. Their last name was difficult and never pronounced correctly by anyone except the French teacher, Mrs. Brandcamp. To everyone else, they were "the Le Moe cousins." I really liked these girls, and tried to be with them whenever I could. They made me laugh. They made me happy! For the rest of my life, I did not often enough get to meet such innocent and kindly people, and I would occasionally think of Les Cousins Le Mieux, and I'd inevitably smile.

# CHAPTER 40

"You're gonna do what?" Sally and I and some friends walked out of the boarding stables where we'd all met to see Sally's new and first horse. The nervous mare's name was Charlotte, a small bay that Sally adored. We planned to go for ice cream sodas after seeing the new addition to Sally's stable, and I also decided to tell them I'd be going to a slumber party at Gloria Gatti's house the following night. When I did, the group stopped walking, looked at me, and then at each other. They smirked and raised their eyebrows. One of them laughed outright.

"Well, what's so bad about that?" I asked.

"A *slumber* party? A *pajama* party? Are you serious? Come on, Court, didn't we stop doing that in grammar school? And exactly what did you say her name was?"

"Gloria Gatti, and who says you can't go to slumber parties when you're in high school? I think it'll be fun."

"Gatti? Gatti? Isn't that what George Raft used to call his gun in those old movies? A gat? What, is her family in the Mafia or something?" The girls all laughed. I was not amused.

"No," I said coolly. "Her father is a brick layer" a muffled snicker here— "and her mother is a teacher at another public school around here. They're really nice people, and I've never been to their home, and I'm looking forward to it. What's so damn—darn -- funny about it anyway?"

The girls simply smiled indulgently at me, which infuriated me even more, and then they laughed a little louder.

"Why are you laughing? What?" My heart beat harder and my fists clenched beneath the sleeves of my linen jacket. "Oh, go bite a weenie," I said. The girls shrugged and turned to the malt shop.

Over their ice-cream sodas, we old friends talked excitedly about away hockey games, the upcoming Academy school play (a production of Gilbert and Sullivan's "Pirates of Penzance") and the senior prom. As I sat listening to them, I felt a pang of loss, since I would miss all of it. My friends didn't seem to notice my sadness, nor did they notice that they spoke of things that did not include me. I joined in the conversation as best I could when I could keep my voice from wobbling. Sally bubbled and babbled joyfully about her beautiful, darling Charlotte, and I tried to enthuse about the mare too, so my friends wouldn't notice how far apart from them I knew I had become.

The next night, my father dropped me off at Gloria's for the slumber party. He told me it was no trouble since he was on his way to visit a friend anyway, although he changed the subject as soon as I asked who the friend was. I waved goodbye as he pulled out of the driveway, but he did not wave back. I frowned at the departing car, wondering why he was so evasive lately. *Lately? The man is nothing but evasive. I wish I had a real father.*

It was dusk and the light was soft and threw a blurred cast on the neighborhood. Gloria lived on a busy highway in a small, one-story home. In the center of the modest front lawn lay a rubber tire, painted white, the top side cut into scalloped points. In its center stood a large clump of plastic flowers, faded from years of weather exposure, but once they had been red, blue and yellow. On the other end of the lawn a tall cement half-shell stood on its end, painted robin's egg blue on the inside, white on the outside. Inside stood a life-size statue of Mary, the mother of Jesus. The veil over her bright blonde hair was white, her gown the same blue as the shell in which she stood, her long, graceful hands rising from deep, flowing cuffs, palms up, arms slightly extended. Her facial expression was serene, the lips and cheeks shiny red, the eyes cast down. Another profusion of plastic flowers lay at the feet of this Madonna, and a small white crescent-shaped bench stood in front of the shrine for anyone wishing to sit and pray or sit and ponder about that statue and maybe even the meaning of life. I wondered if the family actually did worship at that shrine with traffic roaring by no less than three yards away.

Next to this plaster of Mary was a huge grass-covered mound. I squinted. In the dusk it looked like a gigantic grave, but oddly, there was a door in the side of it.

"What on earth...?" I murmured.

"Hiya, Queenie!" yelled Gloria from the open door in her home. A bouncy, sweet kid whom everyone loved, she came from a large, loving and loud Italian family where everyone screamed in lieu of talking, and where hugs, affectionate head slaps and playful punches were commonplace. Everyone equally received and delivered bruises. Everyone dearly loved each other.

"Hi Gloria!" I was happy to be there. I'd packed my pink baby-doll nightgown, two boxes of cookies and all the toiletries I owned. "Am I early?"

"No! Come on in. I'm *so* relieved! My obnoxious brothers and sisters went out for the night, so we've got plenty of space to sleep. That is, *if* we sleep!" We both laughed delightedly.

Petite, curvaceous and having endless enthusiasm and energy, Gloria had won a coveted spot on the cheerleading squad. Every time the spirited New Town Cheering Team came in last at the annual cheerleading competitions in New Jersey---and they did year after endless year-- Gloria wept loudly with all of her sister cheerleaders. But the losses didn't dampen the squad's enthusiasm.

They'd have stood a better chance at winning if only Miss McArdle allowed them to show their black nylon panty-tights. Being forbidden to do this severely curtailed their cheering activities. They were denied the liberty of turning cartwheels, performing high jumps, flips, splits or any moves where their skirts might fly up. Miss McArdle thought those moves suggestive and unseemly: "If that's what it takes to win these competitions, then we at New Town want no part of it, do we ladies?" But the ladies stayed silent and sulked because in fact they did want a part of it. And because Miss McArdle considered it improper for a boy cheerleader to hold a girl by the ankles high over his head (because of the very real and sinister danger he'd sneak a quick peek up her skirt, which might very well turn him into a rapist), yet another part of the cheerleading competition was denied them. The principal was convinced that to invite this sort of temptation went against everything she stood for, and as far as the fuming girls on the cheerleading squad were concerned, she stood firmly against absolutely everything they desired to do.

Before I entered Gloria's home, I stopped and looked questioningly over at the huge mound in the lawn.

"Hey Glo, what is that thing?"

"Oh come on, Queenie, you live on Mars or something? It's a bomb shelter, jerk. You know all those drills we have in school? Well, if the bomb falls and it's on a weekend and we can't dive under our desks, well then, we can go down into the bomb shelter. Although," she lowered her voice, "for my brothers it's something else, but they think I don't know. It's their passion pit!"

I laughed, looked again at the huge mound with the door cut into its side, and back up at Gloria.

"And Queenie, we've got it stocked with enough canned food and water for all of us to survive at least six months in case The Big One falls on our heads. We got beds, a portable radio, and games down there and everything we could ever need. Boxes and boxes of batteries, too. I'll show you sometime!"

What Gloria suspected about her brothers was true. When her father had finally discovered the secret of his progeny's very un-Catholic shenanigans within the bomb shelter, he immediately retrieved the key from them, thus cutting off their special and clandestine activities and a great deal of their popularity.

"Come on, come on!" Gloria pulled me into her home. "Mom's out--she'll come in to meet us all later. She's left a ton of food in the fridge and a couple hundred gallons of ice cream in the freezer. We can make floats and sundaes and anything we want. It'll be a ball! I've got the popcorn popper upstairs, with the butter and oil an' everything. Come on, Queenie, hurry! The others'll be here soon. Lemme show you the house."

We entered the small kitchen, where the walls were covered with motivational quotations laminated to rough-carved squares of varnished pine. Racks of souvenir spoons, vivid plastic flowers in vases which hung from thick, braided cords...every available surface had something decorative on it, so much it was impossible to see any of it clearly. The house shone with cleanliness.

Over the kitchen table hung a shocking painting, a rendering of the face of Jesus Christ, eyes rolled up nearly into his forehead, and a crown of long, viciously pointed thorns on his head, each stabbing deeply into his forehead flesh. I shuddered and looked away, then felt compelled to look back. From the lacerations made by the thorns, thick purple blood poured down Christ's cheeks, into his eyes, into his beard, onto the shoulders of his white robe. The artist had given Jesus a look of such horrendous agony, it was hard to look at him for any length of time. Christ's mouth was partly opened, turned down at the corners, seeming to scream with the suffering the thorns caused him. It was an appalling and ghastly painting which the Gatti kids were requested, by their devoutly religious parents, to contemplate each morning during breakfast. I could not imagine being able to swallow oatmeal or poached eggs or any food at all while gazing at this appalling

266

apparition. It was impossible to look at, yet impossible to look away. This painting hurt my head, and my eyes, too.

I followed Gloria out of the kitchen, relieved to leave that tortured painting. The Gatti living room was filled with too many pieces of overstuffed furniture, their arms and backs draped with crocheted antimacassars, an extra-large example of which covered the top of the television in the corner. Gaudy handmade Afghans were draped over everything, including the piano, and pictures of Gloria's family were everywhere. I heard the tinkling sound of cascading water, and searched the room to see where it was coming from. In a gloomy corner next to a window heavily draped in layers of fabrics of different textures and colors, stood a small fountain! I could barely hide my amazement. It was made of imitation grey stone material which rose from the floor at different levels. Positioned all along the sides of this stone were groupings of plastic tropical plants. The water trickled out from the mouth of a tipped jug, which was held on the shoulder of a naked, chubby, winged Cupid. A fig leaf covered Cupid's indecorous area, and water splashed down sweetly onto each level, then into a bright green pool at the bottom, where dozens of tiny, shiny plastic goldfish floated around, some upside down. A few imitation birds and flowers were scattered about to add touches of realism, I supposed.

There was lots of white in the room. White lamps, white furnishings, tables, china closets and lots of gold highlights. And on all of the furniture, (underneath the antimacassars) was a covering of clear, fitted plastic. I imagined the backs of everyone's legs sticking to that plastic during humid summer months. Mrs. Gatti was very like Mother Nature; she abhorred a vacuum.

Sylvia arrived next, followed by the Le Mieux cousins, and Pansy Junko. Without warning, and right under the portrait of the profusely bleeding Christ, Pansy stripped off her sweater and then her bra, which she shook in front of her the way cheerleaders shake their pompoms. Pansy's popular breasts bounced furiously with each shimmy, and she then waved the bra in circles in the air so everyone would know she'd left her beloved Elizabeth home. The corpulent mouse was in the desk, with an extra ration of mayonnaise jar-top goodies to keep her from feeling melancholic at being left behind. We girls howled with glee at our crazy friend's antics. With Pansy starting things off like this, we knew it would be a night we'd never forget.

Gladys was next to arrive. I felt embarrassed and guilty that I'd always danced with her in Miss Ginocchio's Friday dance classes when

I was trying to avoid Nettie. My throat tightened at the thought of Nettie. *When will this pain ever go away? Oh, how Nettie would really have loved being invited here tonight.* But I knew that poor dear Nettie would never have been included in this gathering.

Next came the Le Mieux cousins and we then all hung out in the kitchen, devouring everything we could stuff into ourselves. We drank the Gatti's entire inventory of soda pop, and finished it all off with vanilla ice cream sundaes, made so generously we had to put them into individual mixing bowls. We covered these mountains of ice cream with marshmallows, maraschino cherries, chopped walnuts soaked in a thick maple syrup, whipped cream, thicker hot chocolate sauce, butterscotch sauce and corn flakes. By the time we got upstairs, none of us felt too awfully well, but the nausea eventually passed and we all settled in for a long night of hell-raising.

Gloria had scrounged up sleeping bags to supplement the two beds already in her cluttered room, and three ancient mattresses crowded the floor to accommodate anyone else who might decide to show up. After we changed into our baby-dolls, we brought out 13 shades of nail polish and began the pin-curling of hair-do's accompanied by long, serious discussions of boys.

Eventually, when these rites were finished, we sat cross-legged in a circle on top of the mattresses and settled in for an even longer analysis of New Town's male population. And later, in hushed tones, punctured by the occasional shriek, we spoke profoundly of sex. Sylvia, her head turned slightly away, remained aloof.

"Perhaps," she said, "I have higher ideals than most, and choose to save myself for someone of perhaps a touch more refined character." We all laughed loudly at her, but Sylvia kept her remote expression.

"What Sylvia? You're saving yourself? What in hell for?" Pansy looked at her in amazed disbelief. "You mean, you're saving yourself for sex or for the perfect man *plus* sex?"

"Both," said Sylvia Frothingham, flipping her long hair back from her face. She'd recently cut her hair into bangs across her forehead. The look was adorable and gamine-like and she knew it.

"You know Pansy," said the perfect Sylvia, "you're cruisin' for a bruisin'," and I covered a grin hearing this uncharacteristic remark from the porcelain Sylvia, "but I shall try to effectively answer your crude and nosey question. So, yes, Pansy, regarding sex, I am doing both of the things you suggest. When and if I have sex, it shall be with a gentleman, a man of learning, a refined young man." I thought, *now you're cookin' with gas, Sylvia!* And as I always did when Sylvia spoke, I wondered how a girl like Sylvia was attending New Town High School and not The Academy.

"Oh, hardy-har-har," Pansy retorted. "Come on, Syl, lighten up. The reason you ain't havin' sex 'cause no one's asked you yet, right?"

Sylvia, pulling up with haughty pride, admitted that this in fact was a fact, but one of which she was not ashamed.

"But Pansy, my dear," Sylvia went on, after her stately confession, "I must be totally honest with you. Just being asked by a boy really isn't enough reason to just do it, isn't this true? I mean, isn't there supposed to be some sort of feeling between the two people? Or, do we all just do it for fun--or maybe money, you know, like some people I know."

"Oh my doodness," Pansy trilled, "you hoot widdle Pansy wif doze nasty woods. Oooo, I tink I'm gonna cwy." Pansy screwed up her face in misery and then laughed. "You know Syl, I'm not in the least ashamed of the way I earn my lunch money, and another thing, Miss High and Mighty, you know damned well that I've never made a secret of it. So up yours with a beach umbrella, Cookie. Opened!"

The room was still. I watched Pansy and felt a rush of pride for my brave, promiscuous friend.

"And, Syl ol' Pill," Pansy went on, pleased that she had the floor, "when you do get around to it, don't forget to tell the lucky guy to use the white balloon, OK? An' if he's too much of a pussy to buy some from the drugstore, tell him to filch his old lady's Saran Wrap. It's messier, but it does the job OK. Yeah, I know what you're thinkin', an' you're right. I DO know what I'm talkin' about!" Pansy laughed heartily, picked up a hand mirror, preened and smiled at herself.

Seeing this discussion was not going well, Gloria cut in. "You, Pansy," she said, "are a bad motor scooter. Put a zipper in it." She turned to me. "So! Queenie! What's with you and Dom, anyway?"

"With Dom and me? What do you mean, Glo? There *is* no Dom and me."

My six companions rolled onto their backs and hooted.

"Oh, come ON, Queenie, you know he's got hot pants for you," shouted Gladys.

"Gladys, that's a very crude expression. And Dom does not have hot pants for me. Besides, he's a disgusting pig and a greaser and a hood, and why would anyone want to go out with him anyway?"

At this, they all raised their hands and shouted in unison, "Ooooo, me, me, I wanna, let it be me, me, me, I'll take wunna Dom's hickies any day o' the week, dozens of 'em!"

"Queenie, what's the big deal?" asked Gloria. "So the guy likes you. Give him a break. We know that Bobby the Undertaker really likes you too, but, yuck, how can anyone think about him as a boyfriend, when everyone knows what he does on weekends?" Gloria leaned closer and waited for an answer.

I looked around the group. "Look, girls," I said, "could we talk about something else? I really don't want to waste our good time tonight talking about that big jackass."

"Sure. We can dig it," said Gloria, and she turned to the other girls and began a lively discussion about the possibilities of several other choice New Town boys.

"Well, ladies, listen up," Pansy said, getting up and pulling her chunky, square cosmetic bag toward her. She snapped open the latches, opened the mirrored lid and pulled out a small paper bag. We all watched her curiously.

"Ladies, I have here a little something that will make us all happy to be alive, and I will share it with you at no cost to yourselves. Consider it a gift." Pansy sat cross-legged, her white fluffy mule slippers on her feet looking much like small, soiled sheep. She opened the bag, and poured onto the bedspread a profusion of crooked cigarettes. Some of the loose tobacco spilled out onto the fabric even though most of the papers on those weird cigarettes was rolled tightly closed at each end.

The Le Mieux cousins got up and leaned over the pile. "So?" Myrtle said, "so you've brought a bunch of weird looking ciggies. Big deal. We've all tried smoking, and it stinks. Makes me dizzy and sick."

"Ladies. These are not your everyday coffin nails," said Pansy. "Prepare, please, to take a trip to Paradise." She produced a pack of matches, and placed one of the oddly shaped cigarettes between her lips, lighting it with a flourish.

270

"How do you know which end to light Pansy? The paper's kinda twisted on both ends."

They all watched her suspiciously.

"Is this what I think it is?" asked Gladys.

"What do you think it is?" asked Pansy.

I began to suspect. "It's that cigarette that's called...I can't pronounce it--it's, what -- I forget--you know, *everyone* knows about it -- it's..."

Heather looked bewildered. Myrtle looked annoyed. I know I looked confused.

Pansy smiled patronizingly at her friends. "Ladies, dear clueless, innocent ladies," she began proudly, savoring the moment "what we have here, purchased at great expense just for you, is marijuana. Grass. Dope. Reefers. Mary Jane. Pot. Joints. Happy Tobaccy. But no matter what you call it, it's really fun, and I dare the rest of you to smoke with me. Now ladies, watch me. Pay close attention and learn. I'll show you how to do it."

Pansy put a cigarette into her mouth, and flipped open a Zippo lighter with a flourish and a loud metallic clack. It had a pink flamingo on it and the word "Florida" in vivid green scroll. She lit the end of the twisted white paper and it flared for an instant. She then dragged deeply on the cigarette. A few sparks fell to the front of her nylon nightie, but it only melted a few spots. The others stared at her, awed. Pansy drew the smoke deeply into her lungs and held it, her cheeks puffing out. Everyone waited for her to exhale and finally she did, very slowly, and passed the cigarette to Heather.

Heather looked down at the glowing joint, then up at her cousin. Myrtle nodded hesitantly, wanting Heather to try it before she did. Heather put the cigarette directly into the center of her puckered mouth, and sucked the smoke into her throat. With her squashed, chubby cheeks puffed to the maximum, she held onto the smoke the way Pansy had done, her face gradually turning blue.

"Exhale, exhale!" everyone shouted, and she did with the force of a Nor'easter, her cheeks deflating like bursting balloons. She looked around the room, her face blank. "So? What's the big deal? I thought I was supposed to get, what, get something. I forget."

"High, Heather, high," shouted Pansy, impatiently. "Jesus God, you're a dumb bunny."

"Oh. Hi, Pansy," answered Heather, looking at her with wide eyes, as if Pansy had just walked in. The group laughed, and as the joint was passed around to the rest of us, it grew so short and hot it had to be clamped and held with a bobby pin. When the last girl had tried it, coughing mightily, we continued on with our conversations. However, each sentence from us was now punctuated with bursts of shrill laughter followed by clapping of hands to mouths and astonished looks.

"My folks are due home soon," said Gloria. She stood and wobbled precariously on the mattress. I wondered why my friend's voice was so piping high. "They won't let us make too much noise so let's put on some records before they get back. I wanna dance The Slop an' I just got the new Everly Brothers record, `Bye Bye Love,' you heard it?" Without warning, she flipped backward onto the bed, her mouth opened impossibly wide and emitted a horrendous belching laugh that no one had ever heard from Gloria Gatti before. I jumped with surprise when the rest of the girls flipped frontward, backward or sideward onto the beds, sleeping bags, or mattresses, like a bunch of hooked fish. The laughs that exploded from our guts took so long our breaths ran out and we began to suck air loudly, strangling in great rasps of mirth. We rolled over onto our bellies, raising ourselves to our hands and knees where we bucked and flipped, still laughing hideously, out of control. My guffaws were so deep and wrenching, I wet my pants and they became so drenched my urine dripped down my thighs. I slapped at Gloria and hung onto her, fell up and down, and gasped and gasped and gasped for air.

Then, as if someone had suddenly turned down a volume knob, the room became quiet. All the girls sat where we'd landed, gazing dizzily around at each other. At some signal, I never knew for sure what it was, we all leapt to our feet and scrambled around Pansy, who scooped up and handed out the remaining unsmoked joy sticks. Pansy lit the ends of the joints for the girls with a more exaggerated flourish of the pink flamingo Zippo. Considering ourselves seasoned marijuana users now, we sat and inhaled as we'd been taught, coughing only a little, holding the smoke until we thought we'd explode and finally exhaling with a slow, sophisticated nonchalance. Then we sat, waiting for `it' to happen, and happen `it' did. We doused the tiny remaining cigarette in Gloria's cold cream jar. And again, all of us cried out with laughter, each tiny movement causing another onrush of shrieks. Our smiles were so wide our cheeks ached. The room looked beautiful to us, and we looked beautiful to each other as we pledged eternal friendship and undying love, swearing that nothing, not even boys, could get in the way of our unending devotion. A couple of us wanted to prick our thumbs to exchange "forever-sisters" blood, but all they could find for a dagger was a large comb which no matter how hard we hammered and shoved the teeth into our flesh it simply would not draw blood. This set off another gale of bellowing laughter, followed by blubbering tears. It was sweet and lovely and totally exhausting, and eventually, we all mercifully fell asleep, wound and tumbled around each other like a gaggle of warm, tired puppies. In sleep, we smiled at the strange and pleasant things dancing on the backs of our eyelids, and eventually my underpants dried.

The next morning, under the bloody portrait of Christ and the intensely suspicious gaze of the Gatti family, we girls ate ravenously, scraping our plates, asking for more, stuffing rolls and butter, eggs, ham, orange juice, cereal, cups of sweet tea and creamy coffee into our starving mouths. The Gattis were pleased at this healthy display of appetite but concerned they were running out of breakfast foods. They listened politely to our cursory, rambling fulminations, and were noticeably relieved when we finally stood, thanked them for a wonderful time, and with our bags packed filed out the door to our parents waiting in cars in the driveway. Mrs. Gatti was perplexed when she went upstairs later on to clean up what she knew would be a huge mess, to find all her daughter's bedroom windows opened wide. The room was cold.

# CHAPTER 41

Dear placid mother was angry. More precisely, she was livid as we stood in the dining room, glaring at each other.

"But mother, I WANT to go and I AM GOING! Please. Don't try to stop me. It's perfectly OK. Everyone's going. We'll be going in a big bunch. Someone's father will drive us. What could happen? I'll be home in time for dinner."

"YOU ARE *NOT* GOING, YOUNG LADY!" *When did she ever learn how to yell like that? She has no emotion at all! Now she's yelling??*

I immediately tried another tack. "Mother," I said calmly, forcing a sweetish smile to curve my lips. "Dear Mother. Why do you object so to my going on television with all the kids?"

"First of all, `dear Daughter,' do not patronize me. I will not have it. I object to it because no one in the family has ever done such a common thing before."

"But Mother dear," I smiled back, "that is because there *was* no television before now."

My mother, momentarily unhinged by such logic, looked back at me, her face a pale blank.

"Courtenay dear," she sighed. "I've seen that disgusting American Bandstand display, and our sort of people simply do not *do* that sort of thing."

"Oh, Mother, how *sick* I am of that phrase! Honestly, whenever `our people' don't want to do something they don't like, they say `We don't do that sort of thing.' Well, *I do* `that sort of thing' and I *want* to go, and I'm *GOING!*"

"Now Courtenay," my mother answered, "please do not use that tone with me. After all, I am still your mother, and while you're living under our roof, you'll---"

"Yeah, yeah, yes, I know mother, as long as I'm under your precious roof, I'll have to follow your rules. So why then, Mother dear, did you and Father ever send me to New Town in the first place? You

274

sent me there, and now all you do is object to my doing things with the kids from school. How come? I'd really like to know that." I stood waiting, tapping my foot, arms folded across my chest.

After one minute with my mother staring at me and making no comment, I went on. "If you wanted me to go there, you should have known I'd end up doing public school things. You didn't expect me to keep on doing Academy things, did you? Well? Well, did you?" We again stood looking at each other in silence. "Come on, Mom, get real. Use the old bean. I'm getting more out of touch with my Academy friends every day. You must know that."

My mother, the proper Mrs. Wolcott took a deep breath, straightened and stood tall before me, her recalcitrant daughter. When she spoke, she used her Royalty Voice.

"I do *not* have to answer any of your questions, Courtenay Wolcott. You are the child, and I am the mother, and let us please not forget that important point. That shall be that, for now. I will remind you that we did allow you to go to that awful little house out on the highway for that pajama party-- or whatever it was called." She sighed so deeply her chest rose high. "Now, you will not appear on that dreadful television show where everyone dances those suggestive dances for all the world to see. And that, Courtenay dear, is that." Lady Helen Wolcott began to walk majestically from the room.

"Mother! Please. Stay here and talk with me. Don't walk away. You ALWAYS either walk out of a room, or just sit and stare when things get difficult." It was the usual airy blank dismissal. A walnut-sized lump formed in my throat. But my mother did stop, and kept her back to me and I knew she would.

"Remember the time," I shouted, fighting tears, "that you and Father told me I had to leave The Academy and go to New Town?" I could see my mother's back stiffen, but at least she stopped walking away from me.

"Do you remember how you just sat there staring into the fireplace? I begged you to talk to me, Mother, to fix it, but you didn't move! My God, you were like a piece of stone. You just sat and stared. Remember? Into the damned fireplace! You just goddamn sat there, Mother. It's always the way you do things. You sit and stare, or you walk away. It's how you cope. You just won't face things." I paused, exhausted. My mother turned, and we stared at each other. My

275

mother's face was drained of all color, stricken. She pulled in a breath which was more like a sob.

"Well, maybe that's a little bit true Courtenay, but you know me, I've never liked conflict. I'm not particularly good at it, you know." My mother's voice was now a rough whisper.

Realizing I had a toehold, I deliberately took advantage of her weakened moment. I gently took her hand, and led my mother to the living room couch, where we sat. I could see that she was becoming frightened. She kept her head bent low. *Why is she so scared? My God, I'm not gonna kill her.* I smiled gently at her.

"Mom, Mommie--can I ask you something?" I kept my voice soft. I reached out and tenderly turned my mother's face toward mine. "Can't we just talk for a couple of minutes? I know we can work this American Bandstand problem out, but there's something else I've just got to know." I saw my parent wince as if warding off a blow she knew would come. I pressed on anyway.

"Mother, can you tell me, once and for all, why I had to go to New Town?" My mother began to turn her head away. "No!" I said. "Wait! Don't turn away from me, Mother. Please. Tell me. I know something's going on." I stood and began to pace. Helen Wolcott remained silent, seated, and refused to look at me.

"Mom," I said, louder now. "Look, you don't have to worry. I'm not mad anymore. As a matter of fact, I like New Town. Yeah! Really!" I beamed my widest smile down at my mother. "I've learned a lot and I've made lots of friends. So you don't have to worry that I'm gonna be mad at you. I'm not, really. But I still don't know *why,* and I want to know so badly. Will you tell me now? Please Mommie?"

My mom suddenly looked sad, beaten down, afraid and deflated. She ran her hands over her pale, short hair and I saw that they shook. I frowned as I looked into her face. I'd never seen my mother flatten like this. Something bad was going on, something I didn't understand.

"Courtenay. Darling. I--I just don't know what to say. It was the money, we had a problem with money and we couldn't afford to send--"

"Oh God, mother, stop it!" I stood up so forcibly, my mother jolted backward on the couch, her hands reaching behind her to grab for support. I began to pace rapidly around the big room, never taking my eyes off my mother's face.

"Do you think I'm a total fool? All the things you and Father warned me about have never happened. Emma is still here. So's Mary, and Fred, too, and the others. We never sold a car, and you've taken lots of trips, and you've even hired more people for the grounds. So it wasn't the money, and Dad didn't sell any old jewelry from a box in a bank someplace. You've both been lying to me all this time. Why can't I know? Aren't I old enough? If I'm not, when for heaven's sake *will* I be?"

Tears welled in my mother's eyes. I sat down next to her, and took her trembling hands in both of mine. We sat for some time, the only sound my mother's stifled, soft sobs. I could see that she tried to stop weeping, but was unable. I reached to hold her but she pulled back from me. I knew one of her most insistent personal rules was to display an air of sweet serenity on her face for the world and to never ever break down or show emotion. I understood the rules. She turned her contorted face away again, so I would not see that her primitive emotions had taken control, and finally, with great effort, she began to speak.

"I'm so sorry Courtenay, that you had to go to that terrible place. I was against it from the start, but your father thought--well, he was afraid you'd--oh Courtenay, I don't know what to say. I just can't. It's too awful."

"What's too awful, Mother?" A coldness flowed over me, thick, like cooled oatmeal, and I was afraid as I awaited the answer.

"Maybe you're old enough--I don't know. I can't tell you, I just can't--it's just too terrible. No." My mother stood and began to walk from the room, then turned her head wearily toward me.

"I had no idea when I first met your father, well, you remember I told you once our two families thought we should marry, but no one knew about... What could I do? I wanted to protect you--I thought I could raise you and you'd never have to know----oh Courtenay." A sob ripped from her throat, and then she said softly, "Oh Courtenay" once again.

Then, quite abruptly like a door slamming in the wind, my mother regained control. Years of "thoroughbred training" came quickly to the fore just in time to pull her back from the edge of commonplace vulnerability. She pulled herself tall again, reached up and smoothed her hair, took a deep breath and became still. I could actually see the familiar, invisible door slam shut, as it had between my mother and me for so many years. I sighed. It was all just so hopeless.

I had to try one more time. "Mother, please! Wait! What is this terrible thing? Can it be so bad? What did it have to do with my having to change schools?"

My mother, composure regained, could be regal when she chose.

"Courtenay," she said, "I'm so sorry. I just cannot discuss this with you any longer. But, if you're so dead set on being on that dreadful television show next Saturday, then you may. But please, do not tell anyone in the neighborhood or at the Club. I should be horrified if anyone saw you doing that." And, with a limp wave of her hand, she stood, and swept from the room.

I sat alone on the couch, angry and confused. I was utterly determined to learn the truth no matter what it took or how I had to go about it. I mean how bad could it be?

The gang of New Town kids and I arrived at the TV studio where The American Bandstand show was to be televised. This large group of raucous friends was joined by hundreds of anxious, restless kids eager to hear their favorite bands and singing groups, and, best of all, to dance on TV for all of America to see. I immediately learned that the red light atop every TV camera might make me a star at least for an instant. It meant the camera was seeing us. It was a heady feeling, and when that red light and the black, round lens was pointed at me, I danced with far smoother and jazzier moves than the ones I'd practiced in front of my bedroom mirror with my Webcor record player blasting.

My heart pounding out of my chest, I even got to meet the ageless Dick Clark, and later The Comets and their leader Mr. Bill Haley, his sharp dark curl plastered at the center of his forehead. Sally and I had bought all the Comets' records. It was disappointing to discover the groups that day would not sing a single word, but would "lip-synch," to their popular hit records. Apparently it had always been done that way. Clark explained it all before the show began, saying it was too expensive to bring an entire band in for a performance, and that the studio was too small to accommodate them anyway. And so, Mr. Bill Haley and his Comets lip-synched "Rock Around the Clock" in a performance that looked just fine to the audience at home, and even to the worshipful kids who were in on the charade. I gyrated sweatily with a hulking Polish boy who sported an enormous black pompadour and a practiced sneer. I never learned his name, since he seemed quite

278

unable to relax the sneer long enough to speak, but I loved watching his lip curling so ceaselessly but only to the upper right hand side of his face. (After some hours, however, the crimp occasionally trembled from the strain. I was pretty sure he was getting a seriously painful lip cramp.) The young man jerked and lurched in a fair imitation of his hero Elvis, and I had an absolutely splendid time.

Much later that evening, I arrived home, breathlessly excited about my TV debut, and eager to tell my mother. I was expecting that she would be cold and annoyed with me for going even though she'd granted me permission. But I was not expecting a response of wrathful indignation. I had only just burst through the door when my mom told me in rage-tightened tones, without even saying hello, that the camera had panned down from my face to catch my dancing feet, and then focused straight up my twirling skirt. The world, it seemed, got a nice long look at my young, firm and rollicking bottom of which I'd become quite proud of late, and the camera apparently also caught my jiggling within my white nylon, pink lace-trimmed underpants. I laughed. "You mean you actually watched the show?" I shrieked. My mother was not amused.

# CHAPTER 42

I thought American History would never end, but it was a required course, so everyone who wanted to graduate reluctantly took the deadly dry subject. People told me the study of history was exciting and absorbing and perhaps that was so but it seemed New Town High hadn't gotten the word. My history teachers seemed to studiously work at making it deadly boring.

Most of us slept through it, and for those who did, cheating on the tests was routine, that being the only way to pass. The teacher, Mr. Herbert Broderick was short and stout with a large wardrobe of business suits, all dark grey except for a pale grey he wore for occasional variety or to, he hoped, pleasantly surprise his teaching colleagues. They never once noticed. Mr. Broderick's teaching methods and subject matter were also grey, his white shirts were grey, and his neckties were mostly grey with a smattering of vapid color sprinkled throughout. Even his face and hair matched in their greyness. In short, the short Mr. Broderick vanished in a crowd. In fact, he vanished when there was no crowd. He was so boring he defined the word, and he taught American History in the greyest, most wearying way he could, nearly disappearing in front of the grey blackboard at the front of the groggy, stupefied class.

His method of teaching was to open a history book and to write down every single word on the blackboard from the assignment we'd read the night before, and to drone in a grey monotone every single word as he wrote it. American history should have been incredibly exciting to all of us, but Mr. B. made absolutely certain it was excruciatingly paralyzing to our minds.

Mr. Broderick had one small, strange hobby, which he often practiced while sitting at the front of the room during history tests and final exams to the pleased distraction of his pupils: he would pass those long hours working and reworking knots on a long shank of white clothesline, only occasionally keeping an eye on the kids so that they did not cheat. They could, and often did, since Mr. Broderick mostly concentrated on tying and untying an endless variety of knots making it extremely simple for us to copy our answers from each other or even from a book on our laps.

I found watching him create these knots was mesmerizing and it made it difficult to focus on the exam anyway. Mr. Broderick would eventually become so engrossed in this hobby, he'd stop flicking his eyes upward to trap cheaters until he jerked to attention from his concentration by the ringing of his personal wind-up alarm clock, indicating "time's up." The sound made most of the students also jerk to wakefulness. He'd walk down each aisle to collect the blue books, the rope dangling from his hand, dragging across the floor, a fancy knot tied at one end. He could tie every knot ever invented by humans, and he dreamed of inventing new ones of his own and finally achieving some deserved fame; he so wished to be famous for creating new knots, maybe even one day writing his own book of his invented knots. I, along with everyone else in the school, thought he was nuts.

One afternoon, I struggled to stay awake through American History, my last class of the day. I had stayed up far too late the night before, willingly seduced by the television set, and had watched a late night talk show starring Steve Allen. He'd lined up some intriguing guests that night, including the famous Dagmar, whose desperate grasp for fame depended solely on her super-sized mammaries. It worked. She was in great demand by TV and radio, even magazines and newspapers. That night, I watched Dagmar read some ludicrous poetry and the camera panned around the audience as they ogled her chest while Mr. Allen's other guests spoke in breast innuendo. Many other New Town students had also stayed up to see this biological phenomenon, and throughout the day my girlfriends and I had to endure a multitude of rude adolescent commentary from the tittering boys: tits, boobs, knockers, headlights, dugs, jugs, paps, mams, boulders (strapped into their "over the shoulder boulder holders") knobs, udders, fun jugs. The list grew as the day wore on, some of it funny, much of it boring by day's end. We girls accepted it without rancor, because we understood (and pitied) the sources. It was, after all, only the bellowings of skanky, immature boys, and we girls had learned from the cradle that it was best to ignore most of what boys did, said and were.

Mr. Broderick droned especially slowly that day. I knew he was talking about the Bill of Rights, but my mind ebbed in and out like a torpid ocean, and eventually just stayed out. My eyelids were pulling down as if a tiny weight were attached to each lash. The struggle to keep awake was arduous. Tomorrow, I'd ask one of the more zealous students if I could copy his notes. I pulled in great swigs of oxygen, trying to keep from passing out or tipping head first onto my desk. Then, I suddenly jerked to attention with a very visible jolt.

Two rows over, one seat down, Tony Alloya had found a novel way to get through the eternity of American History without falling into a stupor: He'd begun to slowly and casually masturbate. His right hand was buried deep in his pocket, and he'd slid down low in his chair to hide the action beneath his desk. As the minutes went by, Tony's activity became less and less casual, and then much more urgent.

Intensely interested, I could not stop staring. I wanted to laugh, but dared not and had I, this remarkable show would have ended. Tony would discover I was onto him. As Tony impatiently approached his passionately desired orgasm, I watched him become more agitated, the legs of his desk bouncing softly off the floor with each desperate jerk of his fist. *How on earth does Mr. Broderick not hear or see this?* Somehow through the haze of his passion, Tony managed to keep the entire performance miraculously quiet, and since the rest of the class was practically unconscious from the numbing boredom of Mr. Broderick's brutally monotonous version of American History, no one else seemed to notice. Tony's head began to slowly bend back, his eyes first rolled back into his head and then squeezed shut, and he began to sweat heavily as he pumped and jerked toward his personal grail. Mesmerized, I could not keep my eyes from the boy's increased gyrations. My pencil hovered six inches from the paper I'd been writing, and I was becoming a little warm myself. Tony's head bent more backward, his glazed eyes now opened wide and fixed on a spot on the ceiling, his arm working his fist harder and faster, and faster and harder. Other kids were beginning to notice and they too became more alert. Tony's performance was rapidly becoming painful to watch and I began to want to loudly cheer him on. Go Tony! Go, go, GO!! I kept silent, but it wasn't easy.

Suddenly, Tony sucked his breath in, his face contorted, his mouth opened in a gushing, soundless scream, and his thrusting body stiffened and snapped once so forcibly that his hips rammed the desk straight into the air, where it hovered for an instant while his obvious pleasure throbbed through him. The scene was so intense, I thought Tony's ecstasy must be melting his fingernails. And then the desk bumped softly back to the floor. This commotion roused more of the somnolent students and they looked quickly around the room for the source. Somehow Tony had the presence of mind to noisily knock his books to the floor, lowering his head and hands to pick them up,

282

covering his violent trembling. It was finished. Done. The mildly interested kids, realizing the fun had ended, dropped their heads down and they went back to their peaceful slumbers. The whole thing was over in less than two minutes.

Then the worst happened to poor Tony Alloya. Mr. Broderick, roused by the sudden stir, glanced down the row at the boy.

"Ah, Mr. Alloya. Will you come up here please, and help me with the map? Please, will you take the pointer and show us where the original capital of the United States was? I know the class will be quite surprised." Mr. Broderick pulled at a large rolled map of the USA, which as usual, refused to release. It was so old that many students laid bets that some of the American states weren't even on it. The teacher gave it another yank and the ancient map rattled down.

I just loved this whole scene! It was the most fun I'd ever had in American History. Maybe even the whole time I'd been in public school. I watched Mr. Broderick, and then turned to look at Tony, but once again, the young boy was in control. *This has happened to him before. He's been practicing!* He grabbed his pile of books, and held them across his lap where the dark stain was spreading rapidly from hip to hip.

"Gawd, Mr. Broderick," Tony said, his voice a little hoarse, edged, and panicky. "I was just gonna ask if I could go see the school nurse. I don't feel so good. Honest. If I don't get outta here, I'm gonna let one, I'm gonna puke, I think I got dire rear, I'm gonna--" with that, he got up, clutching his books rather lower than normal and without permission or a hall pass or even a thought for the consequences, bolted from the room.

The show over, I turned back in my seat, grinning and suppressing the urge to hoot with laughter. With a broad grin I turned and looked around the room. Everyone except Sue Lewis was back to snoozing or doodling on their papers, half listening to Mr. Broderick as he whirred on like a summer fan. And, oh joy, Sue was smiling! Evidently, she too had been witness to Tony Alloya's actions. Sue's eyes locked on mine and her smile continued, friendly, warm and conspiratorial! I didn't know if I should look away or keep smiling. Had Sue forgiven me the ethnic insult in the lunch room last year? Sue raised her hand slightly, still locking me in her gaze, still smiling. It was apparent that Sue had decided it was time to reach across the breach of ancient Christian/Jewish discord. I relaxed, and with gratefulness knew I was finally at peace with the girl I'd so stupidly and ignorantly damaged a year ago. We both turned our faces back toward Mr. Broderick. I thought how I'd always be grateful to Tony Alloya!

Several months after I'd graduated from New Town, I read in the paper about how a suspicious and nauseating smell had begun to drift from under my old history teacher's apartment door. When he had not answered his neighbor's knocks, the police were summoned. They recognized the odor, and forced the door, discovering Mr. Broderick lying stark naked upon a grey rug in his apartment tied tightly in a long, tangled length of grey rope, knotted at different intervals. He had apparently tied himself up, perhaps to amuse himself sexually since he was lonely and unattached. Somehow, the news article said, he'd knotted the rope around his neck and then his ankles and hands, and the rope had slowly begun to tighten. When he must have realized to his horror what was happening, he was unable to extricate himself, and gradually, he strangled to death. It was further reported that his starving, angry grey cat charged out of the apartment door, between the legs of the policemen and down the street, and was never seen again.

# CHAPTER 43

Sue and I sat on the bleachers in the early spring late afternoon sunlight. Trees had just begun to push out pale green buds and the world was awash with singing birds and tender pastels.

"Sue," I said, "you know if you hadn't kinda, well, reached out to me that day in American History, you know, after Alloya..." we looked at one another and erupted into nervous giggles, our hands over our mouths.

"Yeah," laughed Sue. "I know. That was a great show, wasn't it? And I was pretty terrific, wasn't I?"

"Well it was awful nice of you to smile at me, Sue," I said, trying to be serious. "I've wanted to talk to you for so long about that awful thing I said that day. I've wanted to fix it, to tell you how sorry I am so many times, that I was such an awful pill, such a loser, but I was always too chicken. I didn't know how--- and I'm babbling, right?"

"Yeah, you are, Queenie," Sue said, laughing and touching my arm. "Kinda just like you did back then about that Miss Jewish American." She smiled kindly at me.

"But y'know Queenie," she said softly, "the thing that bothers me mostly is this: I kinda don't think you really know *why* you shouldn't have said what you said. Right now I know you're feeling bad about it, but you really don't know why, right? For you it was like sorta being real impolite, right?"

I nodded. I knew Sue was right and I had to try to explain. It was not without shame that I began telling Sue Lewis how my father was unable to go through a single waking hour without negative reference to a person's religion or color, and very frequently, their being homosexual. I was ashamed for "telling on him," but knew I needed to. I went on to tell Sue that my father never used correct religious titles. Instead he used only the slurs, words that hurt, words he'd tried to teach me. I tried to say those words but stammered, unable to repeat them, especially the ones that branded Jews. Sue softly told me that she'd heard them all, and that I had no need to explain, because she understood. With a wisdom and kindness that brought me nearly to tears, Sue told me that she knew I was also apologizing for my father.

"So," Sue said, "let's go get a soda, no, maybe a burger. Call your folks and tell them you won't be home for dinner, OK? You got any money? I do. I can treat."

We walked to a public phone, where I called home, surprised that the line was clear. Emma answered and I told her I'd be home way after dinner was over and that no one should worry. Sue and I went to a restaurant we knew that didn't have a large clientele, so we could sit and talk without interruption or glares from tip-desperate waitresses.

We ordered hamburgers, Cokes and fries and while we were waiting, Sue slowly and gently began to tell me how it was to be a Jew. She told of the sacred holidays and spoke of things that had happened to her people, even to some of her own family only twenty or so years ago in Nazi Germany, things so horrifying, so indescribably awful that they did not at first penetrate my mind. I listened but her words were like balls bouncing off thick walls. I could not make the words go into my brain. These things could not be true. No.

I sat in the booth, one arm up over the back, the other on the table while I played with a fork and spoon, my eyes riveted on Sue's face.

"Sue," I said, my voice rough. "You must be making this stuff up. This could never have happened. How come I never heard about any of this?"

But as Sue continued, my mind flashed unexpectedly to something my Social Studies teacher at the Academy had said one day. "If a nigger robs you, and they put him in a room with a lot of other niggers and ask you to identify him, you won't be able to because they all look exactly alike." No one in class had reacted when he'd said that. He was our teacher; it had to be the truth. We sat impassively listening to the teacher, accepting.

As I sat and listened to my now new friend, I also flashed to the time my parents took me for a short vacation in the Catskill mountains. My father advised my mother and me that there was nothing but Jews in those mountains.

"Don't buy anything from those Jews," he'd said as we drove, "because they will automatically triple the price. And don't forget," he pontificated in sonorous tones, "if a Jew storekeeper sees us coming in our Cadillac, he'll automatically raise the price of everything. They're nothing but thieves and Christ killers." I recalled sitting curled in the back, listening intently, my father's words pricking at my mind, back,

286

deep beyond my consciousness, leaving a tissue of curious guilt. Just at that point a car suddenly shot out of a dirt road to our left; neither driver could see the other because of a large overgrowth of foliage on the corner of the road. My father and the driver of the other car both slammed on their brakes, and the two cars lurched to a stop, inches from each other's bumpers. The men rolled down their windows. The other man was smiling with relief that they'd both avoided a potentially bad crash. But my dear father Mr. Walter Wolcott, enraged, rolled down his window, opened his mouth and as loudly as he could, shouted "KIKE!" He then shoved the accelerator down and in a spray of pebbles and dirt, our car sped away from the stunned man. I remembered sliding down in the back seat, feeling appalled and ashamed of my father, but not quite understanding why. But now, these years later, and on this day, I was beginning to learn.

Sue told me her immediate family left Germany to come to America in the late 1930's and that they had lost many family members in the Holocaust because they'd chosen to stay behind, not believing that they were in any more peril than their Jewish ancestors had been. Some of the Holocaust survivors made their ways to America some years after the war's end, and as a souvenir of their time in the camps and for the rest of their lives, they carried purple-black numbers tattooed on the insides of their arms and wrists. Some kept them covered always, even in the hottest weather. Some kept them exposed always, even in the coldest weather.

"You know, Queenie," said Sue, her voice low, scratchy, "so many of my relatives suffered in horrible ways. I mean you just can't imagine anything as horrible as what they lived through. Y'know, the survivors, our relatives who came back finally gave up trying to explain, because their stories were so incredible, everyone doubted them."

I looked across the table at Sue, unable to speak, wanting to offer some comfort, but knew it would sound stupid and forced if I did. Sue took a breath, deep and long, and she told me stories of the tortures people endured at the hands of the Nazis. She was graphic, her words were colorful, dripping. I was able see it all happening, as if I'd been there. I could smell the endless, billowing smoke from the ovens, see the starved bodies, hear the screams. My mouth dried out, my heart was suspended. I clutched my hands together, wanting Sue to stop, yet knowing I had to hear it all, every terrible word. It had quite quickly become my job to learn. My eyes remained so wide, so fixed on Sue's face that they dried out, and when I finally blinked, they hurt as if filled with sand.

I'd been born in 1940 and so was very young when it was all happening, but I clearly remembered the patriotic songs, the parades, the things people saved and had to do without. I remembered my father screaming at the dining room table about President Roosevelt and his "goddammed Social Security, may the bastard die a horrible death." I remembered having to be very still during dinner while the sonorous voice of Lowell Thomas on the big wooden radio in the corner of the good parlour enraptured his audiences with the latest war news. I knew there'd been a big war and that it had had ended with two terrible bombings in Nagasaki and Hiroshima. I remembered hearing about the heroic returning soldiers and the words "our glorious defeat of America's enemies." But I had never heard any of the horror stories Sue was telling me now. My mind was spinning slowly as Sue's soft bitter words entered my ears and mind and heart. My parents had never said anything about it, but surely, they knew. Why hadn't my Academy teachers ever said anything about the Holocaust? Surely they, of all people, knew of it. Had Mr. Raleigh instructed them to avoid it? Did everyone think if they didn't talk about it, it would be forgotten forever? Or was the message that the Jews and others who'd suffered in the death camps were expendable and deserved what they got anyway?

My mind began to spin faster now, as my memories twisted with Sue's words about the the horrors of Hitler's final solution and of how well he'd succeeded. Afraid I might get sick, I swallowed some Coke, now warm and flat.

I thought about the war's end when my father took me on a rare father-daughter excursion into New York City to see a gigantic, thundering parade of returning soldiers. He'd held me up high from his perch on wooden bleachers where I saw what seemed to be millions of soldiers, Jeeps and tanks blasting past me in an endless khaki river. The noise of the roaring war vehicles smashed so violently on the pavement, I could feel it rumble deep in my teeth and guts. I remembered a tiny, grey haired woman, wearing a black coat with a ratty, worn fur collar, who suddenly burst from the bleachers, crashing down, falling, stumbling, shoving people out of her way. Screaming and crying, she raced alongside the column of marching soldiers, frantically waving a white handkerchief. One of her shoes fell off and lay on the street. A young man from one of the uniformed marching rows leaned forward and laughed joyfully, waving at her but he did not break ranks, and kept marching. The woman ran alongside the parade until it ended, blocks away, all the while waving the small white hankie and weeping, shrieking "My son, oh my son is home!"

Sue's words penetrated my thoughts. She was spinning a long, endless ribbon of horror, a soft wail, but still I could understand every word, the impact of the terrible history lesson knocking my center away. I felt icy fingers of burning guilt slide into my senses, forcing me to think of how I'd been a rich child, oblivious, while people a few thousand miles away were dying hideously, in ways I was unable to comprehend.

Tears began to pour in shiny, crossing paths down Sue's cheeks.

"Queenie," she said. "If you ever see a Swastika carved or drawn anyplace in the world, please find a way to remove it. Promise me! Promise you'll do that."

"Yes," I said. "*Yes.*" I reached across the table and grasped Sue's hands and we two clung tightly, and I was afraid that if I let go I'd sink into a gallery of horrors from which I would never be able to escape.

Sue Lewis would spend the rest of her life working to keep the memory of the Holocaust alive in the world, and quite often she was successful. It ended for her when she was murdered, along with three dozen other attendees at a small-town Synagogue while she was making a speech entitled "Let Us Never Forget." It was all over in an instant. The bomb had been very well made and was extremely effective.

# CHAPTER 44

My dear blando non-mother had barely recovered from seeing my underwear on television when one Saturday morning I came bouncing downstairs on my way to New Town to work on the yearbook. As I rounded the landing, my mother stopped walking so quickly her head snapped back. She looked as if she was staring at a stranger.

I had pulled my hair back into a ponytail high over one ear, and I guess to my most horrified parent it must have looked like an antler. I'd tied a bright red bow around it at the base, and I had cut bangs into a jagged row across my forehead. The pixy cut was in, and I was considering whether to cut all of my hair into sharp points around my face. That morning I'd cut my bangs just to get a feel for it, and to allow my New Town girlfriends to first pass judgment before I continued my hair butchery.

It wasn't just the bizarre hairdo that made my mother stop in stunned silence. My eyelids were blue, and the lashes layered with chunked mascara, some flaking onto my cheeks in tiny black stipples. I'd drawn a deep black line around the edges of my eyelids and had thickened it to points at the outer corners. I rather fancied I looked like Cleopatra. My cheeks glowed with a feverish incandescence, and my lips were smeared a deep vermilion. Bright red plastic hoop earrings swung from my newly pierced lobes and were so large they bounced against my shoulders. It had escaped my mother that I'd gotten her ears pierced one afternoon several months ago by my friend Gloria who had performed the operation with the standard tools of the trade; cork, long needle, cigarette lighter, ice cube, and length of thick white thread.

"Wait Gloria!" I'd shrieked with laughter as my friend approached me with the needle raised murderously in one hand. "Sterilize it first, you idiot! Don't you dare stick that filthy thing into my earlobe 'til you've burned it first with the lighter. You hear me?" And I rolled away across the bed.

"Oh. Yeah, well, you're right Queenie. Sorry 'bout that. I'll just do that little thing. Meanwhile, hold that ice cube against your earlobe so it'll get numb, OK?" And I did that while Gloria stuck the needle into the cork and held the end of it in flame until it glowed orange.

"Here it comes, Queenie. Deep breath now. Be brave!" shouted a delighted Gloria, and she grabbed my earlobe and slowly inserted the red-hot needle into the spot she'd marked previously with a pen. I'd flinched, waiting for the pain, but it was only dull. The ice cube had done the trick. The threaded needle went through my earlobe as if it were cheese, Gloria pulled the string through, made a loop and a knot and snipped it free.

"Look," said Gloria, "no blood. Well, nearly no blood. OK, a little. Oh well, tough noogies."

"How the heck can I see my own earlobe, you jerk? And what do you mean by `tough noogies?' Did you make a mistake?"

"No, no, no. Don't have a bird, turd. Put the ice cube on the other earlobe and get ready, Queenie."

I had been able to camouflage from my mother the string Gloria had threaded through my lobes by keeping my hair hanging long. When the mutilation had healed and the encrusted strings slowly eased out, the holes were quite small, and even now, my mother did not notice that the gaudy earrings were piercing my earlobes, and were not clipped to them.

But there was more. My mother's widened eyes raked up and down my body, from scalp to toes. I had finished off my ensemble with a white short-sleeved Angora sweater, tight, bright Capri pants, and white flats. I was happy and excited. Without a single doubt and without too much effort, I had triumphantly achieved the "cheap" look, so maligned by my Academy peers and yes, me too, and I felt wonderful and sexy and proud.

"Courtenay Scott Wolcott!" my mother shrilled. "Where did you get ... I mean, where on this good earth did you ever get those--those--things, those--" she could hardly say the words – "*clothes*? That---that—*costume???*"

"Oh, you mean this stuff?" I looked down at the outfit I'd spent at least an hour putting together. "Charge cards, Mommie."

"COURTENAY SCOTT WOLCOTT!" my mother bellowed. Uh oh. Middle names again. I was in trouble but I didn't care.

I sashayed through the dining room, shaking my butt and heading for the kitchen, intending to con Fred into driving me down the hill.

I turned back to my mother. "Yeah, Mums, what can I do ya fer?"

"Where exactly do you think you are going?" my mother's voice, now higher than usual, pierced the air.

"Out."

"Out? Out where, young lady? Stand still and talk to me."

"Ma! Get cool! I'm goin' down to New Town. The photogs are there today because we're doin' that spread for the middle of the yearbook and I won the 'Personality Plus,' contest, remember? Me an' Kenny Yzquierdo. He's gonna sit on my shoulders with a funny hat on and we'll yuck it up for the camera. You remember. I told you at dinner last night. Oh. Yeah. I forgot. You guys never listen to me when I'm talking to you at dinner. Or anywhere else, come to think of it. Oh but, well, not to worry! I'm used to it. I'm not bothered by it anymore. Much. Anyway, Ma, I gotta go. They're expecting me. Oh--one more thing. I'm takin' Driver's Ed in school, 'member I told you? Ooops. Forgot again that you don't ever hear me. Or see me either for that matter. Well look Mommie, I get it. It's taken me a lot of years to figure this out, but I finally understand that I'm just not there when I'm with you and Dad." I shook my head and then smiled kindly at my mother.

"Well, anyway," I went on, my voice full of resignation, "Can't do anything about all that now. It's too late. But, as you don't recall, I'll be getting my permit in a couple of weeks, so then I'll be wanting to take my driver's test, so would it be OK if you gave me a car for graduation? I saw one in a showroom in New Town. A nice '57 Chevy convertible. Red. 'Course Fred could drive me to college because we can't have cars there, but then they probably don't allow Negroes on the campus anyway, so that's out. Oh well, I could just keep my new car here, and use it when I come home for vacations. No need to answer right now, Ma. Talk about it with ya later on. Next time you're in New Town. Oh yeah, you never go to New Town. Only I go to New Town. Hmmm--wonder why. Well, if you ever change your mind and go there, take a look at the car in the showroom. It's a real doozy! The guy's card is on the kitchen counter so you can get the address of the showroom. Well, see ya, Ma."

I walked back to my dumbstruck mother and gave her a quick kiss on the cheek, then ran through the swinging doors into the Butler's Pantry and out into the kitchen. As I went through the back door, I thought I heard my poor stunned mother call out weakly, "Oh no you don't, young lady, get upstairs and take off--" but by then I was out in the driveway, calling to Fred, and getting into his car. My mother was left mewling impotent threats at a large, empty room.

The graduates-to-be who'd won the yearbook contests were all at New Town that Saturday afternoon, dressed in ridiculous, exaggerated outfits they thought appropriate for their contest photos. They called themselves the "Senior Celebrities" -- Most Popular, Class Geniuses, Best Dressed, Most Flirtatious, Most Sophisticated, Class Citizens, Best Natured, Class Athletes, Best Looking, Best Hair (Dom won that one), Best Dancers, Best Musicians and of course Personality Plus Boy and Girl, (I'd won that with Kenny Yzquierdo, a boy of Spanish descent so well-liked that some students and teachers would weep when he graduated a few weeks hence.) Kenny would immediately go on to work for UNICEF, and over the years raise millions of dollars for hungry children everywhere, because it pained him immeasurably to see them suffer. He adopted those he could, loved and nurtured those he could not, and the boy who won Personality Plus in high school lived a long, happy life that made a difference to many.

I was just ecstatic when told I'd won Personality Plus Girl. I had not expected it and was thrilled that now I was so thoroughly accepted.

The kids horsed around all morning, driving the photographer into a babbling rage. The frazzled man was on a tight schedule with other yearbook jobs that day, and he didn't have time to chase the kids as they roared around the school, clowning and playing. He spent far too many hours screaming at them to settle down and get into the poses that would best demonstrate to history how they'd won their immortal labels. Finally, the job completed, the exhausted (and shaking) photographer packed his gear and hurriedly left, his face tight and pale.

We all then wandered into the lunchroom that had been opened by Mr. Wright who'd reasoned he had to wax the linoleum floor anyway. It was, in hindsight, a small error in judgment: we seniors charged the kitchen area, and like the starving Armenians to which our parents were always alluding, devoured every scrap of food the taxpayers had provided. We discovered a large cache of hot dog rolls, wrapped and stored for Monday's menu of Hot Dogs and Beans, and with something like divine inspiration, we wadded the rolls into dough balls and happily blasted one another. The balls splatted ferociously onto various of our body parts—none were off limits—but our school chum's hair was the most effective hurl, causing the best of all screams! A few were thrown with mighty force into the darker corners of the room where they remained for decades, endlessly painted-over testimonials to the Class of 1957.

As the day sped on, the group became rowdier. One would think we'd get tired but we gained more energy as we expended more energy. Harkening to the old Judy Garland/Mickey Rooney movies, my classmates and I began shouting, "Let's put on a show! We can hold it in the barn!" We put together an impromptu play, using the long metal counter that divided the kitchen from the lunchroom as the stage. One popular young man with the improbable first name of "Three," (his parents had been unable to think of a name for him, their third child) performed an obscenely hilarious ad-lib act about a fat woman stuck on a toilet, her gargantuan weight causing a powerful, unbreakable suction. His facial expressions and anguished gyrations were so authentic we all collapsed together in smothering mirth, falling to the floor and knocking over chairs. I laughed so hard I became panicked I'd lose control of my bodily functions. I tried to stop but that made me laugh harder. Finally, Three explained to his captive howling audience, the woman's husband came home, discovered his wife's problem and was only able to release the suction by ramming a crowbar between her large buttocks and the toilet seat. Sitting on the counter, his butt jammed into one of the food warming bins, Three sprang up and out of his perch, making a startlingly foul noise mimicking quite accurately what probably was the exact sound of an obese woman's backside breaking free of a toilet seat. For the rest of my time at New Town, I was not able to take food from those bins.

Finally, one of the more level-headed of us suggested we get down to business and write the annual Class Will. This list was always printed on the final page of the yearbook, after the local and personal ads we kids had dunned from businesses and parents. Its purpose was to leave behind certain items and wishes to the younger students (and some teachers). The list included giant economy sized bottles of aspirin, a collision-proof Chevy, a water pistol, a pogo stick, an extra ten minutes at the end of all classes, an invitation for all students to take endless Regents exams, a huge box of late passes free for the taking on a table in one of the hallways, bottles of Air-wick. The list grew longer, louder, more creative and then went completely out of control. Finding this exercise to be enormously funny, we competed to create the most disgusting, repulsive and obscene Class Will gifts, surprising ourselves with our colorful imaginations and rich lewdness. I loved being in the midst of this maelstrom and knew I would never forget that day. I also thought for an instant about The Academy and wondered if my friends there would have enjoyed these sorts of shenanigans, and thought "no" and stopped thinking about them. Their loss.

Finally, we began to tire, our ingenuities draining like wrung sponges. Mr. Wright stood in the doorway glowering and trying to shout over the melee. As ever, he was ignored. Finally, someone bellowed that maybe we all should go for hamburgers and stretch the party a little longer. With a raucous shout of accord, we trooped off, loudly tumbling through the red-painted metal doors like a throng of dogs newly out of their kennels. We all moved instinctively toward Bacci's, the joint that had the best burgers, dogs and fries within a hundred miles, and had a huge, gaudy and loud Wurlitzer, too.

I loved Bacci's, named for its owner who'd had the good sense to keep the interior old-fashioned enough to look appealing, but current enough to avoid being square, thus possibly losing the teen age trade. There were booths, and small round marble-topped tables and chairs with heart-shaped backs of twisted metal. The large dance floor was covered in a wildly designed linoleum that gave the dancers a good surface on which to twist or jive or jump. Or even to slow dance. Along with his burgers and dogs, Mr. Bacci sold ice cream sodas, sundaes, candy, soda pop and bucket-sized milk shakes, two flavors. Wednesdays were "All You Can Eat" night from 5 to 8 p. m. and it was common for some of the kids to fast for two days in preparation. We never could quite empty the kindly Mr. Bacci's larders, but a few times we came close.

On our way to Bacci's, my friends and I talked and laughed, tramping through the side streets surrounding New Town High. One young student grabbed me roughly around the shoulders, but recoiled abruptly when my Angora sweater left stray hairs on his beloved black leather jacket. He stopped, looked down in horror and spread his palms.

"That's gross, Queenie," he shouted. "Look. Ya roont my jacket heeya!"

"Go pound sand, honey!" I called over my shoulder, and I actually skipped away, turning once to look at him and laugh. "That chick needs the men in white coats," I heard him say.

"Yeah," said another. "A real candidate for the funny farm!"

The spring air was soft and sweet, and the brown-grey of winter was vanishing beneath new, green life. I knew we all felt our blood pumping urgently through our bodies, a sweet but confusing sensation. There would be much to look forward to after graduation we knew, but also much to fear and much to hate. We all longed for happy, productive lives, and most of us knew we'd have to work hard for our shot at the American Dream. I knew most of us also fantasized about achieving greater successes than our parents had found, even mine who I knew were not happy people, but some would never get out of the ruts dug by their families for generations. For now though, it was spring, graduation was near, and we were on our way to eat, to dance, and play. The world was new and fresh and washed clean, and it was ours alone to grab and from which to wring life. That day, I felt that nothing, absolutely nothing, could mar this special moment.

"Hey schmoes," someone yelled. "Which one of youse assholes wants to go to the drive-in tonight?" And all chorused yes, we did indeed.

"Great idea. I'll get my old man's wheels. Who volunteers to ride in the trunk? Gotta be a fewa youse small ones."

A few voices volunteered.

"No way, not you, Timmy," someone else screamed out. "You got the gas bigtime. I wuz inna trunk witchoo once an' I damn near croaked. You drive up front widda windows open."

Dom and I walked side by side, not talking much, but bumping together a little and occasionally smiling and snatching glances.

Mr. Bacci was standing in the window of his restaurant watching the laughing and shouting group of young people approach. He squinted his eyes and mouthed "Queenie," and I smiled, flattered he knew my name. And then, the air turning cold, very cold as if the world had just lost the sun, I abruptly stopped moving with the group and looked up the street. My arms fell to my sides, limp and with no feeling. I could feel my face looking alarmed and scared. Mr. Bacci craned his neck to see what was causing my sudden anxiety.

Coming toward us was a group of Academy kids, Remington Nathaniel Richardson amongst them. I realized then that this exact instant was exactly what I'd been dreading for the past two years.

Stiff as a wooden puppet, I slowly looked around. There was no place to run or hide. Some of the New Town kids had stopped now too, and were looking back at me, waiting for me to catch up. I took a couple of steps toward them. The gap between the two cliques was narrowing and there I was, standing alone between them. My eyes darted forth and back. Then I made a quick decision: I would go to the Academy kids, speak with them, and then introduce everyone. And I would hate it.

Head high, a big eager, fake smile plastered across my face, I approached the private school crowd.

"Hi!"

I flinched at my own sweetly false voice. Some of my old friends failed to recognize me at first. As soon as they did, they brightened.

"Courtenay! How terrific! Wonderful to see you! What on earth are you doing here?" Their eyes swept over my clothing, and then they looked at each other, their breeding disallowing them to register shock. But a few could not control the involuntary raising of their eyebrows.

"Oh, well, we were just doing some stupid yearbook stuff," I said, "and the only time the photographer could give us was today, so they opened the school for us, and, well, we got done, and so, well, well--here we are. We're gonna go get some chow... dinner. So! Hey! What on earth are *you* doing in New Town?" I was smiling too brightly, too eagerly and I knew it. The Academy kids surveyed the New Town bunch solemnly. No one spoke. The silence between them was as thick as fog.

"Oh," my old friend Sally finally answered, "we wanted to see `Marty,' and it wasn't playing at the St. George. So we found out it's playing down here in New Town. Hey, you wanna come with us? You know, like we used to?"

"Oh um, thanks, I'd really love to, but I--I can't." I moved closer to the Academy group and cupping my hand at the side of my mouth, whispered, "You know, I'd really *much* rather go with you all, but I've kind of promised these idiots I'd go with them. I hope you understand. You know how it is." And I was filled with a self-loathing so immediate and strong it stabbed my stomach. I squeezed my hands into fists and bit my lips, hoping no one from New Town had heard my traitorous, shameful statement. I was afraid to look at them to see if they had.

"Yeah, sure, Courtenay, sure," Sally said, coolly surveying my outfit, her face registering open distaste. "We understand." From the back of the crowd, Remington Richardson called out to me with exaggerated cheerfulness, "Hey, Court! Why don't you introduce us to your nice new school chums?"

I turned and gave him a forced, sweet smile. "Sure," I said cheerfully.

Anxiously faking a bigger smile, I beckoned to my New Town friends.

"Hey you guys. Come on over here. I'd like you to meet some old friends of mine." *Oh God, how I hate this, and oh God how I hate me!* Swiveling my head from one group to the other, I tried to send each meaningful looks of loyalty but as the moments passed, I became confused and was unable to sustain the cryptic balance I so desperately wanted.

Warily, the two factions edged together. The New Towners, dressed in their ludicrous yearbook picture outfits, approached the impeccably outfitted Academy kids. The contrast was stark and glaring.

As I made the introductions, I found myself growing angry at the way my Academy friends were behaving and I was becoming more and more uncomfortably aware that I myself had behaved exactly this way once myself. I hated their cold superior attitude toward my public-school friends. I hated that their behaviours made me feel defensive. And I hated myself for desperately trying to convey to each group that I thought the other was a bunch of losers. It seemed that time was frozen in that place, on that sidewalk. Neither group seemed to understand my frantic dance. Both sides frowned at me as I stood between them, confused and becoming exhausted by trying to send my overt double messages. Shame came easily to me that day. And I genuinely hated who I was even though I did not at that moment quite know who I was.

I saw The Academy kids stare at Dom, then smile derisively. The way their eyebrows went up as they looked at him, and then back at each other with superior but slight smirks coldly infuriated me. I had an urge to scream.

But then to my clenching horror, Dom began to act like a thorough jackass. He postured, preened and sneered, combed his hair repeatedly with elaborate flourishes, and looked at The Academy kids as if *he* were the superior one. He then suddenly began to dance grotesquely on the sidewalk, to no music, though the New Town kids soon provided it, clapping in rhythm and singing Big Joe Turner's "Shake, Rattle and Roll." Staring at Dom's ridiculous and mortifying display, I ground my teeth so forcefully my jaws ached. My stomach hurt. I hated him, hated them, hated everyone, and mostly me. I wanted to turn and run. Why was he putting on that horrible display? I wanted to die, right then, right there.

After accepting the wild, snorting applause of his classmates, Dom walked over and put his arm possessively around me, grinning widely at The Academy kids. I was incredibly mortified but I smiled brightly to make it seem like a huge joke. My attraction for Dom disappeared like hot vapor. He had embarrassed me. He was dressed as usual in his T-shirt, leather jacket, tight jeans and black boots. His greased back DA was bunched higher than usual for his Best Hair yearbook photo. Worst of all, he continued to preen and run his comb through his hair again and again and he swaggered even while standing still.

But then a sort of meager serenity crept through me as I began to understand that each group suffered from their own personal style of snobbery. I looked down at the sidewalk because I now knew I was the worst of them all for trying to be a part of both camps, instead of remaining faithful to one. The trouble for me that fateful and fated afternoon was that I had succeeded to some degree with this sham, and therefore I could never again belong to the inner circle of either.

Eventually, awkwardly, the groups made feeble attempts at good-byes, and they separated, heading in opposite directions and leaving me standing alone on the grey cement sidewalk, looking from one to the other and not knowing which way to go.

With one long, expressionless look at my Academy acquaintances, I finally turned and trotted after the New Town contingency into Bacci's and settled into a booth, the day's luster forever shattered. When our meals were finally served by the good Mr. Bacci, most of us attacked them with something close to starving savagery, but I could not. The acrid taste of disloyalty and two-facedness, mine, turned the food to ashes in my mouth.

# CHAPTER 45

I sat on the edge of my bed, holding the phone tightly to my ear. It was Saturday morning, and I had nothing to do so thought I'd call Sally and make a plan. I was anxious, wondering if things were still OK between us since the episode on the sidewalk in front of Bacci's. I knew I'd be able to tell by the tone of Sally's voice. I could always read my best friend. As I heard the burring of the phone ringing, my heart began to thump against my ribs. The rings stopped and I heard Sally speak.

"Hi Sal! How ya doin'?" My voice was thick. I cleared my throat and tried again. I kept the phone shoved tightly against my ear, trying to detect any special tones, a coldness maybe.

"I'm fine, thank you, Courtenay," Sally answered coolly. Or did she? Was I hearing something that was not really there?

"Well, Sal old pal, glad to hear that. Whatcha doin' today? You want to go to the Down Beat? Bet they've got a whole lot of new 45s since we were there. How about it?" I loosened the phone. My ear had begun to ache.

"Well, no Courtenay, I really can't." Sally answered, giving no reasons. Her voice was slightly higher pitched, her words slightly more polite than usual.

A pause. "Uh, well, OK, Sal, umm, how about a game of tennis? Maybe the grass courts are open, and we could try that. Grass is a drag, though. So hard to play on. The ball hits the ground and just stays there, y'know? Ever noticed that?"

"Yeah, yeah. It's really hard to play on grass. But when you fall, it feels better. But no, I can't, Court. Sorry." Again, Sally made no excuses and the empty spaces between our words was heavy and long.

"Sally,--is something wrong? I mean, is it because of what happened in New Town? I mean, I just didn't know--I was dressed like that because of yearbook pictures--I didn't—I--"

"Oh, no Court. Please, don't worry about that. Umm, well, let's see--"

I knew my old friend was struggling to get out of this awkward conversation. Sally was lying, struggling to be polite. It was obvious she had been badly affected by that sidewalk scene, and I understood that my old friend no longer had a choice. For Sally and everyone else in her world, the rule was simple; loyalty always and only to Academy friends and connections. I had broken this sacred rule and I knew it.

But I was counting on my long friendship with Sally. We'd been dear friends from infancy, when both families were neighbors in a different town, a handsome area yet not quite as elegant as our current neighborhood digs. Back then, some would have called where they lived, "shabby genteel."

Both of our fathers came into the world swaddled in old money. They'd begun their marriages in homes that were wedding presents from their respective fathers, who had the antediluvian idea that roughing it in homes of only 10 or 12 rooms with one or two servants, instead of mansions with 30 rooms or more and countless house staff, built character. Our fathers were both willing to go through with this amusing charade, knowing that quite soon they would be moving their families into a mansion on a very respectable estate, the very kind they'd always lived in while growing up. Sally's family moved first, followed shortly by ours. A year after they'd moved, Sally's beloved father Charles had died unexpectedly of heart failure while in the hospital for a slipped disc, and we two friends shared a terrible grief, both having loved him.

Our friendship had been further strengthened by a bond formed one rainy summer weekend. We were both playing at my house, and were bored the way young people are bored whether the weather is fine or not. We decided it would be fun to go up to my extensive attic to play with "all the old-fashioned stuff." I asked my mother for permission to rummage around in the attic. My mother, in her standard telephone pose, nodded in unconscious assent. We raced down the long hall to the attic door and charged up the long flight of steps to the treasures that awaited.

Hours later, we were still up there, going through boxes and trunks, dressing up, looking at old books and magazines, laughing, pretending, imagining. We cleared a corner and created a grand parlor from the pieces of old furniture stored in the shadowy attic. We pretended we were great ladies, talking great lady stuff with grand, old money accents. We poured air tea from an old china tea pot with no spout, drank it from two matching fragile china cups the color of snow at dawn, our pinkies stuck out and slightly curled. We served air crumpets from a yellowed and cracked Limoges dish, politely refused seconds, and said in rich lady voices, "Oh well my dear, if you insist. Just one more."

As we pushed an old, crumbling swooning couch back in place, something kept it from sliding across the widely planked floor. I got down on my hands and knees to investigate and discovered a white wicker box jammed underneath. We two girls, both wearing softly faded satin and veiled glamorous hats from the second World War years, sat on the dusty couch and opened the basket.

It was an old sewing basket that had belonged to one of my grandmothers. Its double lids opened like a book, and one of the looped handles was missing. Inside we found scraps of thin fragile silk in a profusion of shimmering colors and heavier scraps of a richer texture. Stuck into the tufted, faded blue velvet that lined the lid were rusted pins and needles, with many curls of silk thread still caught in their eyes. We found antique safety pins, the design of which we had never seen before, and decided they were probably the first ever made. The old basket also contained enchanting items not related to sewing. A filigree shoe buckle looked as though it had once been attached to a flapper's red silk shoe. (We immediately made up a story about how it had flown off during a wild performance of the Charleston, and its owner, a tragically dying young Parisian damsel, had insisted she be buried in her beloved dancing shoes at the end of her short, tragic life. The scene was too delicious, and we were nearly in tears as we created it.)

The basket also contained a collection of Civil War brass buttons, a dog's collar with the name "Coalie" on an attached tag, a crocheted book mark, a broken piece of tortoise shell, and a tiny, beautiful gold compact, no larger than a sugar cube, with a mirror inside its lid. Its top was a cameo of a white-faced Grecian damsel on a pale pink shell background. Her eyes were cast down, her hair flowed in long, waving tendrils, and tiny flowers had been carved between those curls. Inside remained some solidified face powder, and when I touched it gently with my finger, it smudged softly, just as it must have for its now departed owner. It was beautiful and delicate, and I slipped it into my pocket when Sally looked elsewhere, and later kept it hidden deep in the back of my dresser drawer. I never asked my parents to whom it belonged, but was certain it had lived through sweet yesterdays. When I held it in my hands, romantic tales about its history flooded my mind so thoroughly, I would become unconscious to the world around me.

We found something else in the basket on that day. At the bottom of the sewing box lay an old diary, with a small broken brass lock, its maroon cover stained with pale grey mildewed patterns and streaks. Inside, in familiar, feathery script was the name Helen Avis, my mother's name before her marriage to Walter Hancock Wolcott. In fervent, passionate words, the young, tender-hearted and romantic Helen had poured out her soul onto the pages. The ink was black. On some of the pages there were tiny, sunburst-shaped blotches in the words, and I knew before I'd read them that the stains had been caused by my mother's tears. I began to read the words, and my throat thickened as I discovered my mother had once been filled with the same longings and worries and dreams that I had myself. Sally and I, heads bent together, our hair touching lightly, read without speaking. Even with the words in front of us, we could not get a clear picture of young Helen Avis. It all seemed too abstract, too distant and we could not fit the Helen Avis Wolcott of today to the young, fragile and hopeful girl on those pages.

Along about the middle of the diary, our eyes widened with disbelief. Reading the penned sentences faster and then faster yet, we discovered that my mother, Helen Avis, was once briefly and passionately engaged to Sally's father! We gasped in unison, stared at each other and went back to the words. It had been a tumultuous although fleeting affair. Juicier yet, it had been an intensely kept secret. A ring had been given (we tore through the box trying to find it, but it was not there) and a few friends had been sworn-to-the-death secrecy.

We sat on the dusty attic floor, the diary opened on our laps. We read how my mother had planned to "tell the family soon," but the engagement had to be kept secret for a while longer, evidently because her fiancé's mother was "difficult." On the sepia, crumbling pages of the diary, Helen had written of their many plans and dreams, of how the couple had hoped for a large family of perfect children. But soon, the pages revealed that the romance was cooling as Helen admitted that Charles was far too attached to his mother. He could apparently make no decisions without consulting her, and assumed without asking that she would live with them after they were married.

Helen Avis ended her diary with the words, in huge letters, THAT OLD WITCH WILL NEVER LIVE WITH US, NOT EVER, NEVER, NEVER, NEVER!!!!! There were stabbed pen nib holes in the paper and many more tear blotches in the ink. Thus the engagement ended, and Sally and I were destined to be best friends. But not sisters.

Now, as I talked on the phone with my old friend, I sensed that Sally was thinking of that day in the attic too and was trying to be warm to me. I knew Sally valued our friendship. I heard my friend pull in a deep breath.

"Courtenay," she said. "I'm gonna be in a horse show today, down at the Winkworth stables. How's about if you come down to watch? I'll be jumping Charlotte for the first time. Gee, I hope I'll win. I know, I know what you're thinking. You don't have to tell me. I can always tell what you're thinking, Court!"

Sally's words were forced and I could not ignore that, but still, I so warmly appreciated my friend's efforts.

"You're thinking," Sally went on, "that I already have a zillion ribbons, so how come I want more. I dunno. I guess when you're hooked on horses, you're hooked for good. So, will you be there? I'd love to see you there, honest I would, Courtenay." I felt uneasy.

"You always bring me good luck. You always do!" Sally's voice was now too forced. "I'll tell Mother and Cecil you'll be there, and you can sit with them, OK?"

I smiled into the phone, relieved that we were still friends, edgily knowing we were not. Not really. Not anymore. I knew it was done.

"Of course, Sal," I said. "I'd love to see you win a *thousand* more ribbons! I really bring you luck? Honest?? Neato-mosquito! This'll be like Charlotte's debut, right? I wouldn't miss her coming-out party for the world. Yeah! Charlotte, Debutante Horse of the Year!" When I hung up, happy again, my doubts and worries were gone. So then why did I turn and look down at my bed pillow, fold myself face down into it and howl with long, drawn out sounds and tears so profuse the pillow became soaked?

# CHAPTER 46

I found it hard to pretend otherwise, but I tried for as long as I could. It was painfully obvious I was not being invited to The Academy events as often as before. The phone did not ring much and when it did, it was usually my New Town friends calling to talk or to invite me places. I tried pretending it did not hurt. It did. A lot.

I worked at keeping a cheerful countenance, and focused on the happy events of my life instead of these new, dark pulling-down ones. Since the incident outside Bacci's, there had been a slight but distinct shift in my old friends' interest in me, and I knew it. It existed. The memory of my two-faced behavior on that day nagged hard at me. I had rationalized The Academy kids' behavior, and my own too, but the truth kept surfacing, just like the faces that floated to the lake's surface in my dream. Exhausted from endless self-examination, I could come up with no more excuses, and had to accept the truth; I had behaved inexcusably. But, I felt I had been forced to toady to both groups. I struggled to get around it, to make it right in my mind, but it simply would not feel right.

One afternoon the phone rang, and I raced for it, my heart pounding with hope. It turned out to be Montgomery MacDowell ("yep it's me Court, yours truly!") an Academy acquaintance and quite possibly the most boring boy I had ever known. His five favorite words, which he used until they were as flimsy as the tongue of an old shoe, were I, Me, Myself, My and Mine. He never talked about girls or school or the world's problems or God or anything at all, except as to how they all might relate to him.

Normally I would have avoided Montgomery. He was so intensely boring he actually caused my teeth to ache. If I saw him waiting for me anywhere, I changed my direction even if it inconvenienced me and made me late to wherever I was headed. He had to know that everyone avoided him, but it was increasingly obvious he did not.

On the positive side, Montgomery was extremely handsome. Tall, freckled, with curly reddish blond hair, he looked so much like Van Johnson, he could have been his son. But rather than bestowing him with something which might temper his unattractive personality, his good looks only added to his problems for he was extravagantly conceited. It did not hurt that he was also obscenely wealthy.

Montgomery spent an inordinate amount of time in front of mirrors, or any surface that could send back any sort of reflection, even distorted or foggy. He could never pass one without giving himself a smiling salutation, even from the backs of spoons and the blades of knives. A dazzler, at least until he opened his mouth, Montgomery could make a marvelous first impression when he entered a room, if the place were filled with people he'd never met. But Mr. MacDowell, smothered and blinded by his ponderous vanity, never noticed that everyone he came near slowly edged away or that his presence cut a swath through crowds.

I so wanted to be fair about Montgomery MacDowell, so I tried to separate his boringness from the fact that together we had to endure dreadful, interminable Children of the American Revolution meetings on too many Saturday mornings. But whenever I heard his voice, I couldn't help but think of those awful CAR meetings. My parents forced me to go because they thought it was important I belong to an organization that acknowledged the family's status in the American Revolution and the history of America in general. (And, my father never failed to add, only the *right* people belonged to the CAR, meaning, of course, that no Jews or Negroes or Hispanics or Irish or Asian or other lesser folk were ever members.) After all, they'd told me repeatedly, "you are directly related to Benjamin Franklin and your father's middle name is Hancock, and you know who had the largest signature in the center of the Declaration of Independence, remember?"

I was later told, much to my amusement, that old Ben F. had allegedly fathered a large number of my supposed ancestors with ladies to whom he was definitely not married. I'd always wondered about the Hancock connection, too, and rather regarded the owner of the Declaration's most flamboyant signature as a man with a severe need to flaunt, in which case my father qualified perfectly as his relative.

"Oh!" I now said into the phone, disgusted at the chirpiness in my voice. "Hi there, Montgomery! How the heck are you?" I didn't really care how the heck Montgomery was, and knew better than to ask, because he was more than likely to tell. *God, he's such a dink. I just can't stand this. Why did I ask him that? Stupid, stupid, STUPID!!*

"Well hi there Courtenay, I'm just fine, and how are you? You know what I've been doing? Father bought me one of those gigantic model airplanes, you know the kind, it's attached to this long cable and you stand in a field someplace and make the thing go round and round and round. Father paid someone to make it for me. It's big and yellow, and boy, you should hear the noise it makes. I just love it. Deafening, that's what it is. Just deliciously deafening! I may even enter it into one of those contests, you know?"

My eyes began to burn and I knew my blood pressure was building. I was staring hard at the ceiling, not blinking, willing myself to listen to Montgomery MacDowell. *How can I make him shut UP?* I blinked, finally, and the lids felt chalky. I sighed. It was my own stupid fault.

"So how are you anyway?" said Montgomery, who did not wait for an answer. "I'm fine. Yes. I am. I'm working hard, I'd love to go to Harvard, but I'll take Yale or Princeton if they'll accept me. Where are you going? Father and Mother are giving me Europe for graduation. Will you be going there too? A lot of us are, well, maybe we could all meet in Paris or someplace. Surely you're not going to go back to work at that YMCA place again, are you? I heard about that, you know. Remington told me."

I lay back on my bed, and put the phone on the pillow next to me. I could still hear Montgomery's voice, but knew better than to try to answer any of his questions, because he wasn't in the least interested in the answers and he never heard them anyway. *Gee, maybe he's my father's secret bastard son. They're both so alike and so boring. Oh my God no---then he'd be my brother. Gag me!!* Montgomery exhausted me. I dozed a little.

"So do you think you'd like to go, Courtenay?...Courtenay?"

"What? What?" I came to, sitting up. "Oh, Montgomery, the phone went dead there for a second. What was it you asked me?"

"I *said*, would you like to go to the movies with me on Saturday night? It's a three D-er, and they're having a replay of *Bwana Devil*. I never saw it when it came out four years ago, and now it's back, and I'd like it if you'd go with me. They give you those glasses free you know, and when you put 'em on, everything looks like it's coming right out of the screen at you and---"

"A what, Montgomery?"

"What?" answered Montgomery.

"You want me to go to a what kind of movie with you?"

"Oh. Yes, a three-D-er. You know, 3-D. Three dimensional, Courtenay, you dope. You haven't heard of them? I've never seen one, have you? I'd like to go and so I thought about you and I thought you'd maybe like to go with me, and I'll bet you never heard of 'Cinerama' either, did you? So anyway…."

I had to stop his machine-gun delivery. "Of course, Montie, I'd love to go with you. It'll be fun," I lied. "Actually, I've never seen one either, and I hear it's real george. Let's go. What time will you pick me up?"

"Wonderful. I'll come by for you at six-thirty. We can go out afterwards for a soda or something. Father is giving me the Rolls, oh it's really only the old one, but it's great fun and it's sort of funnish to drive to a movie in a Rolls no matter what the age of it is, don't you agree? You know, I--"

"See you at six-thirty, Saturday night, Montgomery. I gotta go now. I'm really pooped out. Remember me to your parents. Bye now!" I hung the phone up, and sucked in a big breath of air, loudly exhaling with relief. "Schmoe," I said. Well, at least one old acquaintance from The Academy wasn't shutting me out, but Saturday night was going to be an ordeal.

Montgomery arrived exactly on time, driving his father's aging Rolls Royce. As we left the driveway, Montgomery gaily tooted the horn. ("Is this cool? Can you dig it?"), and what was even more anguishing for me was that he did it in the "Shave and a Hair Cut, Two Bits!" rhythm. I begged him to please stop, which only added to Montgomery's glee, and he honked more.

Mercifully, we finally got to the St. George Theater, but only after Montgomery, being obnoxiously pompous, made a hideous scene in the parking lot so that everyone there would notice the Rolls. I felt my guts shrivel. I lowered my head and ran into the theater.

We put on the cardboard glasses with colored gel inserts, green on one side and red on the other, and watched the most incredible visual affects we'd ever seen, so realistic that we ducked and jumped, our eyes telling us we were actually a part of the action. It made me heady, sick, thrilled. I loved the sensations and didn't notice Montgomery's muscular arm snaking slowly, so casually around my shoulders until his hand lightly, ever so lightly, grazed my breast. It was so fleeting I could not accuse him because it may have been an accident or even my

308

imagination. I decided to ignore it, and allowed him to leave his arm over my shoulders because it seemed senseless to make an issue of it.

Soon though, his arm became heavy, like a log, and it hurt. And once or twice I again felt his hand brush so lightly across my breasts but it was so slight, and he was paying such intense attention to the movie, I convinced myself it was just an unintentional mistake. It did kind of seem though, that each time something especially exciting happened on the screen, making the audience jump and laugh in their seats, Montgomery's hand would again barely brush across my right breast. But—but it would be terribly embarrassing to reproach him and discover he didn't know what I was talking about. So when the movie was over I decided to ignore Montgomery's hand brushing lightly across my buttocks as we slowly made our way up the crowded aisles. I really began to suspect my date's motives, which I was beginning to not ignore, when we were sitting in his car in my driveway and he reached across me to open the car door. Once again his hand and arm just ever so lightly glanced across my breasts, while he continued talking about himself without missing a beat.

What I had no way of knowing was that the young Mr. MacDowell had been locking himself into his bedroom for a year, practicing his technique with two tennis balls placed on the edge of his dresser. He'd sit and brush his arm or hand gently across the surface of the balls. If they rolled away, he was doing it too strongly. If they stayed still, he'd gotten it right, and he'd soundly congratulate himself in his dresser mirror, for being so skilled. For copping a feel so adroitly.

When Montgomery MacDowell eventually found someone desperate enough to marry him, he rewarded her sacrifice with everlasting impotence. He could only become virile in the company of whores, but even then, not all the time. They made him pay anyway.

Looking angrily at myself in my bedroom mirror that night, I, Courtenay Scott Wolcott swore out loud that I'd never, not ever, go out with Montgomery MacDowell again in this or any other lifetime.

Eventually, the phone calls and invitations from The Academy group dwindled until there were none. I asked myself if it was because they'd seen me with my New Town crowd, or was it just natural that my old friends should drift away since I was at another school. I really tried to be grown up about it, but maturity, I found, is hard when your heart is breaking. I went over and over the scene on the sidewalk in front of Bacci's in New Town, trying to find in it the reason for The Academy kids' abandonment of me but I was not sure anymore. They all knew I'd been sent to public school against my will with no reason given to me. Why were they turning away from me now? Why couldn't we stay friends? I considered talking to Sally about it, but was afraid if I brought it out into the open, I'd have to face the truth, and I was not ready for that and was not quite sure what "the truth" was. Not yet. Not ever. But when?

# CHAPTER 47

I was awfully scared as I approached The Academy soccer field on Friday, wishing I'd never come. My heart pounded hard, and I casually passed my hand lightly over my chest to see if the beats were showing through my sweater. It was the same feeling of helplessness I'd had on my first day at New Town. But this time, I was approaching people I'd known always, familiar faces.

*Why do I feel this way? Why, why do I feel like this?* Walking along the edge of the playing field, I approached a crowd of kids, every face well known to me. The walk seemed longer than I remembered. A couple of the kids turned their heads and looked across at me, but they said nothing, looked away and went back to their conversations. I wanted to turn back, but couldn't: It would have been too obvious, too wimpy. So, I kept walking, my head turned toward the field as I pretended to watch the game with great interest, but as I moved across the grass, my feet felt like lead.

I rounded the end of the playing field and walked behind the white wooden goal posts, making a wide semicircle in case a ball was kicked through. *That would be so embarrassing, horrible, the ball would hit me and everyone would stare.* I was getting closer to my old crowd. I thought about the dream, of being unable to walk, to run and having to get down on my hands and feet to scamper away, but the idea of doing that here was, well, bizarre. I kept on, because there was no other choice. *My head is spinning. I feel sick. Why don't they still like me? We've been friends for so long.*

Mr. Raleigh stood at the edge of the crowd watching the game. He turned as I came near, smiled and walked toward me.

"Well, well, well, Courtenay, my dear, how are you?" he inquired kindly. I was so grateful to be acknowledged I quite nearly hugged him but, embarrassed, lowered my arms.

"I'm very well, thank you Mr. Raleigh." I thought it odd how different my words sounded when I was with Academy people than when with the New Town gang. "Thank you for asking. And, how are you?"

"Quite well, thank you, Courtenay. And tell me, how are things at your new school?"

"They're just fine, thank you, Mr. Raleigh. I've been on the honor role every quarter."

Mr. Raleigh looked sharply at me.

"But of course," I said quickly, "the work isn't nearly as hard as it is at The Academy." *Damn. I'm doing it again. I am a betrayer.*

"Well, then," my old principal answered, satisfied with my qualification. "I'd expect not. How are your college plans coming along, Courtenay?"

"Fine, thanks. I've been accepted at a number of them, two of the Seven Sisters, as a matter of fact, but I've decided to attend a small girl's school in New Jersey because they have a very strong journalism department."

"Oh? Well, well, well, then Miss Courtenay Wolcott. So you've got journalism on your mind, have you?"

"Yes sir, I have." I knew what was coming.

"Hmmm. That's a very nice romantic idea, Courtenay, but isn't that rather a man's job?"

I stared up at him, stifling my rising anger, but its heat reddened my face.

"Oh, I don't know, Mr. Raleigh. Maybe it was back before World War II, but I don't think it is now, do you?" I did not wait for him to answer. "I've seen pictures in the newspapers of lots of female reporters. As a matter of fact, there have been female reporters and news writers for many years. And, you can see lots of them during the President's press conferences too, and the President even calls on them sometimes and answers their questions. I'd really like to be a part of all of that, Mr. Raleigh. I mean, it's so exciting!" *God, what a fucking, fucking yo-yo.* I looked modestly down at the ground, knowing this move would please him.

"Well, well, well, now, my dear, yes, that's true, Courtenay dear," said my old principal, and I knew I had in fact pleased him. *Gross old fart. And why does he keep saying "well" three times?*

"But Courtenay dear, are you not at all concerned that you're taking a job away from a man with children to feed?" I looked up into the man's eyes sweetly, and then cast mine down again, knowing from long experience how pleased he was when kids cast their eyes down

312

after he'd corrected them. I knew what was coming, and he didn't disappoint.

"Well Mr. Raleigh I have thought about that but I know you know that there are many women out there today who no longer have husbands and are caring for children with no father and..." The man looked away. Code for, "stop talking like that. You are being impudent and rude."

"Now, then, yes" he growled. "That is true, my dear. And I know there are a great many capable—harrumph—women in the newspaper business. But they appear to be so--so aggressive, rather a bit too masculine to suit me. I've often wondered, Courtenay, if women in that business ever find husbands."

"Oh, I don't know, Mr. Raleigh, I mean, it seems to me that for some of them, maybe a career is more important. Maybe they're already married anyway, or maybe they don't even want to get married." Again, Mr. Raleigh bestowed one of his famous sharp looks on me. I chose to ignore it. "That's why I'm so serious about this all-girls' college. They really are tuned in to girls and what they want to do with their lives. Anyway, it's what I want to try, and so I will." Feeling my resolve weakening, I softened my words by saying, "I mean, I guess I will. Maybe. I don't know."

"Well, my dear Courtenay..."

Again, I knew what was coming, and whenever my former principal wasn't looking, I mouthed the words along with him, stopping the instant he looked at me. "Journalism really does *not* seem suitable for a young lady." *Sweet God in Heaven, you are such a complete donkey. Do you ever hear yourself?* "Furthermore, what does your father, I mean, --- your parents, what do your parents think of all of this?"

"Well, they're not too crazy about it, Mr. Raleigh. They're afraid I'll never be able to find a nice husband from a good family, too. But I guess I'll have to take my chances." I backed away. "Well, Mr. Raleigh, it's been really wonderful seeing you again, but if you'll excuse me, I think I'll go on over to the benches to visit with my friends. May I please be excused?" *Why did I ask that? I don't go to his goddammed school anymore.*

"Of course, of course. Run along, my dear. I know they'll all be so glad to see you again. Off you go!" He gave me a gentle, playful shove

313

in the direction of The Academy students. As I walked away, Mr. Raleigh called out to me. I turned to look at him.

"How's your father doing, Courtenay?" he called.

*What an odd question, Ah, but then he's an odd guy.* "Oh, he's just fine, thank you sir."

"Well, remember me to him, will you my dear?"

"I certainly shall, Mr. Raleigh, I shall. And thank you for asking about him. 'Bye!"

*He doesn't want to be remembered to my mother too?* Relieved to have had this brief opportunity to gather courage, I turned and walked toward the bleachers.

Cheering the Academy team, the kids barely glanced at me as I approached. I assumed a look of enthusiasm and cheered weakly along with them. No one asked me to sit down or join them. No one even spoke to me. I wanted to disappear. At the far end of the bench, Remington turned and looked at me, then leaned over and whispered something to the girl next to him. She, in turn, looked at me, then whispered to the boy next to her, and like the old child's game, *Telephone*, the word of my arrival spread down the line. I had not known anything that could hurt the way this did.

"Courtenay darling!" I was thrilled to see beautiful Margo Whiticomb, the mother of a boy I'd once briefly dated, walking toward me. She was tall and tanned, and her thick prematurely white hair was a stunning contrast to her dark skin and shining, azure eyes. I had worshipped Margo from the moment we'd met at a ballroom dancing class I'd attended with Sally when we were nine years old.

Sally had been given the unimaginable honor of being permitted to call Margo by her first name, and when she introduced her to me, this gracious woman dazzled me by suggesting I do the same. From that instant, I had always loved the shimmering Margo, and her big, kind, homely husband.

There were a number of other reasons I had always adored Margo, and one was that she had a unique gift: she listened. Because of that, young people were always at her door, wanting to be with her.

I grinned as Margo's long exquisite legs took her rapidly across the ground. *Oh God, what a thoroughbred. When Mother keeps using that*

314

*word, she has no idea she's describing Margo.* Margo moved gracefully as if she were modeling clothes, and in a way, she often was, for Margo Whiticomb dressed every single day as if she would be having tea with the Queen. Her husband never arrived home from work to find his glamorous wife in anything other than her finest ensembles replete with stockings, high heels, jewelry, and perfume, all perfectly coordinated. I had never seen Margo disheveled or sweaty, even after a long tennis match.

"Margo! Oh Margo, I'm so happy to see you. It's been such a long, long time!" I was almost beside myself with pleasure; I really meant those words. We hugged. I knew this kind old friend had seen that I was being snubbed and needed rescuing. And so, despite errands to run and important things to do, Margo stayed next to me for the duration of the game, encouraging me to talk and to be at ease. I knew exactly what Margo was doing, and wanted to thank her, but I was too humiliated to admit that The Academy kids were ignoring me. Instead I looked adoringly at Margo, and we sat and chatted about my life, both of us pretending what was really happening, wasn't.

As the game neared its end, Margo, with her usual grace, smoothly drew several of my old friends into our conversation. Soon we were all laughing and talking like the good friends we were, and it felt good.

When Margo Whiticomb saw that I was safe, she excused herself and left. I turned to watch her walk away. The kind, classy lady smiled back at me, winked, got into her shiny car, waved and drove away.

We all sat for a while, watching the remains of the game together. I still felt something different, a slight chill or tension pressing invisibly against me. I wasn't completely at ease and I wanted to be, but at least I wasn't being ignored.

After some time, the group broke up, going off in couples and small groups, not inviting me to go along, and leaving me sitting alone by the edge of the empty soccer field. The sun was setting and in the waning daylight, the air grew chilly. I began to tremble. Something had ended and I would not say what it was, although I knew. The shadows lengthened and I felt so very, very tired. I stood and began to walk slowly, and I stared down at the ground all the way home.

# CHAPTER 48

"Will you shut up, Goon, for God's sweet sake?"

I was in study hall in the auditorium trying to study for my final exams. Books piled around me, and my final grades were important to me. If I didn't come through, my dream of being a journalist would be gone for good.

The room was hot and many of the students dozed, unable to stay alert in the oppressive heat. The windows were open, but the air was thick, heavy and unmoving. The dreaded final exams were coming in less than a month, as was the highly anticipated prom. Most of the kids had secured summer jobs. There was a great deal on my mind, and the idiot Goon was making a racket behind me, not allowing me to get on with my studying.

Somewhere along the way, Gerard G. Grenella had been renamed "Goon" by his contemporaries. No one knew where this name came from since he wasn't really "goonish." He was however, foppish, weird and utterly unforgettable.

Goon did not "fit in," and he savored this fact. His attitude, and his being "a point off the curve" made him wildly popular. He was a misfit and a rebel and all these things made him beguilingly attractive to all the girls. He had a curious, bizarre charm. He was possessed of (or maybe by) an immense, thick pile of coal black hair that grew to just below his ears. He combed it straight back to the nape of his neck, keeping it liberally slathered with what he called "bear grease" so it looked like a patent leather helmet, unmoving in the strongest wind and so shiny we girls always quipped that we could see our reflections and put on our make-up by looking at it.

Slim, somewhat short and graceful, Goon walked around his world with an attitude part Fred Astaire, part cowboy, part Beau Brummell. He dressed in his own unconventional style that combined all of his parts rather neatly, if not confusingly. His pants were creased to a razor's edge, and they were always very tight. His shoes were shined to nearly the luster of his hair, and he'd applied taps to the heels so everyone would always know old Goon was a 'comin'! His socks were long, to his knees, and frequently of a wild and unexpected color. Something in his outlandish outfits always matched the color of those socks--an ascot, a silk handkerchief, a belt. The Goon was given to wearing long silk scarves about his neck, and he liked them to flow out behind him in the style of a World War I Flying Ace. Or Isadora Duncan. Or Oscar Wilde, his true hero. He wore jackets he fancied old dead poets wore, with billowing sleeves, and a loose, swingy cut. He often sported long black velvet capes with slippery, shiny red satin linings, even on hot summer days. And, his most cherished sine qua non was an ebony cane with a deeply carved silver knob that could be unscrewed to reveal a long lethal-looking, slender sword. This gave Goon a rosy sense of security, and his peers protected his secret so none of the faculty ever found out or confiscated his treasured weapon.

Somehow, Goon was always able to get himself excused from all sports or gym classes. He was not predisposed to sweat and disliked being seen in the school's embarrassing required athletic outfits. Besides, his legs were pathetically skinny, hairless and dead white.

Goon Grenella would live into his nineties, to the end an active, well-loved and famous pimp in one of the nation's largest cities. He flaunted his profession, driving golden, jeweled Bentleys, and his distinctive manner of dressing was catered to by the finest clothing designers. He received all of his ensembles free for the asking, since these creative clothing geniuses were shrewd enough to understand that Goon's high visibility and enormous popularity was the finest kind of advertising.

Right now though, Goon's charms were getting nowhere with me. And, it wasn't just Goon. Something was setting off all the boys rather more than usual, making them behave more nincompoopish than usual Dom of course was as usual being one of the loudest. I simply could not concentrate.

"Could you stupid farts shut your flapping mouths for a little while? Some of us are interested in improving our minds, you know." My put-down was met with derisive laughter. I expected nothing less.

"That Queenie chick really flips me out!" yelled one of them.

"Yeah!" said another. "She's cool. If she could see what we got here, she'd probly get all embarrassed, kawz she's A LADEEEE!"

"Lissen, don't show her what we got here," said the first boy. "I wanna look at them some more. I'm gonna cream my shoes from these things. Where da fuck you gettem, anyway, Goon?"

317

"Oh, now, never you mind, gentlemen," Goon Grenella answered in what he hoped was the way Oscar Wilde would speak. "I have my ways. I have my connections, don't you know."

"WILL YOU SHUT UP??" I knew that things were getting out of hand, and there were no teachers anywhere. Balled notebook paper, pencils, paper airplanes, food, and rubber bands shot through the air. Clearly, this was the dawn of a riot. The school year was coming to an end, the natives were restless and no one in authority was around to stop a potentially full-scale donnybrook.

And then quite suddenly, all the kids except me crowded around Goon. Screams of fake shock came from the girls as they discovered his secret. Grunts and obscene shouts of delight from the boys. There was even some applause.

I finally gave up, closed my books, looked up at the ceiling and sighed. I stood and worked my way to the end of the row of seats, determined to have a look at what everyone was admiring.

Goon sat in the midst of his subjects like a pompous king. He was wearing his famous cape, tied round his neck with a silken, tasseled cord and tossed back from one shoulder to reveal the red satin lining. In his hands was a deck of cards, spread open like a fan.

"So? What's the big deal?" I said to Three, who stood next to me. "What? Is Goon taking bets or something? Maybe a poker game? What's the poopis, Dupis?"

"God, Queenie, sometimes you can be such a stupeedo. Can't you see those cards?" Three looked away in disgust.

I stood on tiptoe and craned my neck to peer over the kids in front of me. From where I stood, it looked like an ordinary deck of cards, but I could see from the kids' reactions that there was something very interesting and likely very unusual about them.

Goon looked up from his throne, and noticed me jumping up and down, trying to see over the tops of the taller kids.

"Ah, little Queenie! Well, my dear, would you like to see my new cards? Yes? Well, everyone, please, give our little royal lady some room. Come on, now. Clear a path for The Queen! Come on Queenie dear, come see Daddy Goonie's pretty new playing cards."

318

Laughing, the kids parted to make a path for me. I boldly moved toward Goon which was not easy since I had to slide past the row of seats with kids in and on them. As I came close to him, Goon stood, ever the gentleman. With a flourish, he stacked the cards together in a neat pile, then handed them to me over one arm, the way a waiter shows diners a bottle of wine. The New Town kids laughed appreciatively, but when I reached for the cards, they stopped laughing.

My pulse began to hammer in my temples as I looked through the cards one at a time. On one side of each card there were the usual markings: diamonds, hearts, numbers, kings, queens—everything I expected to find. However, on the backs of all fifty-two were pornographic scenes, the likes of which I had never seen or imagined in my short and clearly far too innocent life. But I did not scream and flounce away as I think the boys thought and probably hoped I might. No. Instead I took the time to examine each one with intense interest. The room remained silent and no one moved.

There were men on those cards, with penises so huge I thought to myself they might very well need slings. Indeed, one proud young stud's organ was so gargantuan, he was twirling it around like a lariat. There were women having sex with men, women having sex with women, men with men, women with dogs, women with donkeys, dogs with donkeys. Chimpanzees had favorable billing, too. I never dreamed in all my life people could get into, never mind create the sexual positions on the cards. And the clothing! There were crotchless pants, leather penis covers, hoods, whips in holsters, spike-high-heeled cowboy boots, bustiers with long, beribboned garters. I wondered who the couturier was for the models on these remarkably creative playing cards. They were simply awe-inspiring. I was actually enjoying seeing these cards. Had I been shown them a year ago, I'd have thrown them across the room, run away and maybe even vomited. But now I was actually very very interested. In fact, I was so absorbed I never noticed how really silent the big auditorium had become. My head bowed, I whispered, "Hey Goon, you queerbait, where did you get these things?"

"Get them, Miss Queenie? Where did *I* get them? *You* brought them in to show all of *us*, if memory serves, my dear."

"The hell I did, Goon. Where would I ever get hold of raunchy stuff like this?" I laughed, raising my head. And that's when I saw her and that's when I understood what Goon was up to. There stood the silhouetted form of Miss McArdle at the auditorium's entrance.

319

"What, may I ask is going on here? It was my understanding that this room was a study hall. It appears that all of you must have learned everything you need to know for your final exams. Is this correct? I am so very, very pleased to know this. Amazing. Just simply amazing. Well now, isn't that nice. Yes, yes indeed, isn't that *nice!*" Miss McArdle relished nothing more than a captive audience.

Her lips pursed, hands folded nunlike in front of her sunken stomach, Miss McArdle glided down the aisle like a tall scrawny bat. The group shrank back from me, sinking into seats, hastily opening texts, writing in notebooks. I froze, the deck of cards in my hand. Goon melted away, evaporating like a liquid butterfly into the shadows, leaving me stuck with the goods. I had no choice but to face my vanquisher squarely, but I still managed to hiss "you filthy, shitty pig!" to the grinning Goon.

"Well, Miss Wolcott. I'd hardly thought you were the type to roughhouse with the students. We've always thought of you as the model pupil. Now Missy, what is going on here? I insist upon knowing this instant."

When she got no immediate reply, I looked down at my hands. "What have you there, Miss Wolcott?" she asked sweetly. "Come. Show me, if you please. Step smartly, now."

I looked down at the cards, up at Miss McArdle, and back at the cards. "Oh," I said, smiling innocently. "Oh, we were just going to play some cards after school, Miss McArdle, maybe some gin rummy or go-fish or something." I held out my hands in a disarming gesture. "They're just some cards, that's all." I smiled brightly. "Just cards."

"Really? Oh well, if they're just cards, Missy, you won't mind showing them to me, will you? So? Might I see them please?" The principal's chin was up, her long eyelids down. Her slitted eyes bore into mine as if they were glaring out of Satan's head. Her long, bony arm slowly reached out, the sharp fingers pointing straight at my heart. I froze, except for the hand holding the cards which then dropped slowly, slowly to my side and behind my skirt. *Isn't one's life supposed to flash before one's eyes just about now?*

"Oh, Miss McArdle," I croaked, "you don't want to bother with these. They're just some old cards. Well then, I'd better get back to my studies. Finals coming up--oh, haha, of course you know that already, right? Yes. Well. Hmm. I guess I'll just go back to my books, now. So, if you'll excuse me." I paused. "Please?" my voice wavered.

320

Miss McArdle was not one to be denied, especially when she knew there was dirty work afoot.

"GIVE THEM TO ME!"

Trembling, hoping it didn't show, I handed over the deck. I kept my head low and my eyes lower in the submissive posture that sometimes worked for me but apparently, not today. The room got quieter. The kids, pretending to study, stole glances at me with gleaming vulture eyes, loving this moment.

Miss McArdle took an inordinate amount of time to look through the deck. When she was finally finished, she squared her shoulders and looked up with a white, blank-angry face. I saw her lip tremble slightly.

"Where did you get these--these things? I absolutely insist upon knowing."

My eyes swept the room. I was unwilling to confess. I looked into the Judas faces around me, and fought the urge to grin while they worked so industriously over their books. No one offered to take the blame, and Goon was amongst the disappeared.

"Did Mr. Grenella give them to you, Miss Wolcott?" the principal asked, looking around the room. "He's done this sort of thing before, you know. Now where did that boy get to? I've never known anyone who can disappear the way he can." She turned back to me. "Again, where did you get these pieces of filth? If you refuse to tell me, then the entire group of pupils shall stay here, if it takes forever. And, I mean STAY. No one shall go to the lavatory, no one shall eat. No one shall get a drink of water, no one will be permitted to go to the lavatories, (that's with a V, my dear students,) and no one shall go home. I am prepared to stay here 'til Hell freezes over, if you will forgive my language, ladies and gentlemen. I intend to know, before I leave this room, who brought these disgusting cards into my school."

I tilted my head and looked thoughtfully at Miss McArdle, then around the room once more. The scene on the sidewalk outside Bacci's inexplicably flashed across my mind. Standing before this disagreeable old bat, I thought this might be a good opportunity to clean up my conscience a little, and so in one swift instant I decided to be noble and take the heat. Besides, looking like a martyred heroine in front of the kids was not an unattractive idea. I smiled calmly up at Miss McArdle standing like a marble statue at the top of the study hall stairs.

"Yes ma'am," I said. Adopting a lofty "up on the hill" tone, I held my chin high, just as I'd seen Katharine Hepburn do in a movie where she'd had to be very, very brave. I pulled in a long, slow breath and said "I bought the cards from an ad I saw at the back of a dirty magazine, and I brought them in to show everyone in school."

The studious heads surrounding me suddenly shot up from their books as if jerked on strings. There were murmurs, rustlings, a few gasps. A voice from the other end of the room softly said, "Wayda go, Queenie Baby." I turned to look. It was Dom, up in the last row where he'd bolted when the principal had appeared in the doorway. He was, as ever, slouching and grinning.

"Well, well, well," Miss McArdle began. "I see. Miss Wolcott, you will be hearing more about this." Her lips were pulled back, thin as wires, her face ashen with rage. "Will you please follow me?" She glared at me, her eyes wide, white. I returned her look boldly, until I realized it was a mistake to do that. I lowered my head and looked as humiliated as I could manage, under the circumstances.

"Yes, ma'am," I answered, gathering up my books, hanging my head even lower. I shuffled up the aisle and out of the room behind the principal. All eyes were on me. It was a shining moment and I was loving it.

I followed Miss McArdle through the outer office and then through the inner door, the one marked with the two words that struck terror into the hearts of countless miserable students for countless miserable decades: *Principal's Office.*

Still clutching the hot cards, the despot McArdle walked around to the other side of her desk and sat, never taking her eyes off my face. She did not offer me a seat; it was therefore quite natural for me to stand.

Miss McArdle took a deep breath and leaned back in her big leather chair. It barely squeaked under her desiccated frame. She folded her arms over her shriveled breasts and I thought idly that it was a safe bet no man had ever seen them. Or would especially want to.

"My dear Miss Wolcott," she sighed. "Tell me. Where did you get these cards?"

"I told you, ma'am, I saw an ad at the back of one of those dirty magazines...."

322

"Where did you get the magazine, Courtenay?"

"From my brother, Miss McArdle. That little devil is always buying those dirty things. It makes my parents just so angry!"

The principal reached out a scarecrow arm and with a gnarled root of a forefinger, stabbed a buzzer on a black box on her desk. A female voice responded.

"Yes, Miss McArdle?"

"Miss Loefler, will you please pull Courtenay Wolcott's file and tell me how many people are in her immediate family?"

"Yes, Miss McArdle," the box obediently answered, and I felt my heart stop cold.

"Miss McArdle?"

"Yes, Miss Wolcott?" Miss McArdle answered, smiling sweetly.

"Miss McArdle, tell her she doesn't have to look. I don't have a brother."

"Well now, that's what I thought, my dear, that's what I thought." She pushed the buzzer again and told the box to cancel the order.

"Now then, let us get down to business. I shall repeat my original question. Where did you get these filthy cards?"

"I didn't get them, Miss McArdle. I mean, I didn't buy them or anything like that. No one gave them to me. I know you probably won't believe me because of that brother story I just told, but I found them. Yes, I did. On the bus I take to get to school, and they were so--well, gee, I don't know, they were so interesting, you know, I've never, ever seen anything like them. Well, I took them and didn't tell anyone. Then, when I saw no teachers around in study hall, I decided to show them to some kids. And then, before I knew it, everyone in the whole room was gathering around me. Us. It just got out of control. I guess I was trying to be popular or something. You know how it is." I looked down, afraid my last sentence, a veiled insult, had been a step too far. The room began to feel sort of cold.

I went on, allowing an occasional stammer to come into my words. I kept the hangdog look. *This performance is going fairly well!*

"I didn't know you'd show up--well, that is I didn't mean that, ummm, well, I guess I sort of thought no teachers would be around in study hall, so I could show them to everyone and not get caught. Please believe me, Miss McArdle, it's the truth. I found them stuck into a seat on the bus on the way to school. You don't think I'd've been able to tell the bus driver about a thing like that, do you? I would've died if I'd had to do that." Could I squeeze out a tear? I tried. Unsuccessful. I settled for a tiny, almost inaudible sob, a touching, small shudder.

I knew my act was good. I could see that Miss McArdle was close to believing me. I leaned in toward my oppressor, assuming an impassioned, pleading expression and holding my arms out slightly. I even shrunk down a bit with the idea I'd maybe look smaller and helpless. *God, this is fun!* I could see Miss McArdle's icy exterior cracking. Just a hair fracture but still…

The woman sighed.

"All right, Courtenay, you can stop now. I believe you. But allow me to say a few things right now." I took a deep breath. I wished I could sit down. I knew this was going to be a lengthy harangue, and my legs were already beginning to ache.

"May I please sit down first, Ma'am?" I asked.

"You may not," Miss McArdle answered in a fast bark.

"My *dear* young lady. You've committed a grievous sin against God by looking at such filth, by even holding it in your hands for even a second! My goodness, even if your mind touches on this sort of thing, it is a mortal sin. Don't you know that? Decent human beings are forbidden to think such dreadful thoughts, even for a split second. These cards depict abnormal acts and not acts of love between a Godly married couple. I am ashamed of you, that you'd carry such things around and show them to your innocent classmates."

I dug my nails into my palms to keep from laughing, then jumped when Miss McArdle yelped, "Shame! Shame! Are you a Catholic? If you are, I suggest you go to confession to cleanse your soul. I rather think the priest would give you a tremendous penance for this little trick of yours. I suppose you think that just because you come from up the hill you are permitted to do such things."

*Oh God, not that again.* I resumed the hangdog mode, adding a dramatic little twist of my toe into the principal's institutional carpeting.

324

"Well, it is still immoral to do such things, no matter where you come from." Warming to her cause, Miss McArdle licked her dry, thin grey lips and continued.

"Your wealth gives you no special license at all, except for the following; you should set yourself as an example for those less fortunate than you. Teach them goals! Successes! Accomplishments! Objectives! Ambitions!"

I stared in utter shock. How dare McArdle lay such a heavy burden on me? It wasn't *my* job to do *any* of those things. But I said nothing.

"I'm just so very disappointed in you Courtenay, very disappointed indeed."

I shuffled my feet and sighed sadly.

"Yes ma'am. You are absolutely right, Miss McArdle. I'm so sorry. I've done a very bad thing indeed." My neck ached from hanging my head so low. I began wringing my hands together. *Nice touch.* I was the picture of abject remorse, but if Miss McArdle had looked more closely, she'd have seen that my throat was contracting wildly, forcing a belly laugh back to its source. I began to pant from this effort.

"Now. What punishment do you deem fair, young lady?"

I looked up, startled. "Punishment, Miss McArdle? Me? Why? What for? I confessed, didn't I?"

Miss McArdle ignored me.

"Now then, Missy. First, we shall call your parents and ask them to come down here to discuss this matter. With you in attendance, naturally. Secondly, I will expect you to put on my desk, in one week, a three page, typewritten, single-spaced composition entitled 'The Dangers of Spreading Filthy Pornography Amongst High School Students.' Meanwhile, I shall consider whether you should read it to the entire student body."

Recognizing a threat when I heard one, I gratefully accepted my punishment. I knew I could easily knock out the required composition on the hazards of looking at and sharing dirty pictures. It would be fun. I knew Miss McArdle wouldn't make me read it to the entire student body, because none of the students would take it seriously and the whole thing would simply turn into a fiasco of hilarity. The part about calling my parents was troubling, though.

*Negotiate.*

"Miss McArdle?" My voice was small, wheedling. *God, I'm good!* "I know every kid asks the same thing of you, but could we talk a little bit about the part where you tell my folks? I mean, they're a lot older than most parents, and frankly, Miss McArdle"---I'd read that it's good to use a person's name often while negotiating---"they're just not used to this sort of thing." My voice wavered a little.

"Are you suggesting, Miss Wolcott, that your parents are too old to learn of your indiscretion? That perhaps they might suffer heart failure when they learn of this loathsome deck of cards you've been carrying around for God knows how long? Now really, my dear, isn't that a little extreme?"

I amazed myself by managing to finally squeeze out a tear. "No, ma'am. I'm just so afraid of upsetting and embarrassing them. They were older when I was born. I was a mistake and yet they welcomed me and love me so dearly. They're just so very good to me..."

The principal paused.

"All right, Courtenay. I can appreciate your kindness toward your parents in this matter. I think we might be able to keep this between us. Your record with our school is clean, and I still remember your heroics with the Ralphie Volonnino episode. Perhaps you should in some measure be rewarded for that." She paused to take a breath and I began to relax. "If you will write those three pages--oh well, make it two. Well, maybe one will be acceptable. If you'll type me the one page on the Dangers of Pornography etc., or whatever it was I said before, we can close this matter. Have it on my desk as soon as possible. Thank you. You may go."

"Thank you, oh thank you so much, Miss McArdle. I promise you this will never happen again. You've been very kind to me. I am so grateful."

I knew I was laying it on a little thick, and I was proud my act was going so well. To add a final touch of pathos, I reached over the desk and grasped my principal's hand briefly.

I turned, but just before I left the office, I walked back and reached across the desk for the deck of cards. Faster than a speeding bullet, my hand received a stinging slap. I'd never seen it coming!

326

"Just what do you think you're doing, young lady?" Miss McArdle's face was mottled red and pinched with anger.

"I'm taking my cards back, Miss McArdle. Isn't that all right? They are mine after all, and...." I rubbed my hand and looked at the principal with terror and hatred. *She slapped me? Is that allowed? No---and why am I taking the rap for this? When I see Goon again...*

"No, Missy, it is *not* all right. How *dare* you? You absolutely may *not* have them back. I shall personally see they are destroyed immediately so no one else can see them. Now leave this room."

I raced out, relieved to have gotten away clean. As I passed through the outer office, I heard Miss McArdle's high voice. "Hold all my calls for one hour, Miss Loefler." I grinned.

# CHAPTER 49

June. Finally June. "Land of hope and glory/ Mother of the free/ How shall we extol thee? /Who are born of thee." For the rest of my life, I would always be proud that I could sing all the words to "Pomp and Circumstance." Well, me and a lot of other Academy kids. In my first year, the school's music teacher thought the venerable song should be learned and performed since The Academy could not quite afford the Philharmonic Orchestra. So all the students had to memorize it and sing it at every Academy graduation, year after year until they themselves graduated. With the strains of that old song running through my head, I returned to the Academy one last time, a sad time, to watch my old friends graduate.

It was difficult for me, and I was so very glad to be standing next to the regal Margo Whiticomb as my old pals walked up onto The Academy's broad stage to graduate without me. Memories flooded my heart and I had to lower my head to keep the tears from showing. Margo as she always did, understood, and surreptitiously handed me several tissues and once briefly squeezed my hand. Memories like that never go away, I never forgot that tiny gesture and repeated it over the years to those who needed it. Margo Whiticomb was the perfect teacher. How lucky I was.

The graduation was beautiful to watch. It was the typical Academy small class, and the girls resembled Southern plantation belles in their long white swaying gowns, Lilly bells. They were radiant as they floated toward the stage, moving in perfect time to the music. The boys marched proudly beside them in brand new Brooks Brothers suits, shiny and new looking, starched, young and innocent.

I ached to be with them. This old building with its poignant memories was where I knew I really belonged. I'd never really fitted in at New Town. Things just didn't balance or flow the way they had when I was an Academy student. I was sort of happy in New Town, occasionally, but it was an uneasy, less than real happiness. Something was always scraping at me, forbidding me to fully enjoy my public school experience.

After the ceremony, the graduates lined up in the Senior Library, my favorite room in the old building. Ivy-covered stained glass windows

328

stretched from the floor to the high, ornately carved mahogany ceiling. When the sun spilled through those magnificent windows, the room was bathed in a prism of green and rainbowed twilight. The massive oak study tables were long and worn smooth at the edges from elbows and books. There were long, deep scars in the ornate carvings on the table legs, where hundreds of students had rested their feet. Books were on shelves everywhere, and the room smelled and looked mysterious and old, the way rooms look and feel and smell when they have decided to stop someplace in time. This hallowed chamber had the pungent and rich scent of ancient knowledge and I always thought I could feel my brain fill with learning just by standing in its center.

I walked the line of graduates, smiling brightly and shaking hands with my old friends, even Remington, with whom I exchanged air kisses. I tried not to think about how I'd be hugging all my friends that night if I were part of that line, and how they'd be hugging back. Now, they shook hands formally, the way people do with old but distant acquaintances about whom they never cared much anyway. I kept smiling, but my throat ached with a walnut-sized lump. One of the girls said, "Oh Courtenay dear, sweet Courtenay, we all missed you so," but her cloying sincerity made me clench my jaws. After I'd congratulated all of them, I stood awkwardly by while the parents drank Champagne and the graduates sipped soft drinks and ate petits fours. No one talked to me, and no one invited me to any of the senior parties. Even Margo could not help me now. This was my lowest moment since leaving The Academy. When I quietly left the library, no one noticed. I walked into Mr. Raleigh's office. The room's neon lights hurt my eyes after the soft, mellow glow in the Senior Library. Without permission, I used the office phone to call Fred. Would he please come to pick me up, and please, could he hurry? He promised he would. I put the phone down, and went out to the street to wait. As I stood alone in the warm June darkness, I turned to look up at the tall brick Senior Library, saw the moving silhouettes behind the old windows, and heard the muffled, happy sounds.

# CHAPTER 50

The weekend was not going particularly well. My parents weren't talking much, to me or to each other. But I was only mildly perplexed. I understood my parents' foibles about as much as they understood mine, and cared as little.

The weather was warming, but for obvious reasons, I avoided the club's swimming pool.

"If she won't use the damned thing, I'm giving up the pool membership. I can't afford to throw money out the window, you know." It was my father's endless twaddle. I knew he *could* in fact afford to throw money out the window. But still, I refused to go.

Fortunately, there were final exams to study for. I actually enjoyed exam days. Kids went to school just for the test periods and were free for the rest of the day. A heady sense of emancipation came with being able to walk into and out of school whenever we wished. The lunchroom stayed open all day, providing snacks and cold lunches to those between exams.

But there was a high point during that spring. One day, I opened a long envelope addressed to me and squealed with delight. The contents advised that I'd passed my driver's test perfectly, and so I immediately began a lot of serious and not so subtle hinting about a car for graduation. In the meantime however, I was permitted use of the family's existing cars but I became aggravated at the blackmail I had to endure each time I asked for the keys. Everyone, and this included Emma, Fred, and Mary, constantly asked me to "just pick up a couple of things" since I was going that way anyway, and after all, I had the car and they did not. It was all just damnably annoying. These interminable errands greatly interfered with my plans and social life. Moreover, when I grumbled about it, I was tersely advised that I was contributing nothing toward gas and maintenance of the coveted vehicle, and if I wished to begin doing that, then perhaps everyone would ease up on making these annoying little requests of me. Immediately recognizing my miscalculation of the situation, I was savvy enough to quickly withdraw my complaints.

I was finally forced to face the fact that the end of my high school years was fast approaching and as each day passed I feared I would not be asked to the senior prom. I passed a lot of time telling myself it was not that important, that it wasn't the end of the world, and who cared anyway? And besides, I couldn't just go and ask a guy. Decent girls simply did not do that sort of thing. I would have to wait. In my later years when I looked back, I would wonder how many perfect liaisons were never made, proms never attended, marriages never consecrated because of this preposterous dogma.

It was hot in the lunchroom. Unusual and torrential rains had not stopped for days, and things were soggy, especially the moods. I stood at the lunchroom counter waiting for an extra milk. I was distracted, my mind filled with nothingness. I heard my name called out. It was Bobby.

"That's my name, don't wear it out," I grumbled. He approached me shyly, his feet shuffling. I roused myself and greeted him with my biggest smile. I still liked him.

He looked uncomfortable. "Hi Queen," he said. "Can I talk to you for a second?"

"Sure, Bobs, what's up?" I had jammed a chocolate chip cookie into my mouth, and some of the crumbs sprayed out.

"Oh, God, sorry Bobby--yucko, I'm sorry!" I began to laugh, and more crumbs shot from between my lips and landed on his chest. I attempted to brush them off. Bobby laughed too, and took my hand from his shirt. He didn't let go.

"Uh oh, Bobby, this looks serious," I said.

"Well, it kind of is, Queenie."

I feigned horror. "Gee, Bobby, you're not preggers, are you?"

"What? NO! Hey, Queenie, gee whiz. Oh, it's a joke, right? I get it. I mean, oh jeez, well. Uh, look, can you come on over here, Queenie? Let's get away from these losers."

He pulled me toward the end of an empty lunch table, and we sat down. He was so serious, and serious on Bobby Sotirakis was very comical.

"Queenie, would you consider... well, I suppose I'm too late, and you probably won't want to. Anyway, I thought I'd try to ask you--I wish I'd asked you sooner--oh well, it's too late I know--"

"BOBBY!" I shouted at him. "Get on with it. What's the problem? Just say it. Stop stuttering! You're getting me very nervous here!"

"OK, I'm goin' for it. Queenie, if you don't have a date already, you probly wunt wanna go to the prom with me, wudja? To the prom I mean?"

I pressed my lips together. My cheeks puffed. I could not control it and laughter erupted from me.

"Why Bobby! That's the most backward way I've ever heard of asking someone to a prom. Of COURSE I'll go with you. I'd just love to. I'm so happy you asked me!"

Before I could finish he stood and started to walk away, muttering. "Sure--- Hey, it's OK. I knew you wouldn't go for—" Bobby whirled around so quickly he lost his balance and crashed into the corner of a lunch table. Something broke. He looked down at me, his face registering nearly slapstick astonishment. His jaw dropped, slack and limp.

"Wad?" he said. "You *will* go with me? No way! It's a joke, right? Well hardeeharhar. So funny I forgot to laugh. Don't kid around, Queenie."

"Bobby, you sweet big clown. I'm not kidding. I wouldn't kid about a thing like this. I'm not a total boob, you know. I'll say it again, so listen carefully, you big jerk. I'd love to go to the Senior Prom with you. No one else. Just you. I was hoping you'd ask, and I've already got my dress picked out. It'll be pure white so any color corsage you get for me will be just perfect, except one of those huge purple things grandmothers always wear on their furs. Orchids I think they're called, right?" (In truth, I well knew what they were.) "Actually Bobby, I'd sort of like a wrist corsage. Maybe tea roses, little yellow ones?" I almost laughed again at the look of confused amazement on his face, but it didn't stop me. I was very excited.

"Oh no, yellow would be too pale for the dress. Red would be best I guess. Little tiny red roses. And then you can get one for the lapel of your tuxedo, OK? And will you wear just a nice simple black tuxedo? Those colored ones always make guys look like Cuban band leaders, if you know what I mean. You know, like Ricky Ricardo." I came up for breath, and began again.

"And of course, you'll have to come in and meet my parents and they'll take pictures and all of that. Can you stand it? Will you get your father's car? Oh boy, Bobby, we'll have a great time. We'll have a ball. You know, there are tons of parties going on, breakfast parties, too. I know we'll be asked, just as soon as everyone knows we're going to the prom together. You wouldn't play a trick on me and pick me up in a hearse, would you? That wouldn't be funny, Bobby. It really would NOT be funny!"

Bobby waited quietly while I babbled on like a locomotive. When I finally paused, he grabbed a breath and began to speak but I began to speak at the same time. We both laughed. I said, "You first, Bobby."

"OK, OK. Queenie, this is too much. This is far out! Hot damn dog! OK. OK to everything you just said, whatever you said. Umm, I gotta go for now, but I'll remember. White dress? Wrist flower thing? Yeah. Yeah. I got it all. Red T roses. What are T roses? Never mind. They'll tell me at the florist's," he muttered. "No hearse. What, you think I'm a jerk or sumpin'? Black tux. I ain't gonna look like no Puerto Rican waiter in a light blue tux, no sirree. No, Cuban you said. Well, we'll talk about it later. I gotta go now, but jeez Queenie, thanks, thanks a lot. I promise we'll have a great time, great! We'll make plans. Gotta go. Thanks Queenie. Whoopie! Thanks Queenie!" Bobby bent down and for a second, I thought he was going to kiss me, but he blushed and straightened up and trotted off, coming back to get his books, trotted off, coming back to get his pencil, trotted off again. He kept grinning at me, and it was so wide and happy I thought the top and bottom of his face would separate. Then he finally loped off for good, turning once to look back at me. He waved and his books crashed to the floor.

I lay on my bed that night looking up at the canopy, remembering Bobby's awkwardness. I smiled and shut my eyes. It felt nice to be beheld with such puppy-like adoration.

As soon as I told my New Town friends about being invited to the prom, Bobby and I were asked to all the post-prom parties and all the breakfasts too. I was thrilled even though I occasionally found myself thinking it would have been better had I been asked to the Academy prom. No. No I would not think that way. I had no wish to cast a single dark spot of doubt or anger on my happiness.

And then, when I got home from school, my mother gave me the charge card and I'd gone by myself as I knew I would have to, to select my prom gown, trying to pay no attention to the other happy girls in the store laughing and chatting with their mothers as they went through many dress choices. "I don't care, it's OK, I have so many happy things in my life, think think think about those things, I just don't care" I kept whispering to myself.

And then I found the dress and even though I had no one to show it to in the store, I bought it. It was indeed the shimmering white satin dress of which I'd always dreamed--off the shoulder, a wide band of satin across the bust, tight at the waist with a full, sweeping skirt. I'd wear a simple strand of pearls that had once belonged to my great grandmother, and long over-the-elbow kid gloves. I'd wear white satin high heels, sharply pointed at the toes, and it didn't matter how tall I was because Bobby would always be much taller. That my feet might suffer from stabbing, grueling pains all night from those shoes didn't enter my mind and would not have altered the shoe plan had I known in advance. I wanted to be perfect that night, and nothing would stand in my way. I would have my hair done at Jacque's at the bottom of the hill, and he'd put it into a dramatic upswept style, and I'd ask him to weave a piece of white satin ribbon through it to match my dress. My lipstick would be soft pink, and I'd put on just a touch of eye makeup.

I lay on my bed day dreaming and smiling, looking across the room at my dress hanging on the back of my closet door, the protective plastic shining back at me. The phone rang. My parents had been in my father's study for hours with a couple of men and I was not permitted to disturb them. Not much of a problem because I never had any wish to know anything about my father's business affairs. They were probably planning another trip abroad. I yawned. But then I heard my mother calling me.

"Courtenay! Courtenay! The phone's for you. It's your Aunt Esther."

*Aunt Esther? Why's she calling me? I haven't seen her for years.* "Well...what does...OK, I'll talk to her!" I called down the stairs. "I'll take it up here. Thanks, Mom." I picked up the phone and heard the study door close downstairs as my mother went back to join my father and those two mysterious men.

"Hey there, Aunt Esther. This is a surprise. How the heck are you anyway?"

"Hello, my darling little Courtenay. I am just fine, thank you. And how on earth are you?"

"I'm just fine, Auntie E. Gee--it's wonderful to hear from you. I can't believe you're calling me. Gosh, when's the last time we saw each other? A couple of years ago, at least, right?"

334

"I do believe you're right, Courtenay darling. It has been a really long time. Too long, and you're my favorite niece you know."

"Oh, Aunt Esther, I'm your *only* niece!" Her aunt chuckled daintily.

I saw my mother's only sister just occasionally, although each of us wished we could spend more time together. Aunt Esther was always far more interested in my life and welfare than my mother was, and it was one of the many reasons why I loved her so much.

My jolly, funny Esther Nijdam was a short stub of a lady with no neck at all, but this did not hinder her from loading up with rope upon rope of pearls, most long, some "matinee length." Every time I saw the broad shield of pearls spreading from my aunt's chin to her ample waistline I could not help but to always think for just an instant of an armadillo. My Aunt Esther always wore small, stylish, custom-made hats with veils hanging from their rims. Those veils were frequently embroidered with dime-sized designs or sewn-on tiny velvet balls that tended to get caught in my mouth when I kissed my aunt, and occasionally the lady herself would suck one into her own mouth when she laughed which I found to be enormously amusing.

Sadly, Auntie E. was afflicted with dowager's hump, forcing her to pass her days bent over and facing down. Her condition was not helped by her being very short-waisted, and her large breasts drooped nearly to her knees. She had fat, always-jiggling rosy cheeks that hung like a bulldog's because of her stooped posture, and glittering, small navy-blue eyes. Aunt Esther was so continuously covered with expensive jewelry along with her ropes of pearls that I often thought the woman slept in her jewels. All of my aunt's cigar-thick fingers but the thumbs were encrusted with heavy rings studded with every gem found in or on the earth.

Esther and her beloved husband Jan had never had children. Uncle Jan slept in another room from the start of their marriage "because he snores so dreadfully," and Esther spent her life sleeping 'til noon, calling on friends, arranging tea parties and playing bridge and mahjongg with the chapeaued, veiled, wine drinking gang she called "The Girls." She'd not been much disposed toward charity work, but would brag to the end of her life that she'd happily rolled bandages for the Red Cross during World War I. A diabetic, she paid little attention to the disease because to do so would interfere with her nearly daily consumption of sweets. Once I saw her lean across an open display of pastries in a very upscale bakery and, so aroused by the tempting array she drooled squarely and heavily onto a couple of Napoleons. Not in the least embarrassed, Auntie E. just said, "Ooops! Oh, I do beg your pardon" to the Napoleons, daintily wiped her mouth with the little lace hankie she always kept peeping from her cleavage, and went on ogling the display. She never told the bakery lady and I was unable to stop thinking about the people who ended up buying those Napoleons. I thought of them now, the minute I heard Aunt Esther's voice.

Esther Scott had married Uncle Jan, (pronounced Yon) because he'd asked her. He was a Dutch spice importer, a fat, kindly man with an enormous W. C. Fields nose, covered with hundreds of bright red, web-like broken veins. When I was little, I'd sit on his lap and ask him why his nose was all cracked that way, and he would tell me that on a very cold day, it had suddenly fallen off his face onto a city sidewalk where it had shattered into dozens of pieces. He said that a friendly policeman had picked it up and glued it all back together, then stuck it back on his face and this was why there were so many red cracks in his nose. Then he'd throw back his head and laugh and laugh at this story he'd told so often to so many children. I would sit, mesmerized, looking up into my uncle's open, laughing mouth, and count his many big, gold teeth. Unassuming, kind, Uncle Jan learned early in his marriage that it was his place to sit in the background, smile and agree to everything.

During the first month of his marriage to Esther Wolcott, he'd come across some sound advice (in English) that he'd committed to memory and followed exactly for the rest of his life; *"To keep your marriage brimming/ with love in the loving cup/ whenever you're wrong, admit it/ whenever you're right, shut up."* And he'd laugh loudly whenever he said or even thought about those words!

I pulled my thoughts back to the present and lay back on the bed, holding the phone.

"Well, Aunt Esther, you coming down or what?"

"No, my dear, but I spoke with your parents a month or so ago, and we talked mainly about you, and I'd like to tell you about what we discussed."

"Really? You guys talked about me? That must have been pretty boring!"

"Not at all, dear. Do you think you might be able to get away tomorrow, since it's Saturday, and meet with Uncle Jan and me? We'd love to have tea and then a small dinner with you, if you think you can make it. At the Plaza perhaps?"

"Well, sure, Aunt Esther, I can easily get there. But what's all the mystery?"

"Oh there's really no mystery, Courtenay darling. We just want to discuss your future with you. So, shall we say about four-ish?

"Sure thing-ish, Auntie E. See you there. Can't waitish!"

I smiled at my reflection in the car window as Fred drove me to the Plaza Hotel. It would be good to see my darling aunt and uncle again. It had been too long since their last visit. I had always enjoyed teasing my prim Auntie E., and no matter how Esther struggled to keep her aloof, Victorian composure, she'd always end up smiling and then even laughing at my antics. She scolded me endlessly for the disrespectful way I behaved, but I knew she loved it and so did she. No one else in the family played with her or paid attention to her the way I did. I looked forward to a lovely afternoon of tormenting my beloved aunt and enjoying a great dinner while I did it. I was mildly curious, but not terribly interested in why my aunt wanted to meet with me.

Fred let me out at the door of the Plaza, promising to return in four hours. I walked into the big old hotel, smiling at the rows of Hansom cabs lined up outside. I'd always loved seeing the drivers in their top hats and the horses who stamped and snorted with boredom or munched at their grains in the leather feedbags hanging from their bridles.

I saw my Aunt and Uncle waiting for me, looking just the same as they always did. *The Elderly-Ageless.* I'd always called them that. We embraced warmly and I was reminded how I'd loved being folded into the ampleness of these two dear people. *How I do love them. Oh Auntie E, you are such a cliché! You actually smell of lavender!* My aunt and uncle kissed and held me and I found myself wishing once again that they'd been my parents.

We three moved into the tea room, and with a tiny wave of Esther's kid-gloved hand, two obsequious waiters materialized with small, translucent cups of hot tea with lemon wedges, heavy cream and sugar cubes offered on sterling salvers. Larger sterling trays held tiny decorated cakes on Irish lace doilies, all consumed almost immediately by her Uncle Jan who dared not look up at his adoring and frowning wife. Aunt Esther finally smiled and slapped at his hands and then waggled a gloved finger at him. But the gesture was ignored, and the tiny cakes continued to pop, one after another, into her husband's happy mouth.

We three delighted in each other, and laughed frequently. I told my aunt and uncle the most disgusting stories I could think of about life in public school, embellishing lavishly. It was ever so rewarding to see my aunt throw her hands over her mouth to stifle horrified, tiny shrieks, while Uncle Jan sat and grinned, saying very little.

The time passed quickly. My mouth filled with cream-cheese and olive stuffed celery, I finally remembered to ask about why they wanted to talk with me. The smile faded immediately from my aunt's round, jolly face.

"Now come on, Auntie E., no need to go deadly serious on me. What's the deal? Why the long face?"

"Courtenay dear, your Uncle Jan and I have been having some serious thoughts about you lately." I looked over at my uncle, who shrugged imperceptibly and rolled his eyes for my benefit. "You see," Aunt Esther said softly, "we are all quite terribly befuddled as to why your father insisted you attend that--that, ugh, public school. Surely it was not because he lacked the funds to keep you at The Academy... well, whatever his reasons were, we are sure they were sound. Well at least we hope they were. However, your Uncle Jan and I.." I again glanced over at my uncle who repeated his shrug-&-eyeball roll... well, we think you've become overly fond of those, uh, public school people. Now mind, we know we are all God's children, but you see Courtenay dearest, some of us are highly-bred, and some are ill-bred -- it's just the way of things. They can't help it. We can't help it. I certainly cannot explain it, but there it is. You happen to be one of the highly bred, and must act accordingly. You owe it to your family and to society. Your mother and I talk a very great deal on the phone"----*tell me about it!* --- "and we are both very, very concerned, my dear, that you might someday marry someone, well, someone beneath your station, a man of a lesser family, you know--a `Not of Our Kind, Dear. Not PLO, you know, People Like Ourselves.'" My aunt giggled airily.

"And what kind is that, Auntie E.?" I was laughing at my old aunt, but noticed that Auntie E. was not laughing back. Something was not quite right. "Oh, I get it. You and Mom are afraid I might run off with the garbage man or worse, maybe a *Jewish* garbage man, right? Oh come on, Aunt Esther, give me a break, will ya?"

338

"Courtenay," my aunt adopted a stern look. "Please. Do not be flip with me. Uncle Jan and your mother and I are only thinking of your welfare."

"Gosh, I'm only seventeen years old. I have so many things I want to do in my life. Why is everyone so concerned with this marriage of mine, when I'm not?"

"Well, Sweetheart, it's not just your future marriage. Which, by the way my dear, you should be planning for right now. None too soon. Well, anyway, Courtenay darling, we, all of us, just feel that you've gotten too close to those people in public school, perhaps more than you ought---"

"Well then Auntie E.," I interrupted, "they should never have sent me to New Town High School! And by the way, do you have a clue why they did that? I don't. I mean they are just so not PLO, are they? But you know, I had to make friends, after all. If I hadn't, those kids would have---"

"Your mother," my aunt continued, ignoring my outburst, "reports that you occasionally spend time in their homes. Now this is a lovely gesture, and I'm sure your little friends appreciate it, but we all think in time you should separate from all of that and return to where you belong, where your roots are. You are from quality stock, you know."

"'Gesture?' Aunt Esther, I don't go to their homes because I'm making some big 'gesture.' I go because I'm asked and because I like it and I have fun. And what do you mean by 'stock' anyway? That word always makes me think of horses and cows."

"Courtenay, please darling, hear me out. You know we love you and we're in your corner. We only want what's best for you, so let me finish, and then we can have a lovely dinner and Fred can take you home. Now dear," she took a deep breath, "Courtenay, before you go to college, we want you to spend the entire summer in Europe. Mostly in Switzerland where you'll be with a class of people more suited to your status. You can ski, go to Paris, visit Spain and London, and go to all the important museums, concerts, shows and parties. The choices will be entirely yours. And then, if you find you are really happy over there, your parents can contact that sweet little college you were thinking of attending. What was it you wanted to study? Oh yes, journalism, and you can finish up your school in Europe, learning the things that are important for proper young ladies to learn. Journalism is rather a rough trade for a nice young woman, don't you agree?"

I didn't know which question to answer. I looked in disbelief across the table at my beloved aunt. There was a fairly long silence between us while Uncle Jan sat smiling vapidly at the wall.

"Aunt Esther, I'm really overwhelmed. It's wonderful of you to make this offer, and I'll really think a lot about it, I promise. But you know, public school has taught me a lot. I mean, I never knew things--well, never mind, I'll tell you all about that later. But anyway, as for this summer, I can't go to Switzerland. I've really been thinking about going back to the YMCA for my old summer job. You remember, I worked there last summer."

"Forgive me for interrupting you, Courtenay dear, but what does YMCA stand for, do you know?"

"Yes, Auntie, it stands for Young Men's Christian Association, but they--"

"Exactly my point. That organization was started so that nice, acceptable young Christian men might have a place to gather and to play sports. A clean, Christian organization. But now it's become something rather different, won't you agree? I mean, it is not just for Christians any longer, is it?"

"Well, no, Aunt Esther, actually, it's not. And it's not just for men, either. All sorts of kids go there, girls and boys, and it's for all religions. And they even have special programs for retarded kids, and kids with something called Down syndrome. You know, that's when they look sort of Chinese-ish with big faces, thick tongues and stuff. Gee, but they're sweet and loving kids. I wasn't scared of them one bit. But back to what you were saying, Auntie E. They did away with letting only Christians into the YMCA years ago. As a matter of fact, lots of people are starting to call it `The Y' now." I gulped air, hoping if I talked very fast I'd outrun my dear old aunt.

"Precisely what I was saying, Courtenay." Auntie E. was on to my tricks. "You needn't try to talk so fast and to drown me with your words, darling. Now then, I know that all sorts of people attend those places. People not like us, not of our sort. Do you see what I mean?" "Yes, Aunt Esther," I answered abruptly. "I do see what you mean, exactly. And this is why I think that maybe public school has been good for me. I've learned a lot about the people you're talking about, and really, they're not a bad lot, and they work hard. They're nice people who lead good lives. Really, Auntie E. You'd be amazed. You know, before I went to New Town, I thought everyone there was a jailbird or at least a criminal. I can't believe the names I used to call them, the way I used to mock them. I have to tell you, I feel ashamed about that now, Aunt Esther. Can you understand?" I looked beseechingly at my beloved aunt and knew that my dear old relative simply did not get what I was saying. Not at all.

"But darling," and here, Auntie E. lowered her voice so as not to offend the waiters and waitresses in the room. "Darling. these people are the w*orking class.*" She whispered the last two words as though speaking of an unmentionable, dread disease, and looked around the big room quickly and furtively from beneath her veil. "And dearest niece, surely you don't want to be a part of that, do you? I mean working? Like a common laborer? Really Courtenay, you were not brought into this world to *work*, for heaven's sake!"

"Well if not, Aunt Esther, what *was* I brought here to do?" My question was an honest one. I hoped my aunt knew I did not mean any impertinence.

"Courtenay, as your father would say, `There's them wot 'as, and them wot ain't.' Fortunately my dear, you were born to be one of the `one's wot 'ave.' You should be grateful. You were born into this world to make a good marriage, a fine family and to keep --- well, to keep our sort going for generations."

I sighed in resignation.

"Honestly Aunt Esther, I *am* grateful. When I see how those people have to struggle, I am really very grateful for what I have. But you know, since going to public school, I've started feeling guilty. I mean, why are some people just born into such wealth while others have horrible lives, you know? It just isn't fair."

Aunt Esther sat back in her chair and began to fan herself with the wine list.

"Oh dear, oh dearie me. It's worse than I ever suspected." She'd turned pale. Uncle Jan continued to stare vaguely into space. I knew it would be prudent for me to get off my soapbox and try to placate the old girl. I would never accept the invitation to go to Europe, but I knew how to play the game. I reached across the table.

"Auntie E., my dear old darling Auntie. Don't worry." I smiled as winningly as I could, and saw the color come back into my aunt's quivering bulldog jowls. "Really," I went on. "I promise I'll give it a lot of serious thought. I know you're very wise and you mean so well and I

341

appreciate that, honest I do. We'll talk about Europe. Might be a great idea. Who knows? Maybe I'll meet some count or duke and marry him, and make everyone happy. But of course from what I've heard about those jokers, they might not be able to make any babies with me! Or anyone else for that matter."

Aunt Esther fluttered her hand with a pretend slap toward me and delicately screamed, "Oooo, you little muggins! You devil. I ought to take you across my knee. How dare you say such a naughty thing to me? You are the rudest, most impudent ill-bred little scamp this family has ever had! You're just as naughty now as the summer day you got angry and marched over to the fireplace and kicked my priceless Staffordshire dog to pieces. Remember? I should have whipped you with a belt, just as I should most certainly do now."

"Yeah, yeah, yeah, old girl, and you love it, and you love *me*, doncha?" I leaned across the table and planted a loud kiss on aunt's fat cheek, sucking in a considerable measurement of veil and two fuzzballs. And then, reluctantly, my darling Aunt Esther laughed—and laughed---and laughed!

# CHAPTER 51

Emma placed the bowl of cereal in front of me with a loud sniff. I was astonished to see Emma's eyes brimming with tears, and oh, they were so red I thought they looked like blood on mud.

"Hey Em! You've got a cold or something. You OK?"

"Yeah, sure, chile," she said. "Mebbe some kinda pollen in the air or somethin'. I dunno. Eat up, Miss Courtenay. Eat a good brefix. Keep yissef strong."

"Yeah, sure, Emma, I'll keep strong. I'll get fat as a pig if I eat all the stuff you give me. Hey. Where's the newspaper? Father'll go into orbit if it's not at his place, you know that. Want me to check out in the driveway?"

"No. *NO!* --- No, it's OK, Miss Courtenay. That good fer nuthin' paperboy prolly thrown it inta the bushes agin. I'll go fetch it. You eat."

"Sure, Em. Tell Fred I'll be ready in about 25 minutes, OK?"

I obediently ate my food, ruminating on the meeting with my uncle and aunt, letting my imagination loose to daydream about spending a summer in Europe. It was nice to think about that even thought I knew I'd never go. Outside the open breakfast room windows the brilliant old azalea bushes shimmered like petaled fuchsia jewels in the spring breezes, and the forsythia behind them created a golden aura that spread to the sky. My parents' prized tulip tree stood watch, heavily loaded with large creamy and shell-pink blooms, the ground beneath blanketed with the fallen petals. The sight made me think of weddings after all the guests had gone home. The air smelled thick, dizzyingly and mysteriously sweet as it drifted softly through the windows, and as I sat lost in pleasant thoughts I listened to my two favorite spring sounds: the droning of cicadas, and the melancholy, velvety five-sectioned call of mourning doves.

Fred had taken advantage of the few minutes he had while I ate my breakfast, and was mowing the back lawn, the mower blades clicking and whirring crisply together like a mechanical cricket. It was a musical and glowing moment for me, and it pleasured something underneath my heart. I was happy.

I smiled and carried my dishes from the breakfast room into the kitchen. Emma was nowhere to be seen. The sounds of the lawnmower had ceased, so I dropped my dishes into the sink with a clatter, splashed some water on them, gathered my books and went out to find Fred.

I saw Emma and Fred talking earnestly out on the back lawn. I called out, and the two turned abruptly, startled. *That's odd.* Fred spoke a few more words to Emma, and the woman answered and touched his arm. They looked at one another, and then Fred turned and walked toward me smiling. Together we walked to the car.

"Hey Fred. What's the skinny? What were you and Emma talking about out there? You and she aren't, you know, you guys aren't--" I elbowed Fred and winked. Fred smiled broadly, his teeth contrasting white against his ebony skin.

"Now Miss Courtenay, don't you go 'round thinkin' such things, you bad chile! How you do go on! Why, you know Emma's a lot older'n me, and besides, my wife would take a shotgun to me if I's ta fool 'round. Shame on you, you bad chile! Why, shame, shame!"

"Sure, Fred, you old rascal you! Well, I won't squeal on you. You can count on me. I'll keep your bad secret, you devil! Let's go!" Smiling, but not answering, Fred held the door open for me, walked around the other side, and started the car. We drove to the hiding spot behind the stand of trees above the bus stop. Fred had not spoken during the drive, but I hardly noticed; I had been too absorbed in the warm, pastel spring pouring through the opened car windows. I hummed softly, then jumped from the car and ran down toward the bus stop, where the kids were engrossed in conversation, heads bent closely together. I bounced close to them and they suddenly stopped talking. All heads turned toward me.

"Hey you guys, don't do that! If you stop talking when I show up, I gotta think you're talking' about me! So? Are you? Huh?"

Silence. I stopped moving and looked at each face, smiling quizzically. "What?" I said. I began to feel vaguely ill at ease and my smile became forced. Surprisingly, it was Winona who spoke first.

"Hey Queenie. Don't be sucha ego maniac, girl. No one's talkin' about you. We jest, umm, we jest talkin' about the King and Queen of the senior prom. Y'know what? They're thinkin' of nominatin' me. Haw! Me! Whatchu t'ink?" Winona placed one hand on her hip, another at the back of her head, and strolled around in a circle, wiggling her ample behind, shaking her substantial breasts. She was a perfect black Mae West. The kids guffawed loudly and applauded this unusual performance from the normally reclusive girl. I grinned at my friend. Winona was obviously feeling a little better about life, for even she was going to the Prom. Not about to wait around to be asked, and having no problem with cultural propriety, Winona had asked one of the school's best but shyest basketball players, and to her astonishment, he'd said yes. On Prom night they wore matching tuxedos and tall silk hats, all in the color of fuchsia, head to toe, and this astounding couple had more fun than anyone there.

The bus screeched to a stop in front of the kids and everyone crowded on board. The ride was as bumpy and swaying as ever, and I stared, unfocused, out of the window, daydreaming again about Europe. I knew I wouldn't go, but I'd always loved to fantasize, even about things I knew would or could not happen. Maybe especially. I shifted in my seat and looked around at New Town friends. I just could not seem to catch anyone's eye, not even that of my pal Barry who was sitting right next to me and looked away every time I glanced at him. The uneasy feeling pushed at me again, this time harder. *What on earth is the matter with these dorks today?*

As the bus rattled past the huge Catholic church, the majority of the kids, as ever, crossed themselves, never looking up or stopping what they were doing or saying. I grinned, remembering my horrified confusion at this performance so long ago. Now the familiar, nonchalant gesture gave me comfort. But the quietness of the bus was unnerving. Was it the spring weather? The idea that school was ending for the year? No one was cursing. Things weren't flying through the air. What? The non-sound in the bus was the sound that comes after a tapped tuning fork; it goes away but is still there. *This is weird.* I closed my eyes and leaned my head back on the seat.

Finally in school, I smiled and greeted my friends, many of whom laughed and whispered as I passed them. *What the heck is going on?* The chatter in the homeroom ceased as I walked to my desk. I sat down and, perplexed, gazed around the room at my friends and then stacked my books uneasily on top of my desk.

"What's goin' on with everyone today anyway?" I directed the question to the entire room. A couple of kids giggled, and a few mumbled. Getting no real reply, I shrugged, opened my desk and began to rummage for a pencil. Whispered mumblings caused me to raise my head and look around again. Marty was staring at me like a snake about to strike and she did not blink. I turned back to the open desk and saw a newspaper lying on top of my books. *How did that get there? Who did this?* I picked it up. *Why are my hands shaking??*

"LOCAL BUSINESSMAN, SCHOOL PRINCIPAL, TEACHER, AND YMCA DIRECTOR, ALL INCRIMINATED IN ABUSE OF HANDICAPPED CHILDREN. The headline roared across the page in thick black letters. My eyes moved woodenly down the column.

*"Walter Hancock Wolcott, wealthy local businessman, was arrested early this morning at his home for alleged involvement in a handicapped child abuse ring. Also arrested were Winston Raleigh, principal of The Academy, and the school's Latin teacher, Harold Tonnaschell. Clare Savage, director of the local YMCA was arrested at his home at approximately the same time."*

A frigid calm spread through me. I frowned in confusion. These words were talking about my father. *My* father? No, no no no, it was someone else's. I shook my head, the gesture small, like a bird shaking water from its beak. I looked down at the paper again, and the words pulled at my eyes, blurring and yet stingingly clear. They said that my father and his golf buddies had procured young boys for sexual favors, photographs and home movies. It was alleged that the boys were selected from the retarded and Down syndrome groups brought by their families to the Y each day for crafts and physical activities. The article went on to explain that "Director Savage" had made all the horrific arrangements. The reason they were discovered, the words said, was that one of the boys overcame his terror and told his parents. He said, through hysterical tears, that these men had threatened to kill his parents, his brothers and even his dog if he told on them. An investigation was under way to discover if the incidents were local or more widespread.

I had to swallow, but my throat was cement and I could not. I had to cry, but my eyes were wooden, and I could not. I had to scream, but my voice had disappeared, and I could not. I had to run, but my legs were leaden weight, and...I *would* run.

I shut my desk, and stood. I focused on the door to the homeroom. Like a robot, I walked toward it. It was miles away, miles, but I continued toward it. My homeroom teacher's voice drifted into my deadened brain like a phonograph record winding down and down, deep and slow: "Courtenay Wolcott, where do you think you're going?

346

Sit down this instant!" But I kept slogging through a terrible muddied miasma. Finally, the door, the door, I opened the homeroom door, walked through it, down the hall and stairs and out through the red-painted metal doors. The bright sunlight blinded me, but I walked from memory. I'd left my purse, money, lunch, bus pass and books behind, but I did not think of those things. Those things no longer mattered.

As I walked away from school, I heard another teacher's voice calling me back. I began to run. I ran fast, but I felt as I were going nowhere, just like in the dream. I wanted to get down on my hands and feet, to gallop like a horse over the cement sidewalk. The voice, faint now, was still calling me. Was I running? I did not look back. My breath came in harsh rasps, so I slowed to calm my heart and lungs. I walked through the side streets, and then past my bus stop. I kept walking until I reached the bottom of the hill and then I began to climb. And climb. I walked on, past the estates, the wide sweeping lawns, the grove of trees where I'd seen the dazzling bluebirds nearly two years ago. I kept walking, neither looking nor seeing.

Someone was crying. I could hear her. Who was that? Someone who could not breathe through tears. I passed by my home without looking at it. I walked down the manicured paths through the terraced gardens toward the golf course, then stepped off the path and into the woods where I'd spent so many safe, quiet hours. The woods were dark and soft, embracing me, and the black earth was spongy under my feet. I walked toward the stream, and sat on its banks, and watched a small turtle sunning itself on a rock at the bottom of one shaft of sunlight pouring through the canopy of the trees. I wanted to stroke his shell, to feel its smooth, sunbaked hardness. I raised my hand weakly toward him, and he slid from the rock noiselessly, slicing into the water like a black marble pancake, leaving no ripples. I peered into the dark depths and saw the puff of mud billowing silently from the bottom. He was gone.

I hugged my knees to my chest, jamming my face between them. I heard someone howl and scream, and my throat hurt for that someone, whoever she was, as I sat at the stream's edge, rocking and rocking and listening to the faraway, wrenching sobs. The trees, my old friends, silent and sad sentinels bent their branches to me and whispered soft comforts.

When my aching muscles at last begged for release I sat up straight and now my head ached as if it had been hammered, and my eyes were nearly shut from weeping. I did not know how long I'd been there, but noticed dully that it was dark now, the sun had left. I stood and wobbled, pulling in some long, deep shuddered breaths as I looked up the steep sides of the wooded ravine I'd always loved so well. I was glad it was dark. I wished it would stay dark forever so no one would ever have to see me again. Slowly, I climbed my way up to the house. I stopped and looked into the goldfish pond my father had installed in the back lawn. It had recently been cleaned, and the cement sides were the clear, beautiful green of a traffic light. Even in the dark, I could make out the shapes of the slow moving goldfish, big, fat and lazy from Fred's constant overfeeding.

I walked around the house toward the back door where I could see lights in all the windows and a black and white police car in the driveway, its engine running. I glanced at it, blinked, opened the door to my home, and walked through the vestibule into the kitchen.

"Oh, my God, she's here! Thank you Jesus, thank you Jesus!" It was Emma, who crashed into me like a huge brown bear, enveloping me, crying, scolding and crushing me so hard my breath burst from my lungs.

"Oh, chile, my baby, baby darlin', where you bin? We've called and called and went to the school, even called the po-leese. We've been sick with worry, oh my darlin' Miss Courtenay. Ah, Gawd, someone went an' tol' you about what's happened to your daddy, I know it. I knew someone'd tell you. I tol' Fred this mawnin', I told Miz Wolcott to tell you, but no, no one wanted to, so you had to find out in such a mean way. Oh baby, baby, that was bad for you. They tol' us at school how you found out. But you're safe now. You're safe with ol' Emma. I won't let nuthin' happen to you."

The old black woman rocked me gently, standing there in the middle of the kitchen. She crooned to me and the tarry black and terrible hurt loosened its grip on my heart. *Oh, now I can be safe.* I pulled my face from Emma's soft shoulder. Standing behind us were my mother, Fred, and Mary, and behind them was a tall, young policeman.

My mother turned to the officer. Her voice sounded as if she'd been crying too.

"Thank you so much, officer dear," she said to him. "As you can see, our little girl is back home safely with us. You may go now, but thank you so much for responding to our call."

"Well, ma'am," the young officer began, and I saw that his face looked sad for them, "you know, I'll have to make out a report on this, but I'm glad your daughter has returned. I'll use your phone if I may, please, to call headquarters to tell them to take the APB off. Oh, uh, that means the All Points Bulletin. May I please use your phone?"

"Of course. Just around that corner there. But officer, please, does this all have to get into the newspapers?"

"I'm sorry ma'am," he answered. "I'm afraid the newspapers already know about this. Did you not see those ---- sorry, those headlines? As soon as the word came in that your daughter was missing, the papers started calling us down at the station. I don't know how they get this kind of information so fast, but by gum, they surely do. Well, if you'll excuse me, I'll go make that call and then get out of here and leave you nice folks alone."

Emma released me and I turned toward my mother. "Oh, Mother, Mommie, I'm so scared."

I reached my arms out, but my mother stood stiffly where she was. I walked toward her anyway and began weeping. My mother reached out, took hold of one of my outstretched hands and patted it.

"My dear Courtenay," my mother said in a choked, tight voice. "We are the Wolcotts. We are of good stock, strong stock, and my dear, we shall weather this. I have known about this—this little problem, shall we say, for years, but your father promised me this dreadful practice of his had ceased. Apparently it's always been a lie." My mother sighed softly. "But," she went on, "as you well know, we are thoroughbreds, Courtenay. We shall hold our heads high, and our life will go on as usual. We shall stay here and defy anyone to speak ill of this family. This is but a small and ugly episode, and we will move around it and go on. It is forgotten. We are the Wolcotts."

I felt my head cracking. I had never heard my mother speak so passionately or at such length. The speech over, my mother dropped my hand, turned, and walked away.

# CHAPTER 52

Sleep was impossible. I twisted in my blankets. At one point during the night, Emma came in and felt my head. I knew I was hot, but not from fever. Too many thoughts of my father and what he'd done, and how I felt, and what I feared everyone would think, writhed like snakes in my weary mind. When dawn began to nudge the dark back, I sat at my bedroom window, staring out, neither knowing nor caring that it was a breathtaking sunrise, the sky filled with delicate, streaked Easter egg colors and framed by a profusion of spring flowers. It was time, I knew, to make decisions.

As I'd rolled and twisted in the night, the phrase "good stock" kept surfacing in my roiled thoughts. I thought about my mother's remarks from the night before, about the so-called class they supposedly belonged to. Well, I would now have the chance to prove to everyone that I was indeed from "good stock."

I had important things to do, and I began to list them calmly, pushing them into my brain the way I used to draw pictures in mud with a stick. There were final exams to take, there was the prom, and graduation. Following those, I would attend the college of my choice, and then become a fine journalist, famous, my pithy stuff read and argued about by everyone. I would not go to Europe on Aunt Esther's invitation, but instead would go back to the YMCA and ask, beg if I had to, for my old summer job. Only this time, I would insist I work exclusively with the handicapped, retarded, and Down syndrome kids, returning to the scene of my father's crime, to make right what he had made wrong.

My mind wandered to Bobby Sotirakis, and I wondered if he'd still want to take me to the prom, considering all the bad press. But then I smiled. I knew Bobby would remain loyal to me no matter what people said. *Thank God for people like Bobby.* I lowered my eyes and wondered if The Academy kids would have stood by me this way.

I sighed and wanted to remember the glittering things, the happy high school events and not the dark ones. I wanted to look back at my final high school years and smile, but my father had stolen that from me now. Now, when I'd think back on these years, the memory of what he'd done would swim first to the surface, like the dream, and I'd have to search beneath for the happy times. I pulled in a large, deep breath, squared my shoulders and raised my chin the way I'd seen Joan Crawford do in *Mildred Pierce,* and went to take a shower.

Later while Fred was driving me to the bus stop, he reached across the seat and grasped my cold hand.

"How you feelin', Honey?"

"I'm OK, Fred, I'm OK. I guess I've known for a long time that something weird was going on with my father. I never thought it would be this awful, though. I just don't know what's going to happen to all of us. I'm scared, Fred, I'm just so scared."

"I know, Honey, I know. You a brave one, fo' sho', goin' to school right away like you're doin'. Best thing, best thing. An' you're right--you don't gotta hide about this. Ain't your fault. It's his fish to fry, Honey, his own. Proud o'you, little girl. You'll be OK."

We arrived at the stand of trees, and I slowly got out of the car. With my books and purse left behind at my school, I carried nothing but a small paper bag with a lunch Emma had lovingly made for me and a dollar bill taken from her own shabby purse. I hesitated by the car, now afraid. As I took a few slow steps, I felt the same kind of cold fear I'd experienced so long ago on that first harrowing day.

No one spoke. Then someone within the group yelled "Hey Queenie! How's yer fairy father?" Another shouted, "Shut your ass, or I'll shut it with my foot, fuckhead." I stopped a few feet from the crowd.

"OK," I began, my voice faltering. "OK. You all know my father's involved in something bad. Really bad. I don't know what to do about all of this but I know it's not my fault so I'm not gonna take any blame for it." I took a breath and stood taller, again squaring my shoulders. "So now that it's all out in the open, let's just go on to school and forget about it, OK? I still want to be friends with all of you. If you don't want to be friends with me because of what you've read in the paper, well then that's too bad. There's nothing I can do about that." I looked away, wishing the damned bus would show up.

For a long moment, no one spoke.

"Ah, screw it anyway," one of the boys said. I could not focus so did not see who it was. "So your old man screwed up," he went on. "So he's a shit. So what? Ain't got nuttin' to do wid youse or us. Hell, my old man's been in the slammer for three years for beatin' up a guy and robbin' him! An' he only got seven bucks for his trouble." This boy was my instant hero.

The group laughed, and as the tension slowly broke, I looked around for the boy who had made things OK.

"Thanks," I said when I found him. "I really needed that!" The kids laughed and the bus finally arrived. When I boarded, it was wonderful for me to hear the old bus driver growl, "Where's yer friggin' bus pass, girlie?"

"Sir, you may shove the bus pass," I said pleasantly, and grinned as I walked to the back of the bus.

# CHAPTER 53

It was all over. Finally. I put down my pen and folded up the blue book. "I aced it," I whispered. "Yeahboy!" During the American History test, I'd watched Pansy Junko spread Necco Wafers all over the surface of her desk. Everyone knew she'd written important historical dates on one side of all of them, which she turned upside down before the test began. I really admired her ingenuity. Whenever Pansy forgot a date, I would watch her pick up some of the candies, take a quick peek and when she found the answer, it went immediately into her mouth.

There was a brief moment of terror, however, when the supremely bored teacher-in-charge walked lazily down the aisle and saw the candies fanned out next to Pansy's blue book. He politely asked her if he could have one, and, her face suddenly sucked dry of color, she'd weakly said, "Oh, by all means." He squinted down at Pansy and said, "Miss Junko, are you all right?"

"Oh yes sir," she answered in a little girl voice. "I'm just exhausted from all the studying." I suppressed a chuckle, knowing my good friend Pansy Junko never studied an instant during her entire 12 years of schooling since she was so adept at cheating she never felt the need. She'd once confided in me that after graduation, her life's dream was to work in the great gambling casinos of Las Vegas.

"I could show those guys a trick or three," she'd laugh.

I watched with great fascination as teacher-in-charge reached for a yellow disc and before everyone's horrified eyes, chewed and swallowed the dates of the Magna Carta and the Gettysburg Address. He then coyly tossed back one more, a pink disc this time, and contentedly munched the days, month and year of the bombing of Hiroshima and Nagasaki. Pansy Junko received a C in the course and if that very bored teacher hadn't had a sweet tooth, she probably would have gotten a B.

I walked out into the hall, stretched and yawned. It was remarkable, I thought, how one small action, such as handing in a test's blue book can begin a new life. I felt renewed, light, reborn. Now I could get on with my life, go to the prom, graduate, work for the summer, go to college. I walked out through the red painted metal doors, and toward the bleachers, where I sat in the sunshine to think, dream... and to wonder.

Everyone expected a long trial for my father and his accomplices. In the meantime, the men were all out on bail, and my father was staying home, hiding in his bedroom. He kept the door locked, the shades pulled to the sill. I didn't much care--I had little to say to him. Once or twice, I'd tried to show him some understanding and compassion when we passed in a room or hallway, but he'd turned away and rejected me. I was quite used to that kind of treatment from him, so it didn't hurt as much as it might have...not as much, at least.

My mother told me he was talking about moving the family away, but said she would have none of it. She had loyal friends here, her sister, her entire life. To Helen's delighted amazement, she found she was now more sought after than ever. With salivating mewls and clucks of sympathy, all of her friends devoured every detail of the sordid mess, and Helen happily supplied them. She told them that "all along, she'd known about her husband's disgusting other life, but she had her position, after all, her status, and of course, (as a quick afterthought) there was always Courtenay." Helen had no intention of leaving. She'd brought a lot of money to the marriage and our big home, and she could survive quite nicely by simply clipping stock coupons for the rest of her life, thank you very much. She told her friends both at home and away from the weekly mahjongg table that she had held her head high after learning of her husband's perversity many years ago and had long since determined to keep the vulgar secret until her death. After all, he'd promised her "the problem" was under control and would never happen again. Having said that, she'd managed to shed a few melodramatic tears for the clucking sympathetic ladies, and they'd rush to her, pat her with muted, cottony thwumps from their white gloved hands. Cooing and murmuring comforting sounds, they called her husband "that terrible man" and Helen, "you poor, poor thing," and they would then beg for more details. The telephone ran red hot.

Leaning back on the bleachers, I was getting sleepy in the warm sunlight, recalling how Dom had reacted to the news. He'd met me in the hallway after school, greeting me with surprising compassion and sweetness. "How's it goin', Queenie?" He wrapped a strong arm around my shoulders.

"Oh, it's goin' OK, Dom, I guess. Looks like your Marty Commesso really got even with me, didn't she?"

354

"Howzat? And whadda you mean, `my' Marty?" He looked sincerely puzzled.

"You remember last year when Marty thought I was taking you away from her, God forbid? Well, she was the one who put the newspaper in my desk. Yeah, she got even. You should've seen her face! Talk about happy! She nearly popped her---well, her whatevers."

"Yeah?" said Dom. "Yeah?" He bristled, seemed to stretch taller. "I'll break her fuckin' face. I'll slap her neck off!"

"Oh, Dom, don't go all stupid on me. She's been waiting a long time to do that to me. I had to find out eventually, right? I guess she's still mad that Winona kept her from strangling me that day. Let her have her moment of glory. I really don't give a hoot at this point. She isn't worth the trouble. Honest, I'm just too sick of the whole thing to care."

"OK, OK, Queenie. I'll leave the bitch alone, if you say so." Then suddenly, unexpectedly, he said, "Hey Queenie, if you ain't goin' to the prom wit anyone, you wanna go wit me?"

I pulled away from under Dom's arm, and looked up at him. My quick answer surprised even me.

"Dom, I'd have loved to have gone with you, really, I would. But you're too late. I'm going with Bobby Sotirakis. He asked me a long time ago. I wish you'd asked sooner--honest, I do! I'd have gone with you in a split second!"

Dom smiled down at me, shrugged, and said mildly, "Oh hell, that's OK, Queenie. I'll ax Pansy, an' that way I'll be sure to have a good time after, if you get my drift."

I felt my face grow hot. "God, Dom, you're such a jackass sometimes. They're gonna come after you and take you to the funny farm one of these days. But hey, thanks for asking me, anyway." We walked a while longer in silence. He put his arm around me again.

"Hey Queenie you remember when you preached at me about how I should treat even queer-baits like they're human bein's or sumpin'?"

"Yes, I remember."

"Well, I just wanna say that it's cool with me that your old man's a fag who likes to hurt boys. Well, now--- wait a sec. Lemme say that again. I don't think that what he done with the ree-tards was good, but, well, I guess he can't help being a – well, whatever he is--- kinda like

355

you 'splained to me." I smiled. This was the closest thing to outright humanity I'd ever heard from Dominic's lips, and it touched me. My eyes filled with tears and he saw that.

In general, the student body reacted to the news about my father better than I'd expected. I'd overheard comments and quite nearly wept when a boy shouted an ugly remark about my father during lunch period because Rosie, dear Rosie, advised the boy rather loudly to so something that impossible to do himself. Some unpleasant things had been scrawled in ink across my locker too, and another newspaper about the case was stuffed in my desk. I knew without looking that Marty was again watching and grinning, but I refused to give her the satisfaction of a reaction. In the main, however, I didn't feel a need to hide or run away any longer, and I began to relax although I knew it could never go away in all of my lifetime. The New Town kids had showed their own sort of class to me, their kind of grace, and I found it nothing short of majestic.

# CHAPTER 54

I heard nothing from The Academy kids since my father's arrest so after days of grinding indecision, I called Sally. My hand shook as I dialed the number and I hung up twice before it started to ring. On the third try I decided to stop being such a chicken and let it ring through.

Sally's mother answered, and when I identified myself, this woman I had known all my life, was terse. Distant. "Just a moment please, Courtenay. I'll get Sally for you." I heard some intense whispering between Sally and her mother before my oldest friend picked up the phone.

"Hi, Courtenay," Sally said, her voice brittle. *Am I imagining that?*

"Hi, Sal. Hi--umm--how are you? I haven't heard from you in so long-- well, since you guys graduated. Gee, I wish the public school system would get out that early. I've still got a couple more days."

"Oh? Really?" *No, I'm not imagining that. No.*

"Yep," I said, pretending to not notice the ice in Sally's voice. "And then comes the prom. I'm going with that guy I told you about. The undertaker." She waited for the laugh. It didn't come. I panicked. My mind thrashed for something to say.

"What are you doing this summer, Sally?" It was the best I could do.

"Well, some of us are going to Europe... graduation presents, you know. Oh--I told you that already. What are you getting for graduation?"

Finally! A spark of interest.

"I don't know, Sal--actually, they haven't told me. I mean, my mother hasn't said anything about it..."

"Right," said Sally. "Right. Well. Uh, what are you doing this summer?"

Before I could think, or catch myself, I answered.

"I'm trying to get my old job back at the YMCA. Of course there's a new director there, a woman, I haven't met her yet, but I hear she's great. Anyway, I've called her and asked if I could work with the physically handicapped and retarded kids...you know, the kids who..."

A long silence filled the line. My toes curled into a cramp. I'd blown it. How could I possibly have brought up the retarded kids, or the YMCA? *Ogod, ogod, ogod. What was I thinking? O god.*

"At the YMCA Courtenay? With those... retarded kids? I'd have rather thought your family would be quite finished with those people. I mean, you're actually going back there after all that's happened?"

I clenched my teeth, began to answer, hesitated. I had to answer. *Will Sally hang up on me?*

"Sally. We've been friends for so long. Do you think we might be able to talk about all this? No. Wait. Don't answer yet. Please, don't talk. Just listen. This has been really ... hard." I swallowed. My throat began to ache and tears stung behind my eyes. I put my hand on the front of my neck and cleared my throat.

"Not one of my old friends from The Academy has called me," I said, "and it makes me feel like you guys blame *me* for what happened. You *know* it's not my fault. I never knew this stuff about my father. If I'd known this, I'd have told you! Are you angry with me, Sally?" I pulled my breath in with a backward sob.

There was another long pause, and then I heard Sally begin to cry softly. "No, no, Court, I'm not angry with you. I guess I was for a while, but it was stupid because natch, it's not your fault that your father is a--well, you know, a--well, I don't know what to say. You see Courtenay, what happened is...oh God, I hate to say this to you... but well, we all sort of feel that our last year at The Academy is ruined because of this horrible mess. I mean, like, now, when we get older and think about--you know, kinda remember The Academy, this is what we'll always think of first, you know? So, I guess we were all mad at you. You were just easier to blame than Mr. Raleigh and Mr. Tonnaschell, I guess. My God Court, they've been teachers there since forever. We all grew up with those guys. I'm sorry, Courtenay. I'm really awfully sorry."

"Oh, Sally, don't cry. I'm not crying!" I half laughed, half sobbed. "Oh, thanks so, so much for telling me that, Sal. You are just the living end! I know that was hard for you to say. This whole thing has been a nightmare. I don't know what to do. I've decided to just keep moving, just go on with my life. I've taken some flak at school about it, but it hasn't been too bad. The kids have been pretty good, kinda, well--- majestic really. But I know how you must feel."

We snuffled together for some moments.

"Sally?" I said, my voice hopeful. "Do you think we could sort of get together? Tonight? Tomorrow?"

Sally didn't answer.

"Maybe in a couple of days?"

Sally had pulled back. I couldn't see her, but I knew it was happening.

"I'm not sure, Court. Look. Let's cool it for a while, OK? My folks are--well, they're sort of hung up about all of this, and they've told me not to, oh God, this is so hard, they've told me I can't see you. Well, for a while, maybe. I know they'll calm down, Courtenay, and this'll all blow over. God, my father can be such a tool. I mean, they understand that you didn't have anything to do with all of that awful stuff. But they keep telling me that--they keep saying something about `the acorn not falling far from the tree,' whatever that means. And they also keep saying `A person is known by the company she keeps,' and I do know what that means. So hang loose, Court--I'll call you, OK? I promise. Really. Don't worry. We're still friends, but you can't call here anymore, OK?" Sally was beginning to talk fast now. "I'll call you. I'll tell you all about the new headmaster, and the new teachers replacing Raleigh and Tonnaschell. They're both complete lame-brains. I gotta go now. 'Bye Courtenay--so long." And Sally, my best and oldest friend, hung up.

I stared at the phone in my hand, and with a sharp, deep twisting of my heart I understood that far more than that conversation had just ended.

# CHAPTER 55

I knocked on the partially opened door to my father's bedroom, and when he did not answer, I entered the room. *I've never had the nerve to do that before!* He sat in an old wooden armchair in front of the windows overlooking the fishpond, and beyond that the gardens and golf course. It was a sight I knew he loved. An old, frayed lap robe drooped around his hunched shoulders. He was wearing his pajamas as he had been since his crimes had become public knowledge.

My father had become wizened and ancient looking. His eyes had sunk back into his head, the eyelids blue-white and half closed, his expression vacant. He did not look up or react to my presence. I was not sure what I should do so I waited awkwardly at his side and soon my gaze also went to the view from his window. Minutes passed. I could hear his uneven, labored breathing.

As we gazed out of the window, a large long-legged bird swooped down and stood on the decorative rocks surrounding the fish pond. The big bird stared into the pool, motionless, and then suddenly dove headfirst into the water. Flapping his wings wildly, creating a tremendous turmoil of splashing water, he rose with a fat, wriggling goldfish in his beak. I looked down at my father. He did not react.

"Hey, Daddy, did you see that?" I asked my father, desperate for a dialogue between us.

After a minute, he looked up. His eyes were heavily ringed, the whites dull yellow, and they had no shine. They looked like the unseeing eyes of a dead animal. The corners of his mouth were turned down. He was grey and a few dry wisps of colorless hair fell over his forehead. He'd lost a great deal of weight and I pulled my head back and wrinkled my nose because I just realized he smelled very bad.

"See what, Courtenay?" he asked.

"Oh, nothing, Father. It's not important. I just came up to see if there's anything you need or want." I reached out and touched his shoulder tentatively. He looked at my hand, and shrugged it off.

"Oh, come on Father," I said. "Don't pull away. Please. Can we talk a little? Just this once? I mean so much has..."

He sighed deeply. "What do you want to talk about, Courtenay?" he asked. But I knew he knew. How could he not?

"Well, Father, I guess you'd rather not talk about--well, about what's happened and everything. I guess I just want to tell you that I'm sorry you're having this awful trouble, and I hope you'll--well, I hope it'll all just--I don't know. I hope it'll work out OK for you. I wish you didn't have to go to jail next..."

He looked dully at me.

"Yes." He turned back to the windows.

I didn't want to leave. I felt rage, then sadness, and then hatred shot through with tiny bright shafts of unexpected love. But something needed completion, so I cleared my throat, and tried again.

"Father... Daddy, can I ask you something?"

He didn't turn his head, nor did he acknowledge the question. I was left to decide whether this was a yes or a no, and I chose yes.

"Do you remember when you told me I had to go to New Town High School because the family was running out of money?"

My father continued to stare out of the window.

"Well, umm, sometimes, I guess I think there actually was no money problem Dad, and I was wondering if maybe you made me leave The Academy because you were worried something bad might happen to me...at my old school...maybe even in the neighborhood, if people---you know--- found out. Was it something like that? Is that why you wanted me to go to public school?"

My heart was beating hard, and I felt very scared. I'd never spoken to my father about anything on a deeply emotional level, and I never, in my wildest dreams, thought I'd be talking to him about such a terrible issue as this.

My father took half of forever to answer and I began to think he'd chosen not to. He sighed again. Finally, he turned and looked up at me.

"What do you think?" he answered, his voice scratchy, thick.

"Well, Father, I sort of think that maybe was the case. So, I should sort of... well, like maybe thank you because I think you were kind of, umm -- protecting me?"

The man aged more before my eyes, right there in front of me. I could see that years had been added to him. His face crumpled like the cover of an old leather book left out in the rain. He opened his mouth, but no sound came out, closed it, and opened it again.

"I'll be quite frank, Courtenay." Finally. His voice was hoarse, his words nearly amusingly formal. "I thought if this thing ever got out, you might be in some danger. I was afraid that perhaps your schoolmates might think you were somehow involved, and might do something to harm you. I wanted you to be invisible, in a huge crowd where no one really knew you, where this mess could just go away and you'd be.... I simply thought it was better for you to be away so no one would think you knew about it. And frankly your mother and I thought those ---those kids you went to school with at New Town would – maybe---maybe protect you more. You know, they're all such tough guys, gangster types. I wasn't sure the people at The Academy would have had that sort of----well, grit---something. I guess I wanted to hide you in plain sight----or ---.

"Oh—you know, twenty-twenty hindsight. We should have sent you to Europe or somewhere but I couldn't bear to have you go so far away." I was stunned at that last sentence. *This is my father saying these things? He didn't want me to be far from him? What? Am I in a dream?* I almost laughed but looked hard at my parent and I saw he meant those words he spoke.

"And besides," his voice faltered, "people—the neighbors--- would have noticed you were gone and would have wondered. They'd have suspected something. Your mother and I had to be so careful..." *Aha! There it is, the real reason! I should have known—I'd almost begun to believe him. I'll just never learn.*

And then I again felt the urge to laugh—or to cry---this man always managed to let me down. His record remained unblemished!

"We should have let Esther and Jan take you to Europe, to live there until this mess--- until ----

"Sometimes," he went on, "I even tried to think of ways to get your mother to go away too, even with Esther and Jan if they'd have had her. But she wouldn't. We should have taken you to Europe when we knew this---this---thing was about to break.

362

"Your mother has always known about…well, right from the beginning, but she --- Well Courtenay, that's it, ---that is all."

"But Daddy, you'll have to go to prison. You and the others. Your lawyers say they can't save you. Prison Daddy, --- oh no--- "

He went back to staring out of the window. I understood I'd been dismissed, that I was expected to leave the room. I began to feel tears running down my cheeks although I wasn't really crying, and I did not know why I could not quite believe my father's story about his trying to save me by sending me to public school. *Why? Why am I feeling like this? The man is trying.* But, I reached out and touched my father's shoulder again, very gently and shook my head. *He's never cared that much about me or my feelings. Never. I know that will never change. Maybe I'll never know the truth.*

"Thank you, Daddy. I love you too," I said softly, and turned to leave the room.

"Yes," he said.

# CHAPTER 56

If I were to sprout graceful, white wings, I could not have felt more exquisite. I looked at myself in the full-length mirror on the back of my closet door. The flowing white dress stood out from my cinched waistline in a full, shimmering circle. My shoes and gloves and pearls matched perfectly, and my mother had surprisingly contributed a small pearl-studded evening bag. My hair was massed high in dark, shining curls, with a white satin ribbon woven through, and the hairdresser had added some small sprigs of baby's breath. The hairdresser had helped with my make-up also, and when I looked at myself, I thought "OK now. I look positively regal!"

To sweeten my glorious night, the student body had actually nominated me for Prom Queen, and in a secret place in my heart, I wanted to win, although I acted completely bored by it all and told all my New Town friends that I really "didn't give a hoot." When Miss McArdle had told me of the nomination, I had feigned tremendous shock, managing to sputter a well-rehearsed "Why on earth me? The only thing unusual about me is that I can wiggle my eyebrows one at a time," which I proceeded to do forthwith. The principal studied me for a long minute, and then sighed and walked away, shaking her head.

The memory of that tiny interlude with the severe principal made me grin. I wondered why my friends had nominated me. I wasn't stunningly pretty, and the other two nominees definitely were. Perhaps they'd bestowed the honor out of sympathy because of what had happened with my father. No matter. If something this good could come from that terrible mess, I'd grab it and be grateful.

I turned from the mirror, picked up my white rabbit stole, and waited for the doorbell to ring. I heard a car door slam outside, and soon after heard the doorbell chimes and the cultured voice of my mother greeting Bobby at the door. I peeped over the upstairs railing and silently gasped. Bobby looked surprisingly spectacular in his crisp black tux. And now--- this was my moment.

I walked slowly and deliberately down the winding staircase, my long dress trailing. With great drama and flourishes, I imitated Scarlett O'Hara in *Gone with the Wind.* Bobby, utterly besotted, looked up at me in goofy awe. This was exactly the reaction I'd hoped for and expected to get. *The big old goofball never disappoints me!*

"Good evening, Bobby," I said, hoping I was floating down the stairs the way the ladies in the movies did. I marveled how terrific Bobby looked in his crisply pressed black tuxedo and his starched white pleated shirt with maroon studs that matched exactly the color of his cummerbund. My mother stood off to one side, smiling happily, and the entire staff had lined up in the arched doorway to see this special occasion.

Bobby reached for my hand, and bent close to my ear, his eyes rolling for a quick look at their audience."Sheesh, Queenie, I've never been in a house like this. Holy God, you *live* here? Or are we in some kind of hotel or somethin'?" *Does everyone I know think this is a hotel??* "I mean Jeezum, Queenie, how many rooms you guys need, anyway? And," Bobby's voice got quieter, "who are all those Negroes over there?"

"Oh. Those. Yes." I glanced over at the people I loved, praying they hadn't heard Bobby. I felt my face grow hot with embarrassment. "Well, I'll tell you all about it in the car, OK?" I looked meaningfully at the clear plastic box in his hand.

Bobby looked at and then followed my glance to the box, as if just remembering he was holding it. "Oh. Right. Yeah. Well, Queenie, this here's for you." I did not reach for it. Bobby held the corsage out awkwardly. When I still did not take it, Bobby finally said, "Oh, yeah." He took the top off, removed the small wrist corsage and dropped the box on the hardwood floor with a clatter he didn't seem to notice. My mother frowned briefly. The staff turned their heads to hide their amusement. Bobby grasped my hand clumsily and carefully slid the corsage onto my wrist. It was exactly right. A cluster of tiny red rosebuds with soft ferns, it would contrast perfectly with my long white kid gloves. Bobby wore a small rosebud in his lapel, too. Everything was just perfect.

"Come on, Bobby, let's go into the living room so Mother--Mom-- can take some pictures, OK? I'll be sure to have some made up for you, too." As we walked hand in hand toward the huge fireplace with the carvings all around and the enormous copper etched tray hanging above it, Bobby's eyes widened considerably.

"Come on Bobby, you can handle it. Don't faint on me, now," I whispered, propelling him toward the fireplace. He was speechless.

My mother took too many flash pictures, causing big blue spots to float in our vision, and finally, we started to get ready to leave. I handed my stole to Bobby, who accepted it with a blank smile. He held it, stroking it absently until finally I turned my back to him, gesturing with my hands that he was to help me on with it. As Bobby clumsily pushed the jacket onto my shoulders, I smiled as I saw my mother purse her lips at his shocking lack of etiquette. Dear good Bobby had not once asked if my father was around.

Finally, we were on our way and I was actually weak with relief. Bobby had his father's car, and had spent the day washing and polishing it and I was silently so thankful he hadn't brought a hearse. Bobby drove carefully and kept looking over at me in disbelief. It could not have been more flattering and sweet. I put my hand gently on his thigh and the car lurched dangerously so I quickly removed it. We both laughed awkwardly.

At precisely 8 o'clock and holding hands, Bobby and I ran into the beautifully decorated gym. I could hear the music in the air and recalled that magical long-ago summer evening with Remington on the club's patio. I shook my head and grinned up at Bobby. The theme for the 1957 New Town Senior Prom was "In the Good Old Summertime," and old-fashioned songs were mixed haphazardly with the rock tunes of the day. "In the Good Old Summer Time" was played often, along with "East Side, West Side," and "Down by the Old Mill Stream." We danced with "Casey Would Waltz with the Strawberry Blonde" and "Mary, Mary, Give Me Your Answer True." The large crowd loudly mocked me because I knew all the words, and at one point, made me stand and sing two songs all alone, which I did, with appropriate gestures. I sang, "Come Josephine in My Flying Machine" and swung immediately into "In My Merry Oldsmobile." Far too young to know how to play these songs, the musicians scowled as they tried their halting best to play along, mostly off key and always on the wrong beat. But this chaos just added to the fun and made me feel giddily happy. I stumbled and mugged through the tunes, and when I was finished, my friends clapped and cheered. I was overwhelmed with happiness.

In the center of the room stood a fifty-year-old open-top car in pristine condition. The worried owner, dressed in vintage long white duster, goggles and cap, had insisted on standing next to his treasured automobile all night. He'd anxiously overseen the dismantling and transport of his car to get it into the gym, and he had personally reassembled it on his own. Later that evening, the Prom King and Queen would sit proudly on the back of the leather seat and wave to the crowds of their pals as they were slowly driven around the dance floor. I just couldn't wait. I decided that when I won, I'd even be able to accept Dom as my consort if he were chosen king. Oh what a night this would be. I was thrilled to my bones.

Trees in big wooden buckets of dirt (no flowers this time) lined the gym. In one corner there was an old-fashioned ice cream parlor with marble-topped tables and chairs with heart shaped backs donated by Mr. Bacci who, dressed in a soda jerk outfit replete with white paper cap dispensed huge, melting ice cream cones from behind a long counter lined with stools. The band members were dressed in 1880s bathing gear, the men in itchy, striped, one-piece woolen outfits stretched tight from tank top to the knees and the women in equally short heavy dresses with petticoats, puffed sleeves and sailor collars. The ladies polished off the look with loose lace caps black tights and bathing slippers. Without being asked, the pianist performed a fairly accurate rendition of Fats Domino's "Blueberry Hill" which then inspired a comrade to stand and sob dramatically in a good and highly exaggerated imitation of Johnny Ray's "The Little White Cloud That Cried." The performances were hilarious, and the musicians were rewarded with tumultuous applause.

At the door, everyone received straw skimmers. The boys' hats were plain straw with a black band; the girls' were wider brimmed with two long black grosgrain ribbons hanging down the back. All wore their hats contentedly for the first couple of hours but then inevitably the hats became flying saucers, rocketing around the room, flying into the trees, landing in the punchbowl, on the dancers' heads, on the floor to be stomped, and on every table.

Even with skimmers floating in it, the punch was spiked as usual, so it was emptied, refilled, and guarded by earnest parent chaperones also dressed in old fashioned summer garb. One set of parents, to the agonized embarrassment of their child, rode wobblingly around the gym on a bicycle built for two, swerving into and occasionally knocking over the dancers, trees and other decorations. There were balloons and kites and streamers, and the lights strung around the walls were blinking pastels. I thought I had never felt such happiness and anticipation. Soon, the votes would be counted for Prom King and Queen.

*I lost?* I could not say the words aloud, but kept repeating them in my head. My mouth ached from my forced smile and my hands stung from clapping for the girl who'd been declared Prom Queen.

After a booming fanfare, the bandleader had made the announcements, and my name was not spoken into the microphone. I had been so absolutely sure of winning, I'd even begun walking up to the stage but thankfully had caught on soon enough and prayed that in the commotion no one had noticed that I'd quite nearly made a total ass of myself. Even then, I'd waited for several moments for the announcer to come back to the microphone absolutely certain he'd return to tell everyone there'd been a terrible mistake. I silently rehearsed how to smile understandingly when he confessed to the crowd of this terribly embarrassing mix-up, how I'd reach gently for his arm, how I'd stand there on the stage and forgive him, how I'd smile lovingly at the girl who thought she'd won, but hadn't. After all, I was Queenie Wolcott and I'd been nominated at a very difficult time in my life, and so it seemed that after all, I *deserved* to win. *I did! I did deserve to win. Goddammit, I've been through hell. I am Prom Queen!*

But I'd come in second, and second wasn't the same at all. Second is not winning! I'd lost, and that was that. Bobby consoled me by telling me that I was, after all, *his* queen, and besides that, I was much prettier than Gladys, the girl who'd won. To make matters all the more bitter, Dom was voted Gladys' King, and by a landslide. A landslide!!!

I watched with a frozen smile as Dom and Gladys were driven slowly around the room in the antique car, the driver smiling and waving as if he, too, had won something. My throat ached with a pain I'd never thought possible to endure and my cheeks burned from my great big brave smile. But I had to grudgingly admit that the couple looked good together. Both tall with an abundance of shiny, black hair, Dom and Gladys radiated absolute cool. They wore their rhinestone-studded crowns crookedly on their proud heads and they waved their scepters that occasionally crashed together, sending sprays of rhinestones and sequins onto the leather seats of their carriage. Their long red velvet capes, hastily attached to their necks with fake ermine ties, had seen better days, but in the prom's mellow lighting, they were resplendent.

Gladys and Dom's dates, Pansy and a young gawky basketball player named Arnold, stood across the gym from each other. Eventually, they locked eyes and before too much longer, both had vanished for the rest of the night. Fortunately for him, Arnold had been enterprising enough to have five dollars in his pocket, and it was burning a blazing hole there and in his groin. In a very short, torrid and thumping time in the back seat of someone's car (they never did find out whose), he was pleased to realize his money had been very well spent indeed. Pansy Junko was happily the gift that just kept on giving!

# CHAPTER 57

We protested. We put up posters. We asked for private audiences, but Miss McArdle would not budge. She refused to permit the graduating class to wear caps and gowns and she was deaf to the students when they pointed out that it was the standard graduation attire at high schools everywhere. Her school would be different she squawked, proper, and the clothing would be appropriate, according to her rigid definitions of propriety. With a curious lack of consideration for many students' financial difficulties, she commanded the boys be attired in dark blue suits with blue and red striped ties, white shirts, shined black shoes and dark blue socks long enough that the skin of their ankles not show. Hair was to be cut as short as possible; pompadours or obvious DA's would result in the young man's not receiving his diploma. The girls were to wear short, modest pure white dresses, medium high heeled, pure white shoes, stockings and small white purses to be carried in hands which would be encased in short, pure white gloves. On this subject, Miss McArdle adhered strongly to the tenets of a dictatorship. "Democracy" was not in her daily lexicon, and it was absolutely nonexistent when it came to the subject of graduation attire. Miss McArdle refused to budge on this issue for her entire tenure as principal of New Town High School.

Armed with my mother's charge accounts and seated behind the wheel of one of my father's cars, I drove off in pursuit of my graduation dress. When I saw it on the rack of the big department store, I knew immediately it was The One. Made of starched white Piqué, the dress had a scalloped hemline and a wide V neckline, outlined by a second scalloped edging. Here and there throughout the dress were shapes in eyelet lace, and the waistline was held tightly by a huge bow of the same material tied in the back. I immediately loved it. I decided on a pearl choker and pearl earrings, matching white high-heeled shoes, a tiny purse and a small amount of make-up to placate the formidable Miss McArdle. I was absolutely determined I would do nothing to jeopardize getting my diploma. I would die before I gave Miss McShit the satisfaction. I drove home with my treasures, exhausted and smiling to myself, the car's radio blasting some very good rock and roll.

Graduation night was oppressively hot and far more humid than usual for that time of year. As we all dressed in the starched clothing dictated by our tyrannical principal that hot, wet day, we New Town students angrily envied the graduates of other high schools who would be attending their ceremonies wearing only underwear beneath their cool, loose fitting black gowns. We would-be graduates felt cruelly mistreated and abused.

Emma sprayed starch on my graduation dress and pressed it several times so I would look fresh and crisp for the ceremony. When I came downstairs in my chosen regalia, I knew I looked terrific. My father, clad in his pajamas as usual, emerged from the self-imposed exile of his bedroom and took a number of photos, posing me in front of the huge livingroom fireplace. He even suggested I stand with my back to the camera looking coquettishly over my shoulder so the large bow tied at the back would show. He hardly spoke and never smiled, and as soon as he'd finished, he put the camera down and walked heavily back to his bedroom. My mother watched him retreat, an expression of deep distaste on her face, which she made certain he saw before he left the room.

I heard my father's footsteps approach his bedroom door, heard them stop and come back to the top of the stairs.

"Courtenay?" he called. I looked up the long staircase to where he stood. "Yes Daddy?"

"Your mother and I have a small graduation gift for you. I left it in the garage." And he walked back to his bedroom. I looked at my mother but she'd assumed her usual Helen blankness and looked back at me. And then maybe, just maybe there was a tiny smile on her face. Her pale head gestured slightly in the direction of the garage. I walked from the living room, through the dining room, through the butler's pantry, through the breakfast room and pulled open the heavy back door to the garage. There stood a beautiful, shining brand new 1957 maroon and white Chevrolet.

I was beyond stunned. Speechless, I stood holding the door open staring at this glorious chariot. I could hear Emma chuckling behind me. My mother walked toward me, and I said "Mother— Mommy, what is---I mean—is this mine? My car?"

"Yes my darling Courtenay, it is our graduation present to you because we love you." I could not determine just then what made me burst into tears, my mother's strange words or the sight of that magnificent, shining new car waiting for me to drive and own and love, and I didn't bother to sort it out. I stood staring at my new automobile as I heard my mother walk to the front hall telephone, sink into her chair, and dial.

When my name was called from the long list of New Town graduates, I walked nervously up the steps to the stage and accepted my diploma from Miss McArdle. The principal's handshake was strong to the point of being painful. I could not know that Miss McArdle squeezed hard rubber balls all year long, an hour each night, with her cats watching, so that her hand would be up to the task of shaking so many graduates' hands. She was determined that her students' lasting memories would include the tough, strong handshake of their principal. Few forgot. I looked directly into the principal's eyes and saw her mouth twitch in a faint smile. I was gratified to hear loud applause and a few whistles when my name was read. Finally, as my two years in public school were ending, I felt truly a part of New Town High.

Three smiling brown faces grinned up at me and waved as I left the stage. I grinned back and pretended it didn't matter that my parents, or anyone else from my family or childhood friends, were not there. When everyone gathered after the ceremony, I calmly introduced Emma, Fred and Mary to everyone, making no apologies or explanations. I was genuinely proud to have them there, and knew they were proud of me. When Sue Lewis walked by and saw who was with me, she grinned and clasped her two hands together high over her head in salute.

The graduation parties went on all night and none of us wanted to think about the supremely painful fact that we may never see each other again.

At three AM, I slowly, reluctantly, left a raucous breakfast scene. I said goodbye to no one, slid onto the pure white vinyl of my beautiful, wonderful new car and quietly drove away, up the hill, past the huge estates and country club, and back to my home. It was done.

# CHAPTER 58

I'd learned the meaning of "ironic" in English class, and the word was in my mind as I walked into Miss Piacentino's office on a hot morning at the end of June, 1957. I pretended I had left a few things in my locker I wanted to retrieve, but I really wanted to walk around the old school by myself, to memorize it and say goodbye. I looked down at my clothing and grinned, remembering the stiffly preppy way I'd dressed that first hard day. This day I had on a full grey skirt with a silly poodle sewn on the side. My crinolines were hot but I didn't care, and they held the wide skirt out in a fluffed circle. The shiny black "flats" on my feet matched the belt that cinched my waistline, and my bright white blouse was ruffled down the front. *Wouldn't I just love for The Academy kids to see me now!* I shook my behind a little so the big skirt would sway as I walked.

The crooked old woman sat behind what just had to be the same huge messy pile of papers that had been piled around her two years ago.

"Yeah?" she asked. "Aw Gawd, you hereta register AGAIN??"

I laughed, happy the woman remembered that day nearly two years ago.

"Hi Miss P." I began.

"Miss *P*?" the woman asked with obvious annoyance.

"Oh. Sorry, ma'am. I just thought that since I'm graduated and all, and that we're such old friends, you'd maybe let me call you that."

"I ain't allowing any such crap," the woman answered, but she smiled. "Holy Kee-riste, girlie, I remember you a coupla years ago. You was one scared rabbit, I can tell you. I never saw sucha pussy in my whole life. Well, you done good, and I read in your papers that you're goin' ta collitch. Good. No sense to not. I went to Cornell myself you know. Wunna the first colleges in America to take women, even from poor famblies like mine was. Ezra Cornell was wunna them liberal thinkers. Got a degree and worked my way through, too."

I looked with surprise at the woman behind the desk. In two years, this is the most I'd ever heard her speak.

"Well, um, that's terrific, Miss Piacentino. I hope I can do as well as you've done."

The woman smiled at my obvious white lie.

"Miss Piacentino, I seem to have left a couple of important items in my lockers and I was wondering if you'd give me permission to go get them."

"Yeah, sure, sure," she said. "I let a few of 'em in every summer to say goodbye to the old place. You might's well go in too. Just don't take too long. If McArdle finds out I'm doin' this, she'll have my ass."

The building was cavernous and silent as I slowly walked along the hall. Bright sun shafted in from the tall windows outside the registration office, and swirls of dust drifted through them. The huge, hard yellow shades trembled slightly from the summer breeze and the sun gleamed crookedly through their long, jagged cracks. Many of the heavy cords to pull them up and down were missing. The memory of my old fears made me feel silly now. How could I have been so frightened of this benign old building? The entire school was poignantly familiar now, and painfully lonely without the crash and grind of the student body. I looked into my classrooms and at desks I'd used, and stood silently at the doorways to the auditorium and gym. Memories of the kids swept past my mind's eye, and I heard the music of their accents and voices. *"Chicky, the cops". They always said that when Miss McArdle was coming.* I recalled the dances and sports, the learning, the teaching, and discovered I regretted nothing. Even the unpleasant things had toughened me and somehow prepared me for real life, giving me a depth I had not had before. And, with creeping surprise, I realized I rarely thought about The Academy anymore. I thought about my father, blinked, and then did not.

I walked past the girls' room where I'd spent so much time crouched in a stall, eating squashed lunches. I smiled and shook off the old unpleasant memory and retraced the steps I'd taken so often down the short flight of stairs to the lunchroom. Standing in the doorway, I looked out over the big room. The tables and chairs were stacked along the walls, silent soldiers awaiting the next onslaught. Memories flitted through my mind like a fast-moving motion picture. I inhaled the scent of stale food, and grinned up at the atrophied balled hot dog rolls and the straw wrapper stalactites hanging from the ceiling. (A favored lunchroom recreation involved wetting one end of a still-wrapped straw and blowing mightily into the other end so the paper sheath shot up to the ceiling and stuck there. When the ceiling was thoroughly covered, Mr. Wright would climb his ladder and sweep them off, clearing the slate for another season of wrapper shooting.)

"Queenie!" I jumped so hard my feet nearly cleared the floor. Dom stood behind me, chuckling softly.

"Omigod, you scared the hell out of me, Dom. What are you doing here anyway?" I'd been so deep in thought I had not heard him walk up behind me. My hands were shaking. I stared at him.

"Calm down, Queenie. I just came by to get some gym stuff the coach wanted me to get fer'm."

"Oh-- sure," I said, breathing easier now. "Right, Dom. Come on. You wanted to say goodbye to this nasty old place too, didn't you?"

"Who, me? I'm not such a pussy I'd hafta go an' do dat. Dat's for girls. Girls dodat, not guys."

"Oh, Dom, are you never, ever, going to get rid of your Big Man attitude? I mean, what's the big deal in admitting you want to see the school one more time? It doesn't mean you're not a guy, for heaven's sake. Can't you ever let go of that tough guy image you carry around? Doesn't it get too heavy sometimes? I guarantee you it sure gets boring! I mean no one's even here to see you strut your macho stuff. Only me! And you still do it. What is *with* you?" I looked him over: tight jeans, cigarettes rolled into the sleeve of a white T-shirt, black boots, chains, greased-back hair and that curl! *The guy stays in uniform, I'll give him that!*

"Jeez, Queenie, lay off, will ya? Don't you never stop tawkin'?? Christ, you bin on my ass trynna to improve me all year. OK. OK. So, I wanted to see the school one more time. Yeah. You happy now?"

"Yeah. I'm happy now. Oh Dom, you are such a phony!"

Smiling, I reached out and took his hand.

"I never did congratulate you on becoming Prom King, did I? Well, congratulations now, anyway. I'm glad you won. I really and truly am. You looked --- well-- you looked just wonderful. And so did Gladys. You made a fabulous couple. I was really jealous!"

"Yeah. Well, I figured I'd win. But I'll tell you a little secret. I was sure hopin' you'd be my queen. Then I coulda cawlt you Queen Queenie."

I giggled, and as it had happened once before, Dom shyly and slowly reached for me. We kissed and it felt so, so good. I could have stayed forever in the warm safety of his arms. I was at once thrilled and amazed at the softness of his mouth.

Suddenly Dom scooped me up and carried me to the long, stainless steel counter that divided the lunchroom from the kitchen. He sat me there, and we embraced once more and the kissing became something more, and yes, I wanted him to go on, yes, yes. Dom shoved his hips between my knees. He undid my summer blouse, unhooked my bra, and his big hands were scratchy and rough on my breasts. He reached beneath my skirt and pulled my panties off and I helped him, and he tossed them over his shoulder where they caught on the corner of an upturned table and hung there like a small pink flag. He fumbled at his fly. The stainless steel counter was warm beneath my skin. I held onto him tightly, and he to me, and as if something beyond me pulled at us, I wrapped my legs around him and he was inside me, again and again and again. *I won't say no, I won't say no!* It did not hurt at all and it sent waves of something joyous all through me and straight down into my heels, and a sound I never knew I could make I did make and it came from a place I never knew I had, and from him, too, and YES! I shouted, and the sweet pleasure vibrated and exploded in me like pieces of sea glass thrown into the sun and I thought it could never, oh no never, be as glorious or wonderful again. I sat in the spreading pool of his warmth and slid against his stiffening, and he pushed into me again, and I was wrong; it *was* more glorious than the first time.

Afterward, Dom held me tightly, his face pressed hard between my breasts, my arms tight about his neck, my fingers tangled in his hair. We were both crying, and we murmured each other's names over and over.

And then--a familiar clanking noise, accompanied by a tuneless song. We jumped apart. Mr. Wright! He was coming down the hall toward the lunchroom. His pail of ancient water squeaked and rumbled, and he was singing the Janitor's Lament, the song only he knew.

Dom and I looked with terror toward the door. Frantically, we looked back at each other and began to laugh with high, shrieking hysteria. With shaking hands we tried to button ourselves and each other too. Our clothing came together crookedly. He pulled me off the counter, and we both looked at the shining mess left behind, and we laughed even harder, shoving our hands against each other's mouths, trying to cover the sounds. I grabbed my underpants hanging from the corner of the table, balled and shoved them between my legs to soak up Dom's fluid. Then we grabbed hands like two guilty children and ran out of the lunchroom, nearly knocking over the stunned Mr. Wright.

"Hey, Mr. Wrong," we both shouted as we ran past. "Wait a sec, wait a sec," I screeched. Running back to the startled janitor, I kissed him hard and loudly on his cheek, grabbed Dom's hand again and raced off. I ducked into the girls' room, rapidly cleaned up with cold splashed water and a few paper towels, pulled on my underwear and ran out to meet the nervously pacing Dom. The hem of my skirt had caught in the elastic of my underpants, and Dom jerked it out and we laughed more, and shoved against each other as we tripped and bumped past the astonished Miss Piacentino in her office. Together, we burst through the red-painted metal doors.

Outside, finally, the hot sunshine blinded us as we stood on the steps and we pushed the palms of our hands against our eyes. Suddenly shy and embarrassed, we dropped our hands and stepped away from each other.

I took a deep breath. "Well, Dom, umm--you know, I've got a car now. How's about if I drive you home for a change? I mean, you've driven me home an awful lot."

"No thanks, Queenie, I got somethin' to do in town today. Thanks anyway." *How on earth could we be talking so casually like this, so normally, after the thing, the good, oh the good thing that had just happened?* I grinned.

"Sure, Dom."

We parted. We both turned back once toward each other, and smiled for a long minute. Dom finally turned, and I watched him walk away.

"So long, Dom. It's been good t' know ya!" I called out.

He turned. "Yeah. Right, Queenie," he called back. "You're right. It's been good ta know you, too. I mean dat. I always will. Well, I guess I'll see ya sometime." He waved and disappeared around the corner and I knew I would never see him again.

Except in the news. After graduation, Dominic Nuncio Di Russo went into the sanitation business and rose through the ranks rapidly, catching the attention of the Mafia, who recruited him. He lived a long and fruitful life under their tutelage, his last years as an aging, respected and very vigorous Don. He died instantly one late morning while dozing in a barber chair having his ear hair trimmed. A disgruntled member of the opposition had been waiting in an office window across the street, focusing tightly on Dom's neck through a telescopic lens attached to the barrel of a high-powered rifle. He took him down with a quick clean shot that only barely nicked the end of the startled barber's large nose.

# CHAPTER 59

I worked hard to prove my worth at the YMCA during the summer of '57. Maybe harder than I had to. At first it was difficult to come to work because I felt all of the stares. The new director of the YMCA treated me coolly at first, but in time, the matter of my father was put aside and I was able to enjoy a long and productive summer.

Caring for the retarded, handicapped and Down syndrome kids was hard and stressful work, and I had to be alert every second. Many of the tiny physically handicapped kids had been stricken with the dreaded poliomyelitis virus and would never be able to walk unassisted. And they were the lucky ones. Some polio victims spent the remainders of their lives trapped on their backs in iron lungs, never to get out or breathe on their own, looking forever into a mirror above their faces tilted so they could see the people coming to visit them, the dwindling visitors. As years passed, they would be left alone with just themselves, their medical attendees and the mirrors.

Some of these young kids had been appallingly spoiled by their worried parents, and they learned to milk a situation for all its worth. It pained me to see these children drag themselves across the floor by their hands and elbows to get to the edge of the pool. Once in the water however, they were quite capable, thanks to their overly-developed shoulders and arms and they could play and splash easily as long as they could hold onto the sides of the pool. Nevertheless, it took me a while to catch onto a trick a few of them played on us, their counselors.

They would drag themselves to different sections of the pool edge where they'd pull several colorful, plastic inflatable inner tubes over their wasted bodies. At a signal, they'd all take a huge gulp of air and fall head first into the pool, where they'd hang upside down, their puny, thin useless legs draping over the inner tubes like wilted plant stems. Frantic, the counselors would blow their whistles and dive in to pull the kids upright, seconds before their air gave out. They'd be dragged out of the pools and the plastic rings jerked off their bodies.

Once I was on to their game, my fists would clench in anger whenever they tried it. I knew I could not beat hell out of them, but I wanted to rather dreadfully, and the kids well knew this and would laugh and clap at having "gotten" the counselors one more time, knowing they'd never be punished, and would always be saved. It was a way for them to be mischievous and obnoxious like ordinary kids for a few seconds. I knew that, but I took away the plastic rings anyway.

I loved those children, and my job, and wept when I had to leave at the end of the summer. There were only two more weeks left for me to pack and prepare for my departure for college, to begin my new unknown.

Forty-four years had passed, in a twitch, a blink. Now my hands throbbed as they gripped the BMW's steering wheel. My throat ached and my eyes too as I focused hard on the old red painted metal doors. I had pursued my dream, gradually overcoming the roadblocks of my parents' endless objections. After graduating from college I'd won an astonishing golden plum: The New York Times offered me a job as hack writer, proof reader, gofer, mailroom clerk, and occasional obit writer, all for $48 a week after taxes. I had been eager and willing and did not let the woman offering the job finish the last sentence before I happily and nearly hysterically accepted.

I smiled wryly, now recalling the impossibly tiny, cockroach-infested apartment in Greenwich Village I'd rented with two college chums. We'd felt quite grand to actually have an elevator in our building, and that it rattled frighteningly and almost worked added to its nerve-wracking charm. And to make it all even more debonair, this dangerous contraption was run all day and most nights by a huge, perpetually laughing old black man named Rufus who watched over us, clucking and scolding when we came home late from a date.

I rested my head gently against my hands on the steering wheel, remembering my utter, indescribable joy when, after starving and working endlessly, one of my columns was finally accepted, appearing on page 43 of the Sunday Edition of the Times. My first byline. Nothing after that ever came close to measuring up to the feeling of that exalted moment.

I'd written books after that, and a couple made the bestseller list of the Book of the Month Club and stayed there for over five months. I seemed always pregnant with a new book before the old one was given publication birth.

380

I married my college sweetheart who never once in all our years together suggested I stay home to cook and clean, and so I never did. We parented three terrific sons who grew well and became productive good people in spite of the fact that their mother worked at a big newspaper during their formidable formative years.

It constantly amused me to remember that my parents had never approved of my marriage to a young man who had actually worked his way through college and who'd come from what was then called "modest circumstances." I knew they'd waited and hoped every day of their lives for me to announce my divorce, but I never did, never had to. My marriage flourished while my parents' relationship foundered and eventually, slowly deteriorated into colorless wreckage.

My father had died 16 years before after lying in his bed for four years, the result of a paralyzing stroke he'd suffered while in prison. Unable to care for him properly, the prison authorities, making sure the press would not find out, allowed him to go home to die. He had been unable to speak during that entire time, blinking once for yes, twice for no, and three times for Get the Hell Out of Here. My mother had refused to care for him, hiring 'round the clock nurses to feed and bathe him, until one day he blinked three times, turned his head, looked out of the windows at the sights he loved, sighed and died.

Because of some extremely wise investments in the early years, and stock shares sold for 35 cents per, we Wolcotts were well-oiled financially and always had been. My father's strange lie about our having to "tighten our belts" was ridiculous. In fact, the riches had rolled in endlessly in something just short of vast amounts. I had long ago accepted the fact that I would never fully understand my father's reasons for sending me off to public-school. What I did most clearly understand was that it turned out to be the finest gift he could ever have possibly given to me. Unknowingly, he thoroughly enriched my life.

Emma, Fred and Mary finally retired or moved on, and I helped my aging, cranky and loudly protesting mother move into a posh nursing home. The vast amount of work cleaning out the big old house was now thankfully behind me and the estate was on the market. Realtors had drooled over it, happily advising me that a "small village" could be squeezed onto that property in "no time at all" the beautiful terraced gardens leading to the golf course and the steep, hiding ravine and gentle woods that had been my tender sanctuary would be removed to make room for rows of identical ranch houses and maybe even a recreational vehicle park. I cringed. The grand and stately old neighborhood was irrevocably changing forever. I would never return to see that. Never.

I stared out of the BMW's windshield at New Town High School where I'd spent two important, formative years, and my eyes spilled silent tears. Sights and sounds went through my mind like the spun dial of a radio and the memories were as clear and vivid as if I'd stepped from them that morning. The faces of all the kids I'd known there moved around my mind in slow circles. Dominic Di Russo's came to me more often than the others and I thought of how he'd taught me so much more of his world than I'd ever taught him of mine. It was better that way and I knew it. His chances of entering my world were slim, but I'd spend the rest of my life bumping into his.

I regretted nothing and understood, finally, that I was meant to go through this. Ultimately, New Town High School had been my consummate preparatory school.

Tears again stung behind my eyelids, and then slid down my face into the corners of my mouth. I started the car, gazing sadly at the big old building once more before I drove away. I drove through the side streets, out onto Main Street, across the railroad tracks, past my bus stop and on to the bottom of the hill.

Ω